YOU KNOW HER

D. E. WHITE

Storm
PUBLISHING

Ebook ISBN: 978-1-80508-210-1
Paperback ISBN: 978-1-80508-212-5

Cover design: Lisa Horton
Cover images: Arcangel, Shutterstock

Published by Storm Publishing.
For further information, visit:
www.stormpublishing.co

PROLOGUE

"Five years ago, during the July heatwave, YouTuber and social media influencer Joy Maddison disappeared. A perfect wife, mother, daughter and sister, Joy's final video, posted by her devastated husband, Emile, has now been viewed over a hundred million times. In the final frame she smiles for the camera, signing off with her familiar, 'See you all later, my darlings. Love you all!'

And then she was gone..."

I lean forward and touch her face on the TV screen, tracing her movements with a steady forefinger as she smiles for the camera, turns to open the gate to the woods.

The evening sunlight catches her long blonde hair, turning the strands to threads of true gold. Her laughter always makes me smile, as though we share a private joke. Which in a way is true, isn't it, darling?

My TV screen is a large one, and this time I'm not on her YouTube channel re-living her last post, I'm watching a documentary, made for the five-year anniversary of her disappearance.

She would have loved this, being centre stage on a Saturday night. She looks so beautiful.

I used to watch her every day and night. I know everything about her. Joy's whole life was played out on social media and there is nothing we have missed. She had so many devoted fans but really, in the end, I was the only one who loved her enough to take the next step.

But I knew at the time I was doing it for all of us.

PART ONE
MATTIE

ONE

There was blood under her nails.

Dried, crusty dark flakes stuck on her hands as she flexed her fingers. Her eyes hurt, straining to focus as the harsh July sunlight streamed through the broken window. She looked down at her arms, where the half-healed scabs showed signs of fresh scratches, recent injuries. She blinked hard, and slowly, painfully, began to push herself upright. Every bone ached, and her body was heavy.

Outside, the seagulls squawked and circled. She glanced at the window and watched them for a moment, focusing on the rise and fall of their white wings, gathering strength before she made a final effort to stagger to her feet. The dirt from the rough floorboards had coated the base of her bare feet, making every step uncomfortable, sticky. Where the hell were her shoes? And her phone? It was like regressing to babyhood, she thought angrily, as her brain reluctantly clunked back into full consciousness.

The photograph, lying face up on the grimy floor, one edge fluttering gently in a draught, made her wince. Had she taken her treasure trove out last night? Or had she just plucked this one, stunningly beautiful picture to stare at while she sat in a drunken stupor, slumped in front of the screen? The anniversary was over. With gentle fingers, she picked it up now and took it back to her little shrine in the cupboard. Safe now. She mouthed the words and smiled. The woman in the picture smiled back at her. *"Love you, Joy,"* she whispered. And this time her words were clogged with tears.

Her battered old phone was lying in the sink, she saw now. How had it got in there? With fumbling, sweaty fingers she wiped a few drops of water from the screen, checked her missed calls. Work. She had missed her first shift back since she had fallen ill. Mattie took a deep breath, finding comfort in the fact her chest no longer wheezed and the heat that had swept across her body, engulfing her in waves of pain, had gone.

She still felt like shit though, and her throat was dry and scratchy. Last night must have been a bad one. After six weeks of lying on the grubby mattress, sweating out some kind of vicious flu bug, Mattie had dropped into the pub to see if anyone had heard from Jono. Most people ignored her, only paid attention when she mentioned Jono McQueen.

It had been a dead loss. Nobody had heard from him or seen him in weeks. They had just looked at her, in that pitying way, or with a glint of malicious amusement, telling her without words they thought Jono was too good for her. He had left her, of course he had.

Pushing her hair out of her eyes, she scrolled down, smearing the screen even more. Still no messages from Jono. The sadness inside her shifted, reminding her it was there, poking at the raw place that never seemed to heal. Her boyfriend had been gone a whole six weeks now. Deep down, Mattie knew he hadn't left her; she knew he could be dead – probably was dead, in fact.

No more Jono to help her score drugs. There were plenty of others who would do that though, as long as she gave them the money. But last night she had spent her last wad of fivers, and the plastic box wedged under the double mattress was empty. If she was completely honest, she hated what she had become, what people saw as they passed her in the street. She had kidded herself Jono really cared about her. In her head she could still see him laughing in the sunshine as they sat on a bench next to the sea and watched the sun rise over the port. The drugs had still been throbbing around her body, her heart beating too fast, her breathing erratic, after a long night of partying. But she had been safe because Jono had been beside her. He had always been beside her, had laughed with her, and called her his party girl.

When Jono first went missing, she had struggled to pay what he owed. Rumour had spread that he had left her a large sum of money to pay off his creditors. Not bloody likely! She rolled her eyes as she remembered hearing the gossip from Denny at The Dragon. Violence was commonplace in her life, and people went missing all the time. Sometimes they came back, but more often than not they just disappeared forever.

After Jono's dealers put the pressure on, she had turned the house upside-down in desperation, finding at last a plastic bag full of smaller bags, divided by weight, carefully marked in blue pen. Fifty wraps of crack cocaine, with a street value of around a thousand pounds, she hoped. Jono had cleaned everything else out. It was her first time as a wannabe dealer, and she was caught in a drugs raid, and banged up for the night. Terrified, she had cowered in her cell after the interview, trying to control her pounding heart, her raw, shaky breaths. She was small time, a tiny fish in the wider net, and she wondered why they had bothered. She hoped it was all a mistake.

Then Abs had come down, spoken to her, told her he knew all about Ned, had worked with Jono. She'd known her boyfriend was a police informant, because he liked to boast to her about it. That was where the real money came from, he had said, and he loved screwing over the very players he depended on for his livelihood. He liked being the big man, the one in control of someone else's life.

Normally, Abs explained, there would have been a formal interview with the DI, but she was away, and the management was changing, so it was him and another man, whose name she instantly forgot. They explained her role, told her to sign the agreement, even gave her a fake name. Abs would be her official handler. She'd got off with a lesser charge and was free by lunchtime. Still shaking, she bought a three-litre bottle of cider for a couple of pound coins from the off-licence and necked the lot. And hated herself just that little bit more as she limped home that day, drunk and alone. Her bad leg was always sore when she was worried. An accident long ago that she barely remembered now had left her with a limp and long twisted scars across her kneecap.

She looked at her phone again. The screen had gone blank. She tried to plug it into the charger. Nothing. Moving to the cupboard on the other side of the room, she pulled her work phone from a broken drawer. This one was smaller, less battered. A lifeline. There were two missed calls from Abs, and he had left his usual curt voicemail. That made her shake a little more. Less from hangover, more from guilt at what she was doing.

"Mattie, where the hell are you? I need a meeting today at Carats. Tell me what you've got on Ned right now and I'll double your pay for this month. Call me back when you get this."

That was good. Very good. This way it didn't matter she'd missed her shift at the fish market, though Ned would be pissed off. Naturally her boss had no idea she was also working as a police informant. As usual the thought of the police made her stomach clench, her heart race like she'd taken a load of amphetamines. She took a deep breath and reminded herself she hadn't, and she wouldn't.

She called Abs, and he picked up immediately. "I can meet you now if you want?" she offered.

"No, I need an hour to sort some stuff out, so be there for eleven, usual place." Then he hung up. He was always short on the phone, had told her even though the phone was safe, she needed to be careful, always imagine someone was listening, watching.

TWO

It wouldn't take long to walk over the road to meet Abs, which gave her time for a shower, to sort her head out.

If Jono was still around, still protecting her, she would never have fallen into the informant trap, never been in contact with the police, risking her sanity and liberty. Jono had it all worked out, and despite his arrogance and bluster, he *loved* the thrill ride of being so close to the police.

She didn't need any thrills in her life, she just needed to survive, to start crawling her way out of the pit she had found herself in. From party girl to down and out. How had it happened?

Mattie knew about death. She also knew about clinging to life, even though sometimes it seemed, deep in her heart, that it might be easier to let it all slip away, to forget the pain. It bothered her that she felt so at home hiding on the tattered fringes of society, in the shadows of many different worlds, not properly belonging to any of them. Some people laughed at her, some spat at her, and many more walked straight past without seeing her. She was invisible to well over half of them, which was just the way she liked it.

Feeling thirsty, Mattie grabbed a mug from the draining board on her way to the bathroom. The handle fell off and she hurled it across the room in sudden frustration, tears running down her face. At the sink she took a deep breath and turned on the tap, letting the water gush out and spatter her face as she leant down and drank, quenching her thirst. Mattie let the tap run, until her bony rib cage couldn't bear the pressure of the cold hard enamel of the cracked sink unit any longer.

As usual the mornings were tough. Pretty much the only reason she worked at the fish market was because she didn't have to go to bed. She clocked in at 2:00am and was finished by 6:00am. Most of the time, she managed it, taking other shifts only when they needed more cash. Before she got sick, before Jono left, she hadn't always been sober at work, but she had worked hard and said little, cushioning herself from the outside world with the ebb and flow of artificial stimulants. Now she found herself seeing her world through new eyes, and it was terrifying.

She rubbed her hands along the insides of her arms, avoiding looking at the scarred and bruised skin, the wrecked veins. Something had been missing last night. No drugs. Lots of booze but no drugs. The craving was still there, but the desperate, sick longing was missing. It was pleasing. A little victory maybe?

It was weird too, she thought, hands braced as she raised her head from the sink. Mattie shivered, enjoying the feeling of the icy water dripping down her T-shirt, cooling her sweaty skin. Through the cracks, the sun was blasting through, bathing her in light and heat. This much she could see from the filthy, half-boarded-up window. The only glass still in the frame was cracked, with wicked shards glittering in the daylight. A summer heatwave. Just like the one five years ago.

Her hangover made her wince at the flash and dance of the sunlight, but her heart wasn't racing, and she felt a little burst of childish excitement that she might be starting her climb out of the life she had fallen into. A life she had to admit she had been perfectly satisfied with until her boyfriend vanished.

She turned from the window, tasting the day, breathing the salt in the air, on her cracked lips, even inside the house.

The hot summer air drifting in through the broken window brought scents of the fast-food outlet on the corner of her road, the smoky tendrils of the huge factory chimneys that lined the port, and a faint odour of fish. A train roared past somewhere behind the house. The trawlers would have long brought their catches in, and she should have been there, plunging her hands again and again into the crates of ice, the slippery strong-smelling bodies, sorting the fish, labelling the containers.

Sometimes it wasn't just fish, and Mattie and Jono were amongst the workers trusted with dealing with another kind of cargo Ned liked to bring in. She and her boyfriend had worked side by side for so long, lived together for so long, she still found herself talking to him, even though he hadn't been in touch since he left for that night shift with Ned.

She grabbed a threadbare towel from the draining board, first patted her face gently, then scrubbed it fiercely with the rough, smelly fabric. Ned seemed really pissed off Jono had vanished, refusing to answer her questions, insisting Jono hadn't been working that night.

She knew her boss dismissed them both as junkies, as manpower only. But Mattie wasn't stupid, and she sometimes noticed things the others didn't. At times when she had been off the drugs and booze for a few hours and the fog had lifted, her brain processed things Ned wouldn't have wanted her to put together. Jono would have been surprised too. He had always looked out for her, but he was patronising as well, and he under-estimated her.

Although her muscles ached and her head throbbed, Mattie tidied the kitchen area, before heading upstairs for the shower.

Jono had left one thing in the house, apart from the drugs. His old green jacket still hung on the back of the doorframe. She touched it with light, trembling fingers as she went past. It was the one he wore down the fish market, and she had left it, dangling from a rusty nail, like a grubby talisman drawing him home.

The fungus on the back wall in the shower was getting worse, but she turned her back on it as the icy water trickled out in a sullen stream. It was just toadstools anyway.

Naked, she inspected her bruises, her scars, her tattoos, studying her battle-scarred body with a detached kind of interest. The tattoos were pretty, the rest were not. At least she was still breathing though. So far, anyway. Bobby was still here, and Abs needed her. She had some money, and she had been off the drugs for nearly two months now. Nearly two months sounded better than six weeks. It was a proper milestone, something to feel proud of, she thought.

Mattie had a tally on the wall downstairs, written in marker pen on the faded wallpaper. Each day she didn't take drugs, she added another mark. The small black strikes were a source of pride.

She closed her eyes now, tilted her head, letting the feeble trickle of cold water wash over her face. But as she did so, she felt she was being watched. Confused, she opened her eyes, blinking and whipping round as her heart rate sped up. There were no windows in the bathroom, no cupboards, but the door was now shut. Surely she had left it open? Mattie had a phobia of closed doors, of being locked up in the darkness.

Fear caught in her chest, and she turned the shower off, trying to listen through the pounding of her heart. The house creaked as it always did, the seagulls screamed, and a train thundered past. Mattie grabbed her thin towel and wrapped it around her body, stepping out onto bare, dusty boards, wet feet leaving prints as she padded towards the door.

"Jono?" She took a breath and flung the door open, half expecting to see her boyfriend there, laughing at her, telling her it had all been a joke. He was always laughing at her. Maybe he was back. The relief washed over her body and she almost smiled. Of course, he would never really leave her. "Jono... come on, stop messing with my head. I know you're out there."

But there was nobody on the landing. Bewildered, with disappointment biting deeply, she searched downstairs, calling occasionally. But nobody answered, and nobody laughed from the empty rooms. She was all alone. The door must have blown shut of its own accord, she told herself firmly, rubbing herself dry, banishing the goosebumps of fear with common sense. There were no ghosts in Number Forty-Two, Kingston Lane. She was okay, she really was.

Dressed and back downstairs, her hair framing her face in limp curtains, her heart rate calm again, she told herself that so far, she had done a good job of picking up the informant work, right where her boyfriend had left off. Proper rent and a nicer place without holes in the walls were out of the question for so many reasons, but at least she would be able to live and eat as she added her strikes to the wall.

She checked her work phone. Twenty minutes until she had to leave. After her shower, and her scare, she unexpectedly felt quite calm. It was like the whirlpool that was in her mind was now still and calm as the summer sea.

Maybe it was the lack of drugs, or maybe even just that she wasn't sick anymore. These moments were so rare, when she was gifted one, she usually liked to clamber up to the old attic bedrooms, and sit cross-legged on the floor, either staring at the sky or painting and drawing on the old and peeling walls. She had begun with some brushes and paint left by the previous occupants of the building. It had only started as she began to recover from her flu, this urge to create, so Jono had never seen her draw. He'd never known how it made her feel to be covering a blank space with her own translation of her world.

Even if the weather was bad, she would be up there, looking through the holes in the roof, entranced by the cloud patterns, the glitter of sunlight, the pounding of rain or the remote, sparkling stars high above the city by the sea.

The house, part of a terrace of three broken buildings, was derelict, shuttered, locked up, structurally unsound. Jono had found a way to get in at the back, through some broken boarding. A previous owner had left a large rusting boat on a trailer in the back garden, and it blocked most of the rear of the house. There was a metal gate covering the kitchen door, also rusty and backed with plywood. They had levered it open, manoeuvred the frame so it could be wedged a little way, allowing proper entrance and exit of the abandoned site. The wildness of brambles and weeds grew well over head-height, and ivy was winding its poisonous way across the roof and walls, with tough, fibrous tentacles thicker than Mattie's arms.

The path leading from the former back garden wove behind the factories on the industrial estate, the new development after the traffic lights, up to Kingston Lane. The main trainline to London was metres from the house, the trains screeching and rattling long into the night, early in the mornings. After a few months of living there, Mattie found she could get home in whatever form of consciousness she was in. Sometimes she woke up in the nettle-covered garden under the boat, sometimes in the house, but she always got home.

Her other phone buzzed now, and she picked it up and tapped it gingerly. At least it was working again. There was a text from Bobby:

> Are you still alive, doll? Ned's super pissed you
> weren't at work. Will be round later if you like.
> Love you xx

Jono had always hated Bobby, but Bobby was the only person she would trust with anything and everything. Almost everything.

They were an odd pair, but there had been an instant connection from the first time they met. They had supported each other, both at work and at home. Bobby had recently found the courage to leave his abusive long-term partner and Mattie had been cheering him on the whole way. He stood up for her at work, looked out for her when she was sick. And nagged her to start going to addiction counselling. Jono had laughed himself stupid when she had timidly mentioned she wanted to get clean, to stop spiralling, flailing around in the darkness.

Now Bobby was single, had space in his tiny flat off Boundary Road in Hove, and Jono seemed to have gone for good, Bobby kept telling her she should move in with him. But that would mean being back in the real world, where you needed to register for things, fill in forms, be a fully functioning member of society. There was another, deeper and darker, reason she couldn't do that.

She felt the now familiar tiny spark of something deep inside her chest, and every time, it almost felt like she was waking up, checking out her world, her life, like an observer might have done. Looking in from the outside, she didn't like what she saw.

Quickly, and carefully Mattie checked her meagre food supplies, the oil for the generator, and bagged up a few items and the bedsheets for the laundrette. She checked her phone, surprised how little time had passed. Still ages until she needed to meet Abs. Her mind wandered, sifting memories.

The information on the trafficking of girls at the beginning of this month had led to her first real pay packet from Abs. She had gorged herself on a McDonald's burger and fries, revelling in the unfamiliar sensation of being able to fill her belly. It had been two weeks after she had signed on that dotted line in the dimly lit room at the police station.

The poor, lost girls from the container ship had never led back to Ned. He was far too clever. But at least they got a proper burial, Abs had told her. Mattie wasn't really surprised the police couldn't find any evidence leading to her boss. Disappointed perhaps, but at the end of the day, she was just glad to pocket the money she desperately needed.

Abs had asked her if she was okay after she found the bodies, if she wanted to talk it out or something. It was nice of him, but she had also felt little bubbles of hysterical laughter welling up, along with the guilt. He thought she was such an innocent. But he had no idea what she had done.

Mattie bagged up the rubbish from her kitchen, yanked the ties firmly and dumped the bag next to the door. She would chuck it over the fence down the way, into one of the huge containers in the recycling depot. Yeah, she thought, with a twist in her stomach, Abs had no idea at all, but it wasn't the first time she had seen a dead body.

THREE

Mattie pulled on her trainers, and slipped out of the house. On the way she ditched the rubbish bag in a green bin. Jono had laughed at her, said she should just chuck the rubbish in a hedge somewhere, but Mattie insisted it went in the proper place.

The thunder of traffic hurtling along the coast road, the shouts and chatter of people passing by, and the occasional deafening hooter from the port, were a soothing background to her turbulent life. Carats Café and Bar was always packed, the car park busy with surfers, gathering to ride waves. The outflow pipe from Shoreham Power Station created unique conditions, and a pack of tousle-haired water-lovers was present from dawn till dusk during the summer months.

Mattie slipped through the crowds, dodging girls and guys carrying heavy boards, stumbling a little on the gravel near the door. She walked with her head down, shoulders hunched, hair falling forward to hide her face. In her grey T-shirt and faded jogging bottoms with one hem hanging loose, she felt invisible amongst this jostling, laughing, summer-tanned crowd.

Abs was there already, sitting with his back to the wall, chair facing the huge glass windows that looked straight out onto Southwick Beach. He was tall, with a sharp, chiselled face, intense dark eyes and a shaved head. When he spoke or moved it was with a kind of barely contained nervous energy, like he was expecting to attack or be attacked at any moment.

"Hi! Do you want a sarnie? Cuppa?"

To be a CHIS, a Covert Human Intelligence Source, to give the job title its proper name, she had needed a fake name for the records, for the reports, but Abs wouldn't call her by it out in public, where she was known by her given name. Martha was a rubbish fake name anyway, but she hadn't argued when they suggested it. Her whole being had been itching to get the hell out of the police station as fast as she could. So, Martha it was. Any communication directly with the police in the line of duty, and she had to remember to introduce herself under her cover name. But not in public.

Mattie nodded shyly at Abs in greeting, ducking her head, keeping her eyes downcast. She caught a waft of his aftershave. It was a nice citrusy scent. Even after her shower and clean clothes, she probably didn't smell nice at all. She really hoped she didn't smell of fish. It was a hazard of her job.

It didn't used to matter, she thought suddenly, but since Jono had gone, she had started to notice things more. And to worry more. It was like someone had pushed back the shower curtain and instead of daily events happening through a steamy haze, she saw and felt things far more acutely.

Abs came back from the counter with her bacon sandwich, and a large, chipped mug of tea. She was instantly aware of the hunger pains in her empty stomach. She took a huge bite and started munching, wiping a blob of ketchup from the corner of her mouth with her fingers.

"Any sign of Jono yet?" Abs asked, keeping his voice down to the general level of chat.

She shook her head, finishing her sandwich at speed, then worrying she had looked like a starving dog while she did so.

He fitted right in here, Abs did, Mattie thought. He had his rucksack, faded Eighties band T-shirt, surf gear that looked like he wore it every day, and just the right amount of muscle to pass for a regular gym user. Perhaps he was a surfer in real life. It wasn't like they ever talked about personal stuff. His name wasn't even Abs, but she would never know who he really was.

"You got something for me?"

She darted a quick look around the busy café before she spoke. She had been told mistakes meant death. Hers, Abs' even.

"Hey! You still with me?" Abs caught her attention and she realised she'd been drifting. It was something that happened from time to time.

"Yeah." Mattie took a shaky breath and told him, keeping her voice low, their heads close together over the sticky vinyl table. It was basic information: the when/where/how and who was running the show. But it was gold dust for the police. And she liked the idea of being able to help prevent dealers using innocent kids to deliver. Kids on bikes, like a bloody pizza delivery service.

"That's not the info I wanted about Ned," Abs remarked, but his eyes were bright and interested and she knew she'd hooked him. Double pay would mean food and drink for a week, maybe some diesel for the generator would be a good idea.

"No, but this is for real. I heard it last night. You know I've been sick, like really sick, since I last saw you... I need more time for... for the other thing with Ned." She raised her eyes from her mug and stared at him. "You could get hooks into this operation though, couldn't you? Before people get hurt, more stuff out on the street..."

He nodded slowly, eyes narrowing, "Maybe."

She was a little discouraged but reminded herself he never

did give a straight answer. "I just need more time for the other stuff," she repeated.

His eyes were above her head, voice raised and slipping accents. "I know you said that, but that loser boyfriend of yours is not coming back, is he? Let's go out tonight properly. My shout!"

Bewildered by the flash fire change in his whole demeanour, she felt her own eyes widen as a heavy hand came down, fingers clenching cold and cruel on her thin shoulder.

"Mattie! What happened to you this morning? I thought you'd recovered from the plague and were going to be back at work..."

Through the cheap fabric of her T-shirt, she could feel nails digging into her skin. She winced but she didn't dare move.

Mattie swallowed hard, willing her voice to pass as normal, casual. "Ned. Sorry, I slept in. Late night, you know. This is Abs, my... friend." Her voice trailed off and she hoped she had done it right. Abs had coached her over and over with their cover story.

Now Abs smoothly picked up the slack, leaning forward. "You Mattie's boss then?"

"Yeah." Ned finally let go of Mattie's shoulder and moved round the table. His cool grey eyes mocked her, but she knew he was sizing up her companion. "Got yourself a new man already, Mattie?"

Mattie stared at him; her head twisted round so that her face was close to his. His face had all the sharp lines of Abs' but his eyes were different. An emotionless, vacant pale grey fringed with thick black lashes. His mouth was thin and his lips the palest rose pink, and the hand, still clasping her shoulder, was white, blue veins standing out in relief.

She couldn't help comparing the two men. Abs was slim and muscled, but Ned, although of similar physique, was all raw bone and sinew, so deathly pale he looked unhealthy. A ghost, out of place in this hustling crowd filled with cheerful gossip and flushed cheeks.

As though sensing Mattie was struggling to reply, Abs smiled easily at Ned, filling the awkward silence with ease. "She has but she doesn't know it yet. I was just telling her I reckon Jono's long gone now. He said something after Christmas about heading over to Ireland again, but I didn't take much notice. He's full of shit, isn't he?"

Ned nodded, eyes still narrowed, but his hand relaxed and dropped away from Mattie's shoulder. "Always, man, always. So, you know Jono?"

"Cousins. You know how it goes. Hadn't seen him in years until I met him in the gym again."

Mattie found she was holding her breath, and slowly reached for her mug of tea again, sipping so she didn't have to talk. She was blown away by how good Abs was, but then, he did this for a living. And he wasn't really Abs. He could be anyone. He had emphasised often enough, if the cover story was blown, people died, and he and Mattie would be first in line.

She only half listened to the rest of the conversation, trusting Abs to make it right. Ned was saying something about boxing, gesticulating with his right hand, the other hand slipping out of his pocket to rest on the edge of the table. Abs was talking about his personal trainer job and how he liked to do a bit of business in the clubs in his spare time.

It was terrifying. Mattie's whole body was frozen, shoulders rigid and her heart beating so hard it hurt her chest. She sipped her drink through trembling lips, trying to stop her hands from shaking, and had finished her mug of tea by the time Ned was ready to move on.

Her boss fixed her with that cool, assessing gaze, "Found yourself a better man than Jono, haven't you? Be on time tomorrow though. No shagging lover boy and missing your shift." He grimaced, presumably at the thought of her having sex, and Mattie cringed into her seat, feeling her cheeks burning.

After Ned left, Abs stuck rigidly to the cover story, chatting about nothing, before he suggested they take a walk.

The heat hit her face as they stepped outside, beating in waves through her thin top, so that she could almost feel her skin burning. Her lips were salty with sweat and the lazy sea breeze, which today was just a breath from a furnace. The vivid blue sky arced above, without a trace of cloud. Just as it had five years ago, on the day it happened.

FOUR

The road was busy, and Abs took her hand as they dodged the traffic and pedestrians and turned right into the scrubby, litter-filled area between the scrap metal piles and the marina. Some kids with skateboards had made a ramp, and the concrete bollards, easily circumnavigated by those who knew about such things, were decorated with colourful graffiti.

"It's better in here. A bit quieter." Abs smiled reassuringly, as a couple of sweaty runners sprinted past, heading for the path along the marina, earbuds in, flushed faces grim with concentration. A group of teenagers were sitting, and standing on, a bench, hoods pulled up despite the burning heat, eyes focused on their phones.

Mattie opened her mouth to say something, but Abs was too quick, his words a little louder, a little clearer than maybe they needed to be. She was sure Ned had gone the other way. But was someone still listening? Still watching?

"So, I'll see you Friday, chick?"

Chick? She nodded, unable to see the danger he had obviously clocked, but trusting him, as he had said she should in this situation.

He peeled off his own hoodie and draped it around her shoulders. "I'll get you some nice stuff soon. Jono never treated you right. I know he's family an' all, but it's true you deserve someone better than him."

She needed to speak, needed to play the game. Mattie licked her lips. "What if he comes back?" There was danger. She could see it in Abs' bright, alert eyes, his tense body.

Abs shrugged. "He'll have to deal with it. Shit happens, doesn't it?"

Mattie nodded again, limp as a kid's rag doll as fear still coursed through her veins like poison. The remnants of the flu had left her weaker than she had ever been. She must keep up her strikes on the wall, day by day, hour by hour. It was the one thing that brought her closer to escaping from this terrifying and claustrophobic life. She could do it, she really could.

Without any warning Abs leant in, kissed her hard on the lips, and then called, "See you later!" as he walked away.

Crossing lines. That was what he had called it once, telling her if there was danger, she must never be surprised at anything he did. There must be danger now for him to go that far, Mattie thought, still shocked by his action. She pressed a finger to her lips and hid behind her curtain of wispy brown hair. Invisible, now was the time to be invisible.

She turned quickly and walked back towards the gates, trying to look casual, not peer into the shadows of the scrap metal, the high walls topped with razor wire, or the makeshift skate park.

There were plenty of people around, but she was craving the crumbling four walls of her home. Too many people was almost as bad as nobody at all for her. She stumbled a little on the dusty, uneven pavement and winced as her bad knee twisted.

Had Ned really swallowed her cover? Did he actually think Abs was her new boyfriend? Beginning to trust that the threat had passed and she was safe, Mattie found an embarrassed choke of laughter bubbling up. As if. Mattie knew how she looked, knew what she was and for a bloke like Abs to get involved with her... Hilarious. But, she supposed, if anyone could get the better of her boss, it would be him.

Her phone buzzed and she checked the text from Abs:

U ok?

She tapped back with unsteady fingers:

Yeah

Her phone buzzed with a quick reply:

Go home now. Spk soon.

Mattie stashed the phone away in her baggy pockets. As she began to walk the long way home, doubling back twice as she had been instructed, she passed the corner shop. The one that sold cheap vodka and under the counter knives with no questions asked. She passed the house that sold sex in the attic and drugs in the basement.

The police were always trying to clean up the area, but recently spent more time focusing on the more infamous, busier places further into the city: New Road in North Laine, or West Street where the under twenty-fives were fair game as they staggered from club to bar and back again.

Although her heart raced and a shadow of that itchy, prickly feeling raced across her body, she was just too tired to go inside, and the craving was dull enough for her to ignore. *You can do this, Mattie.* And she was now stone broke until Abs paid up for this latest information. Food was a priority, and she needed coins for the laundrette up the road. She wanted clean sheets and clean clothes and some strawberry shower wash from the Co-op. But food and the strikes on the wall were top of the list.

She stuck her chin out and pulled her shoulders back as she walked. One foot after the other, allowing her mind to wander over her journey so far.

Before Jono had left, she had pretty much existed on a diet of cocaine, ketamine and, occasionally, MDMA. Drugs to make you high, drugs to put you to sleep, and drugs to help you leave your real life so far behind that they became your life. Jono had supplied them all, and they had enjoyed the uppers and downers together.

Now she could see the lifestyle for what it was, and she winced as she passed a young girl in a cheap mini dress, her eyes dead, thin arms hugging her skinny body as she hung out on the doorstep of one of the dingy clubs on the west side of the factories.

Mattie had never paid in kind for drugs, and the thought made her shrink into herself. Jono, whatever his faults, had never allowed her to get into that kind of trouble. Sex was a cheap, rough currency and anyone was fair game on the city streets. Mattie sighed as she passed the warehouses, kicking an empty beer bottle away from her path, fine dust rising, coating her tatty trainers as she did so. She imagined she could still taste the sour sweetness of last night's binge. Shame flooded her chest, making her gasp out loud. It was up to her to make changes, and she could do it. She really could.

The drink was another matter. She could walk on past these various vendors now, but when it got to the evening, she worried the sweats would start. A different kind of sweats to the ones she had dealt during the long, long days and nights when she had been sick. Relaxing a little now, surer whatever the danger had been near the marina had now passed. Mattie glanced quickly over her shoulder. Nobody was following her, and she relaxed further, allowing herself the pleasure of enjoying the sun on her face, on the back of her neck, the brightness making her squint as she dodged round a motorbike parked on the pavement.

She crossed the road again and took a shortcut home up behind the factories, pushing through the brown scorched stalks of brambles, nettles and hogweed. The plants released clouds of brown dust that made her cough.

As always, Mattie cut through the backways for this last leg, staying in the shadows, walking along the overgrown footpath by the railway to get home. She was okay, she thought to herself, she was actually okay. Alive, and starting to question her choices, make proper decisions; surely that was a good thing?

Ten minutes from home, she turned a sharp corner, overhung with limp brambles and scrubby, parched trees. From nowhere, heavy, sweaty hands grabbed her arms, pinning her wrists painfully. She gasped, fear and pain overwhelming her as another hand came over her face, nails digging in as her vision blurred.

One thought slashed through her brain. Ned had figured out she was a grass, and now she was going to pay for it.

FIVE

It's a hot evening, after another sweltering day. The faint smell of smoke, scorched landscapes and dusty pavements drifts in the air. Outside, tourists are swarming, their chatter and screeches mingling with the calls of the birds circling high in the azure skies. It was hot when Joy disappeared too. Another 'unprecedented' heatwave, and another summer of sweltering unease.

I turn back to the TV. The news is full of the weather: the drama created by the long drought, the train lines that have stopped working, the old people most at risk.

But the next announcement makes me hold my breath in shock. A little piece of news but a headline if ever there was one.

"In breaking news, the police announced today they have a new lead on the disappearance of Joy Maddison and are currently searching a building site in West Hove, where a body has been discovered..."

I lean further forward, heart thumping faster, palms sweaty, squinting at the screen. Shit. I mean, really? All these years I've been waiting, watching the news, the police, and now it comes...

The presenter explains that she has been missing for five years, and police have had no new leads on the case during that time. The picture changes to footage of police teams and their dogs searching the area, and for a moment my heart stops but then I realise I've seen this before; this is old footage, from the aftermath of her disappearance. Even the presenter looks saddened now, as he tells us sombrely that the day after Joy went missing, her necklace was found in a rubbish bin at a local beauty spot on the South Downs. It was the little gold charm one she wore the most, a gift from her devoted husband, Emile. The jewellery was found ten miles from Joy's usual running route, from the route she was supposed to take that night. I push down my irritation; we know all of this. But I suppose they have to add the details. They show a graphic mapping her run, and it's done well, but they get her route a little wrong. She never made it that far. And the actress they chose is a poor, faded copy of my glorious perfect Joy.

I take a swig from my can of lager, sufficiently distracted until a photo of Joy is back on the screen.

And then they show the area being searched and I lean in to try to see it closer. It's one of the new social housing developments on the A259. These have been springing up across the city for a few years now, edging their way down towards Southwick and Fishersgate. They pop up on previously derelict brownfield sites, and yes, I think it is a good thing, but they are building on tainted land. They are developing land where maybe people might think broken buildings would lie undisturbed for years. Perhaps forever.

I recognise the place as the camera pans in, and my stomach knots. Crucially, frustratingly, the presenter doesn't say what new evidence has come to light, but their white tents and police cordons are everywhere. Everyone at the scene is dressed in plastic suits and booties, making them look like they've just dropped down from a space station.

Their faces are sombre with self-importance, shuttered from those who have a right to know. Keeping secrets from us.

I grab my phone and check Twitter, always the best place to get information. Sure enough, the tabloids are already speculating now a body has been found. Is it Joy's body? And if it isn't, what's the link to her disappearance? Lots of comments from keyboard warriors who know nothing at all but love to sound off behind a screen.

There has always been a two-way split amongst her fan base – between those who believed she was killed the night she went missing, and those who are convinced she ran away with a new lover. A few murmurs that the pressure of fame led her to take her own life, but people don't really like this one. Because if she had committed suicide, it would be partly our fault, wouldn't it? We don't want to feel a trace of guilt that our constant adulation, or conversely, our constant trolling, might have contributed to the death of a mother, a wife, a daughter and a sister. Some of us really don't like that at all, and so we go back to chuntering behind our keyboards.

As I watch, listen to the commentary on this new discovery, my heart rate speeds up even more, and the worry makes me grab another can of beer, but twist it round and round in my hands, not opening it. When I do snap the ring pull, I cut my thumb, and the beer froths everywhere, mingling with the blood. My hands are shaking. For Christ's sake, I should be cooler than this.

Gradually though, as I wipe the blood away and clear up the mess, I find I can rationalise. Whatever they may have found, it will be okay, I'm almost sure of it. How would they even find me, anyway? The time the police should have discovered what really happened was the night she went missing, or when they discovered her necklace. There is no sign they have any further information on those crucial few hours.

But coppers are tricky and, like anyone with a bit of power, you can't trust them an inch. I need to be careful.

I still have my ways of finding things out, so tomorrow I'll put the word around, ask a few casual questions, and the first sign that this might lead to something bigger, and I'm off. I've had it planned for five years after all, so it won't be hard to put into play.

The programme ends with a close-up of Joy's face. It's a shot I recognise from her Instagram account, and a plea from the presenter to get in touch if you know anything or saw anything the evening she vanished. By now I'm calm again, reassured there is no big reveal they are hiding from us, that this is a minor interruption to my annual pleasure.

I wait, drink in hand, sure they will go for a dramatic ending, the money shot, and let out a sigh of pure satisfaction. The programme closes with the shot of Joy, filmed on her own camera, the one she positioned on the gate and left behind. She laughs, before turning to run into the woods, blonde ponytail flopping across her neon-pink running vest, feet thudding on the dry summer path.

And then she was gone.

SIX

"Make sure you do show up for work on your next shift." The rough voice in her ear was familiar from the fish market. Ned's boys. Ned's crew, who breathed violence as naturally as they breathed oxygen. "We know what happens to people who bail on us. We're a team, aren't we, Harley? A family. And families stay loyal, Mattie Woods."

"Because if you don't who knows what might happen to your new boyfriend?" The other man, she recognised him too, stood in front of her, barring her way. He smiled, pushing his red, sweaty face close to hers. He wasn't someone who was usually violent, but at this moment in time he was clearly out to prove himself with Harley. "And don't start talking in your sleep, Mattie. Jono couldn't keep any secrets, and now the little bastard's gone, hasn't he?"

"I don't know what you mean! Do you know what happened to Jono? Where is he? *Do you know where he is?*" Mattie managed to say, and she could feel her voice going shrill with terror. Her limbs still ached, and her brain still felt a little foggy, a side effect of her recent illness, she assumed. Whatever the reason, she didn't feel in control, and certainly not ready to be interrogated by Ned's pet thugs.

She could hear the rattle and thunder of an approaching train. The embankment to her right was separated by just a shoulder height strand of thin, rusty wire fencing.

Harley bent down into the bushes and hauled a body from the brambles. It was a boy, no more than a teenager, his head lolling back, and the man hoisted him over his shoulder.

Mattie recoiled in horror, feeling her mouth and eyes widen in shock. She took in the small burns along the boy's naked arms, the red raw marks where he had been restrained. His T-shirt and jeans were covered in mud and blood, but his chest still rose and fell. He was alive.

"Who's that? What are you doing?" She tried to push forward, towards the kid.

"Someone who couldn't keep secrets, just like Jono." Harley grinned, as he lowered the wire fence down with one hand. With a twist of his massive shoulders, he adjusted the boy on his back and began his descent towards the track. "Nobody likes a fucking sneak, Mattie," he called back to her. "Costs us money, costs us deals, costs lives."

"No! What are you doing?" Mattie couldn't stop a cry of distress. She was struggling feebly while the men held her back, laughing at her horror. She could feel nausea rising and tears raw in her throat.

The noise of the train came nearer, approaching the tunnel, and, reaching the halfway point on the embankment, Harley threw his burden out onto the line with an obscene grunt. The boy rolled several times, coming to rest half on, half off the track, at the entrance to the tunnel.

"He's still alive... You can't do this!" Mattie screamed at them, lashing out as hard as she could, desperate now to prevent the tragedy, but her words were lost in the roar of the oncoming

train. The driver, coming from dark to light, on a blind bend out of the tunnel, would have no chance of seeing the obstruction on the line.

She was still struggling frantically, consumed by the need to do something, dimly aware she could do nothing. Another death, another day of violence. Her captor was laughing, containing her with ease in the loop of his arms.

Ignoring her screams, Harley climbed casually back up the embankment, and they pushed Mattie into the overhanging trees with them, turning her face with cruel fingers squeezed into her cheekbones, forcing her to watch the execution, the horror. She shut her eyes in defiance and concentrated on the fuzzy black swirls in her head. But the swirls were laced with scarlet threads and the noise from the outside was inside too. Her face was wet with tears. The train roared past and was gone.

"Just a little warning," Harley told her as the sound moved away, his mouth close to her ear, words ringing in her brain, and they dragged her swiftly away with rough, heavy hands.

Numb with fear and sickness, her bad knee protesting with every stride, she stumbled along with them, unable to speak, breathing so fast she wondered if her racing heart could keep up. Did they know she was an informant? Had they known about Jono and killed him? Her phone, her precious work phone, seemed to burn against her in her pocket. She always deleted the messages, and it was filled with enough random numbers and apps to make it seem like her own personal phone, but what if they knew?

It seemed like forever, staggering along with her captors, listening to the noise on the trainline behind her, and the crash and grind from the industrial estate to her left.

Suddenly Harley spun her around, and before she could react, the other man delivered a quick, vicious punch to her abdomen, just below her ribs. As she doubled over in agony, they let her drop to the ground before heaving her roughly over the fence. A swift boot to her back and she, in her turn, rolled helplessly down the railway embankment.

For a long time, Mattie lay amongst the weeds, a sprinkle of pollen dust from the trees above, spitting on her upturned face, the burning pains slowly subsiding from her body. One hand slowly unclenched from her phone and the other moved slowly to her face. She traced the scar on her cheek, the line of her lips. *Alive. She was still alive.* It wasn't the first time she had been beaten up. Hour by hour, day by day, she reminded herself, she would get away from all of this. She had to.

Further away, behind the treeline, she could see blue flashing lights, hear shouts and engine noise. The boy's face would haunt her. He had been alive too, but maybe, just maybe, he had stayed unconscious. She hoped with all her heart that he had stayed unconscious.

Mattie vomited painfully into the brambles, one hand clinging to the wire fence, swaying slightly, waiting for the nausea and shock to pass. Her face was wet with sweat, and she still felt dangerously close to passing out.

It took a long time to get the last hundred metres home, but she made it, experiencing the kind of gut-tearing relief of a marathon runner reaching the finish line. Tears poured down her cheeks, and she was still shaking. That poor boy. Not much more than a child!

The tiny spark of confidence she had been nurturing had gone, and she scrabbled desperately around the house for a bottle or a wrap of something. There was half a bottle of cheap vodka under the sink in the bathroom. The cap was missing, and a film of dirt lay across the liquid, but she drank it anyway.

She shoved her work phone back in the drawer, ignoring everything, everyone.

By late afternoon, enveloped in a haze of alcohol, she was able to take out her scrapbooks, tracing the beautiful pictures with clumsy fingers. She and Jono had loved to do this when they were wasted, and this way they could enjoy them without the terrible stab of guilt and regret that came if she looked at them sober.

Joy Maddison stared out from every page. She was so beautiful, so confident and happy with her long, wavy blonde and brown hair, her aquamarine eyes, Mattie thought now, drifting gently along on the tide of vodka.

Again, she touched her scars self-consciously. Joy would never have taken drugs, have drunk so much she turned from an exuberant party girl to hopeless addict, lost her own self in a whirlpool of self-hatred.

She picked up her personal phone, now mercifully dry and working again, and comforted herself by re-watching the documentary from a couple of weeks ago. So sad, so very sad. On Twitter, Joy was still trending, as she always did around the time of the anniversary and for a few months before and after.

Jono had said they must never say a word to anyone. The only way to cope was to keep it between themselves. It was terrible what happened, he said, but they weren't to blame. Not really.

Mattie's attention was drawn to the breaking news, which flashed up a header as she scrolled. She clicked, fingers slipping across the screen in her haste.

Joy's sister, Lucy, was being interviewed again. DI Lucy Merry. Mattie sometimes wondered if Joy had been as proud of her sister as she always claimed. Online, there had been rumours of tension between the sisters, due to Joy's choice of lifestyle. The police were only good for handouts, Jono had told her, useless at solving crimes. Or good for thrill-seeking, if you were a CHIS, she supposed. She waited impatiently for the link to load.

Jono was, or had been, a thrill-seeker. Mattie was... What was she? She didn't really know. A follower. A puppet. As the effects of the alcohol began to wear off the familiar sense of paranoia began to invade her brain, reaching snaky, treacherous tendrils into her thoughts. Why was she even still here after what she had done? She deserved to die. The thought echoed through her brain, the words of her nightmares. Who had said that? Jono?

'You don't deserve to live.'

'You are evil, but there is a way to make everything better...'

'Tell me what you did. Tell me what you DID!'

Mattie shivered. The harsh voice normally only came at night. She focused on the screen in front of her as she huddled on the large grubby double mattress on the floor, which had served as their bed.

The video still wasn't loading properly, and she re-clicked on the tantalising link, frustration rising in her chest, hot and sour. The house they were squatting in had some furniture and some amenities. The owners, whoever they were, had forgotten to turn off the water supply, and the generator provided electricity. Compared to where some people had to live, huddled in shop doorways, in the shelters on the seafront, or under the pier, they had it easy, Jono had always told her.

Finally, the link opened and she watched it, almost holding her breath. DI Lucy Merry had short, wavy brown hair instead of long blonde extensions, but her bluey-green eyes and the curve of her mouth when she smiled made her the image of her lost sister. Mattie found herself wanting to touch the screen, trace the figure with her rough, weather-worn fingertips. Lucy's voice was all at once different but the same, and she was taller, more angular, but had a similar build.

It was eerie seeing Joy's sister, and Mattie always wondered if it might bring comfort if Joy's family actually knew what had happened. More and more since Jono left, she had considered phoning the helpline, leaving an anonymous tip, but terror of her phone being traced, of having to face up to reality, stopped her every time. So far. Frowning, she listened to Lucy's words. This was old stuff, surely, edited from the documentary, which she had watched over and over.

But then the screen divided and the breaking news part hit her like Harley's fist in her guts. The remains of another poor woman had been found, the same age and with similar physical characteristics as Joy. She felt the tension build, clawing at her throat, making her heart race, as there was the TV presenter, live at the building site.

"It was initially believed the body may have been linked to the disappearance of Brighton influencer Joy Maddison, but new information received has led police to believe this is not the case, and the search for the identity of the deceased continues..."

It wasn't Joy. Mattie could feel wetness on her cheeks, but was only vaguely conscious that she was crying in great rasping sobs. Of course it wasn't Joy. She forced herself to continue watching.

DI Lucy Merry was speaking again. "If anyone knows anything, can remember the slightest detail that might help us to find out what happened to my sister—" She broke off, took a breath and continued, her voice a little stronger now. Or was it simply a little more desperate, Mattie wondered, after the news that the family still had no body, no idea what had happened. She couldn't help the relief flooding her body. "We need your help. Joy's family need your help. It's been five years since her children lost their mother, her husband lost his wife, and my father lost his youngest daughter."

It was heart-breaking and Mattie stared, transfixed, tears drying, itchy on her skin, drinking in every single nuance of Lucy's voice, every tiny facial movement from the flicker of her lashes to the curve of her mouth as she spoke – just as she and Jono had once done with Joy, greedily devouring her perfection. She couldn't look away.

SEVEN

The sun had set, and the long shadows of night encompassed the port. The night was hot and air dense with city smells and drunken laughter. Mattie found it hard to breathe as she trudged along the main road, trying not to think about what she had witnessed. Her feet, in the torn and battered trainers, were sweaty and uncomfortable, and she had a blister on her right heel. For some reason, it was this tiny hurt that brought tears to her eyes. *Get a grip, Mattie.*

Bobby was waiting by the main gates at the fish market, and he pulled her into a hug as soon as she walked in off the road. He was a very tactile person, and he had once told her he found it reassuring, grounding even, to be able to hug his friends, having never been encouraged to hug anyone during his childhood.

Bobby was like that. He was open and he shared stuff. Mattie didn't share anything if she was coherent and not under the influence. Unlike her boyfriend, she watched her mouth. Unlike that poor kid on the train tracks... Once again, she tried to shove the memory of the limp body away.

"What was that hug for?" She extricated herself from his welcome, wincing as her bruises complained, hoping the alcohol fumes hadn't reached him. Despite cleaning her teeth until her mouth bled, she was sure she must reek of it. And she was ashamed. She knew if the little blue bag of cocaine wraps had still been in the house, she would have blotted out the horrors with a load of powder too. Oh God, the sounds of the train screeching to a stop, the shouts, and she could easily imagine what a few tons of metal would do to a human body. *Stop it. Don't think about it.*

The darkness contrasting with the harsh floodlights as the catches were unloaded made her blink. The huge three-metre-high orange plastic shrimp, which stood to the left of the gates, near the 'Ramon and Sons' fish market sign, seemed to be leering at her. Someone had perched a pink cowboy hat on its head, and she blinked, half convinced she was hallucinating.

The stench of fish and diesel, the shouts of the workforce employed by Ramon and Sons, brought her sharply back to reality. Her feet crunched grit and dust as she and Bobby followed the concrete path around the back of the main buildings.

Mattie, still dazed from the trauma of the day, not to mention the quantity of alcohol she had knocked back, suddenly became aware her friend was speaking.

"Wake up, doll, I've been ringing you all afternoon!" Bobby, tall, slim and beautiful with cropped bleach-blonde hair, always looked out of place in his red work apron, like a model wrongly cast for a photoshoot. He held her at arm's length now, studying her bruised face with concerned blue eyes. "What happened to you, Mattie? Did you feel sick again? How did you hurt your face?"

"Nothing... Tell you later," Mattie hissed, before adding in her normal voice, "Sorry, my battery ran down and I couldn't find the charger," which was a lie. She didn't want to tell Bobby how she had spent the afternoon. The shame and nausea made her head feel hot and achy. Sweat was making her head itchy. She pulled her hand away, dragged a rubber band from her baggy pocket and tied her lank brown hair into a knot on the top of her head.

His eyes narrowed, telling her he knew she was bullshitting him, but to her relief he let it go without further comment, swiftly changing the subject, as he took out a pair of gloves from the plastic boxes. "Hey, guess what? I've got a gig!"

Genuine pleasure at his excitement chased away her fuzzy head, the events of this afternoon and the nausea. "That's amazing. I'm so pleased for you. When?" Bobby had been trying to break into the comedy circuit for months, writing his own material, reading it to Mattie on their breaks.

"Tomorrow night at the Ship and Anchor. It's off Walton Street. You know – the one that does open mic nights? You will come, won't you?"

"Me? Do you want me to come?" She was pleased for him, but surprised. Bobby had been working on this for so long, but every time she had asked if he was going to get a slot at the festival or perform in one of the comedy clubs or bars in the city, he had brushed her off, saying he wasn't ready.

"Of course I bloody want you to come!" He rolled his eyes. "You might be the only person in the audience. I want you to tell me how fucking wonderful I am, in case nobody else does."

She grinned at him, enjoying his excitement, before she caught the supervisor's eye and turned to grab a red plastic apron from the hook. With the addition of big, smelly red gloves, she was ready to heave and sort the slimy fish into iced containers. She hated it, and she especially hated the dead eyes staring at her as she sorted their lifeless bodies. But cash in hand no questions asked was hard to come by.

When she had explained this to Bobby, he'd pointed out the fish were dead so they couldn't be staring at her, and made her laugh, saying that years from now they would be sitting on the beach eating chips, looking back on this shit time as the point that brought them together.

"Hey, Mattie." Ned appeared in front of her, smiling blandly like they were best friends and he'd never given orders for a kid to be thrown under a train, or for her to be beaten up and threatened by Harley and Lucas. Just another contender for boss of the year, the bastard.

Beside her, Mattie felt Bobby slow his work and stayed close, probably feeling her shivering with fear and anger. He knew how terrified she was of Ned but had no idea quite why. She wouldn't tell anyone about what happened today. If she kept it locked inside, it never happened. It was the same with her nightmares, and the voice. As long as she didn't speak about them, they weren't real.

Bobby wasn't at all terrified of Ned. Outside of his toxic personal relationship, he had a core of steel Mattie admired. He frequently told Ned and his merry men to fuck off and shrugged off their 'pretty boy' insults with singular, rather elegant, disdain. Nobody but Mattie had known that for many years after work until recently, Bobby went home to an abusive partner, who lashed out whenever he felt insecure.

"Mattie, I want you to come along with me, I've got another job for you tonight." Ned made a mark on his clipboard, and stared at her, lips parted in a smirk. He was challenging her to protest, to step out of line.

She couldn't stop her face from registering fear, from freezing inside at the thought of working alongside Ned. Or worse. Did he know?

"Don't look so worried, Mattie! Come on, let's get on with it." Ned was clearly enjoying every minute of making her squirm, laughing at her as though he was just the best boss in the world and she a reluctant employee. "Bobby, you get on with this container with Cain. Lucas, Harley and Karl, you come along too."

Safety in numbers, Mattie thought hopefully. Had he tortured Jono, before he killed him, she wondered now, as she followed her boss into the shadows. Had he laughed as he murdered her boyfriend?

EIGHT

DI Lucy Merry was flicking through the files, working on the backlog of emails that had accumulated during the past seven days, forcing herself to concentrate. But her sister's face was everywhere. On every screen, or every wall, as though Joy was trying to send her a message. When Lucy pressed her hand to her forehead and closed her eyes briefly, she could see a reel of early childhood memories, so much more precious since her sister had vanished. She saw the two of them laughing on the pebbly beach, eating ice-creams on the pier, on the double tyre swing in the garden...

Not knowing what had happened was unbearable. She had seen it over her years as a police officer, but not really believed when the families told her they would rather know the worst, so they could grieve and move on. Anything, they had explained, was better than the endless waiting, the false hopes and the inevitable crash of gut-wrenching disappointment when a new lead proved to be useless.

Well, now she knew, and if the victim happened to be a little bit famous in her own way, it was much worse. Everyone had seen her, everyone had their own theory as to what had happened and everyone wanted to be involved.

The TV screen in the corner, silenced but still showing the local news, was moving from a fire in Worthing to a suicide of a teenage boy on the train tracks in Portslade. Sadness and desperation, Lucy thought, picking up the remote control. She didn't need to take on board anyone else's grief just at the moment. She hated summer, hated the heat Joy had loved, hated the fact the sun beat down and the city was busy with people getting on and living their lives. Her life seemed to have frozen when her sister went missing. She still carried on day-to-day life, managed, Christ knows how, to get it together enough to nab a promotion. Although she still suspected it was a bit of a pity offering, designed to put her on another track, away from the more public investigations.

For the anniversary she had taken a week off work to be with the family, as she always did. The remains of the family. Her dad was a mess at this time of year and her brother-in-law, Emile, was trying hard because of the kids, but he needed her too.

She couldn't concentrate. Instead of signing off on the new CHIS that had been added to the books in her absence, and checking in on her source handlers, she found herself looking back at photos on her phone. Her beautiful little sister, with her perfect smile, and bleach-blonde hair falling in perfect waves. Even with the slightly superficial Barbie look she had cultivated towards the end, nothing could take away Joy's genuine smile, her sweetness and the way she could make anyone feel happy without even trying.

Who would have wanted to hurt her sister? Lucy hated that the answer was immediate. Lots of people. So many people would have wanted to topple her from the higher echelons of the influencers. Joy had been semi-famous, a celebrity in the world of influencers and the kind of magazines Lucy avoided. Z-list they called it, but her following had brought her money, and a career in a space where twenty years ago, the word 'influencer' certainly wasn't used in the context of a job description.

The media might be divided on the pros and cons of influencing as a career, but nobody could deny it when money came rolling in. That was the real success. It was business, and suddenly Joy had been a businesswoman, not just another wannabe. Her sister had always disliked the word 'influencer', said it had negative connotations.

Nobody but Emile and her father knew Joy had also been filled with insecurities, moved to tears by trolls, struggling to hold it together for the last few months before her disappearance. None of this had shown in her bright, happy vlogs, or her beautiful, carefully crafted photographs on her Instagram feed. Being signed as the face of a clothing brand, with her own edit, had been huge and it had tipped her over into the big time. Not just a local celebrity now, but someone who had to hire a PR agency to deal with numerous requests for appearances and collaboration.

There was a particularly nasty little online forum that had sent Lucy personal messages after Joy's disappearance, urging her to check out the posts. She had, and Cybercrimes had been through the lot, interviewed people, discarded people. There was nothing there. And yet every year, on the date Joy had vanished, her family would receive a little reminder to check the forum.

She knew she shouldn't. It was masochistic and self-destructive, and she should be working, not wasting time on this shit, but her hand moved towards her phone as though disconnected from her control...

The NatterJack – Welcome to our forum, dedicated to influ-

encers, *public figures and celebrities. Please keep your posts
clean and follow the rules. Happy nattering!*

@JustAnotherNatterer: *Thanks to admin for welcoming me as a
new member. Like many of us, I am sick of these influencers
taking us for complete idiots when all we give them is love and
positivity for their brands.*

Here is my April contribution to Joy's thread:

*In the last month Darling Joy has been showing us round her
garden, exhorting us all to get out in the fresh air and do some
gardening. This is mainly so she can show off her new free
clothes and blag some free garden equipment from Barley Mow,
the company she seems to mention in almost every post. (I know
some of us are complaining as she isn't declaring #AD enough.)*

*As usual Emile has been chained to the kitchen counter, making
his special French salad dressing or tinkering with the new AGA.
I know he's a chef but come on, all the poor man seems to do is
cooking and washing according to these vlogs. Not very
advanced cooking either.*

*The kids have been encouraged to pose with the new chickens, in
a very picturesque hen run, but they are only really allowed
airtime if they are advertising some new range of clothing or toys
that madam has blagged or been paid to promote.*

*Darling Joy is looking rather sparkly and fresh-faced after a
course of beauty treatments from Casey's Spa in The Lanes – bet
that didn't cost her anything! She must think we're stupid the
amount of advertising she's doing in every vlog and not coming
clean with #AD. I know a number of us have now pushed this*

along official channels, and hopefully instead of raking in the
cash and laughing at us, she will eventually pay the price with a
bit more than money.

The bitchy hate thread went on and on, with others chipping in on the comments section to agree how much they despised and hated Joy. And yet they still watched her, followed her, picked her life apart like crows at a rabbit carcase. Lucy put her phone down and picked up her mug of tea. It was cold so she set in down again, pushing away the nausea she felt each time she read something derogatory about her sister. Joy's fame had not just affected her personally, it had spread tentacles across family, friends, neighbours. Many had felt the light but poisonous sting as a side effect of being connected to Joy Maddison.

Lucy was desperate not to give up hope, but in her heart, and from her experience, she just knew. Joy was not coming home. Someone had found a way into her life, probably killed her that same evening she went missing. She was dead and gone, and her family could only hope one day, they might have a body to grieve over, get the closure they were desperate for. On her desk were photos of Emile, her parents, her nieces and nephew, in laughing family groups, and one single picture, a totally spontaneous one of her and Joy on the rainy beach in Brighton, the year it had happened. They were laughing, hair messy and eyes watering. No make-up, no filter. Beautiful.

With an effort, she turned back to her files, to her job. The news about the woman's body had stirred everything up again, but she had to force herself to focus. And it wasn't even the poor victim that had raised her blood pressure, it was the DNA that had been discovered on the body. A tiny thread of clothing, lodged in a fingernail.

Right, DC Miles Parker was going to have to go. He was

burnt out, a loose cannon, caught up in the criminal world and unable to resist the temptations it was offering him. He was sinking fast, and it was time to cut him loose before he did any major damage. Operating under four different aliases, he had been one of the best six months ago, but things changed quickly under pressure. Abs, Diego, Lennie and Bailey would all have to go. False names for false lives that had served their purpose. She made a note about transfer opportunities.

She tapped on the keyboard and pulled up another file. DC Alia Mattez could take over the new CHIS, Mattie Woods, if she was willing. It would be tricky, and several of Miles' contacts would just have to be ditched, but this one was a fairly new acquisition and she had access to Ned Carthy. Lucy badly wanted Ned; even though she had made the move from Major Crimes, and technically was no longer part of the team, she still wanted to see him shut down. It was unfinished business. The sly bastard had fingers in so many illegal pies he should have his own bakery. And he was getting overconfident. At long last, at the beginning of the year, she had felt they were making little inroads into his business dealings.

Lucy picked up her phone and placed a call to DC Alia Mattez, fingers tapping the table, her eyes fixed on the blank TV screen in the corner as her sister once more filled her mind.

Her source handler didn't pick up, so, ignoring her emails and stack of paperwork, Lucy gave in to her craving for information and rang her contact at the lab instead. The discovery of the body was something she couldn't get out of her head, coming as it had two days before the anniversary of Joy's disappearance.

The body was female, early thirties, the skull obviously showing signs of violence despite having been in the ground. So far, the police had managed to keep it under wraps, issuing a standard, vague statement, so that even the journalists had no idea what had really been discovered at the building site in

Hove. The press statement was true, the body wasn't Joy's, but it was a potential brand new lead, one that would certainly not be communicated to the media at this stage.

"Hi, Jess." Lucy tried to push down the rising hope in her heart, crushing her emotions.

"Hi, love." Jess was an old friend. "There's no doubt at all in my mind."

"But you can't tell how old it is? I mean, Joy could have been abducted and kept with this woman, and buried somewhere else or moved on? Or are we thinking secondary contamination?" She rattled out the questions, brain working furiously.

"Take a deep breath, Lucy. It's unlikely Joy would have been trafficked. Think about it. She was famous, she was hot property, and a totally different demographic to this poor woman. You know DI Armstrong already got an ID and traced the victim's parents?"

"Yes. Elise Vorunchuk." Lucy leant on one elbow, propping her chin in her cupped hand. She did know really, rationally, that a woman with millions of YouTube followers was not going to be trafficked like these poor anonymous victims. It was just that her professional knowledge seemed to fly out the window whenever her sister was concerned, and emotion took over.

"Right." Jess's sharp Northern accent sliced through Lucy's doubts. "She was a Polish student, and according to her parents she signed up to one of these websites that claims to fix girls up with jobs as nannies or bar staff."

"I saw the report. Her parents were under the impression she'd landed a job as a housekeeper to a rich ex-pat couple, who had a villa in Calvia. It's in Mallorca, Spain and they took it for the summer. They said she told them the couple were very private and didn't want their details circulated, so Elise couldn't give an exact address. After she left, they had regular texts until August. August five years ago..." Lucy knew the report off by heart. The summer she lost her sister. It didn't seem like five years ago.

She kept as close to all the investigations into Joy's whereabouts and was aware she was a pain in the arse, but she wanted answers. The family wanted answers, and they couldn't see why Lucy, as a serving police officer, couldn't provide them. She had failed them.

"We've sent the samples off for specialist testing and I know the DI is still talking to Interpol. In answer to your other question, yes, secondary contamination is possible. Hold onto that hope and we'll get as much as we can."

"Thanks, Jess. Sorry, I just wanted to touch base." Lucy could sense her friend was busy. In addition, as she wasn't officially on the case, for obvious reasons, Jess was going out on a limb to share the information. "It just throws up so many questions. My dad and Emile have been going crazy, trying not to hope, but equally wondering if she really is in Spain, living it up with another bloke. I had to stop my dad booking us all plane tickets last time there was a sighting." She sighed.

"I get it, honestly, I do," Jess paused, and Lucy could hear the light rattle of a keyboard. "If Joy's DNA was discovered on Elise's clothing and body, firstly how the hell did Elise get from Mallorca to Brighton, and secondly, did Joy come with her?"

Lucy put her phone away in her bag, thinking hard. There had been reported sightings of Joy in Spain since she vanished. But also in Ireland, Scotland, Wales and parts of the USA. Whatever her sister had done, whatever reasons she had for running away, if she was still alive, Lucy felt she could forgive anything.

She replayed the initial conversation with DI Armstrong in her head, as she had done a hundred times since he first rang her with the news.

"Forensics have found a trace of your sister's DNA on the body from the Hove building site. It's being fast-tracked at the

lab. We don't know how old it is, and there is currently no sign of another body, but we're still searching.'

No other body yet, Lucy thought, as she switched off her computer, picked up her bag and slipped her car keys out of her pocket. They were all still searching. Everyone was always still searching.

NINE

The gig had been a washout. Bobby had been right when he said hardly anyone would turn up. The open mic nights were held in a crowded pub. Just a tiny, raised area in one corner with a microphone was supposed to announce to everyone there was a comedy act in the house. Names of acts were chalked onto a blackboard. In Bobby's case some joker had changed his name to Booby by the time he had got to the microphone.

Four people paid attention to Bobby's 'tight five' introduction, including Mattie. She thought he looked like a rabbit caught in headlights, but the material was sharp and funny. He staggered to the end of his slot like a true professional, and she felt a glow of pride. It also occurred to her, watching with crossed fingers and a bitten lip, that she had never realised how long five minutes was before.

Two of the other audience members were pissed, homophobic blokes, and the other an elderly lady, who sat on her hard chair right until the very end, watching with pursed lips and a piercing stare. She approached the corner of the room and beckoned to Bobby, whispered something that made his face crumple and walked swiftly away.

Mattie sought out her friend, shoving her way through the two blokes, who swore at her. She swore back. The noise and crowd, the familiar smell of beer and sweat was nearly too much for her, but her focus was on her friend, which helped prevent her from toppling off her self-imposed sobriety wagon.

She found him outside in the alley by the bins. "What did she say to you, that woman?"

Bobby was wiping away make-up, and he looked up, all glittery eyes and red lips as he shrugged. "She said I had a beautiful voice and was quite funny."

"But that's good," Mattie said robustly, "I know the turnout was bad, but you were the first on, and everyone is still at the festival event up the road. Plus, in a pub everyone wants to drink, not watch an act. You were *funny*... You were!" She was just so proud of him for following his dreams, she was nearly in tears herself.

He finished with the make-up remover, pulled off his wig and ruffled his hair before pulling a sky-blue hoodie over his head, snuggling into its soft folds, despite the heat of the night. "I know, I do really, but I was just hoping for a few more... It took a lot for me to get up there on stage and now I'm wondering why the hell I do it in the first place, or if I should ever bother to do it again."

"You will do it again, because you have talent," Mattie told him fiercely. "You just need a bit of luck. And this was a last-minute slot. You'll get more and it will be better next time. Just... maybe hang on for an actual event instead of the corner of a pub next time. But if you can do it here, you can do it anywhere. It was your first time, Bobby, give yourself a break!"

They started for the street, arm in arm, and Bobby smiled suddenly, relaxing, the corners of his mouth wrinkling in the way Mattie loved. With his blue eyes and elegance, she often told him he was a lot like a rather beautiful cat.

"They say that about sex, don't they?" Bobby said. "The first time is always the worst."

She leant her head briefly on his shoulder, relieved he still had his sense of humour. As always when the past was mentioned, she felt a pang of loss. After years of addiction, she had lost a lot of memories. Sex was a perfect example. She kind of remembered sex with Jono, but nothing before that. Mattie had no idea whether she'd had loads of partners, how crap her first time had been, if she had ever been in love – absolutely zilch. An ambulance flashed past, blue lights and sirens shattering the usual buzz of nightcrawlers along the pavement, the driver expertly weaving in and out of the oblivious Friday night traffic.

Mattie had learnt it was better not to try and delve into the past. She became frustrated and tearful at her memory loss, but also afraid she would stir up the voice and her nightmares. Perhaps it was better she *didn't* remember her first time. Or her first anything. The blackouts were a consequence of years of hard drinking, the drugs she forced on her body. Now she was older, she was paying the price. An addict. She was an addict, and she didn't want to be one now Jono wasn't around.

Bobby left her at the main road, walking slowly, zigzagging up the hill to get the bus. She watched him until the darkness swallowed his slender, hunched figure. The familiar dizziness engulfed her as she in turn tried to direct her feet homeward, but she pushed it away. It was happening less and less, but Bobby's sadness had affected her and now she wanted a drink again.

She wouldn't.

Hating herself but this time powerless to stop the craving, she nipped into the off-licence by the traffic lights, sat outside and snapped the ring pull, snapped the next one, craving the feeling when the alcohol hit her bloodstream, giving that hazy, warm, relaxed state. A group of teenage girls, dressed for clubbing in miniskirts and bra tops, swaggered past in high heels. A group of men eyed them up.

Couples wandered along arm in arm. In a shop doorway two men were making out, and in the next shop doorway a homeless man was sitting on his sleeping bag, a plastic carrier bag next to him. He stared vacantly into the road, his face pale and sweaty as it was caught in the neon lights of the takeaway next door. The tide of people flooded onward, headed for other parts of town, but Mattie and the homeless man stayed put.

Invisible, she thought. *Me and him both.*

After she was done binging, she shoved the cans unsteadily into a bin, and headed for home. As she turned the corner it started to rain, a light spatter that barely marked the road, but promised one of those summer storms. Aware she was still at least ten minutes from home, she swore at her pathetic self. Too weak to resist the booze when things went wrong. *You're weak, Mattie. You'll never get out of this mess now.*

As she finally turned onto the coast road, the rain became a downpour. Ahead, a group of teenagers were standing huddled around something in the drainage gutter. They were laughing, chucking beer cans. Mattie took little notice, staggering along in the shadows, avoiding trouble, until she was right next to them. A beer can bounced off her arm and she hunched deeper into the rain-soaked folds of her hooded top.

She heard it then, piercing through the comforting haze of alcohol. A tiny mew of fear. Mattie stopped, swinging round to face the kids. There was a creature flinching in the gutter. A ball of sodden fur, terrified and trapped.

Without thinking, Mattie gave a roar of rage and launched herself at the group. *"Fuck off, you little shits!"*

They jeered and laughed but she ignored them, and such was the force of her onslaught they backed away, chucking a few beer cans, still circling her and the cat. Keeping a wary eye on the attackers, she reached down and plucked the creature from the gutter, tucking into her cardigan. She could feel the terrified patter of its heart, the shivering and its tiny form against her larger one.

Mattie took out her knife. Lots of people like her had a weapon. On the street it could sometimes be the only way to survive. Only ever for emergencies, Jono had taught her. Well, nobody was taking this poor baby away from her. A rush of familiar yet strange emotions made her chest and throat tighten as she backed slowly away from the danger zone. The teenagers advanced, following her down the road.

"Hey, mad bitch, whatcha gonna do with that? Eat it?"

"Nah, she's just a loser junkie... She wants to *smoke* it!"

The laughter and the taunts continued until a police car emerged from the side road that led to the port, cruising slowly towards the town centre. This was a familiar patch for trouble, a regular beat for local law enforcement. The teens legged it over the chain-link fence into the industrial estate, clearly having their own reasons for not wanting to confront the law.

The police car moved on, accelerating along the stretch past the petrol station. Mattie hastily, clumsily, slipped her knife away. She walked slowly and carefully, bent over in the summer rain until she reached home. She was drunk, but concentrating so hard on her precious cargo, she felt almost sober. The rain washed away her tears, turned dusty pavements into rushing streams and drummed loudly on the factory roofs.

In the house, she took her cardigan off, wrapped the cat snugly, taking care that its little whiskered face stuck out, and flicked on a couple of lights. In her hurry, she almost tripped over the flex, and the overloaded power socket, which snaked under the mattress, but at least they had some light now.

Finally, she hurried to bring old blankets and a bowl of milk, with some stale bread soaked in it. She crooned to the little creature as she rubbed it carefully dry with a frayed towel. It was a silver tabby. Pretty. A stab of fear that this might be someone's pampered pet and might be taken away from her.

Mattie pushed the thought aside. The cat had half an ear gone on the left-hand side, and a thick rope-like scar where some fur was missing along one foreleg. Its eyes were green and intelligent, but still bright with fear. It had a pink nose and extremely long, trembling white whiskers. She stared at it, lips parted in a smile, feeling herself light up inside with a kind of childlike enchantment.

For the first time in ages, she sat carefully on the battered old sofa and looked around her, taking in the filth, the mould on the walls. She felt completely sober now, which was impossible after the amount she had drunk tonight. On her lap the cat suddenly looked up at her, blinked and started purring. Tears coursed down her cheeks, and she swallowed hard. She tasted salt as she wiped her cuff across her face, sniffing happily. The cat's eyes were huge, studying her with fear and curiosity. It was perfect, and she ached to draw the delicate lines of the furry face. But not now, they needed to get to know each other first.

They sat together in the yellow glow of the inadequate lights, until the animal fell asleep, and Mattie closed her own eyes.

She woke the next morning to find the cat gone. Desolation shook her entire body, rattling her brain. But as she stirred, pushing off the rough blanket, the cat appeared, purring, meowing, rubbing round her legs. Its fur was spiked out and wet, suggesting it had found its way out, but still returned to her.

"Oh!" She spoke out loud, unable to believe her pure rush of joy at its presence. At the same time the nightmare, always lurking at her elbow, spilled out from the shadows. The voice was back, shouting at her, screaming even.

'You don't deserve to live after what you did.'

'Say it. Admit what you are, what you did... Say it now!'

She braced herself for the panic attack the voice usually triggered, but she focused her attention on the cat, currently washing its white paws, still purring, and gradually the voice faded. She took a deep, steadying breath.

"I suppose you need a name." Her voice sounded different. She pondered the cat. "Cleo? Silver?" Something was pushing on her brain, a weight, or the pressure of being underwater and struggling to reach the surface. "Nuala. That's your name."

It was only after she had repeated the bread and milk meal of the night before that she remembered. Joy had had a cat called Nuala. It had died after being hit on the road, and she had been devastated, blaming herself for not fencing the garden properly. She had been so honest in her vlogs, never trying to gloss over things like that, Mattie thought. Joy would have saved this cat too.

She found this particular memory of Joy didn't tear her apart quite so much. So what if the cat was called Nuala? Animals were old spirits and this one had found her. Mattie found she quite liked the idea of having the reincarnation of one of Joy's pets to look after. Perhaps it was a faint sign she was being forgiven for what she and Jono had done. Mattie traced guilty fingers over her strikes on the wall, pushed down the self-loathing and began another column for today. *Nobody said it was going to be easy.*

The cat jumped on her lap as she sat down on the floor, wrapped in a blanket. "I never meant to hurt Joy, Nuala. Even Jono said that we never meant to hurt her. Because we loved her, you see. We loved her so much. Too much, I guess."

The cat blinked, staring with shining eyes. Under the steady gaze she grew slightly uncomfortable. "We just wanted her to know *how* much we loved her, but Jono, he went too far... He was drunk and a bit crazy. You know what men are like, Nuala, they always want things. They always try to take too much." Her voice was soft, hesitant at times, but she kept talking, soothing herself as well as the cat, blotting away the shadows and the harsh voice that accompanied them.

"I used to listen to Joy when she was a presenter on the radio. She lost her job a few years ago, but she still has that sweet voice, and she was so kind to everyone, Nuala. She said she lived for her job. If the radio station hadn't closed she might never have been an influencer, or she might have moved into TV or something. We would still have loved her whatever she did, Nuala."

Nuala closed her eyes, kneading with her claws on Mattie's lap, and eventually Mattie dozed too, in a ray of sunshine, as the sun broke through after the storm of last night. She could forget the past for a moment, focus on the present maybe. She would have to get food for her cat, more blankets for them both, some more diesel for the generator so they could both be warm and have electricity. Jono had always got fuel before.

She would have to work more hours and maybe do another job for Abs. The fear the cat might belong to someone had dissipated. Nuala clearly recognised her as a kindred spirit, and perhaps would stay with her now. Mattie had always liked cats. The thought came suddenly and weirdly. Perhaps, as Bobby said, if she could stay clean, other things would come back to her and good things might happen, despite the predictions of the voice. But that would mean confronting her past, and Joy.

Was she ready to do that?

TEN

We watched her every day, millions of us. The last big event she did, we were there, clapping and smiling in person and online, as she told us all how honoured she was to be doing collaborations with this business and that business, about her new clothing range, and how she had hit five million subscribers on her YouTube channel.

Instead of watching from behind my screen, I was rubbing shoulders with the others. Occasionally I winced away from their slavering devotion, but I did understand. The girls next to me were cooing over Joy as she stood in the red-carpeted VIP area. Her dress was too revealing, cheapening her beauty. I would have instructed her, forced her, to wear something else, but the colour of the fabric brought out the sea-green of her eyes and her golden tan.

Her long hair was straight and glossy that day, falling down to her waist. She looked like a little doll, ready for someone to pluck from the toyshop shelf. My doll. Pride burnt in my chest and every time she looked across and caught my eye, I revelled in our intimate connection, the part I was playing in making her famous.

I forget whether it was some TV awards or a brand launch, but I knew at that exact moment, she'd finally found the stardom she never knew she was looking for. Joy always insisted she was just another girl-next-door, a local girl who had married well and accidentally found that her own brand of wholesome beauty and friendliness was marketable, loveable.

I was happy and sad at the same time, standing there soaking up the excitement, the fanatic obsessive love some of her fans had for her. They wanted to be her friend, they wanted to be her, to climb inside her world, they wanted to fuck her or work with her. Whatever the reasons, they wanted her.

The jealousy, the desperation emitting from those who trolled her, an equal amount to the genuine love and devotion, I would say, came in great waves, breaking and gushing over her as she posed for photographers before being led away by the security team. As the waves broke, I could almost taste the spray they flung out as they crashed over Joy, soaking her even as she stood, elegant and confident in the sunshine. It tasted sweet and sad and sour all at the same time.

Other minor celebrities, influencers, were ushered along, posed for photos and taken away, but we were there for her. Only for her.

An hour later, clouds darkened the sky, a summer thunderstorm growling in from the sea. It began to rain, but still the fans stayed strong, putting up umbrellas, chattering in groups, taking selfies in front of the security barriers. I knew from experience we would all stay put until she left the event, and that whatever the weather she would stop on her way out, chat, sign autographs, pose for selfies. Because that was what Joy was like. She was genuine, and she was a good person before it all began to unravel.

I'd seen enough that day, so I went home, checked her diary and started to make plans right after the event. We all knew where she would be, and her efforts to keep her home address secret had long been abandoned. Of course, she didn't advertise it, but she filmed her vlogs in her house, in the city, in the surrounding area, and she had become less and less cautious over the years. As she so often said, she was a local girl through and through and we knew everything about her.

We knew her career as a radio presenter stalled when the local stations closed and everything went up to London, and we knew she slipped into being an influencer almost by accident. Joy was genuine, and that's what made her both different and relatable. It was an irresistible combination.

It didn't matter if you lived in Nevada, Melbourne or Hove, if you followed Joy, you felt so familiar with her favourite places, you were with her as she stopped for coffee, lunched with girl-friends, took her kids to the park. The nanny would take care of her kids, while she got her photos done. Perfect, cute shots of a busy working mum. Which of course she was.

Every detail of her life, from what she ate for breakfast, to her exercise routine, to her skincare products was on show. All her fans knew her kids' names, ages, schools, and we could download the floorplan of her house. We could breathe in the wholesome, good-girl essence of Joy by simply watching her YouTube channel, buying her clothing or make-up collaborations, drinking the same coffee brand as she did.

But we preferred to see her in person, to be within touching distance. We wanted more.

ELEVEN

Time had seemed so blurred, previously so unimportant in her life, but now, Mattie had started to wake earlier, to sleep better. Bobby had helped her find her nearest AA meeting, and they had started to look at help available online. She was surprised to find it was there, she had just never looked for it before. Jono had reiterated again and again that they must stay under the radar, must live like this because it was the only way.

It was soon time to meet Abs again, this time on the pavement near Heaven's Gate where she stepped quickly into the car. It was safer than meeting in a café now and she was thankful Ned had so far not followed up on his threats.

"What have you got for me?" Abs asked. As usual the driver stayed silent, taking the long route out of the city, heading for the winding roads across Devil's Dyke and the South Downs.

"Ned's got a big shipment coming in next week." Mattie gave him the scrappy bit of paper she had written the details on. "I don't think it's just drugs either, because there's a buzz going round that it's a bit special."

Abs narrowed his eyes and shifted in his seat. "Special?"

"He doesn't tell us everything, you know that, but I don't

think he did get rid of Jono. I mean, one minute he talks like it *was* down to him, the next he's almost suggesting Jono was paid off and disappeared on his own," she explained. "He's also worried Jono might have talked to someone else, a rival you know, like he was playing both sides. That's why he keeps getting at me and trying to find out about you, I guess."

"You'll have to say I've gone up north for a bit," Abs told her. "The story holds, but not if we want him to carry on thinking the way he does. If he's focused on holding onto all his business, he might get careless."

"Ned's never careless."

"This is a big one though. There's another DI working on this, a new boss for you. She likes to meet everyone." His expression was an unhelpful blank, and she reacted quickly.

"No way! Meet a copper!" Mattie felt panic rise in her chest, hot and fierce. "Fuck off, Abs."

He was amused now, the corners of his mouth turning up, showing a dimple in his right cheek. "I'm a copper. It won't be any different."

"Not really, you're not. I mean not a proper one. Sorry, but no, I can't think..." Mattie rubbed her face with a trembling hand, and said quickly, "This is okay but I'm not talking to anyone else, alright?"

"Okay, I just thought it might bust this one open and this DI is pretty focused. If it really is a trafficking ring, it's massive. And you know the girls you saw in the shipping container could have been saved if we had got this open a few months ago."

"Don't try emotional blackmail with me, Abs, I know what kind of shit is going on," she said coldly, holding his gaze, noticing for the first time the light dusting of freckles across his nose, his cheeks.

He stared back at her, as though seeing her properly for the first time. "Sorry. Hey, you look different, you know. You sound different too."

She shrugged. "I'm getting off the booze and drugs, but don't jinx it," she said with quiet pride. "And I've been going to the AA drop-in meetings. Bobby took me."

"Really? That's good. How are you managing without Jono?" He sounded genuinely concerned, but she couldn't bring herself to mention Nuala. Nuala was now her talisman, her extra motivation to get away from this life.

"I still wonder what happened to him, where he is and why he left, but if I'm honest with myself..." She took a deep breath. "I'm better off without him." There, she had said it, and to Abs of all people. "I'm just going cold turkey, you know, taking one step at a time, one hour at a time." There was no need to mention the sweats and shakes, the vomiting and that her last few attempts had turned into disasters. But since the night she had rescued Nuala, she hadn't touched any alcohol, and she had now been off the drugs too.

"That's good." He was still looking at her in a slightly different way. "I'm pleased for you, but you know, this isn't something you can just leave behind. The one drink will always turn into a few bottles, or the one hit into a week of lost memories."

She found herself looking at him differently now. "You sound like you know?"

"Might do. Anyway, thanks for the info. We'll follow up on it." He paused, still watching her in a weird way. It was like there was an undercurrent of communication she couldn't quite figure out. "I might be getting transferred, so you might need to meet another copper anyway."

"What? *Why?*" Mattie felt the panic in her chest rising again. "I can't do this without you." She found herself cringing at her phrasing, even as the words fell into the tense silence between them. "And what about next week?"

He stared out the window for a moment, then turned back to meet her eyes and shrugged. "It's just a management thing. A promotion. I don't want to do it at all, but I can't turn it down. I'll make sure the handover is done and we can introduce another handler really quickly, so we don't lose any time on this. In fact, now you're coming off the drink and drugs, it makes it even easier. You're more likely to pick up female friends, do normal stuff like go out, and your new handler is a woman."

It was almost as though he was talking to himself, and Mattie saw the driver glance into the rear-view mirror, face impassive, but eyes watchful. His words hurt, slicing at her fragile confidence like little knives. More likely to be *normal?* There was a sharp edge to his tone that she didn't like. Had she not been normal then? Just because she was an addict didn't mean she wasn't normal. It just meant she had an additional load to struggle along with, a disease to ward off, something else to fight.

The wordless communication, and the beginnings of a potential bond had gone. "Are you saying a woman will definitely be taking over as my handler? When? Will she ring me?"

"No, I'm not saying anything. Here, I'll be in touch, and she will too."

Confused, Mattie took the handful of notes he offered, and zipped them deep inside her jacket. There were a lot of notes there, and she couldn't help but wonder if he'd made a mistake when he counted them. But she wasn't turning money down. Not when she had a new family to feed. The thought warmed her from the inside out.

"You know what to do, next Wednesday night?" Without waiting for an answer he went over it again. "I won't be there, but your new handler will want to go through it again, but I want to say... I want to say if you feel like it's too dangerous at any point, you get the hell out of that pub and start running."

"I..." Mattie stared at him. "Got it." Was he expecting it to go wrong?

"Good." He reached out a hand and held her chin lightly

between his fingers and thumb, until she raised her eyes to his. "Be careful. Nobody will give a shit about you except you. Remember that."

His eyes burnt on hers, until she turned away, breaking their connection. The fear simmering away like a cauldron full of poison in her stomach notched up to full-on terror. He was expecting it to go wrong, that was what he was trying to say. Mattie linked her hands and sat up straighter, almost holding her breath. Message received.

They rode in silence for the last ten minutes, and eventually the car drew up on the coast road, about half a mile from where she lived.

"Mattie?" His voice was low and he glanced quickly at the driver.

She paused as she stepped out, glancing in both directions. "Yeah?"

"Be careful, won't you? I mean it. This is really big, this thing with Ned. Dangerous."

For a second, she felt that undercurrent of terror again, but this time he looked away first, and she knew she was on her own. Decisively, Mattie pulled her hood up and zipped her coat up to her chin, even though the storm had long since drifted inland and the day was warming up to be a scorcher. "I'm fine, Abs. I'm always fine really."

She didn't look back as she heard the car pull away, but she was convinced he was still watching her.

TWELVE

Wednesday night, a week after Abs had also abandoned her, Mattie spent an hour upstairs in her house, breathing in the scent of hot summer air mixed with dust and dereliction. She had nearly finished two walls now and the soothing rhythm of sketching and painting kept the terror away, even if her imagery often evoked such a fierce pain after she had completed it.

At some point there had obviously been a fire in this room. A blackened fuse box hung from the ceiling by the door, and the walls were covered in a mix of soot and mould, overlaying the white paint.

As well as the stash of paintbrushes, she'd discovered that if she dipped her brush in water, she could recreate the colours in her head. The unusual heat of the summer had left the walls bone dry, and the mixture of mould and rust-coloured fungus became a thick inky medium she smeared with her fingers. The feeling of the cool, slightly gloopy mixture on her skin, the slight awe as she watched her fingers move as though they belonged to someone else, with skill and precision, transported her.

But the pain was brief, cathartic almost. Something kept

deep inside, someone who only surfaced in her nightmares, could be dragged into reality and slashed onto a wall. She could touch the faces with her fingers, could smear the mould spores right across eyes and mouths. If she wanted to.

But she knew what she had to do, and as the shadows lengthened, and the intense heat of the day cooled slightly, she laid her brushes down. The house was silent apart from the little creaks and groans, which she hoped didn't signify it was going to fall down.

Two hours later, Mattie slipped through the throngs of partygoers, and in at the side door of the Crown and Sword Inn, as she usually did. Ned had been using her as a drugs courier for a few months now, and she obediently passed the heavy shoulder bag to the man dressed in grubby chef's whites.

Abs' warnings were ringing in her head, but her new handler said she needed to be bang in the middle of the danger zone if she was going to get what she wanted. And it didn't get more dangerous than this.

The payment had already been arranged, so all she had to do was stay in the background, make herself invisible. She was pretty good at that, but she didn't want to be in the pub tonight, desperately didn't want to witness what she knew was going to kick off.

The new handler, Emily, had also assured her she just needed to do what she normally did. Both gangs should be present, a big deal going down, but Ned would know if she did the drop and then ran. Her orders were to stay in the pub, hang out with the crew as she would once have done with Jono. A week had not been long to get to know her new handler, and she sure as hell didn't trust her.

But tonight, instead of partying and artificial highs lasting well after the shadows had been swallowed by the fierce glittering heat of the day, there would be a raid. Emily, although vague on the actual details, said it would be loud, there would be a lot of firearms officers around, probably over forty, and Mattie would need to get on the ground when ordered to do so, follow commands and let herself be taken to one of the custody centres with the others who had been arrested. She might be taken away from Brighton, to Worthing, or even Crawley, but she must go along with everything, for her own safety.

Mattie replayed the conversation in her head, hunched over a pint, smelling it, almost tasting it, but not downing the amber liquid. God, she was so proud of herself, fixing in her mind a picture of her cat every time she felt the urge to slurp. Her stomach was twisting, and she was tapping her knee as she always did when she was nervous.

The change from Abs to Emily, intimidatingly sexy with her long dark hair, smoky rock chick eyes and scarlet lipstick, as she gave Mattie a last brief under cover of darkness on Tuesday, also made her nervous. At least she hadn't had to meet the DI in charge of The Unit yet.

An hour crawled past, with Ned's crew all back-slapping, rowdy, and jovial with the other crew. She watched these people, knowing how much street value the drugs in today's deal was worth. Knowing how much misery and ecstasy it would bring. To disguise her fear, she pasted on a smile, pretended to sway as though she was a little drunk, and imagined what the scene would be like if she was with Jono.

But every time the door opened she felt a jolt of electricity travel down her spine; her eyes were sore and every sense was alert and waiting for the raid. They had no idea, none at all, that as they drank, inhaled, swallowed, passed around girls, chips and discreet packages, that they were about to be busted.

At eleven-thirty, just as Mattie was beginning to lose hope, there was a sudden, swift noise of vehicles outside the door and the firearms officers were everywhere, shouting, pushing, as party-goers scrambled to get out the way and the landlady started yelling at them.

Mattie had known for a while that this pub was a major player in Ned's drugs empire, but she had been waiting for the right moment, the right payment. Her tip-off could at the very least take the shine off Ned's big deal, and merger with the other organised crime gang, maybe even lead to his arrest. Fewer drugs on the street would ultimately mean fewer deaths. It had occurred to her she had only started to think like this recently. She saw a lot, but now her mind was starting to actually process what she *did* see, to put puzzle pieces together.

"Get on the ground!"

"Get down, hands behind your head!"

"Now!"

She froze, hunched over, shivering with emotion, and slid to the floor with the rest of them. Her head twisted awkwardly to one side where she lay, and she watched the armed officers speedily searching, separating groups, taking control so quickly, so efficiently, she was shocked even though she had known what to expect. Her pint glass, spilled in the chaos, lay on the side of the table, the amber liquid dripping out onto the sticky red patterned carpet. Mattie hadn't touched a drop in two hours. Another small win in the midst of her current terror.

She could hear a few of Ned's clients, the landlady, the chef, all shouting, see them making a big fuss while the players and the couriers tried, and failed, to get clear. Some seemed to have simply vanished already, whether they had escaped out the back, thus delivering themselves straight into the waiting arms of the police officers, or really gone, she couldn't guess, but she felt like she had a big neon sign above her head flashing the word 'GRASS'.

There were more police inside the pub, now everything seemed to be under control, unarmed officers searching groups, starting to lead handcuffed individuals away. She began to breathe more easily. This was okay, and it had happened just as Emily promised it would.

Suddenly a scuffle broke out to her left, there were shouts and armed officers coming straight to the source of the trouble, but in the midst of the confusion, Mattie felt a strong hand grip her shoulder, a voice in her ear. "Let's get out of here." Harley, with his hood pulled up to shield his face, big shoulders hunched over and a knife vanishing quickly into a baggy pocket.

There was blood in the corner, someone else had also pulled a knife and was waving it around yelling. As Harley pulled her roughly away, and the fighting escalated, Mattie locked eyes with a police officer. A woman. She experienced a jolt of shock so bad that it actually winded her, and her knees almost collapsed under her trembling body.

The woman had Joy's eyes, but short, brown, wavy hair. Her face was familiar from the TV screen. DI Lucy Merry.

The crowded pub was in chaos again and the police were struggling to control them, to regain the upper hand, as Mattie, unprotesting, still in shock, was hauled roughly down to the kitchen. She forced herself to talk to Harley, act surprised, terrified, when she actually felt barely conscious.

"What the hell's going on?"

"You can see what's going on! It's a raid, isn't it? Let's go. For fuck's sake, Mattie, move a bit faster, you bloody cripple!" Even Harley's voice was laced with panic. *"Move!"*

She was stumbling, her bad knee letting her down badly, bashing into the work surface, knocking a pile of saucepans flying with a tremendous clatter.

"Harley, I can't..." Confusion and terror must be showing in her face, she thought, even though thankfully he had no idea of the real reason why.

Mattie was no actress, but it wasn't hard to fake, because she was freaking out at seeing Lucy in the flesh.

What would DI Lucy Merry have said if she knew the truth: that she had just locked eyes with her sister's killer?

THIRTEEN

Harley swung open a door in the floor, shoved the others down the steps into the darkness. Mattie was last to go, hovering, frozen with terror at the gaping space beneath the kitchen, shock at seeing Joy's sister still rendering her incapable of movement. Her chest was tight, she couldn't breathe. She clawed at her throat. The dark space yawned in front of her.

"Mattie! *For fuck's sake!*"

Without saying another word, Harley took two long strides, picked her up and carried her down into the shadows of the cellar, setting her roughly on her feet, where she reeled into the other members of their group. Behind her she saw the big man reach up and swing the door shut behind them, engulfing them in smothering blackness. She was aware only of her blind terror, of warm bodies bumping against each other, and the muffled curses, until Harley used the torch on his phone to light the way.

The cellar was well-stocked with racks of wine, huge plastic delivery crates and barrels of beer. One of the men grabbed a couple of bottles as he went past, shoving them into a rucksack, laughing. Others jogged along shoving each other in their eagerness to escape the law.

With no choice, Mattie followed them dumbly. She was trapped now, unable to follow the plan and get arrested with the others upstairs, stuck with Ned's reprobates, staggering along in a pitch-black tunnel somewhere under Shoreham High Street. There was occasional gossip about old smugglers' tunnels still being used on the coast, but mostly they had been blocked up or used as tourist attractions. She and Jono had visited one place like this in Hastings on a day out. Mattie tried to focus her mind on the memory, blocking out the hysteria that threatened to overwhelm her.

It had been a rare proper date when they had been to a pub for lunch and stayed talking all afternoon. They had been happy, drunk, and run into Jono's mate, who had brought a few wraps and given them a lift home.

Joy's sister still lingered on the fringes of Mattie's consciousness, as she stumbled along with the men, but she ruthlessly shoved DI Lucy Merry to the furthest corners of her mind, afraid of screaming out loud at the shock.

She forced herself to recall every detail of the day in Hastings, and only returned to reality when the group stopped, bumping into one another. Harley struggled with another door. It was rusted into the wall, and he swore, shoving violently against it, shouting at the others to help.

Between them they prised it open and the group passed into another cellar area. This one was newer, concrete and cobwebs, and a set of stairs bore a sign labelled with the fire exit logo.

Mattie was beyond exhaustion now, saying nothing, trying to blend in with the other five members of the group, hoping Harley might forget she was there. Hoping she would get out alive. The ghosts of Jono and Joy were spinning through her brain, whispering, pushing, crowding her. She tried to focus on breathing, on walking. On foot in front of the other. The tightness in her chest had eased, but her nightmares beckoned.

The steps opened out onto a disused warehouse. Bare of equipment or workers, it was vast and smelled of dust and abandonment, she thought, trying to hold in a sneeze.

Harley was laughing as they emerged. "Am I fucking sick or what?"

"What were the police doing there? Did they take the stuff?" Mattie asked, hoping these were the right questions, but feeling like she was transparent, and Harley was just waiting to tell her he was going to kill her.

The dank darkness of the warehouse was eerie. The huge vaulted roof had holes in, reminding her of home, and long chains reaching down to the floor they were standing on were attached to some ancient rusty lifting equipment which loomed, menacing, in the half darkness. The chains swung very slightly, dancing to an inner music, even though Mattie couldn't feel any breeze. There were dark stains on the concrete floor, stretching out from the centre of the warehouse to the hidden corners.

"Aren't you lot the lucky ones?" Harley still seemed to be in a self-congratulatory mood now, and he turned to Mattie. "Be grateful, bitch. I could have left you for the pigs."

"But he couldn't because you might have told them something about the delivery you made earlier." The other man smiled nastily. "We couldn't have the little messenger girl screwed over, could we?"

Mattie said nothing, her head still spinning. At least in the pub the police had been there as a distraction and safety net. But she should have been arrested with the others, questioned and then released, according to the plan. Emily would not be happy with her. Joy's sister, as one of the officers on the raid, would not be happy. Now, she was stuck with Ned's finest, one of whom cracked the neck of his stolen wine bottle against the wall, swiped across the glass with a knife and stuck it to his lips.

She supposed he didn't care about the splinters of glass that were probably accompanying every gulp of the ruby rich liquid.

To her surprise they showed her the door, and she found herself out on the pavement, a hundred yards from the traffic lights, and about a mile from home. "Now fuck off, Mattie and pray that the package you delivered tonight hasn't just been creamed off by the coppers," Harley told her, with a vicious pinch on her shoulder.

She nodded, dazed, stumbling homeward, grateful to be alive, sucking the warm night into her lungs, licking the salt from her lips. There was a slight breeze to push her wispy hair from her sweaty forehead. At least going this way home, she didn't pass any twenty-four-hour shops, especially now she had cash stuffed in her pocket.

Mattie had been so convinced she was going to wind up dead, like that poor boy on the train tracks. The jolt of relief that she was still alive was tempered by the catch of raw emotion that he was not, that she hadn't been able to stop them.

Only now she was alone did she allow her mind to process the shock of seeing Joy's sister. On the TV it was different, but in real life she looked harder, more professional and with a certain tough edginess that told you people didn't mess with her. Less like gentle, straightforward Joy. There had been gossip, she remembered now, that Joy's sister was ashamed of her, didn't like her being an influencer, but watching the documentary, Mattie had felt nothing but sadness emanating from Lucy whenever she was on screen.

The nightmares woke her at 2:00am, barely an hour after she had finally managed to get to sleep.

'You did something bad. You're evil.'

'You killed someone.'

'*You watched her die, while she screamed for help, and you did nothing.*'

'*Say it! Admit what you did, and I'll give you some water. You need to be punished for what you've done, but if you admit it, confess to me, it will be easier. I just need to you say it.*'

The shadows rolled across the ceiling, and she was back in the other room, terrified, screaming back that it hadn't been her fault. She hadn't wanted to do it. But she knew if she screamed back, if she argued, the voice would go on, and she would be stuck in the room forever.

Properly awake, she found herself sitting on the side of the mattress, unaware how she had got there, blinking in the darkness. Her T-shirt clung limply to her hot body. The weird, disjointed feeling that always accompanied waking from one of her nightmares made her light-headed. She fumbled for her phone – 3:00am. The images in her head remained, stronger than ever. The voice had a body and a face now. Although she couldn't see him, couldn't recognise him, he was growing more substantial. The darkness inside her head was becoming real and she was still shaking with fear.

A slight chirping noise from the other side of the room was Nuala slipping back through the broken boards after a hunting expedition. Gradually the lights filtered back into her consciousness, driving away the remaining shadows still staining her mind. The big raw white floodlights from the port, the yellow security lights from the factories, played in a soft kaleidoscope across the mould-encrusted ceiling. But were there other shadows lingering in the corner of the room? Was it Nuala again or a footstep on the stairs?

Mattie rubbed her forehead, waiting for the panic to subside. Weirdly, she was sure she could smell Jono's aftershave. He always wore a strong, almost peppery scent that she liked. Dazed, she turned her head left and right like a questing hound. The torch was next to the mattress, and she shone it carefully around the room. Nothing. Nobody. But the smell was so strong she could almost taste it.

"Jono?" Her voice rang out, echoing across the derelict house. Was he haunting her, or just messing with her head?

The T-shirt and jogging bottoms she wore to sleep in were soaked in sweat, wet and cold against her skin. There was nobody there, but impression of the nightmare presence remained, and he was staring down at her as she lay helpless on the bed. Not Jono, after all, but the faceless entity from her dreams. Her own face was wet with tears and sweat.

When she looked down, puzzled by the pain in her forearm, she saw she had scratched the insides of her wrists again. Blood beneath her fingernails. Blood on her hands.

There had been no blood when Joy died, she recalled, still confused and exhausted in the aftermath of her troubled night. She waited until her heart rate slowed, before making her way, not back to bed, but up to another room in the house, shining the torch carefully in front of her, keeping the beam on the floorboards as Jono had taught her. Any security guards or nosy locals might see torchlight in a deserted house and alert the police, he had lectured. His scent was fading now, carried away on the sea breeze, but she could hear echoes of his voice inside her head.

Carefully, methodically, she sorted through paints, brushes and sticks of charcoal, but selected a pencil from the battered cardboard box on the floor and began to draw.

The smell of damp from the house, the cleaner smell of salt and smoke from the port, comforted her. Jono wasn't there, and sure as hell the freaky nightmare man wasn't there. His face bothered her, blank and featureless. Had he been wearing a mask? It must be her mind playing tricks, but even so she ached to start drawing, to ease the pressure building in her brain. Nuala sat washing her paws, eyes brilliant in the shadows.

Mattie worked on by the light of her torch, wide awake now

in the peaceful hours, those magical hours between night and day. Suddenly, finally, she felt the blessed urge to sleep, and staggered back to bed. As she lay down, wrapping her arms around her body for warmth and comfort, Nuala settling next to her, purring, she thought her phone buzzed.

She put a hand towards the floor to check for a message, but she was so very tired. It was a tiredness so extreme her soul felt battered, and her bones ached with echoes of past horrors. Drifting back into sleep now, feebly questing fingers brushing the filthy floor as she thought her phone buzzed again. But she was so tired, too tired to check...

FOURTEEN

"DI Merry?"

Sitting in the debrief at the police station, Lucy shook herself back into reality. They were all looking at her, waiting for her to speak. "Right, yes, sorry, boss." She quickly, briskly, summarised her part in the partially successful operation, and the role of her handler and CHIS.

A small part, as her new promotion had sent her further from the action, but because this had been tied to her last case, she had still been a cog in the workings, one of the unarmed officers sent in after the scene was secured and the environment safe. As usual she was careful to keep her players anonymous. Police were notorious gossipers, and one wrong word, one leaked name could mean a busted case at best, a dead CHIS or handler at worst.

The success came with the seizure of five thousand wraps of cocaine, as well as ten kilograms of heroin and three hundred thousand pounds in cash recovered from the pub raid. A small cache of firearms had also been discovered in one of the upstairs storerooms. Eighteen people had been arrested and the cocaine could be traced directly back to an illegal shipment which had come into the port two weeks ago. They were inching closer to Ned and his illicit operations; she could just feel it.

Covert video recording devices had been placed in the pub beforehand, showing gang members, transactions between the two main players, and would lead to easy prosecution. Unfortunately, this time, there was still no direct evidence leading to Ned, and several key gang members had escaped, so the game went on. God, she wanted Ned, the slippery bastard.

The Chief Superintendent dismissed the team and Lucy went back to the small suite of offices at the end of the building, further away from the main police station. The Unit also had an office in Lewes, but she preferred working in the throbbing heart of the city.

After grabbing a coffee, she headed straight to her computer, pulling up the footage of the raid. She'd joined in, celebrating the success that had given the multi-team operation such a buzz, but for her it was overshadowed by something else – someone – in the pub last night.

The woman she had locked eyes with. She had been so stunned she had faltered right there in the middle of a major operation. A crucial moment that could have cost lives. Although she had quickly recovered, the guilt remained, and she couldn't help reminding herself it had happened so often since Joy had been gone. A similar mannerism, a toss of hair – she had seen her sister on every high street, in every car park, felt that expectant jolt in the pit of her stomach so many hundred times.

She never realised, until her sister went missing, how many women shared the same bluey-green eye colour as she and Joy, had the same square chin and high cheekbones. They weren't that unusual really, not so special. Joy's eyes had been enhanced in every photo by filters and tints, careful make-up and matched clothing. Lucy wore waterproof mascara and sunscreen, and occasionally styled her hair if she had a date. Not that she'd had a date for months now, she realised, her mind drifting again. Swiping right on Tinder and other dating apps was boring, and she didn't really want to share her life with anyone right now. She was extremely independent and extremely single and that was just how she liked it.

She scoured the footage looking for the woman's face in the crowd.

Her gut told her this meeting was different. She had felt the other woman's spark of recognition, a connection. The direct gaze, so similar to her own, was clear in her mind. She found the piece she wanted, rewound and studied the woman. The footage was grainy and pixelated, but she could see to her disappointment this woman was older than Joy, and being manhandled by a tall bloke, who kept his hood pulled down over a peaked cap.

She stumbled as he pushed her round the fighting group, and while the tactical firearms officers regained control of the main area, the man and woman had vanished behind the mass of bodies. Was she unsteady on her feet because of alcohol, or did she have an injury?

The very last sighting was a partial back view of the man, and a side profile of the woman. The face shape was similar. The curve of her mouth. But there was something wrong. A disfigurement across this side of her face. A scar maybe? A tattoo? Frustrated, Lucy zoomed in, but the footage became even more pixelated, and the woman dissolved into a mass of tiny grey and white squares.

Older or not, she was the image of her sister. Lucy sat back in her chair, careless of the fact it was past 2:00am and she should be at home getting some rest. Part of her was even glad she wasn't at home on her own, sinking a quick bottle she told herself was a treat for a job well done, or a comfort after a long shift, or just because it was Friday.

She didn't drink to excess, she reassured herself all the time, because she was aware of the shifting sands, the delusional grey area between drinking because you wanted to and drinking because you needed to.

There had been so many false hopes, and she was reluctant to put the family through another one. The DNA discovery seemed to have hit a dead end because it was impossible to verify with absolute certainty how old the sample was. Forensics had confirmed it was certainly Joy's DNA and the fact the dead woman from the building site in Hove had been working in Mallorca, somewhere her sister had been supposedly sighted, seemed like a positive step forward.

It anchored Joy to a place, maybe... Lucy shook her head and swept an impatient hand through her short hair, pushing it back behind her ears, as though to clear the tangle of theories, or at least weave them into something more cohesive.

Was it remotely possible Joy was alive, and the whispers had been true? That she had run off with another man, lost herself in another country. Had she come back with Elise for some reason? Brighton was a big city, perfectly possible to vanish in, but so many people had been looking for Joy, surely someone would have recognised her. She had millions of followers, and yet she had vanished. It still seemed impossible that someone didn't know something, hadn't seen something.

The trouble with being on The Unit was she was slightly removed from the main investigative teams, as well as being in a separate building with less bustle than she was used to. It had been a great promotional move, she thought, but took her away from that cutting edge she loved. Now, like her handlers and the CHIS, she moved in the shadows, on the ragged edges of so many lives. The smoke and the mirrors she relied on to keep her team safe could intoxicate or consume.

Common sense told her that the woman from the Crown and Sword pub was not her sister. It was ridiculous. Everyone had a double, as she had already discovered, and the image wasn't even clear on the footage. It was likeness conjured up by her longing for Joy to be alive, and the desperate hope the DNA discovery had released. But still... her eyes.

Her fingertips slid lightly over her phone, and then retracted. She couldn't tell anyone else, not after the DNA findings. Her dad, especially, seemed to be eagerly awaiting his younger daughter to walk through the door, ready to assert he had always known she was alive.

Perhaps this woman had been one of those arrested? She could check, put out a casual word. The moment their eyes had met it was like this person, Joy's double, had felt the connection too. She couldn't dismiss it, no matter how much her the sensible, professional part of her brain was insisting this was just another woman who looked a bit like her sister.

Lucy scrolled back down the documents in Joy's file, briefly immersing herself back into Joy's world.

@JustAnotherNatterer (May): *This month Darling Joy seems totally full of her own importance, with six trips to London, not to mention jetting off to Ibiza, Rome and a freebie to New York. Yes, we'd all love to do that so her rubbing it in with her 'look at me and how wonderful I am on the beach/five-star hotel/Michelin starred restaurant' just really grates. I know some of us have got together and complained to the council about her stupid planning permission for a two-storey gazebo.*

Did anyone notice how she's starting to freak out a little – talking a bit too fast and maybe glugging down a bit too much of the old freebie wine? Emile's TV show has been cancelled but he seems to be picking up the slack by starting his own YouTube channel. Must be tough being married to Little Miss Perfect. I mean, she has no qualifications, yet she lords it over him the whole time and constantly puts him down. He's the chef and she's telling him how to make her favourite salad dressing. Pleeease!

Angry and aware exhaustion was starting to creep in, Lucy snapped the top on an energy drink, downed it so quickly it made her splutter, and continued to scroll. Eventually she found the piece she was looking for:

@JustAnotherNatterer (June): *Darling Joy has taken up running to advertise sportswear brand Elite. What a joke. Does it counter the extra wine consumption and those rumours of marriage problems in paradise? Emile seems to finally be getting tired of having a walk-on part in Darling Joy's show, and he was quite short with her in last week's vlog, and he also took the wine away before she could pour another glass. Maybe she had a few before filming? I see those lucrative healthy lifestyle and whole-some family deals drifting away as she steps onto that particular slippery slope.*

The post on mental health and trolls had me in stitches. She's a vlogger and influencer. Does she really think the world is all candy sweet and sugar roses? Most of us hate her and are only following her to see when she finally trips up and it all comes crashing down. Meanwhile Joy has finally signed to a big one and spent a long time trilling about her excitement. Her own collab with a fashion outlet, and a make-up range to come (vom-it). She looked ridiculous in a flowery dress and Ascot hat for the announcement. The strain is clearly showing – spotty face and extra weight hiding under that belt. Feel sorry for the kids. Does she ever spend any time with them?

@JustAnotherNatterer (July): *More rumours in Darling Joy's circle about her drinking being a problem. A little bird told me everyone is talking about it. We all know she got drunk at the*

launch of a perfume and slagged off a few other vloggers. Big
mistake! Mind you, her sister is a big drinker too. We don't see
them together at all, but she has implied they spend nights in
with more than a few bottles.

Also, did you know, Joy's sister is a police officer? Bet she hates
Joy really and the last thing she would do is share a bottle with
her. And uh-oh, has naughty Joy been seeing another man behind
Emile's back? @PoisonIvy suggested yesterday Joy has a thing
with fellow vlogger Reggie, but I'm going to disagree. I think
she's set her sights higher and might have snatched a certain
billionaire property developer. Does this mean leaving rainy
Brighton for the sunny mansions of Spain? Mallorca sure tops
Soho House down by this particular coastline.

There it was. Lucy frowned at the screen, eyes tired and
gritty after a long day, brain still wired from last night. DI
Armstrong had already sent the whole piece off to his Interpol
contact, and the Cybercrimes team had been through the posts
and comments. A connection. Reggie Holliday, a fellow influencer, had been interviewed at the time of Joy's disappearance
and he had a solid alibi. He'd been appearing at some event in a
club in Manchester, if she remembered correctly. But what if...

She checked in with the last post, dated two months after
Joy's disappearance:

Now you see her, now you don't. Darling Joy has vanished. Or
has she? What a way to go for publicity. And just before the story
broke in the gossip mags about her alleged affair with Reggie,
which was coming right after Emile's little indiscretion... Nice
timing. Kids and Emile crying all over the TV and us all
wondering where she is? Plane tickets to Spain? Well, she
showed us which drawer she kept her passport in, so it makes you
wonder... The police seem to be taking it pretty seriously, so in

advance if anything has happened to her, of course this whole forum is just a bit of a laugh.

Joy's recent comments about her mental health and trolls just made us think she's finally realising she wasn't meant to be on show, and she isn't anything special after all. The thing is, if you put yourself out there, you're almost asking to be knocked down. The tallest poppy and all that. What do you all think?

My last post was deleted by admin (thanks for that @PoisonIvy), but I'm hoping you let this one stay. It's a kind of tribute to our Darling Joy as the family held a memorial today and filmed it for all her YouTube followers. Bad taste but Emile's channel is still up too, and poor old Emile needs to carry on shilling crap to get some cash. It's doing very well in the wake of Joy's sudden disappearance. He seems to have got the sympathy vote... It seems widely accepted now, after the discovery of her clothes and the fact she has just disappeared, that something bad happened to Joy.

She was a patronising bitch a lot of the time, but she gave us all a lot of (unintentional) laughs, and these vloggers aren't known for their brains. If she's planned this and thinks she's got away, we'll hunt her down and find out everything about her new home, new man etc. If she's dead, well, I'm sorry for the family but they'll move on. We've all lost loved ones at some time or another, and maybe this is a lesson for them all.

Don't put yourself on a pedestal because at some point, it's going to smash, and you'll be back amongst the rubble and dirt with the rest of us normal human beings.

This is my last post here, so over and out, and enjoy your lives!

But it wasn't the last Lucy had heard from @JustAnother-Natterer. Every anniversary she and other members of the family received an email from an encrypted account, signed Just Another Natterer. A nasty little reminder even though Joy was gone, her haters and lovers were still keeping tabs on her sister, her dad, her husband and her kids.

But this year, after four years of regular communication, nothing had arrived.

FIFTEEN

I've always been a planner, and this time I was more meticulous than I had ever been. I was absolutely positive I could feel the collective goodwill of our community, of Joy's community, wanting what I wanted too. Later, I wondered if perhaps I didn't want to take ultimate responsibility, maybe I wanted it shared out in manageable pieces so I could carry my part of it for the rest of my life.

There would be no second chances. This was it. But I'm not going to lie, there was a tiny streak of blood-red sadness in the sunrise outside my window that morning. It had to be done, for Joy's sake, and I kept to my routine all day, keeping an eye on my beautiful girl via her social media accounts. She's too famous now, taking herself too seriously when she should be with her family.

It was the new deal with the clothing company that confirmed my fears. It pushed her earnings to a ridiculous level. She was chosen to front the new sportswear campaign for Elite, with Reggie. When the first pictures came out she was standing in front of him in every single one and yet they were supposed to be equal. Reggie seemed pretty pissed off from the cryptic comments he pushed out on the socials.

That evening, in the scorching sunlight of July, I waited on her usual running route, keeping the car hidden, composing myself for our meeting. It was past 8:00pm but the simmering heat of the day lingered in the hot air. Every time another car passed, I winced. This road was usually quiet so late in the evening. It led to nowhere but the footpath through the woods. I checked my watch: 8:21pm. Two minutes, and Joy should come running out of the woods. She would need to pause at the road, a quick check to see if there was any traffic, before she jogged across, picking up the footpath on the other side as it wound its way through the trees.

My heart was pounding, my hands sweaty and shaking. Would my voice stay steady? Would she be afraid? Another question flickered across my mind, an unworthy one that made me cringe inside... Did I want her to be afraid? The answer was just as shameful; I did. I wanted her to realise my power was far greater than hers, that we put her up there, and we could take her down just as easily.

It all went smoothly. In the end my fears of traffic, of dogwalkers, of Joy suddenly changing her routine, were groundless. Nobody else passed through the woods, and nobody saw my car as I cruised down past the footpath at the same time she emerged from the woods. My distraction, a later addition to the plan, worked perfectly. She was surprised, a bit wary and confused, but she never suspected what was going to happen to her. And why would she?

When it was done, I held her in my arms, kissed her forehead gently. I remember thinking how wonderful it was that we could now both be free: her escaping the insanity of her life in the spotlight, me knowing I had done my best to give her what she had been afraid to ask for.

The sad thing was, we all knew that was what she wanted.

She had been pleading with us for months, although it was carefully framed behind her latest posts about this and that. I was giving her the best, and most beautiful gift of all.

Because behind the glamour and the glitz, we knew Joy had struggled and was still struggling. She'd had panic attacks since she was a little girl, had lost her mum when she was seven. She talked about this occasionally, about mental health and about keeping control and it being okay to talk about it. This was the kind of sharing people liked, I suppose. She was wrong though, because it can be dangerous to share what's going on inside your head.

She talked to her audience, to all of us, like we were all invited for some intimate chat round at her house. Never sexy, not like that, although some people will take anything they can to get off. No, that was part of her charm, she was genuinely sharing her life with her followers, and we knew all about her. We know where she went to school, when she went for a smear test, where her passport was kept.

We liked that she was open. She never pretended to be something she wasn't, but the glossy perfect life she had created for herself was starting to eat away at her soul, changing her for the worse.

We knew her so well that we could tell she secretly wanted us to help her escape.

SIXTEEN

The port was busy this morning, and an early pale pre-dawn sea mist was lingering across the harbour. Lots of fishing boats coming in, and the grey Border Force vessel heading out. There was also a huge ship that Mattie was fascinated by. She thought it must be some kind of dredger for the cement works. It was taller than the others, with a high cockpit, and vast machinery all over the deck. It looked like a clockwork ship from a Gothic nightmare.

Two days after the raid nothing seemed to have changed. Nobody jumped her along the railway line, Ned's business appeared to be continuing, albeit at a reduced capacity. But there was tension in the air today. Mattie felt it in the coolness of the breeze, in the way she spun and turned from the broken window, almost breathless with fear, to find nobody else in the room.

She stroked the purring cat, trailing gentle, shaking fingers along the soft fur of her back. Nuala had overcome her fears and was now a constant, if independent companion. Even Bobby, who said he didn't like pets, had been charmed by her pretty face and serious eyes.

She picked up her phone and scrolled down, froze momentarily. Jono's number. A missed call. Freaky. Quickly she rang the number, but as usual, it didn't connect. How was that possible? He rang her, and then switched the phone off? Was it a mistake? It must be... She shook off the crazy thoughts racing through her brain, and put her phone in her pocket, ready for work.

Relishing the peace and coolness of the early dawn, Mattie set off for her shift at the fish market after a tepid shower. At 4:00am, after another night of broken sleep, it was weird to be walking along the pavement sober. Her footsteps seemed to echo on the dusty road as she crossed at the bus shelter. Hardly any traffic at this time of day.

She walked faster, previous calm vanishing as she got nearer and nearer to the fish market. She didn't want to go to work, not here, not with them. Mattie tried to ignore the familiar twist of nerves that seemed to boil up in her stomach, choking her. She had managed it for the last two days, told herself Ned would suspect something if she didn't turn up, but every bone in her body ached with fear. He would surely want a debrief from her soon, but she had hardly seen him around the yard, or the office. Had she delivered the packages successfully? Had anyone seen her?

Emily, the new handler, had gone through all of this with her, patiently coaching her to talk about a feeling of being watched as she slipped in the door. Maybe, she had suggested, tell Ned her contact had seemed more nervous than normal when she handed the bag over at the pub? Because he would ask. Even though Harley must have given a blow-by-blow account, he would ask...

She must sow the seeds of doubt and push the blame onto someone else. Emily had assured her Ned would be looking far higher up than his lowly courier to blame for the Wednesday night raid, but Mattie's knees still shook as she walked, and her heart thumped even harder when she reached the market and Harley informed her with a scowl that Ned wanted to see her in the office. It was happening.

The office was a half cobble, half concrete affair, with a flat corrugated iron roof. It was reached by five rusting metal steps. Ned kept all the windows closed, and the air conditioning unit switched on to max, even in the height of winter. He didn't ever seem to feel the heat or the cold.

She knocked and opened the door, almost falling over a long sinuous body, heavy across her toe, and thicker than her arm. *"Jesus Christ!"* The snake was almost always in its large, luxurious, centrally heated vivarium in the corner of the office. She had watched Ned playing with it before, allowing it to slide across his shoulders like an albino scarf, but had never seen it on the floor. She closed the door hastily and stepped over the coils.

The python flickered its tongue in and out, small cold eyes absorbing her form, before it continued its unhurried route along the grey carpet tiles.

Ned was laughing, the way he always did. Not like it was funny, but just because he enjoyed seeing her fear. "Don't be so pathetic, Mattie, it's just a reptile."

She said nothing, but kept very still, tracking the snake's lazy progress around the room.

Ned stopped laughing abruptly as he met her eyes and sat down. He seemed to enjoy lording over his employees from behind his desk, making them stand like naughty schoolkids. With filing cabinets and plastic boxes all ordered and neat, two laptops and a bank of security cameras, he could have been a successful, young entrepreneur running any old business. Instead, she knew full well what went on behind the legitimate, and prosperous, front of the fish market and delivery service. And she knew Ned had little to do with the hardworking legitimate side, leaving it all to his cousins and half-brother.

"Mattie, we have a problem. Someone is telling tales. We

lost two deliveries last night, and it can only be because someone has been talking. There was the Crown and Sword major fuck-up on Wednesday too." His jaw was tight and his eyes cold with fury as he spoke, as though he was keeping himself rigidly under control. "That was a proper bang-to-rights deal, and now I'm not sure we have our extra turf after all. Nobody wants to mix with a crew who haven't got their own house in order, do they?"

She shook her head dumbly, held her breath, trying to look surprised, waiting for him to continue.

"I thought by getting rid of Rory, we had sorted the rot, but we haven't."

Rory. The teenage boy on the railway lines. She had seen it in the papers as a suicide, the tragic death of a runaway, who had been missing for two years. Mattie was still ashamed she hadn't tried to do more to help the kid, which was one of the reasons she hadn't told the police anything about it. What was the point? They could never prove it, and there wasn't a chance in hell she was going to testify in court. That was the reason she never told the police about any murders she witnessed. She couldn't ever be an eyewitness. "How... How would the police even know about the deliveries though?"

Ned narrowed his eyes, his thin face and venomous expression reminiscent of the albino python, which had now coiled next to a filing cabinet. He was flicking a golf ball from one hand to the other, faster and faster. "Don't be so fucking stupid, Mattie. How would the coppers know about the other deliveries? If I thought it was Dave who screwed me over at the pub, if I thought he was dirty, I'd have killed the deal myself, but..." He paused, and a flicker of indecision crossed his cold face. "I want to know who snitched on me. I'm losing business and losing respect and it's got to stop."

Mattie, transfixed by the golf ball flashing between the thin, cruel fingers, felt her knees go weak and her mouth dry, as she fought to stop the relief registering on her face. Dave Tidy now ran his own patch over Hastings way, but he had once been part of Jono's friendship group. Getting involved in a turf war with a rival dealer wasn't going to end well for anyone involved, but at least Ned didn't seem to think it was her who had grassed him up. What had Emily said? *Divert suspicion. Always sow the seeds...* Her mind spun frantically. "Jono... Jono said he thought Lucas at the Crown and Sword was getting a bit close to Dave earlier this year, so maybe you're right. They both worked in the kitchens somewhere else for a bit, before Dave went out on his own, I think. And didn't he have a family connection there too?" She knew she was babbling but couldn't stop herself spitting out the names.

Ned, clearly rattled by the possibility of further mutiny in his ranks, pounced on this information. "He did? Fucking hell, why didn't Jono tell me before..."

She waited for him to add, *'Before I killed him...'* but surprisingly, although the words seemed to echo in the air between them, he merely added, "If only he'd seen me before he pissed off. Bloody unreliable bastards, the lot of them. Go on, get on with your shift, now, while I sort this shit out."

Mattie, correctly assuming she was dismissed, walked slowly backwards, eyes darting between the snake and its owner, until she could close the door safely behind her. She paused on the steps, trying to control her shaking legs. She really couldn't carry on living this double life. It was getting more and more dangerous.

There were other ways to earn a living, even if you were, well, even if you were Mattie Woods, currently of no fixed address, with no bank account and no records. As Jono had liked to boast, they were off all records, and didn't exist at all. But if there was a chance Jono McQueen might still be alive, if Ned hadn't killed him, where the hell was he?

SEVENTEEN

Bobby had brought a bag of Chinese takeaway and they sat on the battered sofa and watched a film on his laptop. Nuala sat purring between them, tail curled neatly around her silver striped body.

"Thanks, Bobby that was great." Mattie smiled at him as she stacked the foil containers, licking a last drop of sauce from her fingers. The sofa was part of the original furniture, abandoned by the owners, sprouting rusty springs, and mildewed foam. But the old leather covers were still mostly intact, and Mattie had got used to the odd smell. Nuala had cleaned up the mouse problem. She was definitely getting fatter, and her fur was sleek and shiny with health now.

"No problem. We would have been more comfortable at my place though. Hey, you've still got a bruise from where Harley dropped that container on you last week," he told her. "Seriously, you need to get out of that place and out of here. Come and live with me, just until you get back on your feet."

"It's fine, and the container just brushed my face and shoulder. I don't even think he meant to do it," she said, touching her scarred cheek self-consciously. "If he had meant it I'd have been squashed flat like a beetle."

She said nothing more, wondering again if she should unburden herself. But which secret to share? The weight of her fragmented lives was getting hard to bear.

"Don't you want more from life than hiding out here? There must be something you want to do with your life, or want to be?" Bobby persisted now. "You know, like at school when you're a kid and they ask if you want to be a builder or a copper?"

She laughed. "I don't even remember that far back. And I definitely didn't want to be a copper." She dropped her gaze to her hands, rhythmically stroking the cat. "Why would you ask me that now, anyway?"

"Because you've changed," Bobby said bluntly. "Since Jono's been gone you've gone off the booze, off the drugs, and you look better. Happier."

Abs had also noticed a difference. "You think it was Jono's fault I was an addict?" She was aware of conflicting emotions rising. "Because it wasn't, you know. After I was sick, I just haven't felt like I needed anything... Not much anyway, and it's different. The feeling is different." It was so hard to explain, about the cravings, the odd taste in her mouth, how she some-times woke up and felt like she had a hangover, even when she'd had nothing to drink except stale tap water.

His eyes were serious. "I'm aware addiction isn't just some-thing you can kick, but my theory would be that when you were seriously ill, for what, almost six weeks in the end...?"

She nodded, wondering whether she should mention the call from Jono's number. After what Ned had said, she was trying to work out how she might feel if he was still alive. To be honest, after coming face-to-face with DI Lucy Merry, she was trying to work out a lot, and also beginning to wonder if she was cracking up.

"When you were ill, and it was just me looking after you, and Jono was gone, you went cold turkey. Basic, crude rehab. Your body was trying to recover, and now you're getting stronger again, you can carry on the process."

"Maybe. The woman at the drop-in centre said to try and take it one step at a time, even just a minute or second at a time if I was having a tough day." Mattie remembered the sweats, the shaking, and the nightmares making her scream as red-hot pokers stabbed behind her eyes, in her head every time she moved. It had been a big step for her, gathering the courage to ask for help, to accept the advice, but the people at Pavilions had been friendly, non-judgemental and offering lots of things she longed to accept. "I'm going to the place in Hove you suggested, too."

"Good, I'm really pleased for you." He was smiling at her, clearly proud, and she felt herself tearing up.

She had assumed it was just the effects of the flu. Bobby had threatened to call an ambulance several times, but her obviously genuine terror at the idea had thankfully dissuaded him from this course of action. "This woman at Pavilions did say it sometimes depended on how long a person has been an addict, like it can reflect how long it takes them to come off stuff, but that everyone is different."

Bobby nodded and continued, "And you didn't have any help, any medication or anything. You just did it. But I'm sure they went over this, Mattie, but it's with you forever, addiction, so you'll need to always be careful. No magic cures." He looked at her carefully, pushing his blonde fringe away from his eyes. "Don't take this the wrong way, doll, but I do think Jono was an enabler. It never seemed right. He liked to be in control, and he liked that you followed wherever he led. I'm not saying he didn't care for you, in his own way, just that your relationship was toxic."

"I loved him," Mattie said quietly, as she sat, shoulders

slumped, noticing again the smell of decay and damp in house, despite the oppressive heat of the night. As more and more time passed, she had also been thinking perhaps she had just depended on Jono, which was a totally different thing to love. Wasn't it?

Sometimes, she still woke in the night, convinced he was there, desolate when he wasn't. But now, in the daylight, where dreams were burnt away by the hot sun, she could view their relationship more objectively.

"And now?" Bobby picked up his bottle of water and unscrewed the plastic cap. He didn't drink right away, but played with the cap, twisting it one way, then the other. "Mattie? What are you thinking about Jono now?"

Uncomfortable with the conversation, but aware her friend was only trying to help, Mattie frowned, flipping a brown curl of wispy hair away from her sweaty face. She made a sudden decision. "You know I said I have these nightmares?"

"About that guy yelling at you?"

She nodded. "Well, since I was sick, I can see him now too. Not properly. His face is always in shadow, and he wears a mask... Like a surgical mask if you know what I mean? Well, the other night I had the worst dreams ever and now it's like I'm actually in the room with this man."

Bobby's eyes were fixed on her face, a gentle hand on her arm. "That's fucking creepy, doll. I'm not sure what to say. I mean, it could be some older trauma coming out, like from childhood or something? Or, and don't take this the wrong way, an ex, or even Jono."

Mattie shook her head, and uncurled her legs from the sofa. "I don't know where my head is at just now." She wished she could tell him about seeing Joy's sister, how it had thrown her totally off balance, even tell him about Joy, but she could never do that. Instead, she needed to figure things out for herself, and she knew she could do it. Before she was tempted to reveal too much she changed the subject. "Come on, I want to show you something."

"As long as it isn't a dead body."

She stumbled on the loose floorboard as they walked towards the stairs and almost fell.

Bobby caught her arm. "Hey, what did I say?"

"Nothing, it's fine. This way."

A couple of months ago, just before she got sick, the newsagent's on the corner had been giving away a pile of garage sale junk for free, and she had snatched up the plastic bag full of pencils, charcoal, sharpeners and erasers, adding to her art supplies.

She ran a gentle hand across the walls, careful not to smudge anything, but tracing the scenes of the port, seagulls, Nuala of course, boats, fish, and...

"Shit, that's me! That's Ned, the fucker, and Harley and Connie and Lucas... These are amazing. You have so much talent, Mattie." He was looking at her with genuine, untainted admiration, and something else she wasn't used to. Respect.

Mattie, unexpectedly, felt her cheeks burning with pride, and dropped her gaze shyly to the floorboards. She drew his attention to the far wall and as usual shivered at her accurate depictions of her nightmares. It was as though the man she had drawn was standing behind her now, his breath cool and deadly on the bare skin of her neck. She deliberately rubbed her arms and turned away to look at the other pictures.

Bobby drew a sharp breath as his quick eyes took in the images. "You see him? This same man always?"

She nodded. She couldn't explain, she just couldn't even begin to make him understand. And if she did, the respect and admiration that had just made her glow with pleasure would surely vanish. Their friendship would not survive.

"It's not Jono?" Bobby questioned again, peering closer.

"No!" It came out raw and sharp, because she felt a twinge

of guilt. She too had wondered if her boyfriend stalked her nightmares. "I mean, I don't think so, but I don't know because of the mask. The voice sort of echoes in my head, as though I hear it through water, or a loudspeaker at a busy festival or something. It's distorted. It doesn't sound like a real human," Mattie explained.

"Maybe it isn't real at all. Perhaps it isn't a memory, but just your way of dealing with things in your life," Bobby suggested, tilting his head to examine one of the scenes.

Mattie considered this carefully. "You mean the man is like the demon representing drink and drugs? But that would mean I have voices in my head, and that might mean I'm crazy."

"Maybe. Not the crazy bit, you idiot, but the representation of your own personal demons. Or perhaps, like I said downstairs, you have suffered some historical abuse you can't get rid of. I mean, I still have nightmares about Col, and I loved him so much it almost tore me apart." He smiled and she put her arm around his shoulders for a quick hug. "It might be symbolic he's wearing a mask," Bobby continued, "because he *isn't* real so you can't pin an identity on him."

"I don't know, but it's driving me mad I can't see who he is. I feel like he *is* real," Mattie told him.

"You need therapy."

"Probably." The last thing she would ever do would be to see a therapist, or allow anyone to pry into her thoughts, because who knew what kind of secrets they would uncover? Perhaps this was her mind's way of dealing with the guilt at her part in Joy's death. In which case, and if Bobby was right, she would never see who the man behind the mask was, because it was herself and Jono. "Come on, let's go, my brain is fried."

"At least I've got your career sorted now, doll," Bobby said more cheerfully as they reached the bottom of the stairs.

"You have?" She bent to stroke Nuala, who had padded up on silent paws and was watching the pair of them.

"Of course. You're an artist, aren't you? Those pictures are as good as photographic images, and you only had access to some builder's brushes and water. Imagine what you could do with proper art supplies and canvases. You could be famous!"

She smiled at him, enthusiasm and something else rising in her chest. Something panicky and hot. How was she going to navigate her way from her current circumstances to anything at all, without giving everything away... How could she ever re-join society properly, and live in the real world, after what she had done?

EIGHTEEN

When Bobby had gone Mattie stood scrolling through her phone as moonlight poured through the boarded-up window, making a chessboard on the kitchen floor, the soft, pure light cleansing the filthy, rotting room.

In addition to a few photos, carefully stashed in a drawer, her phone had two precious files of photos and screenshots. She and Jono each had duplicates. Every aspect of Joy's life captured and pinned like a butterfly under a specimen needle. There were a couple of videos too, including that last terrible one. She desperately wanted to delete it, but never had. Jono said they must never delete the videos. They each had evidence, which meant they each had blackmail.

But had Jono deleted his? She hadn't questioned his instructions, his answers to her queries. If someone had got to his phone they would have the proof of what they had done. She had never looked at the pictures sober before.

But it hurt that Jono had often called her a poor man's version of Joy. They had found each other at a meet and greet party, and he said he just knew when he saw her that they would be together. She couldn't remember if it had been the same for her. Alcohol and drugs had blurred her memory to such an extent that she had huge blackout gaps, but her short-term memory was good. Mattie remembered lots of wild parties in recent years.

She did look like her idol, it was true, and had at one time bleached her hair blonde to look even more like her. The blurred photos on her phone showed her and Jono at festivals, at parties, laughing, and she thought she could sort of remember the feeling of dancing, letting the music take over your body so you didn't care who was watching.

Mattie poured herself a mug of water, sipped it, standing full in the path of the moonlight, stone-cold sober, turning everything over in her mind. Joy's sister, Jono's possible return from the grave, her own life. Even the shouts of a group of lads outside, the roar and rattle of the late-night train to London, didn't distract her.

After Joy's death, she had wanted to hide away, become invisible and try to find a way of living with her shameful secret. Jono had said it was best if they lived on the fringes of society, with no records, no paperwork, and no authorities knowing they even existed.

She had occasionally mentioned getting some help with housing. The charity St Mungo's had a reputation for helping, not asking too many questions and never judging. Or even, she had once suggested, adding their names to a housing scheme list, maybe using fake names. Some of Jono's friends had moved to Craven Vale, an estate in East Brighton, and reported back the accommodation was fine, and drugs were readily available. Jono had told her to shut up and not talk about things she was too stupid to understand. But she could tell he quite liked the Craven Vale idea.

Anyway, when Jono got the CHIS gig that all went out the window. All he cared about was that he was a player now, and he could move higher up the dubious underworld hierarchy.

Power. Bobby was right, everything had been about power and control for him, but for her, the CHIS payments might mean she could finally change her life.

She needed to hit the jackpot. She already had a rough idea how she was going to get herself a massive pay-out, and get Ned put away for many years. Well, it would either be that or she'd be dead. If she got caught there would be no questions asked, Ned would chuck her body in the sea and nobody except Bobby would notice. How much did she want to turn her life around and how far was she willing to go?

The answer came immediately, bubbling up from her subconscious: she would go all the way, and put her life on the line if that was what was required. She wanted to change her life for the better, to be clean, and to be free. Satisfied she had thought it through, she began to start thinking of the how and when. It wasn't hard, because next week was D-Day as far as Ned was concerned.

Mattie wondered if the man in her nightmares knew her secret and if he would let her escape from this life. Or maybe the voice in her head would stay forever, as a punishment for what they had done, for what *she* had done.

NINETEEN

Joy's house (she could never think of it as Emile's house, even now her sister was gone), was in a peaceful, secluded area, high above the city. DI Lucy Merry flipped through the documents on her laptop as she sat in the sunny, manicured garden, annoyed she had let it get this far in and not yet met the CHIS. One of the first rules she had implemented after her transfer was to ensure she interviewed each one.

New and old recruits were treated equally, which had caused some ructions, but she had laid it on the line in a way that they were not to even think of screwing her around. Those who fucked up, she had cut loose without a second chance. She wasn't popular, but who cared about being liked? The buzz was in a job well done and, hopefully, an added bonus of lives saved from information given.

The contract had to be signed, and there was no shit about only interacting with their handlers. She was the boss now and if they wanted the money they needed to play by her rules. Of course, the true details of the CHIS were kept on a separate heavily encrypted management system, and she had read both.

So now she had to meet Mattie Woods, who had been

signed up while she was away. Lucy flicked through the brief history, noting the boyfriend, Jono, had disappeared, but also noting Mattie had given them some good stuff in the short time she had been an informant.

Jono had signed his contract with a pseudonym, Knob. Lucy rolled her eyes. There was a note Mattie had reluctantly assumed the pseudonym of Martha and refused point-blank to have her photo on file. This was usual, and due to the nature of their role, very few had photo identification.

DC Alia Mattez, using the name Emily, had reported the first two meetings had gone well, that Mattie was nervous and slow to trust, but keen to get her money. As far as Mattez had been able to gather, on the surface, Mattie was employed by Ned on a legit basis, cash in hand, for shifts at the market.

The fact that Ned used Mattie for the illegal stuff too, including the drugs drops, made her all the more valuable. All conversations between CHIS and handler were sanitised and recorded, leaving no trace of identity. This way evidence could be used in live investigations without compromising the CHIS and handler. Lucy thought the system worked well as far as it went. Occasionally, as with Mattie's previous handler, Abs, things went too far, but again there was an easy way of pulling in the reins before things got dangerous.

Lucy flicked down the last few notes from the recent meeting. Although Mattie had been reticent, Mattez said she also suspected Ned was putting the pressure on for Mattie to take part in more of his illegal business, now Jono was out of the picture. According to the paperwork Mattie had been at the raid on Wednesday night, but hadn't been arrested with the others. Mattez, as 'Emily', had been in contact with the informant since, but was still concerned about Mattie's safety.

Her position in Ned's crew meant that hopefully Mattie Woods would be able to give them what they needed to take Ned down. But it was a risk. The whole thing was a crazy risk, and Jono McQueen wasn't the only CHIS to go missing recently. One of the reasons she had been transferred was to help clean up The Unit. It was a valuable police resource, with safe systems in place, but in the last couple of years, it seemed to have become increasingly lax when it came to paperwork and legalities. She would sort that out.

Finishing her urgent emails, she snapped her laptop shut and leant back against the soft grey cushions of the lounger, absorbing the luxurious surroundings. In the near distance the swimming pool gleamed, dappled turquoise and tempting against the backdrop of white marble and purple lavender bushes. The slap of wet feet and triple splashes as her nieces and nephew dived in made her smile. But her mind was still turning over possibilities. Should she tell Emile about the woman in the pub? Ever since that night she had been unable to forget the jolt of electricity she had felt. So what if the CCTV didn't show a great likeness? It was hard to change the eyes.

Although, on reflection, perhaps not. Some of her source handlers wore coloured contacts. DC Alia Mattez had quite a collection, she knew, and the results were very effective. But this woman on the CCTV didn't look like someone who would care about things like that.

Another few minutes soaking up the sunshine, and she had reached a decision. Emile needed to know, if only because she was going to crack up if she didn't share this news with someone in the family, someone who really knew Joy as she did.

Lucy opened her eyes, picked up her files from a huge stone urn filled with lavender and swung her legs from the lounger. The garden shimmered in the heat haze, a mass of green lawns, colourful flowers and neatly clipped shrubs. She loved Joy's taste, and appreciated her sister's flair for design, but was always glad to return to her fifth-floor city apartment, with its glass and chrome and spectacular views of the coastline and the i360. It was a plush pad for a copper, but Joy had insisted on helping buy it outright, arguing that she had the money so why not use it to make her family happy.

"I brought you a drink." Emile's voice came from behind her, interrupting her thoughts. "Sorry, I thought you'd finished working." Joy's husband was standing right behind her, and Lucy turned and smiled.

"Thanks. No, it's fine, I'm done." Lucy pushed her paperwork aside, laid it on her laptop. She hadn't heard him approach, was still trying to get her thoughts in order. Screwing up her face against the sun, she watched the kids messing around in the pool, and took a sip of the iced juice he had offered, buying time. She had failed on her promise to investigate this latest sighting alone, even though, with her practical police head on, she was fighting any hopes it *was* an actual sighting, but... "Actually, Emile, there's something I want to tell you..."

He stood in front of her, blocking the sun, motionless, as she told him what had happened, what she felt, what she thought she might have seen. Then he spoke softly. "Do you actually think it might be her?"

"I can't be sure, Emile, of course I can't, but I thought she recognised me. There was..." She replayed it in her mind for the hundredth time. "There was something, like she knew me too. I wasn't going to tell you, but it was just weird, you know?"

He shrugged. "You shouldn't have to handle these things on your own... and with this coming so soon after the DNA was found, I don't know what to think, Lucy, I really do not." His tone was hopeful, but his eyes were hidden by designer sunglasses. "I'm glad you told me. If it concerns Joy, it concerns me. But say it was Joy, why wouldn't she have tried to reach out to you? If she was still in the city, or anywhere, then why hasn't she contacted us in all this time?"

Lucy could hear the pain in his voice, the bitterness and the longing, because it mirrored her own. There had always been question marks over Joy's disappearance, but her family all hated to think she had run away, had planned to leave them all.

It was this and the constant niggling terror they would get the call telling them a body had been found that had worn them all down. Every waking moment, whether at work or at home, Joy was a ghost at Lucy's shoulder, and she knew it was the same for the rest of the family.

Emile pulled out the chair next to her, and moved the sun umbrella round, shading them from the burning midday sun. He was tall, well over six foot two, and his white linen shirt and trousers emphasised his summer tan. A designer watch peeked out of one of his shirt cuffs, and a discreet gold bracelet encircled his other wrist. "Do you really think she might be here, in Brighton, but hiding from us?"

Lucy frowned, hating the pain, the rawness in his voice. "I don't know. If it was her, she didn't have a chance to do anything. Hell, we were in the middle of a drugs raid. It was a huge operation, and I could hardly manage to function, let alone start trying to keep my eyes on her."

"I do understand. You said you checked the CCTV, and the images didn't look like her?" Emile always looked expensive, perfect, unattainable, Lucy thought. And yet he had fallen for her bubbly, feisty, fun-loving sister. He had been famous long before Joy was. The tabloids liked to suggest Joy had only married him because she was riding along on his coattails, enjoying the luxury lifestyle, the holidays in the Maldives, the double page spreads in OK! magazine when their children were born.

Lucy knew this wasn't true. Her sister had fallen hard for Emile, indeed had expressed doubts about the celebrity lifestyle long before she too became famous. She sighed. The kids were shrieking with laughter now, splashing around with an inflatable pink flamingo. Beyond waving at their aunt and their dad, they were ignoring the grown-ups, engrossed in their games.

Lovely kids, missing their mother, surviving because they had to. Not lacking in any material wants but deprived of Joy. As they all were.

"Lucy?"

"No... I don't know. The images were crap, all grainy, and I don't have anything better to look at." She took another breath of rose-scented sunshine. "I'm looking into it. Carefully."

Emile called out to the nanny to make sure the kids had plenty of sunscreen on, before turning expectantly back to his sister-in-law. "You can find out who was in the pub, can't you? You said it was a raid, so you must have a list of who was arrested or whatever? Which pub was it?"

"I can't answer your question, you must know that. It's an ongoing investigation." But Lucy was thinking the man who had hauled the green-eyed woman away clearly hadn't wanted her involved in the raid. Or was he hiding her for another reason?

"It's a bit hot out here. Do you want to come inside for a drink?" Emile asked suddenly. "Ella will watch them for us."

Lucy nodded, understanding his need for privacy, shrinking away from the further questions that were bound to come. Ella, the pretty nanny, with her long red-gold plait and white swimsuit cut high on her legs and low on her cleavage, was checking her phone at one of the poolside tables, occasionally glancing at the kids, mostly looking at Emile.

Ella was the daughter of a friend, and so was deemed safe to look after the children. Lucy had told Emile several times the girl had a massive crush on him. He used to laugh it off, but more recently had seemed annoyed when she mentioned it.

Which was fine, Lucy told herself. Was she still feeling territorial on her sister's behalf? Because Emile had every right to move on. It had been five years after all... But would he really move on with an infatuated kid? It felt weird and very wrong. Unexpectedly, tears blurred her vision, emotion clogged her throat, and she hastily pulled her own sunglasses out of her bag as she followed him along the brick pathway around the side of the house.

The kitchen was cool and expensive, smelling of mint and basil. Marble worktops and slate floors, with copper bell-shaped lighting strung along an industrial-type beam above the long table. Joy had been so excited choosing her perfect kitchen, Lucy remembered, running an unsteady hand along the smooth, cool surface of the sink unit. She had taken so many pictures for Instagram, filmed so much content for her channels in this luxurious haven.

Emile took a bottle of sparkling wine from the fridge and poured them both a glass. To Lucy's surprise he didn't immediately pursue the subject of the woman in the pub. "You know, I got one of those emails from our friend today. The NatterJack troll is still alive and kicking unfortunately."

"Ah... I thought your agent was monitoring all your emails again?"

He shook his head, dark curls falling across his eyes. "Only the work ones. This was to my personal address. Want to see?"

"Not really, but I guess I should," Lucy said, taking a gulp of wine. It was icy cold and should have been delicious, but the bubbles tasted sour on her tongue. "*I* haven't had one from NatterJack this year and neither has Dad."

Emile opened his laptop and logged in, spinning the screen around so Lucy could see too. "I didn't want to say anything, because we've all had a lot to deal with, and, well, the police can never trace them, can they? It's always an encrypted email and blah, blah..."

Happy Anniversary to Darling Joy! Hope you and the kids are keeping well. We know how much you like secrets, Emile, so watch out for a lovely reveal next month. We wanted to do it this month, but we were too busy looking for Joy. Popping up in Spain again, isn't she? And Kansas? Just like a little Dorothy in pretty red heels. Or is she closer to home than you'll ever know? Anyway, here's a link to our little forum as usual. Enjoy!

Thinking of you on this special day and always,

JustAnotherNatterer x

"Well?" Emile asked, his face tight with worry. "Do you think they really know something this time, or are they still just messing with our heads?"

"Ninety per cent bullshit. But the last line about her being closer to home? That worries me a little. Or they might just have been watching the news story before it tailed off. Looks like it's just you that's being targeted this year. Which again is out of pattern... I'll give DI Armstrong a ring tomorrow," Lucy said, making a note on her phone and taking a screenshot from Emile's device, before forwarding it on to herself. "We can log it, but we've already been through that forum with Cybercrimes a few times now, and nothing came back. Some trolls just love to keep poking the wound, don't they?" she added bitterly.

"With a pointed stick," Emile agreed, shutting the laptop with a snap. "I was thinking about this woman you saw. Are you going to tell the DCI, or DI Armstrong about her? Should we be out searching along the coast?"

Lucy cringed inwardly, knowing he was too kind to add that she had 'seen' her sister twice before and initiated massive, complex searches, only to find the women were nothing like Joy close-up. Tracing the patterns on the marble with trembling fingertips, she shook her head. "I just don't know. Like I said, I only got an eye meet and when I checked the CCTV footage, my first thought was that this person was older than Joy, and the brief impression I had was false. Do *you* think I should escalate it?"

Emile sighed and ran both hands through his dark hair in

frustration. Eventually he said, "No. Not yet. Last time we thought we had a sighting it almost cost you your job. Everyone still thinks she's dead, even with the DNA findings from the body in Hove."

"Which could be old, connecting her with the victim before her own death," Lucy said, trying to crush the little spark of hope that persisted in flickering in her heart. "It would be different if they felt there was enough evidence to reopen the case, but that would require overtime, a team, all the bells and whistles the force can't afford unless it's as close to a certainty as we can get."

"Right." Emile was checking his phone. "We could try the private detective again... And maybe best not to mention it to Frank? He had another doctor's appointment last week. He won't tell me what it's about, but you know his heart isn't great, and he was popping medication last time he was over."

Lucy pushed her hair back behind her ears and picked up her wine glass again, frowning. "I wouldn't mention it anyway, I don't think... He either gets far too upset about things or super excited we've found her. You know how he is, and the DNA findings on the Hove body just made it a hundred times worse."

Her dad had never believed Joy was dead, and his absolute belief that his younger daughter would be found alive and well was unshakable. Both she and Emile had asked him several times recently to stop talking to the kids like their mum was just going to walk through the door.

"I can see why he does it, because then he doesn't have to deal with the fact that she's gone. Give it a week, see what you find out, and then let's talk again. If there is any other reason to pursue this, even the slightest chance it's for real, we can talk again." Emile's brown eyes were bleak, and he turned away to refill their glasses, swiftly changing the subject. "My agent had an offer for a reality show. It's eighty grand for a week on an island somewhere, cooking whatever we can find to live on, doing challenges. You know, standard celebrity stuff."

"I thought you were concentrating on the restaurants?" Lucy was surprised. He had three restaurants, in London, Brighton and Cardiff and she had been under the impression they were all doing well.

"They don't make enough to cover all this." He waved an expansive arm indicating the beautiful oak-framed house and the expanse of gardens. "Plus the kids' school fees and all the staff. I need to make more. I've been using savings to cover the shortfall, but now it's almost run out. To be honest, I don't have the cash for the private detective if we did decide to revisit that idea."

"Understood. But Emile, if you did this show, you would be completely exposed to all the trolls. Everyone would be watching every single thing you did..." Lucy couldn't imagine anything worse. Without thinking, she finished her wine and then felt annoyed with herself. She was trying to cut down. The recent promotion to The Unit had given her the boost she needed to clean up her lifestyle a little, and number one was more exercise and less booze, which in her working environment was a tough order.

Emile didn't reply. She wondered what secrets he was hiding. Everyone had their little secrets, but if you went on a national TV show, they would all come tumbling out. JustAnotherNatterer and the NatterJack forum would wet themselves in delight, she thought. Bastards.

"So, what *are* you going to do about this woman?" Emile eventually asked, his dark eyes holding hers, handsome face expressionless.

"Track her down and see whether she actually is Joy, of course." Lucy straightened up, pulled her shoulders back and picked up her bag. "And it might be best if I did that on my own."

TWENTY

Ned pulled Mattie for a word after her shift. She was already quaking about having to meet the DI today and felt Ned must be able to see right through her. Exhausted from ten hours of sorting catches, lugging heavy containers and batting away Harley's insults, the last thing she wanted was a chat with her boss.

At least the snake was reclining in its tank and not patrolling the room this time, she thought, eyeing it warily. She looked down at her feet, boiling in old tatty trainers that needed resoling. At least she had money for regular trips to the laundrette now.

"Mattie, I need you to come on a little outing with me." Ned smiled, leaning against the wall of his office, finishing his cigarette like he didn't have a care in the world. "Don't panic, it'll only take a couple of hours. We need to pick something up and I need you to do it for me. It's over in Hastings. You can finish the last two hours of your shift when we get back, and I'll pay overtime for the extra."

"I…" Surprised and horrified at the request, she stared at him. What excuse could she possibly have for not going? She could hardly use the classic doctor or dentist appointment, as Ned was fully aware of her circumstances thanks to Jono. People like her didn't have regular check-ups for anything. "I'm really tired, and I was going to the hospital to get something checked out," she said lamely. Last time they took a road trip, it was to meet a rival dealer, and Ned had jokingly told her she was there as a witness if he got shot while he was re-negotiating territory. She remembered asking why the man wouldn't just shoot her too, and Ned laughing. Was he testing her?

He stared at her now, vacant grey eyes raking her face, stripping her bare of lies and secrets. "Go later."

She stood in front of him, her mind working frantically, but nothing happened. No miracle was going to get her out of this one.

"Go and get in the fucking van, Mattie." Ned slipped a hand into his rucksack and shoved a wad of ten-pound notes into her hands. "You lot are so tight, won't do anything without cash up front." He grinned suddenly, nastily. "But I suppose it means you have a tiny bit of business sense. Maybe there is hope for you after all. I'd hate to see you go the same way as your ex-boyfriend. How's the new one, anyway? Abs, was it?"

"Oh, we broke up..." Mattie mumbled. She turned, stuffing the money into her pocket, shivering with fear as she passed across the yard and climbed into the passenger seat of Ned's van. The seat was hot, and she wriggled uncomfortably, wincing at the touch of burning plastic against her skin. This particular pair of jogging bottoms had holes where the fabric had worn thin. She could do with some new clothes, too, she thought randomly. It would mean a trip to Primark in her most presentable outfit if she could stand the stares.

Ramon and Sons, the fish market and delivery service, had a fleet of logoed vans for deliveries, but this one was the one Ned used most. Mattie tried to drag her racing thoughts together.

What the hell was she going to do now? Did she have time to tap out a quick text to Emily, explaining she couldn't make it?

But just as the thought crossed her mind Ned jumped down the steps of his office and jogged over to the vehicle. Dust swirled from his swift feet. Expensive trainers for her boss, designer clothes and not very discreet gold jewellery at his neck and wrist.

He turned the engine on and the music up loud. It was a rapper Mattie didn't recognise. She liked rap, and she liked jazz, but this was all harsh cruel lyrics and the music pumped through her head, seemingly picking up on her anxiety. She shrugged into her threadbare T-shirt and picked at the ragged sleeves.

"It's not everyone who gets to go on little road trips with me, Mattie." He caught her horrified expression. "Don't worry, I don't want your body. I can do a lot better than you have to offer just by snapping my fingers in the street." He sang along to the lyrics for a while, before turning the volume down. "By the way, I'm really pleased with your behaviour the other night. Harley said you did good and kept your head. If you want to make some more money, you stick with it and remember your loyalties are to me and only me."

Interesting Harley had given her a good report. What was he up to, that he was bigging her up to Ned, just days after beating her up? And today he'd been as vile as ever, laughing when she dropped her end of a heavy container, swearing at her slowness at packing the ice... Mattie passed her tongue around her dry lips, wishing she had some water. She tried to think of something to say. "What are we going to collect?"

"A package." Ned still seemed to be killing himself over some private joke, smirking away and lighting another cigarette.

It worried Mattie that he was in such a good mood, almost as much as it scared her when he was in a bad one. They passed a motorcyclist way too close, and when the rider gave them a Vsign, Ned cut him up so sharply at the next roundabout, the rider nearly fell off.

Ignoring the chaos he had just caused, Ned put his foot down as they sped out of town along the coast road. "It's something I was storing but it needs to be moved and delivered to another location... and I needed someone I can trust. Can I trust you, Mattie?" He glanced across at her, pale eyes locked on hers.

Numbly she nodded, unable to look away from his cold, hypnotic gaze. When he turned back to the road ahead, she folded her hands neatly in her lap, terror freezing her body. It was going to be a long morning.

The long row of terraces in Hastings looked innocuous enough. The road was simmering in the summer heat, and a woman with a double buggy walked wearily in the direction of the town centre. She wore denim shorts and a bikini top, and in one hand she held a large iced latte with the McDonald's logo. Mattie swallowed hard, trying to will moisture back into her dry mouth and parched throat.

Ned parked behind some redbrick houses, backing the van into a large garage, well-hidden from the road. The area was overgrown with scorched weeds and scrubby grass, and dwarfed by a row of huge recycling containers, all well graffitied, dribbling dog poo bags and busted electrical goods.

"Come on, then." Ned jumped down from the driver's side.

Mattie scrambled down and slammed the door, sweaty, shaking hands slipping on the handle.

Ned winced. "Careful! You don't need to trash the bloody van."

The woman who answered the back door was obviously expecting Ned, but she looked surprised to see Mattie and shot a question at Ned in another language.

Spanish, Mattie thought quickly, she was speaking Spanish.

She recognised the language, but the words were too quick for her to catch the meaning.

Ned answered in the same tongue, and another woman called from further inside. The conversation was too fast for Mattie to follow, but she caught a few words she recognised.

"Mattie, I want you to go with Natalie and help bring the package to the van."

Natalie shot her a look of compassion she really didn't like, but she followed the other woman into the side room. Mattie could see a glimpse of a cramped living room, girls in skimpy clothes drinking tea or Coke and staring at their phones. The place reeked of cheap perfume and incense sticks. Huge blow-ups of explicit photographs covered the walls along the hallway. So it was that kind of house. She bit her lip to stop it trembling and pulled her shoulders back. *Come on, Mattie, deal with whatever it is and move on. You'll be out of this forever soon.*

"We wrap him and take him out to the van. Okay?" Natalie said in English, pointing to the floor. Her heavily accented voice was matter-of-fact, but her heavily made-up eyes reflected all the fear Mattie was feeling.

Horrified, gagging at the stench of death, Mattie stared at the deceased man. His face and torso were covered in blood, which had also stained the carpet. His forehead had a strange bloody indent that she assumed had been caused by a blow from a heavy object. He looked familiar. From the fish market maybe... Or maybe the Schooners Inn the other night, or even the Crown and Sword.

"Hurry up, girl! Ned does not like to be kept waiting."

Mattie bent cautiously, wincing as her knee clicked, extended a tentative hand and began to help Natalie wrap the body in some sheeting. She winced when her fingers touched his skin but continued winding the sheets around and around his lifeless body. He was cold and stiff. Not knowing much about rigor mortis, but aware of the process, and its effect on the body, Mattie surmised he had been dead for a while.

Next came a length of blue tarpaulin. He wasn't a heavy man, and when the job was completed, they were able to lift him between them, passing back out of the door at a word from Ned.

Once they had passed into the shadowy depths of the garage, he opened the back doors to the van, waited while the two women loaded the body, and then slammed the doors so fast Mattie nearly lost a hand.

"See you tonight at 8:00pm, Natalie. Make sure they are packed and ready. Mattie, get a move on. I haven't got all day."

Mattie side-stepped a stinking pile of rubbish next to the overflowing line of industrial bins and got back in the van. Within minutes they were heading back towards Brighton with a dead man in the back. Her breath was coming short and fast, and even though she had wiped her hands on her clothes, it felt like they were stained with his blood. Her fingertips tingled painfully where she had made contact with the man's skin.

"Well, that was easy, wasn't it, Mattie?" Ned said in jovial tones, as he crunched through the gears of the old Renault van.

She wasn't sure what to say. No, it hadn't been easy. It had been horrific, and she had been doubly shocked she recognised the man from somewhere. She was pretty sure it *was* the Schooner Inn from the other night. A client who hadn't paid for his gear. Or maybe a rival dealer? Not one of Dave's crew, but there were plenty of others circling the area.

"Do you know who we've got riding in the back with us?" Ned was grinning, as though he could read her mind.

She shook her head. Her lank brown hair fell forward, and she hid under the curtain of a fringe in dire need of a cut. Haircuts were hardly top of her list of priorities. She'd lost her only pair of scissors anyway, and it was hard to see around the back with only one mirror. Usually, she made do with pulling her hair into a ponytail and awkwardly snipping the end off.

Ned was still talking, almost crowing with triumph. "You don't need to know, but let's just say, I'm about ten times fucking richer today than I was yesterday. Mattie, I am the fucking *king* today. And after next Friday's party I might even retire."

Next Friday. She knew exactly what was happening next Friday, but Ned would never know Mattie planned on crashing the party.

He turned the music up and began to sing along again, bashing his hand on the steering wheel in time to the bass beat, shoulders jerking as he swayed in his seat.

Flashing blue lights and a siren made them both freeze.

"What the fuck?" Ned turned to Mattie, who kept her face blank. His showed a momentary flash of panic.

Probably the most genuine emotion she had ever seen from him, she thought, as he indicated and pulled over. Her heart was pounding and she wondered if she was actually going to pass out.

The police officer asked him to get out and at her side another officer asked Mattie to leave the vehicle.

She felt faint, sick to her stomach and irrationally terrified the police officers would know her, or at least identify her, but Ned seemed to have recovered. They stood at the side of the road opposite the skate park, and she fixed her gaze on the kids flying across the ramps, spinning and turning with athletic ease. The sun burnt down, reducing her vision to a blur of vivid colour, and she was so thirsty.

One of the officers was talking to Ned. "Did you know your brake light on the near side is out?"

"No, I didn't. Sorry, I just delivered a load and I'm heading back to the market now, so I'll get it sorted at the next garage," Ned told him contritely.

The officer scribbled a bit of paper, made a note on his iPad and asked Ned to sign.

And then the two traffic cops left them to it.

Ned was laughing so much a glob of spit shot out of his mouth and landed on the steering wheel as they turned and edged back into the traffic. "Bloody hilarious."

Mattie didn't think it was funny at all. Her heart was still beating far too fast, and she could feel rivulets of sweat coursing down her back, T-shirt sticking uncomfortably to her skin and to the seat back. And it had only just occurred to her that nobody had offered her gloves. Her fingerprints must be all over the dead man and his tarpaulin shroud, making her at the very least an accomplice to a crime, and at the worst, a murder suspect. There was a certain irony in that, she thought, but just now she needed to get home, away from the evil sitting beside her, curl up with Nuala and think about what she needed to do.

Ned made her work the last two hours of her shift, stacking cases and labelling deliveries in the office, but at last she was able to escape. At least she was able to down a whole bottle of water, drinking it so quickly she almost made herself sick. He made no mention of the body still lying in the back of the van, and she didn't either, for fear he might involve her further in its disposal. Word was a lot of bodies went out to sea in the fishing trawlers, weighted and wrapped, ready to be dropped into the depths of the English Channel.

TWENTY-ONE

Mattie knew she should tell Emily about the body, about the house in Denver Road in Hastings filled with cheap perfume and girls with dead eyes, but as with Rory's death, she was an eyewitness. She was sure they would want her to testify to what she had seen. Besides, it was too dangerous. It had only been her and Ned in the van, and he would surely guess she had grassed.

Information, she was paid for information, and she needed more without being dragged further into Ned's shitty business. Hence the plans for next week. A clean break, an escape and a new start, that's what she needed.

Walking home in the muggy heat of the late evening, she took deep breaths of salty air, not caring that it was also filled with exhaust fumes from the constant flow of tourist and commuter traffic on the main road.

She was so tired, she actually ground to a halt next to the scrap metal dealers and leant on the wire fence for a few moments, forehead pressed against the hot metal. The port was always alive, and each hour was different. Although the loading docks were quiet, a few trawlers were heading out to sea, and

she could see further along some kayaks and oars lying abandoned by a derelict shed. Probably stolen for a few hours
of fun.

Overhead the gulls floated lazily on the stormy air, wings
outstretched, eyes sharp. Far out to sea Mattie could see the
wind turbines spinning slowly, and the bank of cloudy haze that
might be sea fog or the long-promised storm.

She turned and headed home, her footsteps thumping
heavily on the dusty pavements, shoulders drooping with
exhaustion.

Unable to get hold of Bobby and feeling the heavy shroud of
anxiety and depression starting to draw across her, she
succumbed to the lure of the off-licence on the corner, paying
with a few of the notes Ned had just given her. Blood money
becoming booze money, she thought to herself, spiralling, hating
herself, but unable to stop herself. Not even the thought of
Nuala or all those strikes on the wall could blot out the dead
man in the back of the van.

She could ring Bobby again, she could ring the nice woman
from the AA meeting, or she could try any of the helplines she
had been given, had carefully stored in her phone.

'You don't deserve to be alive.'

'I'm giving you a chance to confess, to start all over again.'

Rolling back home in total darkness two hours later, she didn't
at first realise Nuala wasn't in her usual place, curled neatly in
her blanket. The cat was a creature of habit and even through
her drunken haze, a stab of worry hit Mattie's gut.

She called, stumbled into the door jamb and swore.
"Nuala?"

There was a squeak from the room to her left. Bewildered,
Mattie moved the door with difficulty, where it was swollen
from years of leaks and disuse.

In the far corner, on a nest of old clothing and cardboard, Nuala was nursing four tiny kittens.

"Oh!" Mattie whispered. Bobby had said she was fat, and she had been a bit concerned she was feeding the cat too much or the wrong food, but she had been fat with babies.

But there was distress in the cat's miaows and as Mattie inched closer, speaking reassuringly, she could see another kitten was lying unmoving, jostled by its brothers and sisters.

Without thinking she reached down and picked up the tiny, wet and cold baby, shoving it down the neck of her T-shirt, rubbing it gently. It wasn't moving and she was pretty sure it wasn't breathing.

Nuala made another noise and Mattie spoke to the cat gently, her voice choked with emotion. "It's okay, we'll take care of your baby, darling. We will..."

Gradually, skin to skin, she thought the tiny cat was warming up. It was even smaller than the others. Probably last born.

"I know, I should have been here, not sitting in the bloody road getting wasted." Tears blinded her vision, streaming down her cheeks. But as she was looking down, she saw the previously lifeless kitten was moving its paws a little. She carried on the rhythmic, gentle massaging, hugging it to her skinny chest until the baby gave a little mew.

Crying properly now, Mattie knelt next to Nuala and edged the kitten towards its mother, helping it to latch on, knowing it was vital to its survival to get that first nourishment.

Nuala began to lick the little one, and the other kittens made tiny noises and stretched their pink paws. Their eyes were still shut, Mattie noticed, but at least they seemed warm and healthy. "I wonder if I should move you?" She glanced at the roof. But the cat, with animal wisdom, had found a dry, draught-free spot to give birth. The room was musty and heavy with cobwebs but had a tiny draught of cool air.

She checked her phone. Two missed calls, a text and a voicemail from Bobby. And the binge had almost cost the life of a kitten. She hated herself for succumbing, but instead of weakening her resolve she now found it had made her more determined to sort her life out. She called Bobby, wanting to share the news, wanting to touch base, and he picked up straight away.

"I've been trying to get through to you for ages" Bobby said, concern sharp in his voice.

. "Guess what? Nuala had babies tonight."

"Oh my God! *Shut up!*"

"No, she did. Five and they are just the cutest ever. She's being such a good mum."

"What happened with you and Ned today? Why didn't you call me back?"

"Sorry, I was a bit freaked out, and it was nothing. No, that's not true..." She told him the full story, including the bit about her relapse.

There was silence and she worried for a split second she had lost him. But she should have trusted that Bobby never judged.

"Doll, we said, didn't we, that you're bound to fall off the wagon sometimes. It won't be easy. As long as you pick it up again from here, just take each day as it comes." He paused. "And I don't like that Ned made you go with him and bring a dead body back. Why would he want you to do it?"

"I thought maybe as punishment and a warning. You know, to keep me in line."

"But you haven't stepped out of line. Exactly how much was Jono involved in the shady side of the business?"

"Probably even more than I thought he was," Mattie admitted. "I almost get the feeling Ned has got me taking over from where Jono left off."

"But you aren't him, and the more stuff you do that's criminal is going to make it harder for you to leave and move on."

Bobby didn't seem massively freaked out about the dead body, Mattie thought suddenly, a little nagging fear creeping in where it definitely shouldn't. He hadn't suggested she go straight to the police or anything. She was preoccupied with Nuala and her kittens, but part of her questioned why Bobby hadn't brought up the police. Had he already known where she'd gone today?

Oh God, though, was she going mad? Paranoid even her best friend might be about to screw her over. She took a long, slow breath to calm herself.

"Anyway, doll, I've got to go, but I've got another two gigs booked in now, and I'm thinking of leaving Ned and getting a bar job to tide me over, make a proper go of things."

Her answer seemed to hang in the air, and she forced herself to speak, eyes still fixed on Nuala and her babies. "That's amazing, Bobby, and you know what, I'm going to leave too. I need a couple of weeks to get my head around what I need to do, but I'm getting out." There, she had said it, almost shocked by the words coming out of her mouth. *Come on, Mattie, you can do this, take back control of your life.* She could start again with her strikes on another wall. If she could get away from all this, maybe she wouldn't keep tumbling back into her pit of darkness.

"That's excellent, doll. Nothing we can't do together!" Bobby's voice was warmed with enthusiasm.

She ended the call feeling more optimistic than she had in ages. The momentary paranoia was gone, and Bobby was her trusted friend again. But, she thought, if the fish market job went, so did her secret income as a CHIS. She was only useful if she was close to the danger, feeding the snippets of information that others couldn't get to her handler.

This was why she would change the current trajectory of

her life, moving away from the criminal underworld, re-join society, without revealing her sickening secret. She and Jono had got away with murder, after all.

Now she was beginning to understand, to fight for her sobriety, she could see the real reason she had been content hiding away with this kind of life. She didn't believe, after what she had done, that she deserved anything better. Joy's last screams would haunt her forever, and the voices, the man in her nightmares, he was punishing her inside her mind. She could move house, get a job, sort herself out physically, but inside she would have to deal with her crimes until she died. Atonement, she supposed, if that was even possible. But she would do it.

"And I suppose that's how it should be," she told the six cats, who were purring contentedly at her feet.

TWENTY-TWO

The police, the media, the majority of the fans, nobody has a clue what really happened that hot and sweaty evening in the woods. I panicked afterwards, after it was done, and all traces cleared away. Had someone seen my car? Had I missed a traffic camera somewhere on my route that might identify my vehicle? Worst of all, would my complex alibi stand up to scrutiny if I was challenged?

But the police are overstretched. Lack of funding, they say, don't they? Despite Joy being recognisable to millions, despite her case being high profile enough for extra teams to be drafted in, they scrabbled around uselessly, flailing for evidence.

They did find the necklace later, and to do them credit, I later discovered that Joy herself had left a false trail I never knew about. Clever girl. She must have somehow sensed what would happen during the investigation after the escape. The other conclusion is that she was planning something of her own, without me, which doesn't bear thinking about.

There was a multiple stabbing at a stag do the week after Joy vanished, then the next month a little girl was found murdered *under the pier. There are some truly sick people out there. I think this, and my planning, helped me to avoid detection.*

I still can't quite believe the high when I realised, the day after, the week after, the month after, I had got away with it. Joy was at peace now, I felt like the best person in the world. The horrors of fame, the wealth, the celebrity status that made her step away from her true self, have all gone. I bothered less with following other vloggers, but I still joined in with all the chat discussions on Joy. Oh, the secret thrill of contributing, of being the one person who knew the whole truth. Or so I thought.

Every year on the anniversary of her disappearance there is the feature on Crimewatch, candlelit vigils, talk of fresh evidence and her case reopening. Nothing ever happens. A city that never sleeps, a city that loves a star, and yet this is also a city where thousands of lives and deaths go unnoticed. Despite Joy's famous face being plastered all over the news stories every single year, it seemed that really, just for the twenty minutes I needed, there wasn't a single person who had seen Joy Maddison.

But this year it has been different. Another sweltering heatwave, which left the city uneasy, and now a big discovery and a new lead. Sure, nothing else has happened since the excitement over the body, which wasn't Joy's anyway. Nobody has come banging at my door and I haven't heard any rumours suggesting the coppers are any closer to discovering the truth. But just in case, I set my plans in motion to ensure I'm one step ahead. Sometimes listening to your instinct can save your life, or at least, save you from falling into trouble with the law.

I'm still watching the news, waiting. There is something going on, I can sense it, we can sense it. Coppers are bigmouths sometimes and as we gossip amongst ourselves online, someone has a brother, who has a cousin, who has a friend in the force right here in Brighton. This particular thread on NatterJack went on for six pages of speculation, and it may well come to nothing.

Even so, I'm staying away from the action. I can still watch, still have a ringside seat, but I'm not centre stage.

The gossip grapevine also still mutters about Spain, but if there is something concrete in the lead, they're keeping that well hidden too. Interpol and the Spanish police are saying nothing, not to the news stations anyway.

Sometimes, a mad crazy part of me wants to ring up the helpline and tell them I've tasted Joy's blood, felt it spatter warm on my face and on my lips, seen her stripped and raw, the veneer of stardom smashed away. I see this in my dreams, but I can't tell if I want to confess, or I just want them to know I've outsmarted all of them.

The funniest thing is, I'm still here, still watching, still living my own life. I still love Joy of course, even after what happened that night, and afterwards. I always have. I've kept all her photos, her press cuttings, saved files of digital screen grabs from her social media. Her presence fills my head, but increasingly I worry about another presence... This one is beginning to niggle, first muttering in my ear, now increasing to an insistent shout. It would be a huge betrayal to Joy if I were to do it again. I can't anyway, I tell myself firmly.

I was so lucky in so many ways five years ago. But still suggestions whisper in my ear, and the sugary high I get from my power over all of them is something I crave over and over again. This is real and something I have created. But I think my addiction to Joy means I might have been subconsciously questing around for a new project. Never to replace, just to add another layer. My blood fizzes with excitement. One more time?

No! Only stupid people repeat their actions again and again. I am anything but stupid. I chuck a few empty beer cans into the dirty crate and wipe my hands on my top. The sun is just rising, and it must be around five. I hate the winter, the darkness and the cold, but the summer I can live for. In the winter, the layer of sadness, the cloud and darkness mean I need to use other things to give me the strength to carry on. When the heat of the summer sizzles across the city, the sea and the beaches, and the tourists flock to crisp themselves on striped sun-loungers, I can soak it all up.

I glance in the mirror and smile falsely at my reflection. My hair hangs limp and greasy over my shoulders today, so I grab a band to tie it back. There is nothing I can do about the worry etched on my face, shadowing my eyes, caused by my indecision. Hopefully nobody will notice. Nobody looks any closer than the superficial, do they? A quick scan of the face, and sometimes not even that. I can be anonymous, or I can choose to be noticed, and that's one of my skills. I use it every day.

A text makes me glance at my phone, and I snatch it up, frowning. According to my source, this time, the police really do have something from the DNA on the dead body in Hove. That's why they made such a fuss! But it makes no sense, and I frantically tap out questions, my fingers slippery with sweat and anger. I hate it when people keep things from me to make themselves feel powerful, important. I knew about the DNA, but how can this possibly lead to Joy?

But only question marks come back. My source knows nothing more or will say nothing more. Abandoning my plans to go out, I pull the band from my hair and sink back onto the sofa, trying to put it together in my head. My fingers are busy, tap-tap-tapping on keyboards, on my phone, pulling up news stories on the body. A young woman, well, we all knew that already... She was supposedly working in Spain, but had turned up in Brighton. Rumours of a people smuggling ring, of prostitution, of drugs, blah, blah.

Did they really think she was Joy to start with? It's been five years, and a body that has been underground for that length of time would be well advanced in terms of decomposition. There would probably be no way of identifying it apart from forensic samples. *Maybe this explains the time lapse. It would have taken a while for the lab to run tests. I google it quickly.*

They must have considered it might be Joy initially for it to be breaking news on the documentary, but why have they not now released the DNA finding to the general public? I consider the impact this will have on me and rationalise. It might even work in my favour. I still don't understand how it could have happened, but I do know this will possibly lead them further from the truth. Unless they uncover another body.

This finding, so close to the anniversary, will be in the news for weeks, once the story breaks properly. I need to be sure I react appropriately both on and offline.

I wipe the film of perspiration from my cheekbones and hunt for my shoes. I thought I made no mistakes five years ago, but I could have done one thing differently.

I pick up my phone as I head for the door and place a call:

"Alex? Necesito un favor, por favor..."

The screams of the tourists greet me as I step outside into the blinding sunshine, and I imagine their blood spread across the sand, splashed across the walls and dribbling away into the ocean.

TWENTY-THREE

"So, what do you have for me?" Emily asked, sipping her coffee. She had one for Mattie too. A posh one from Starbucks.

The car moved smoothly away from the kerb, and took a new route, this time heading west towards Worthing.

After nearly getting caught out with Abs, Mattie now preferred meetings in the car and Emily was happy to accommodate her. She sipped her coffee, getting things in order in her mind. She was going to have to nail Ned, wipe that slate clean. The three reasons for that being, firstly, he would come after her, and he could blackmail her if he wasn't banged up, but she also felt a strong urge to atone for her own crimes, to do something good, something strong, before she left this dark world.

If she helped the police stop Ned's relentless progress, shut down some of his prostitution rings, some of his drug rings, she would be helping a lot of people indirectly.

The second reason was money. If she was going to start again, she would need a decent amount to tide her over. Bobby had sent her numerous links to charities who existed in Brighton to help people like Mattie get back on their feet. She just needed to ask for that help. And now she was ready. She could never get away from what she had done, but maybe if Jono *was* dead... If, if. Her nightmares spun in her brain, but she pushed them away. If Jono was dead and gone, Mattie was the only person alive who knew what had really happened to Joy Maddison that night, and she could keep it that way.

Dragging herself away from her thoughts, grateful Emily couldn't read her mind, Mattie sipped her drink, licked the foam from her lips, relishing the delicious caffeine hit. "My cat had kittens last night," she said suddenly.

Emily smiled. As usual she had perfect scarlet lips, and her teeth were very white and even. "Cute."

"Do you have pets?"

"No. Too busy partying, me," Emily said, flipping back her mane of dark wavy hair, her bracelets jangling as she did so. Her eyes were very bright, and such a strong and beautiful colour. Unusual.

Mattie thought Emily had the exterior of a party girl, but sometimes those eyes were a little too watchful, hinting at something else hidden within her psyche. Or maybe it was just because Mattie knew she was a police officer.

She gave her handler more details on clients, and the address of the house in Hastings, adding she just thought it was part of an illegal brothel. Nothing about the dead man. Not yet.

It was time to broach the most important part of the meeting, the one that would set her free if she could pull it off. "How much would you give me if I could give you the evidence you needed to bang Ned up?" Mattie asked suddenly.

Emily, ever the poker face when money was mentioned, turned to look out of the window, before she glanced back at Mattie. "A dead cert? Let me talk to the boss, but I'm thinking six grand at least for concrete evidence. It would have to be bang on though, Mattie, nothing the CPS could pull apart."

Mattie nodded, thinking that with a figure in mind she could at least start to make her plans. It would enough for a

fresh start, to pay Bobby rent, maybe get some kind of training...
Here she was making real plans for the future. A glow of pride
and anticipation slid under her skin, taking her unawares. *You
can do this, Mattie.*

But almost at once the masked man shouted from the
depths of her mind, contradicting her positive thoughts:

'*You can never do anything again.*'

'*You need to admit what you did, or you will drive yourself
mad.*'

'*Tell me what you did, Mattie. Tell me!*'

"Mattie? Are you okay? *Mattie!*"

She became aware Emily had asked a question, that her
handler was leaning close, concern in her eyes.

"Sorry, yeah fine." Mattie struggled to control the panic
attack that was rising in her chest. The heat seemed to be
building until her lungs felt like they were on fire. She pinched
the skin on her left wrist, hard enough to feel the pain, hard
enough to bring her back from that terrifying other world.
"Fine, I'm fine. Can you turn the air conditioning a bit higher?"

"I asked why you might suddenly have access to that kind of
evidence?" Without waiting for an answer, Emily added gently,
"I'm not suggesting you're holding back, I'm just seeing a
change in you, and wondering if that goes with the sudden urge
to get Ned out of the picture."

Mattie considered. The darkness was slowly receding, as
the AC blasted out a blissfully arctic breath, and she could feel
her breathing slowing to a normal rate. "You're right, it does."
She didn't elucidate and Emily nodded slowly.

"Just be careful. Don't do anything that puts you in danger.
Or us. Okay?"

Calm now, Mattie almost laughed. Every time she went to
work, every time she went within Ned's orbit she was in danger.
Every time she stepped out onto the street there was a kind of
danger. That night that Joy had run into the woods, on the

sunlit evening, there had been danger too, crackling in the July air, dancing through the trees. She just hadn't known it until it was too late.

It was only when Mattie got home that she realised she had left her phone in the unmarked police car. Her personal phone. Shit and double shit. She rang Emily on her work phone but got no answer. She left a message, panicking a whole lot more at the thought of all the incriminating evidence on that device. The photos, the videos. Had Emily taken her phone on purpose? Did she suspect Mattie was going to throw in the towel? She seemed so open and nice, but Emily wasn't a real person at all, she needed to remember that. She was just like Abs, and Mattie didn't *really* know her. Or trust her.

TWENTY-FOUR

DI Jack Armstrong was tall, and broad-shouldered, with a beaked nose and lank dark hair falling to his shoulders. A tattoo of a climbing dragon covered his neck and disappeared into his shirt collar, and another peeked out from under his collar. He was well liked and slightly feared.

Lucy, sitting opposite him on one of the desks, was studying the whiteboards, breathing in the stale air. The air conditioning was broken again, and even with all the windows closed it was twenty-nine degrees in the room. This was an open plan area, generally used by the Major Crimes Team. Once, she had been part of it, now she was working in the shadows, behind closed doors, operating her handlers and CHISs like puppets.

"We can't progress any more without further evidence. You know that. There was the phone call last night, but it was unsubstantiated, and you know how many sightings we've had," the DI told her.

Lucy sighed, pushing her hair back from her face in an effort to clear her thoughts. "I do know. Anything on the couple who employed Elise?"

"Nothing. She did take a flight to Alicante, entered the country on a perfectly legal work visa, but, according to two unnamed sources, left via boat in April. After that, we have no idea where she went, and her parents were under the impression she was still in Spain." The DI scrolled down the page of his iPad, reading from his notes, "Her social media too, her friends, all thought she was living it up in the sunshine. No suggestion of any time in the UK. The Spanish address was real but the employer names fake. We know she was somewhere in Costa Blanca, but not why she was there. The address was an empty apartment block, owned by a business registered as The Happy Travel Company."

"You think she was being *trafficked?*" She could hear the shock in her voice.

"Possibly. We will find out where she was working, but the couple she was working for... and I know it is a possibility it was your sister and a new partner, well, we just don't know. It could just as well have been a cover story."

"But how could Joy's DNA have been on her body?" Lucy could feel a headache developing right behind her eyes, the nervous tension shooting darts of pain down the left side of her face, down her jaw. Neuralgia, the doctor had said, which could be caused by stress. He had asked if there was anything especially stressful in her life that might be triggering the headaches. She had laughed.

"Since the Spain angle is coming up the strongest, we are leading on that as the priority, but you know how slow multi-agency operations can be. Your sister could have been hiding out with another bloke the whole time, and somehow crossed paths with this girl. Maybe the girl worked for her." The DI flipped his device closed and leant back, arms behind his head, eyes thoughtful. "It's pretty complex, isn't it? As the local police haven't been able to trace the couple the victim was supposedly employed by, and the agency is denying all knowledge of her. They say she ghosted them, and they took her off the books. It is an agency Interpol have had eyes on previously, and before you ask, they have no known links to The Happy Travel Company."

Lucy picked up her coffee and swirled the remains of the cold, weak brew, staring into the murky liquid as though she could see the truth at the bottom of the cup. "You don't believe they're telling the whole story? Or even that they are lying?"

"No. We have a murder victim, who needs justice, and we have your sister, who needs an end to her story, a conclusion, whatever that might be." His expression was compassionate, but professional. "Lucy, you know yourself, even if it was old DNA, even if we are looking at secondary contamination, it gives us something solid," DI Armstrong admitted. "I think, I want to believe, that we are on the brink of a breakthrough when it comes to your sister's disappearance and I'm going to keep pushing until we exhaust all avenues on this new lead."

"Is it enough to get some bodies, to get the case reopened?" Lucy was almost holding her breath, her heart pounding so hard it felt like she could hear it pulsing in her brain. She had been tempted to tell him about her sighting the other night, but if she mentioned it, might it take the heat off this new lead? As Emile had hinted, and she herself had admitted in her heart, she wasn't in any way sure this woman was Joy. She flashed back to Emile the last time she had seen him. There had been something, she was sure, something he wasn't telling her.

She pushed the thought down. If she spoke up now, with her history of screw-ups when it came to her sister, this could jeopardise the reopening of the case. It would be easy enough to do some digging and reassure herself this was the correct course of action. Right now, she needed to present a professional front, calm and assured. Lucy smiled determinedly at Jack, forcing herself into work mode.

She knew she was a pretty good actor when it came down it. How else could she oversee her own team at The Unit? That thought made her give a little ironic chuckle, deep inside. Emile wasn't the only one with secrets to hide, but perhaps she needed to dig a little deeper on her brother-in-law's current dating status. It was niggling at the back of her mind.

"I've already put the request in." DI Armstrong smiled back, clearly pleased to be delivering the news she wanted to hear. He rolled his shirtsleeves up, exposing intricate artwork, and bulging muscles. He cut an intimidating figure out in the field and many criminals thought twice before trying to screw with him. "Come on, Lucy, I know what you're hoping for, and who wouldn't be in your position? We've known each other a long time, and I hate to see you so... well, not yourself."

He was a good bloke, Lucy thought, smiling at his awkwardness, and he was right, they had known each other for years. She could trust him. His motive was also to find out the truth, to get justice for the victims and the families they left behind. No office politics for Jack Armstrong, "I always wondered at the back of my mind, if one of these online trolls was actually a journo. They seemed to know everything as it happened, and there were a couple who never seemed to leave her alone."

"Names?"

"On file. They were interviewed."

He was still looking at her, expectant, eyes bright with interest, so Lucy tried to explain, her words coming slowly as she tried to sort events into chronological order. "They used to follow her around, the press. Right after she signed the contract with the fashion label, after her appearance on that beach reality show. She pretended it was all okay, but she was terrified. They didn't speak to her, she said, but she could be dropping the kids at school, filling up with petrol, and a van would pull up, doors would fly open, and a photographer would jump out the back, get the shots and then drive away."

"That's horrific. Can't say I'd be happy with my private life laid out for the general public to pick over. A bit like a modern-day torture. You know, being pegged down for the crows to peck your eyeballs out."

"Nice. Exactly what kind of things do you watch at the cinema, DI Armstrong?" Despite the general sombre tone of the conversation, Lucy felt a smile tugging at the corners of her mouth.

"I don't go out, I've got Sky at home," he shot back, but the sparkle of humour in his dark eyes made her grin properly. "Carry on talking about the press and your sister, you never know what you might have remembered, slash forgotten. Memories are funny things, and sometimes selective."

"Well, the photographers chasing celebrities, that's how they get all those shots for the weekly magazines, the papers with gossip columns to fill, and Joy was a great story after Emile's supposed affair."

"Did he really have an affair?" DI Armstrong asked.

Lucy shook her head, remembering. "I don't honestly think he did. I think the press were sold the pictures, jumped to conclusions, and this girl was keen to make a name for herself. It was at a VIP party at a lap-dancing club on East Street: Platinum Lace."

"I know the place. She was one of the dancers there?"

"No! She was with the party group. Supposedly a friend of Joy's. Anyway, it was sorted between Joy and Emile a long time before my sister disappeared. That was never going to be the reason Joy ran away. *If* she did."

"How did your sister cope in general with the fame?"

His voice was quiet, expression almost idle. If you couldn't see the intelligence in his face, you might have thought they were a couple discussing who was going to take the rubbish bins out, Lucy thought, as she answered carefully. "It certainly wasn't on a Hollywood scale, but it is odd for someone to suddenly find out everyone is interested in what they eat for breakfast. It wasn't even that, though, because she had been letting people in for years via her YouTube channel and socials. It was more that lately she felt they were trying to catch her out. It was a very tabloid-friendly level of fame. Joy felt she didn't deserve any of the money and good things it brought, and she almost felt she did deserve the hate."

"Imposter syndrome. She never came across as especially insecure to her fans?" He was doodling with a biro now, making small boxes overlaid with grids, repeating the pattern again and again.

Lucy considered this. "Sort of... She would do these deep chats on her Instagram Stories with no make-up on and talk about mental health, post-natal depression, all things we should be more aware of and educated on, but the only way, she said once, that she could really address her own issues would be to take a total step back, and stop doing what she was doing."

"Her husband wouldn't have liked that?" He put the pen down and folded his arms, brow furrowed, all that inner intelligence focused on her sister. She liked him for it, and she trusted him to be telling the truth for ninety-nine per cent of every conversation they had ever had.

"I don't know. They had a certain lifestyle, but suddenly she was just as famous, as she often put it, for doing nothing, whereas he's a trained chef with a career. The money was pouring in, and all the free stuff companies wanted them to sponsor or feature." Lucy paused, leaning back against the wall, moving someone's paperwork carefully from her coffee cup as she did so. "It sounds like a dream life, but I think in all honesty Joy felt like it was turning into a nightmare escalator she couldn't step off."

"Be careful what you wish for?" he suggested, pushing his chair back.

"Right. My sister was genuinely naïve about the downside

of what she was doing. To begin with, she had this little channel, her radio presenting gig, a few followers who were mostly her friends from Brighton, and then it went absolutely crazy." Lucy sighed. "Instead of getting excited at the next thousand followers, she should have been future-proofing her finances and putting razor wire on top of the walls."

TWENTY-FIVE

Emily smiled reassuringly. "This won't take long, and it really is just going over the contract you already signed. It's a formality, a tick box. Look, and I've got your phone right here."

Mattie grabbed the phone, trying to see past Emily's smiling mask. Had she looked at it? Had she seen? Did she *know*? She was shaking, but if she had been able to find the strength to make her facial muscles work, she would have almost smiled at the amount of cliches the police officer reeled off. All she wanted was to get her phone back, but Emily, obviously sensing weakness, had coaxed her into coming in to sign a contract too. Unfortunately, she knew as soon as she set foot in the police station she would feel the hot, acidic guilt bubbling up in her chest.

But this was a different building, no signs out the front, and certainly not the main police station. The anonymous grey concrete structure was grubby, with straggling weeds growing around the base. Even though she was sneaking in the back entrance, she found she was shivering, scurrying along with her head down. There were no officers in uniform, and in general, this could have been any old office. Any slightly tatty, grubby headquarters for any anonymous Sussex business.

"Just sign to say I've given you your phone back" – Emily shoved a clipboard in front of her – "and then all you need to do is say hello to the DI, sign off your contract and head home."

Mattie scribbled something eligible with shaking fingers. "Why do I need to see her?"

Emily was still smiling, still reassuring, but Mattie sensed a slight tinge of frustration. "Because she's your new boss, essentially, and if you can deliver what you promised all the paperwork needs to be signed off properly and she needs to meet you. We can't promise or give that amount of cash unless everything is done correctly. Do you see?"

She nodded without speaking. She did see, and it made sense. Mattie forced strength into her limbs and thought of all the recent battles she had fought and won, and then focused on the prize. So tantalisingly close. Her freedom and a new life. It was worth everything she had to go through.

Emily led her into a small room off the main corridor. The air was stale and the plastic chairs and table were bare. There were no windows. She barely had time to sit down, perched uncomfortably, ready to flee, heart hammering, when the door opened.

The DI entered holding a file and when she glanced at Mattie her polite smile froze on her lips and her eyes widened.

"DI Merry, this is Mattie Woods. All the paperwork has been checked." In the silence that followed Emily was staring at her superior officer. "Boss?"

DI Merry fumbled with her file and then seemed to compose herself. "Sorry, I'm sorry. Mattie? Sorry I couldn't meet up with you before, but as Emily has told you, I want to make sure I meet every CHIS working with The Unit." The words were rolling mechanically off her tongue and although they sounded right, her face was still pale.

Mattie wriggled uncomfortably on her hard plastic seat, and knitted her hands underneath the table, trying to control her shaking. Even her teeth were chattering. She had never expected to be in the same room as Joy's sister, let alone having a conversation with her. This was about as bad as it could get.

Emily took charge of the interview, clearly concerned about her boss. It took twenty minutes, while Mattie answered all the standard questions, agreed she had signed the contract they were showing her.

The DI slipped the paperwork back into the folder and turned to Emily. "Can I just have a few moments alone with Mattie?"

"Sure, boss." Emily made her way out of the room.

For a long moment the two women stared at each other.

Mattie, finding the courage to meet Lucy's eyes, saw hope and compassion and a raw, strong emotion rose in her chest making her want to burst out crying.

"Joy?"

Mattie shook her head, unable to speak.

DI Merry seemed to struggle to get her emotions under control, then she continued, a quaver in her voice. "Okay, look I'm really sorry, but you can trust me. Tell me if I'm wrong, but you are the image of my sister, Joy Maddison, who went missing five years ago."

"I know... I do know I look like her and I know who she was." Her heart was thumping so hard her whole chest seemed to be shaking, there was a roaring sensation in her head, and red spots danced in front of her eyes. "But if you are thinking that I am your sister, you *are* wrong. I'm so sorry for... I'm sorry, okay? But I'm not *her*." Mattie couldn't get her mouth to shape Joy's name, couldn't bear to say it in front of her sister.

The hope, the sadness, in DI Merry's eyes was almost too much to bear. "You can trust me... Any kind of trouble, whatever you might have done or left behind, I will be there for you."

Mattie stared at her, pain tearing holes in her chest, tears streaming down her cheeks now, and then the words seemed to spill out of her as if a switch had flipped. "I'm not who you want me to be. My boyfriend, he used to say I was a poor man's copy of Joy, and he was right, I suppose. I ran away from foster care, dodged the system, enjoyed myself, and somewhere along the way I lost the reason why I was doing it." She took a deep breath. It was weird, almost like she had always known this day would come, that she was an actor saying her lines. She had thought so much in the early days about what she would say if she was ever asked about Joy. But never in a million years did she imagine this nightmare scenario.

The words were coming from somewhere deep inside her. It felt like she owed Joy's sister an explanation. And the longer they talked about Mattie, the less they would talk about Joy. "I loved Joy. I was like a super fan, and that's how I met my boyfriend. All those events she did, we were in the crowds. Every episode of her vlog, we would watch again and again."

The DI seemed to be listening, but Mattie thought she was struggling. Did she believe her? This was worse than she had imagined.

"How old are you?" Lucy asked.

"Thirty-seven. I know, four years older than Joy, and my birthday is in May, hers was in April. I told you, I was a massive fan of hers. My boyfriend and I met at one of her events. I... I used to try and make myself look even more like her. She was my absolute idol." She was stumbling over her words, repeating herself, wiping her eyes with her fist. Every word was true.

DI Merry was still staring at her, searching her face. "It's your eyes, more than anything. I look at you, and yes, I see physical differences, but it isn't just the colour of your eyes, it's something else," Lucy said. "Your boyfriend went missing, didn't he, I recall? Jono McQueen."

"Yes."

"How long were you together?"

"Ages. Years." Mattie remembered them celebrating a yearly anniversary of getting together, and Jono, slightly weirdly, lighting candles he had stuck into a McDonald's burger to celebrate the number of years they had been together. "It would have been almost ten years this month."

"Are you from this area?"

It could have been a casual question, and she had no reason not to answer, but Mattie was having trouble staying calm, her nerves jangling like she'd taken a bucketload of speed. She forced the words out of a dry mouth, and they felt clumsy, forced. "No. Portsmouth originally. I don't have any family and I like I said, I was in foster care. I ran away, moved up here with a friend when I was sixteen."

"I should apologise," Lucy said eventually, colour returning to her cheeks. "It's a bit of a shock. I saw you at the pub and now seeing you close up, talking to you, it's like seeing a ghost. You're so like her. Your voice... You even sound like her most of the time."

On impulse Mattie leant forward and shyly, in trepidation, laid a hand over Lucy's. "I'm so sorry I'm not your sister, and I really wish she had been found safe and well."

"Thank you, that's nice of you..." Her gaze was still lingering. As Mattie moved her arm, her tatty T-shirt had slipped down her shoulder and she saw that Lucy was staring at the exposed skin. "Mattie, how did you get the scar on your shoulder?"

She shrugged self-consciously, pulling the fabric back so it covered her shoulder. "I don't know. After I got hooked on drink and drugs I had a lot of blackouts. Times where I woke up with injuries, in weird places. One time I ended up in hospital after a car hit me. It was my fault, I staggered across the road absolutely plastered." She touched the scar on her face. "This was the glass from the windscreen. Jono, my boyfriend, had to take care of me when I came out because I could hardly walk afterwards." There was her knee as well, but that had come from a childhood accident, she couldn't remember exactly what had happened, but she knew she had walked with a slight limp for a long time.

Lucy's face was pale again, the shock clear in her widened eyes, her tone of voice. "Joy had a scar on her shoulder in the exact same place. She got it from falling off a swing in the playground at school when she was seven. She had four stitches."

Mattie didn't know what to say. "I suppose lots of people have accidents."

"Yes, they do," Lucy said thoughtfully. Her professional expression was back, her eyes cool and assessing now, as though back in work mode. "I suppose your boyfriend liked you to look like Joy?"

"Oh yes. He said I was the next best thing to dating her." Mattie stopped, unsure if she had said the wrong thing, still desperate to protect her secret. This woman, with her warm voice and intelligent bluey-green eyes, was Joy's *sister*. She had touched her skin, could hear the pain she had been carrying for five years, could smell her perfume. It was light and flowery, and somehow at odds with Lucy's sharp professionalism.

The words were gathered on her tongue, the guilt inching them forward, like a river flowing towards a waterfall. Disaster was seconds away, and she was shocked how much she wanted to tell Lucy what really happened. She liked her, she realised, and wanted to comfort this stranger who was so desperate to believe, desperate to carry on hoping.

But how much would Lucy hate Mattie if she confessed to her crimes?

TWENTY-SIX

While I wait for the police to catch up, to release more information, I find myself constantly running over the events of five years ago. She was surprised to see me of course, but not as afraid as I thought she might be, and I had help. Maybe not help exactly, but more of a distraction. A liability too, and another loose end I had to tie up.

I don't look threatening, and Joy must have been able to read the love in my voice, see it in my face. The timing was perfect. I was able to take her to the building, down into the basement room I had carefully prepared for her.

Later, my voice and her own screams were the only sounds she would hear for a long time. I waited until she was once again fast asleep to make the first cuts, carefully, artistically. The room was dimly lit, and I was careful to shine the torch downwards when I needed light, hopefully preventing any busybodies out at night from wondering what was going on. The first part of my plan was complete, and it had been tough on both of us. The emotion, the noise, but I was getting there. The room smelt of fear and piss.

Now it was time for the physical work. I stroked Joy's pale

hair as it spilled across the plastic sheeting, her breathing slowing, deepening. It was easier with her eyes shut. At this point I
wondered whether to take photos, and paused with the knife in
my hand, thinking. I could even make a video. Or would that be
going too far?

But yes, why not? This was part of our journey together, and
another part shared only by us. It was an intimate moment. One
of many she and I had shared on our journey together.

I admit I may have gone too far. Afterwards I picked up the
iron bar, turned it over in my hands a few times, feeling the
smooth metal cool oagainst my hot skin. She was so peaceful, fast
asleep and breathing deeply, evenly. I lifted the bar and went for
one clean, quick blow, but somehow, I found myself hitting her
again and again. Not just her legs as I had planned, but her
whole body. Again, and again while she lay still on the bed.

After a time, the fire left me and I began to shake, dropping
my weapon, staring in horror at her at her bloodied body, at what
I had done. I should never have done that, not even in my wildest
imaginings and it was at that point I began to feel some guilt. I
deleted the video I had made, ashamed, knowing nobody else
would understand.

Before, I had almost felt the collective force of Joy's fans
driving me forward, urging me to help her, but this one act had
severed our bond. Perhaps forever. It was a low moment, not even
equalled by what I had to do next.

I found I was sobbing, saying I was sorry again and again,
holding her hand, which was slippery with blood. But her eyes
were still shut, and now I thought for a brief, panicked moment
that her chest wasn't moving.

I regret I lost control. It happened once before, and I swore it
would never happen again. Because losing control is a weakness,
and I don't like to think of myself as that weak, crazy person in
the corner of the room. Power makes me feel like a king, ruler of
the world. I am happy, confident in the natural order of things

and I can show love to anyone I choose. What I feel for Joy is love, I'm sure of it, but who can say?

Afterwards I cleaned up as I had planned and left her body alone in the darkness. As I looked back at the destruction I had wrought, I saw that in the shadows the sheet covered her like a funeral shroud and emotion made my chest tight.

Yet it had to be done.

TWENTY-SEVEN

"Dad, I told you to ring if you needed a lift to the doctor." Lucy helped her father out the car and he brushed her off with annoyance.

"I'm not decrepit yet, am I? Come on, Lucy, I'm not even seventy, don't treat me like a doddering old man."

She ignored this, and passed his walking stick. "Emile said you had another appointment about your heart."

"It's nothing to worry about," Frank told her, reassuringly. His expression of annoyance dissipated, and he patted her hand before leaning heavily on his walking stick. "I'm only sixty-eight, and I might not to be able to sprint anymore, but I'm doing okay. If I didn't have heart issues, I'd still be running, and swimming every day, and then you wouldn't worry so much. Come and make me a cup of tea and tell me how that promotion is working out."

She followed him inside, breathing in the faint scent of childhood as she entered the hallway. "It's going well, thanks. A load more paperwork and a lot less of the action, but I suppose that's what comes with being in charge."

"Thank you, love." He studied her face, his grey-blonde brows knitting, pale blue eyes bloodshot. "You're tired out, aren't you? I said that promotion was too much for you. I know exactly what you mean about the paperwork, though. When they gave me the headmaster role, it was great, but I spent more time organising everyone else than doing any teaching."

His square face was flushed with the heat of the day, and his greying hair, still thick and curly, stood up in sweaty spikes. He was a tall man, even accounting for the stoop when he leant on his walking stick, and strongly built. Lucy could remember when they were kids him scooping them up, one on each shoulder, and walking through the woods with apparent ease. Retired from teaching for over ten years now, his health had declined further since Joy went missing, she was sure of it.

"Just don't start telling me I should get married and have kids, Dad," she told him now, and he chuckled, which turned into a cough.

"As long as you manage it before I croak, I'll be happy."

"No pressure then," Lucy responded. "Dad?"

"What's wrong, love?" His quick, intelligent eyes seemed to take in the strain on her face, and the worry in his voice made her want to cry.

This could be her worst mistake ever, she thought, but with her dad's health increasingly frail, and her own concerns, she felt he should know. "Dad, I think Joy might still be alive."

He held her gaze. "Of course she is," he said stoutly, expression clearing. "But why have you suddenly reached the same conclusion? I always got the impression you and Emile thought I was bordering on senility to keep hoping."

"I think I saw her in the street," Lucy invented. She couldn't share Mattie's real history, couldn't compromise her job by revealing the identity of a CHIS, but this was plausible.

"What? *Really?* Did you speak to her?" Her dad was gripping her hand now, eyes intense and shining. "Did you tell your colleagues at the station?"

His questions came like bullets, and while part of her had been desperate to share, part of her knew instantly she had made a mistake. Where her sister was concerned, her professional and personal judgement was shot to pieces.

Lucy answered slowly. "Yes, and that was the weird part. She said she wasn't Joy, and to be honest, physically she looked a lot older when I got closer to her, but Dad, there was something about her. I can't get it out of my mind."

"I always said she was close to the edge before she left us," Frank said, stirring his tea. "There was so many whispers about what happened to her, but all this time, I've known she was alive. But why should she be in Brighton? The police think she's in Spain, so much so they've reopened the case, haven't they? Go on, love, what did you do when you saw her?"

"Nothing, I've got a phone number, but she just says she isn't Joy."

"Perhaps she is, but she doesn't want us to find her, in her new life. Why would she give you her details if she didn't recognise you? Maybe she would talk to me. I could call her..."

"Dad, I'm a police officer, I had my ID on me, and no, I can't have you ringing up a woman who says she isn't Joy. Think how it would make us look, and on a professional level, it would be wrong. It could be a fake number, anyway," Lucy fudged. Of course, it wasn't. She had Mattie's CHIS phone and she had checked out all her personal details again since the interview.

She knew the woman lived illegally at Number Forty-Two, Kingston Lane, in difficult circumstances. Everything they had on file, or had previously held for the boyfriend, Jono McQueen, she had been over and over until her eyes hurt from staring at the screen, willing the sparse information to give up secrets, answers.

"We should visit her then, if you think she might not be

who she says she is. What does she call herself, this woman you saw?" Frank said stoutly, as though the decision had already been made.

"Mattie." The name was out before she realised what she had done. So much for being professional and staying detached.

"Mattie? Like Matilda?" He was leaning closer, expression intense, but eyes reflecting the shock she had felt when she questioned Mattie Woods. "What a funny name."

"I suppose, I didn't think." Lucy put her head in her hands and wiped away the tears with her fingers.

Her dad seemed to recover a little, shambling round the table to put a comforting arm around her shoulders. "Oh love, this has happened before, hasn't it? Us getting all excited about bringing her home and nothing has come of it. Why don't you go and freshen up and I'll find some biscuits? You can tell me about the DNA thing again, because I'm still a bit annoyed the police didn't share it with us right at the start. I know these are your colleagues, but we need to be kept updated."

The suggestion of biscuits made her laugh, despite her concerns. "Dad, I'm not twelve!"

"Biscuits aren't just for kids." He gave her a little push. "Go on."

Lucy smiled as she made her way through the winding, creaking old house to the bathroom, and after she had rinsed her face in cold water, she did feel slightly better, or at least able to cope. Wiping her face on the towel, she stared into the mirror. Her reflection stared back at her, tired and bit ragged around the edges, but still retaining that spark of hope she had nurtured ever since her sister vanished. Unusual-coloured eyes, a legacy from their mother. What were the chances of her meeting Joy's exact double? Or could her father be right, and Mattie was Joy, but she just didn't want to be found.

She always thought there could be no doubt, but since Joy had gone missing, she had realised how many other people shared her sister's characteristics. The scar on her shoulder was weird too. Was it too much to suggest the boyfriend, the former CHIS, had even injured Mattie to make her even more like Joy? Had he been creating, as Mattie suggested, a poor man's version of the woman he really wanted? And where did that leave Mattie? A doll or puppet, who seemed to have followed this man around, hung off his every word.

So much could be gleaned from the files, from what DC Miles Parker had picked up from arrogant, manipulative Jono and what he and DC Alia Mattez had picked up from Mattie herself. The CHIS handlers were great people-readers. They had to be, and as well as assuming their own fake identities, they had to slip into the life of their CHIS. Always in the background, and hopefully rarely, if ever, seen by others in the CHIS's circle or family.

DC Mattez, 'Emily' had been sitting in when she had interviewed Mattie, and she would have known something was wrong, even if Lucy hadn't branched off into a completely different direction with her questions. But she had said nothing afterwards, beyond asking if her boss was okay.

Another call from DI Armstrong had revealed a possible ID on the Spanish villa couple, and this woman also fitted Joy's description. Photofits were currently being distributed and, as JustAnotherNatterer had predicted, things were starting to happen. The press would be crawling all over it as soon as the news was leaked.

Frank had emptied a packet of biscuits onto a plate and made more tea for them both. "Now, you should get a good night's sleep, and enjoy your day off tomorrow, and then decide what to do about this woman."

She looked at him in surprise. "Don't you think I should go and find her as soon as possible? Half an hour ago, you were about to call her and march across Brighton to find her."

He appeared to deliberate, steepling his hands, frowning

into the distance. "Suppose it is Joy, but she doesn't want us to know her. We don't want to scare her off. Whatever happened to make her leave, we need to get her to understand it doesn't matter. I... Love, look, don't take this the wrong way, but we had all this before with that woman you saw in the bar, and the other one at Victoria station." He paused, as though collecting his thoughts. "While I am quite sure Joy is still alive, I do wonder if it's more likely that she is in Spain."

"Maybe." But Lucy knew in her heart there was something about Mattie she needed to pursue. Who would have thought she wouldn't immediately recognise her own sister, even after five years? But if Mattie had admitted she *was* Joy, what would she have done then? "The DNA was found on the victim in Hove, and I saw Mattie in Brighton."

His expression was earnest, concerned, and he laid a hand over hers, warm and strong. "I know, love, I'm just trying really hard to be sensible, so we don't come crashing down again, so *you* don't come crashing down again. Can you force her to have a DNA test?"

Her dad was speaking her thoughts out loud. He was also a good people-reader, she reminded herself. When they were kids he had been pretty clear about who he thought were good friends, good boyfriends, and those who didn't make the cut got short shrift.

"No. She isn't accused of any crime, and she isn't already on the database."

"And she has documents to prove she is who she says she is?" Frank queried, picking up his reading glasses and then putting them straight down again.

He was trying to be calm for her sake, she realised, feeling a wave of love and gratitude for his dependability. Whatever life had thrown at them, he had always been there, even if he was a bit distant about their success. Proud yes, of course, but he always said he could understand her work, whereas Joy's had completely confused him. "From what she said it sounds like she lives rough, or at least in a squatters' community. No, I haven't seen documents. I had to stretch it to get her number." Mattie's driving licence looked legit, and was clean, showing her old address in Portsmouth, but she wasn't prepared to share that with her dad yet.

Lucy had already put in a call to a friend in the local force and Mattie's Portsmouth details should be with her soon. If her dad went blundering in, whether it was Mattie herself or a random stranger, it would be a disaster.

"Take time to think, and if you still believe it could be her, we will visit her together." His face was glowing, and she saw a glimpse of how hard he was trying, as she was, to be sensible, to keep his emotions in check. This had happened before.

"Not now?" Despite her question, Lucy was relieved. Why was it anything to do with her sister and she seemed to totally lose her edge? The logistics of how she knew Mattie and where she lived, coupled with taking her dad to visit, would certainly lose her the promotion, if not her job. And she already had one strike on her rap sheet.

He smiled. "If she wouldn't admit anything to you, she probably won't admit anything to me either. But as I say, I feel more strongly about the Spanish connection." The smile faded. "My heart broke, you know, when she disappeared, but the thing that has kept me going all these years is that I thought that at least if she chose to go, she was happy wherever she was. I still felt I had failed as a parent." He glanced at one of the many framed family photographs, showing the girls snuggled up with their mum and dad at a Halloween bonfire party. "I knew how unhappy she was doing the vlogging thing, constantly abused by those sick trolls. I should have made her stop doing it!"

"Oh Dad, you couldn't have done anything. It was her own choice to do that and if it was her choice to cut ties and go, well, that was it, but I find it hard to believe she would leave her kids. Those babies were her life."

"I know, I know... Have you told Emile about seeing this woman?" His voice was a little unsteady, and the fierce hope burning in his eyes reflected her own.

"Yes, and we kind of reached the same conclusion as you and I have just done."

Frank nodded. "Don't tell anyone else, Lucy, will you? If it doesn't come to anything and those reporters come around to the house again, it would be... It would be horrible," he finished lamely. "They say awful things about Joy, about Emile."

She leant over and hugged him. "I won't. It's you, me and Emile against the world when it comes to finding Joy, isn't it?"

Still arm in arm, they finished the tea in silence, both staring at the kitchen wall. It was covered with family photographs, framed certificates Frank had been awarded for teaching, and even his graduation photograph. In it, he was all dressed up in a robe and mortar board, with her mum, the dark-haired Beatrice, holding his hand and gazing up at him adoringly.

"You've always done your best for us, Dad," Lucy said now, pecking him on the cheek before she released him, "Mum would have been proud of the way you raised us after she died, too."

"You think?" He smiled sadly, his eyes still fixed on the photo of his wife. "I hope so, I do hope so, Lucy. You know what I sometimes think?"

"What?"

"Beatrice is waiting for me to find Joy. I have these dreams where she's asking where she is, and that's when I know I can't rest until we find her." He met her eyes. "But I am trying very hard to be pragmatic and sensible about these new leads. After all the disappointments of the last few years, the sightings all over the world, it's worn me down. I almost believe she doesn't want to be found, but I must carry on so Beatrice can rest in peace."

Lucy woke with a jump at 2:00am, sweating and with her heart racing. It felt like she had spoken in the cool, shadowy bedroom. Echoes of a name bounced off the white walls, danced between the bunch of white roses on her windowsill and the huge poster-sized framed prints of the city hanging either side of the door. Had she spoken out loud in her sleep?

She would be risking everything, but the more she had thought about Mattie, the more convinced she had become. Not in Spain, somehow involved with another man but right here in Brighton, her home city, less than half a mile from where the DNA had been found. Mattie was also part of Ned's network, had access to the criminal underworld, was a part of it, so it would be easy to see how her DNA might have been found on a victim of trafficking.

It was the same single-minded desperation she had felt the last time she thought she had found her sister, and as before it had broken through the veneer of professionalism. Last time it had been the gold charm bracelet that matched the necklace Joy had always worn. The necklace had been found dumped in a bin on Henfield Common, but the bracelet had never been found.

The woman at the bar looked like Joy on the CCTV, and as she lifted her glass, the charm bracelet had caught the light. The bar was part of a trendy nightclub in Birmingham, and Lucy had only seen the footage because she was asked to review some evidence as part of a case she was working on. Her attention had been focused on the barman, until she became aware of the woman in the background.

Hours of police time had been wasted, and, as her dad said, the crashing disappointment when they inevitably discovered the woman wasn't Joy, led to weeks of depression, and a whole lot of embarrassment at work. Especially as this was the third time she had been convinced she had seen Joy.

The craving, the wanting to know, overrode every other sense she had. Searching for her sister was like a drug, and she wouldn't be able to live her life until she knew what had really happened that night five years ago. Unexpectedly, and bizarrely, it seemed that answers might be at her fingertips.

TWENTY-EIGHT

Friday night, and Mattie made sure she finished her shift bang on time. It was ridiculous how urgent it now was that she cut all ties with not only Ned, but with the police. It had never occurred to her, especially in her current state, that anyone could actually mistake her for Joy Maddison, especially Joy's own sister. Every time she thought about her meeting with DI Merry she felt physically sick.

She grabbed her bag, refilled her bottle at the tap and walked out of the gates. Bobby wasn't working until tomorrow, and the others never really spoke to her unless it was to tell her to work faster, or to laugh at her. The pavement was dusty, the shadows lengthening and the crowds heading home from the beaches had long gone, taking with them those precious selfies on their phones, and leaving behind a trail of litter stretching all the way to the sea.

Mattie strolled slowly, enjoying the gentle warmth of the night, not thinking about what lay ahead yet. She had time to kill now. Nobody in her current life had ever suggested she might be Joy Maddison, and only Jono said she looked like their idol. Even he had said it less and less as her looks slipped away and her drugs habit increased. She remembered now, a little sliver of memory she would rather have left forgotten, that he often used to call her Joy when they had sex. She knew why he did it, and she had been flattered. Anger pulsed through her body. Just what kind of loser had she been over the past few years?

Mattie checked her phone out of habit, reassured to see no messages, and especially reassured to see none from Jono's number. Having pushed it out of her mind, she felt she would now like to punch him if he dared come back through the door. He had loved her because she looked like someone else.

She kept replaying the conversation with DI Lucy Merry in her head, over and over. DI Merry. *Lucy.* Joy's sister, who was quite clearly desperate to see her sibling again, who deserved to know what had really happened on that July night, five long years ago.

Mattie still couldn't quite believe she had been talking to Joy's sister. To be fair, Ned and his crew weren't the types to have tuned into a Joy Maddison vlog anyway, so they probably didn't even know who she was, but to Mattie it was beyond her wildest dreams. And her wildest nightmares.

Even Bobby said more than once that she looked a bit like Joy, she thought suddenly, frowning, but he had never suggested she might *be* her. She saw the resemblance in the mirror sometimes, but it was just a passing likeness. Now though, she had begun to wonder, if her boyfriend had ever properly cared about her, or just been using her because he couldn't have the real thing. They had both been obsessed with Joy, but did his obsession go beyond that of a super fan, turning the adulation into something sick and twisted?

She knew the answer to that, if she delved deep. The thoughts made her feel sick, as though she, Mattie, was just some kind of broken and disposable doll. Like a busted-up Barbie she had once seen in a rubbish bin along the road, its limbs missing, hair cut down to the scalp, skin defaced with biro and nail polish.

The videos and photos she and Jono had cherished seemed to prove this theory. Had she gone through the last ten years, with someone who only loved her because he could pretend that she was someone else? That didn't make sense even to her.

Jono, why did you leave me on my own? I thought you loved me.

He had been irritated by her though. Quite a lot of the time. He had told her she was slow, stupid, lame, but they had both laughed about it. Even though maybe, she admitted to herself, she had felt kind of sad and ashamed deep inside. She had laughed because he did, to make him happy.

Memories of Bobby telling her how his former partner, Col, had always managed to make everything Bobby's fault. Col had never said he hit Bobby because he loved him. No, he had been far cleverer. He had told Bobby it was because the dishwasher wasn't loaded correctly, or the cleaning hadn't been done to his satisfaction, going on to say, with a shake of his head, that most people could manage to keep up half decent standards, so why couldn't Bobby just be normal like everyone else?

Bobby, far too close to the situation, had for a long time been unable to see he was being manipulated, and he had even begun to believe he was that person, the one Col saw, the one who 'wasn't normal'. Because of Col's job as a police officer, he had convinced Bobby nobody would believe him if he ever tried to report the abuse. Even when Bobby finally got the courage to end the relationship, he never reported anything, but simply, slowly and painfully moved on.

Had it been similar for her and Jono? Her mind stuck on the physical abuse Bobby had suffered. She was sure Jono had never hit her. Positive. He had laughed at her, but never laid a hand on her in anger.

With so much on her mind, and so much to prove, she

cleared her head as best she could, and focused on the task in hand. This was it, the money shot.

Tonight, she wasn't going home to Number Forty-Two. Instead, she walked through the hole in the wire fencing, and dodged straight down to the loading docks. After a quick and cautious look around, she opened the door of a shipping container and slipped inside, bolting the door securely behind her, wincing at the slight clanging noise.

She knew this part of the port so well, and when it came to hiding places, she had several options. But Ned always unloaded dodgy cargo on this wharf, right in front of the two factories, and the net sheds. It was an older area, built for smaller vessels and sat awkwardly next to the vast newer constructions and mechanised loading equipment.

But it was secluded, never likely to be busy, and the security cameras and lights missing a good part of the shadowy corner. You just had to know where to walk. And where not to fall over the huge chains and winches that formed part of the old lifting mechanisms for oversized and weighty cargo.

Earlier this afternoon, just past the RNLI lifeboat station and the old stone lighthouse, Mattie had spotted both Coast-guard and Border Force vessels moored up. She was now hoping this was not the night when they too were acting on information. It would be bloody typical if they got in first, she thought, with a flash of panic.

Despite the heat of the night, Mattie shivered inside her container, fighting the waves of panic at being stuck inside the dark space. It smelt of rust and fish, and the powdery unpleasant scent of cement floated in through the holes in the side. This particular set of older style blue containers, forming a stack of six, had been in place for at least six months, and she was certain nobody was suddenly going to pitch up and move them tonight. Or she had been certain. Now every creak and wash, every small noise made her wince. A brown spider, descending slowly on a silver thread, swayed gently in the breeze.

Very small, almost finger-sized, holes in the side, perfect for holding her phone up and videoing any action outside, also gave her fresh air and saved her from a full-on panic attack.

The phone she was using tonight wasn't expensive, but it did have an excellent camera. There was a faint but usable light from the floodlights outside the factories. Best of all, she was close enough to get a good identification in any videos or photos.

By 1:00am she was freezing cold and had cramp from waiting it out. She was also having major doubts about her cleverness in doing this at all. Hushed voices alerted her to some action outside and her heart began to pound. She peered through the holes, flexing cold hands, making sure her trainers made no noise on the metal floor. A smallish vessel was making its way in from the harbour mouth. Inconspicuous, faded red, with the look of a trawler bringing in an early catch.

Despite the cloudy night, as she had hoped there was easily enough light to see what was going on, and although Mattie was rigid with fear, she managed to film the whole exchange. She took extra care to add close-ups, and zoomed-in footage of the trawler crews, and the lottery-win moment when Ned slashed the corner of a tightly wrapped brown plastic parcel, drew white powder out on the tip of his knife and held it to his lips and nose.

His face was silhouetted against the pale backdrop of the gleaming waters, the peace of the night. There was no wind, so the audio should pick up well too, Mattie thought, trying to shift silently from foot to foot as her calves cramped and her bad knee started to twinge.

"It's good to go," Ned announced, and stepped aside while Harley, Connor and Lucas moved in to continue unloading. "Get half in the white van, and half in the usual place."

He passed a wad of notes to one of the trawler crew. The

man, small and wiry with a knitted cap pulled down over his face, started to count them out with exaggerated care. When he finished, he said something sharp and heavily accented to Ned, that Mattie couldn't catch. His words fell soft but deadly into the night, and it was clear from his aggressive stance he wasn't happy about the amount.

Ned shrugged and held both palms upwards. "Times are hard, boys. This is the amount I agreed on with your boss. You can take it all back if you aren't happy and give me the fucking money back."

For a heart-stopping moment the tension between the two groups seemed to soar sky-high. Ned's crew paused in their work, and Mattie could see Harley sliding a hand into his pocket. She caught the gleam of a weapon.

Similarly, another crew member appeared from below deck on the trawler, carrying a baseball bat.

Nobody spoke, or moved, and Mattie held her breath. Her mouth was dry, and her legs were agony. Surely, they wouldn't give it back. That would screw up her plans. She didn't want another fight; she wanted a nice, neat exchange with everything caught on camera.

The sound of an emergency vehicle siren on the main road seemed to break the impasse and Mattie relaxed slightly as the two groups dropped their fight stance and the transaction seemed to be complete.

The trawler crew beat a hasty retreat, and she watched the vessel, *Lady Jane*, sailing out to the harbour mouth, probably to engage in some legitimate fishing just in case they needed an alibi. Ned had told her only a few fishermen were on the illegal payroll, and mostly because they were struggling to survive financially. But, like Ned and his crew, there was a legitimate side to every business. Which was why it was almost impossible to detect.

She waited, sinking to her haunches, hugging her knees and

the precious phone. If this had worked, she had finally done it, she was free. And just for once, in a rare moment of confidence and self-congratulation, the dark voices in her head were silent, as though even they acknowledged the magnitude of tonight's work.

TWENTY-NINE

Mattie was awake and up in her special place, painting and sketching by 5:00am. Wired and triumphant, she had watched the video over and over, before falling asleep for a couple of hours. Nuala had woken her, delivering a gift of a small dead bird. But even that couldn't dent her happiness. No need for drink or drugs. She had done this all on her own. Bobby would be proud, and she could move on with her life. She had never felt such personal happiness and the glow inside her heart seemed to match the soft pink and gold sunrise over the port.

No voices, no darkness, as she painted Bobby, Nuala and the port, and slowly the day warmed up and the smooth liquid gold became a fierce glittering heat as it poured through the holes in the roof, the boarded-up windows.

"We'll be moving soon, Nuala," she told the cat, scooping her up. "You'll like it at Bobby's."

Suddenly there was so much to think about, so much to plan she was almost giddy with excitement and hope.

At 7:00am her phone pinged a message. Emily confirming the meet this morning.

Showered and dressed, Mattie set off along the back roads,

winding her way around until she slipped through the church-yard in Shoreham. It was a long walk, and it was hot, but she didn't care. The car was waiting.

When she slid inside and pulled the door closed, she realised there were three people in the car. The driver pulled away quickly as Mattie knew she had walked into a trap.

"Hey, Mattie." Emily smiled at her from the backseat, but her smile seemed a little strained. Next to her sat DI Lucy Merry, who nodded at her, lips just curving in greeting, gaze intense.

"I didn't know you were going to be here," Mattie blurted out, shock making her stupid.

"I didn't either, until about an hour ago," Lucy told her. "I just had some free time, so I thought I'd come along for the ride. I understand you have something pretty special for us?"

Mattie felt her shoulders relax just a bit, and she leant back against the car seat, sliding the phone out of her pocket. "I did it. The video shows everything and the audio quality is good. I checked it like you said," she addressed Emily, who nodded and took the phone.

While the two police officers leant in and watched the video, Mattie studied Lucy's profile, the small nose, the curve of her lips. So much like Joy's. But even as she waited, breathing far too quickly, she knew whatever happened now, she had done it. The video wouldn't vanish, the evidence was there. She could take her cash and walk away.

Except she couldn't.

"This is great stuff, Mattie." DI Merry turned to her, eyes blazing, "This is exactly what we needed."

"So I'll get paid, then?"

"Of course. There is just one other thing I want to ask for before we lose you." Lucy wasn't smiling. "I want you to take a DNA test."

"What?" Of all the things she had been expecting, this was

definitely not one of them. Mattie found she had one hand to her chest, clutching just under her breastbone like a heart attack victim. "Why would you need me to do that?"

"Please understand." Lucy was speaking slowly, carefully. "This is really hard for me, for my family, and even harder to explain, but I would like you to take a DNA test to confirm you aren't Joy Maddison."

"But I'm *not* your sister!" Mattie said, speaking fast, fighting her rising heart rate. This was torture. She should have got straight out of the car when she saw DI Lucy Merry was along for the ride. "You know I'm not!"

"Humour me? Have the test."

Mattie could tell from the faces turned towards her that Lucy knew this was a bad idea; she could see from Emily's expression that she thought her boss had lost it.

She herself was beginning to feel faint with desperation, claustrophobic in the car with the two police officers. "No. You can't make me. I'm not under arrest, I'm *helping* you!" She should never have put herself through this. "You have to give me the money now. That's how it works."

"Okay, I get it. The footage is good. It's perfect. That was a really dangerous and brave thing to do, Mattie, and we can use all of it and hopefully get Ned banged up." Emily eyed her boss warily. "You're right, that's how it works."

"When do I get paid?" Mattie asked, relief flooding over her.

Lucy, who was now watching the footage back again, said nothing. The DI looked up, as though aware of Mattie's scrutiny. "We can arrange a meet-up to give you the money. You could have a swab for the DNA test at the same time."

"Boss, can we leave it?" Emily was clearly getting more uncomfortable by the second with the meeting, and the car, looping back along the coast into the city, was passing back into Hove.

The great sweep of blue and grey sky hung over the greyness of the sea, and on the horizon the wind turbines spun white and futuristic.

"She is Joy. I don't know how or why but this is my sister," Lucy said calmly. She leant forward to speak to the driver, who made a right turn up the next side road.

As she moved back against the seat, her hand touched Mattie's, and Mattie winced and pulled her hand onto her lap. The skin-to-skin connection reminded her of when she had first touched Joy, had realised through the buzz of artificial stimulants that she was a real person. A real person who lived and died just like anyone else. Nausea rose in her stomach, and she found her eyes were wet with tears.

"Mattie?"

"I'm not your sister." She could almost feel the pulse jumping in her wrist as she clasped her hands tightly together, trying to suppress the relentless rise of raw emotion. She could feel Lucy's intense gaze on her and couldn't look round to meet it.

"I understand, but a DNA test will confirm either way..."

Something broke loose inside of her, and she was powerless to control it, suddenly powerless to stop herself wrecking her bright and beautiful future. "I'm not your sister and the reason I *know* that is because I know where Joy Maddison is buried! Okay? My boyfriend killed her, and I helped him. She's *dead* and I can show you where her body is!" Mattie was breathing fast as she turned in her seat and faced them, hands clamped on her thighs.

Why had she said that? Fuck, now what had she done? Sabotaged her future, that's what she had just done. Snakes and Ladders, and she had just jumped on the biggest snake she could find, heading down in a straight slide from CHIS of the year to wanted criminal in a matter of seconds. All her strikes on the wall, all her excited plans, had led to this moment.

She looked at the two police officers staring at her, and she knew then, from the mixed expressions of shock and distrust, she had just burnt through every layer of her new life, exposing a rawness that had never been meant to see the light of day.

"I think we need to go back to the station," Emily said, taking charge, but still staring at Mattie as though she had never seen her before.

Mattie kept quiet on the ride to the police station, and Lucy said nothing more, keeping her gaze averted, looking out of the window. Her jaw was very tight, as though she was holding in all the things she wanted to ask, and her hands lay still and once again tightly clasped on her lap.

Four hours later and here she was, after a formal interview, a confession. She had voiced the horrors she had dreamt of ever since they had murdered Joy. And yet there was also a strange relief in showing them the videos of Joy on her phone, the pictures of her idol, including the final horrific ones she could hardly bring herself to watch.

Lucy had not been allowed to sit in on the interview, as she was personally involved, and Emily, after a vague, reassuring murmur had slipped into the shadows, leaving her with two male officers. Both middle-aged, and both professional and detached. They reminded her a little of Ned, in their cool, emotionless manner, but they were kind enough, offering her a drink, the duty solicitor. She declined both.

What was the point of a solicitor when she had just confessed? She had done it, she and Jono, but as he was probably dead too, it was down to her to face up to it. All her thoughts of a new start, making inroads into starting a journey back into society, had all been for nothing.

The police officers pressed her on representation, and eventually she agreed to the solicitor. She didn't know why they would want her to have representation, but she supposed it was a case of covering their arses. But no solicitor could get her out of this mess.

Perhaps, in prison, the nightmares would stop. Her worst fear now was Nuala, but she prayed she would be able to talk to Bobby, and he would continue with their plans of moving the cat and kittens to his flat. Even when he knew what she had done, she thought he would care for her animals.

"Can you tell us exactly what happened?"

Mattie found her voice. "Jono, my boyfriend, and I went to Joy's house. We went quite a lot. It was a laugh and once she started running, we knew her usual route and routine and we would wait, watch her." She was aware how creepy this sounded, but she knew she had to keep going, and say everything, give up all the ghosts. "That day, the day she vanished, we were just inside the footpath where she crossed over the road. It's... it's a wooded area and nobody was around. Jono was a drunk and he'd taken something new, something one of his friends gave him. A new batch... He was a bit crazy."

"Go on."

"This time when we heard her coming, he jumped up and grabbed her, swung her around with a hand over her mouth, laughing. She was terrified and struggling, her rape alarm fell on the grass before she had a chance to activate it." Mattie paused, before continuing with all the confidence of an actor who knows their lines. That was exactly what it felt like. Whatever happened she knew what they had done. "Jono wanted me to touch her too, he kept saying 'Look, we've got her all to ourselves and she's all ours.'"

"What did you do?"

"I was shocked, and I didn't do anything until he kissed her. Then I got up and tried to shove him away, but we were all

struggling, and he had an arm around Joy's neck, I was holding
her hands. I was drunk, so all I could think of was what Jono
had said, here she was in real life, and we were touching her,
but I became aware she was fighting to get free, and it was
wrong. We were happy but she wasn't. She didn't realise how
much we loved her..."

"Did Joy manage to get free?"

"No. There was a horrible sound, like a click and a crunch
of bone, and she went limp and heavy. The evening was very
still and quiet, no cars on the road, no dogwalkers on the footpath. It was such a hot day I guess everyone was waiting until it
was cooler... I... I knew everything in the world had stopped and
she was dead before Jono did." Tears were pouring down
Mattie's face.

"What happened next?"

"We took her jewellery, Jono said we should, and put her in
the car. Jono always had a car, but never the same one for very
long. This one..." She screwed up her face, thinking hard. "It
was a black car, very battered, small. I can't remember the type."

"Go on."

"We took her to the woods behind the Shack Café, a long
way into the trees, and we buried her. Jono said he had pickaxes
in the boot and tarpaulin, from the work he'd been doing for
Ned, and the ground was wet from the storm that morning. We
buried her quite deep, but all I could see was her blonde hair all
limp in the dirt, her skin was getting all muddy..."

The police officers watched the video in silence, not
wincing at Joy's indistinct screams for help as she struggled
initially, nor the sound of tools thudding against the woodland
turf, digging her grave after she had succumbed to her attacker.
Mattie wondered if she was going to throw up, feeling beads of
sweat gather on her forehead, and her T-shirt sticking wetly
under her arms and across her back. She wiped her lip on the

back of her hand and sipped from the paper cup of water they had given her.

"You filmed this?"

"Yes."

"Why did you carry on filming after it went wrong? I can understand you wanting to capture the meeting, but you must have been holding the camera while your boyfriend dug the grave and laid the victim to rest, as it were. If you were as horrified and upset as you claim, why record it?"

She hadn't ever thought of that and was at a bit of a loss to explain. Why indeed? "I don't know. I was off my head and Jono must have wanted me to, I suppose."

"Did he get off on the fact you both killed Joy? Perhaps that was his plan all along? It would explain why he had the tarpaulin and tools in the car."

"No! Oh no. Jono loved Joy as much as I did. She was the kindest, sweetest person and she used to wave at us at events and everything..." Mattie trailed off again as emotion overcame her. She sat looking at the table while tears dripped down her nose. It seemed like too much effort to wipe them away.

"Okay, that's all for now, but we'd like you to take us to where you buried the victim."

"I can do that." Mattie blinked, her eyes gritty, and exhaustion threatening to overwhelm her. Her bones seemed to ache with tiredness and her heart was sore. Yet, she couldn't help but feel a sense of peace, no, of satisfaction maybe? She searched her mind and came up with the feeling that you get when you've just performed well in a tough exam. Which was odd, but cleansing.

Soon she was just numb and floating along as they processed her, took fingerprints and photographs. Mattie cooperated with everything, said please and thank you, but nothing registered in her brain. She might have been dreaming.

They led her out to an unmarked car. The police officers were calm and reassuring, as one of them put a hand protectively over her head when she dived into the back seat.

"It's okay, Mattie, all you have to do is take us to where you buried Joy Maddison."

THIRTY

She could pinpoint the exact spot. They had visited it for the anniversary every year, she and Jono, stepping over fallen branches, pushing through brambles to the clearing and sitting on the grass with a couple of cans, some gear and candles.

It was their very own candlelit vigil and Mattie had nightmares for weeks afterwards, but Jono had insisted, pushing her to do it with a cruelty that should have warned her. They had done something very wrong, and they should torture themselves a little, think of what might have been, mourn their beloved Joy, he told her, blue eyes sombre, sad and a little bit excited.

The forensic teams were on site, and everyone was dressed in white suits and booties. Mattie remembered seeing the same outfits on TV when they found the dead woman in Hove. The one they had thought might be Joy. The media would go into a feeding frenzy once they realised the police finally had not only Joy's body, but also the woman who helped to kill her.

After she had pointed out the grave site, Mattie was taken a little further away, and she watched, fist in mouth as the turf, the mud and the grit slowly peeled back to reveal the body. It took a long time to dig, as the ground was so hard.

Again and again a shovel would go in, sharp tools would loosen a section, gloved hands would examine. Inch by inch, barely sheltered from the sun's heat by the sparse tree cover, the team worked on, and Mattie felt like she was going to pass out. She waited, as dust so fine it was mere powder stuck to damp, sweaty skin, and the conversations were brief and forced from dry throats.

Water breaks were taken on the other side of the cordon, but Mattie refused to move. She needed to be there, to own what she had done. It was the full circle, and the rest of her life would spring from this moment. No future plans would be made by herself. The court would decide her punishment and where she was going to live. She realised she was crying silently, letting the tears drip off her chin onto her angular breastbones. The heat was all encompassing.

Would Joy's body be a skeleton? Five years was a long time for a body to be in the ground, she thought, but she wasn't prepared for the flashback she experienced as Joy was carefully removed piece by piece from her final resting place.

She had forgotten they had wrapped her in tarpaulin, and underneath... She could hardly bear to look, but she couldn't turn away. She deserved this, the voice had said so and he was right. Not a skeleton, not anything recognisable as human. Pieces of cloth too, hanging in strips. The team seemed to move so slowly, photographing, documenting everything.

Mattie turned away from her escorts and vomited into a patch of crispy, dying brambles, her whole body shaking, sweat mingling with tears and snot on her face.

She was in this place five years ago, could see the blonde hair in the dirt, hear the screams. Was it her screaming? Because Joy had been dead by then. Through it all the man shouted at her. Which was crazy because he hadn't been there, it had just been her and Jono. Or had it? Surely Bobby must be right, and he wasn't real. Was any of this real? Perhaps she was just on a really bad trip and would wake up next to Jono on their grubby shared mattress in Kingston Lane.

Finally, as a man bent to sweep away more dirt and dust with a fine brush, there was Joy, exposed to the world. Her remains were laid carefully, respectfully onto white plastic sheeting, but Mattie could only think of Joy's privacy being violated once again. The body was protected by a white tent, but the side was open to allow officers to come and go, and Mattie could see inside, see what Joy had become in the five years since she had last seen her. A few scraps of faded pink clung to the blackened corpse. In five years, decomposition was well established as nature took back her own, and Mattie, as she gazed at the pathetic remains, could see no sign of her idol in this relic of their obsession.

The scene, set against a scorched, dusty summer woodland, and so similar to the summer Joy had died, seemed to spin out of control, like a TV channel struggling to get a signal. Despite the dizziness, she somehow knew now that she wasn't dreaming. This was the reality of what she had done.

She realised finally, as she wiped her mouth with her hand, she had always half hoped it was all a nightmare, but here it was, proof that she was a murderer. Of the person she idolised. The videos were real, the police had proof and a body. It was all true.

Mattie was taken back to the police station and returned to custody. After the body had been revealed the peace and the floating feeling had gone. Now she wanted to scream, to run away, to tear at her skin with her fingernails. All these years she knew what she had done, but it had been something she had learnt to deal with, push to the back of her mind.

Now she would go to prison for the murder of her idol. People would hate her. She hated herself. It would be on the news and in the papers. She couldn't stop shaking, sinking to sit on the floor of her clean but basic cell. Already she fancied she could hear a buzz outside. Jono wouldn't come and help her, wherever he was, but if he was alive, he would see her blamed. What would he do? How would he feel? She found she couldn't even begin to imagine, but if she was in his shoes, she'd stay the hell away.

The hatch to her cell opened and a couple of times, an officer asked if she was okay, if she wanted anything. She knew it was just to get a glimpse of Joy Maddison's killer. Mainly, she just wanted to be left alone, sitting with sagging shoulders, mouth slightly open, absorbing the shocks of the last twenty-four hours.

She had to call Bobby, so he could look after Nuala and her babies. Tears began to fall as she considered she would probably never see them again, never see Bobby again. Ned would know what she had done too. He would probably love it, be wishing he had recruited her earlier, used her more extensively given her murderous tendencies.

The duty solicitor visited again and explained she could plead guilty of manslaughter. She and Jono had not gone out with the intent of killing Joy, had they, the woman asked.

Mattie, sitting opposite the small, sharp-eyed, grey-suited legal aid, shook her head. "We loved her. It was an accident. We didn't mean to hurt her."

"Whose idea was it to go and meet Joy that night?"

"I don't know. I suppose we both decided." She couldn't remember. Certain parts of the night she knew were true, but others she couldn't begin to piece together.

"And what was your intention?"

"Just to meet her, to talk to her. I expect we were both a bit drunk, had taken something and thought it was a good idea," Mattie said.

"Was anyone else with you?"

"I don't think so... I don't know." She blanked on that, trying to remember. Failing.

"And you said in your statement it was Jono who was holding onto Joy when she went limp? He had his arm around her neck?" The woman was making quick notes, firing the questions like bullets, piercing through Mattie's shock and confusion.

"Yes. I was holding her hands, I think. I was so out of it. I don't know what I'd taken but I remember thinking here I was, touching Joy's skin. It was like a dream sequence." Mattie bit her lip, feeling more tears slide off her eyelashes and seeing them splash on the grey Formica table. The nightmares were roaring in her head so loudly a throbbing pain was stretching from her left temple down to her tightly clenched jawbone. It was hard to tell what real life was and wasn't.

"Mattie, you held the camera while your boyfriend dug a grave for Joy and eventually buried her, didn't you?"

"Yes. He told me to. I think he did. I can't remember that well."

"What was your relationship like with Jono?"

She shrugged. It seemed years ago, meaningless. "It was okay."

"Did he ever threaten you? Abuse you?"

Mattie shook her head. "He cared for me, but then he just vanished, like walked out with all his stuff. Sometimes in the past, he would go away for a couple of weeks on business and then come home. I was sick this time while he was away, so I wasn't keeping track of the days, but it was the week of the anniversary when I realised how long he had been away."

"Anniversary?"

"July the fifth. Joy's death." She explained about the ritual.

As the solicitor concluded their discussion, she laid a few options out for Mattie, which Mattie couldn't even begin to take in. It was only when she casually added, "The police will be referring you for a psychiatric assessment too," that Mattie felt her head jerk up.

Attention snared, she was jolted back to alertness. "What do you mean? I'm not crazy." Evil definitely, but not crazy, she thought bitterly.

The solicitor looked at her calmly. "It's not because anyone is suggesting you are crazy, Mattie, it's a standard procedure. You do say you were drunk, maybe under the influence of drugs, and there are gaps in your statement that we can't, at present, fill in. Important gaps."

Mattie frowned at the woman, unable to think of a reason to refuse, unsure if she had any say left in her life or whether, from now onwards, everything would, as she had imagined earlier, be decided for her.

Her solicitor smiled briskly. "It will be okay, and it all adds evidence to the case."

"But we killed Joy. What else is there to say?" Mattie considered. "Do you think Jono really is dead?"

"I can't say, but from what you have told me it seems he left of his own accord, if he took his belongings. What happened when he reached his destination, we don't know, do we? I know the police are still investigating."

"Jono murdered Joy and I helped him, and then we buried her. I don't think it could get any worse," Mattie informed her. Each time she said it out loud it was getting easier. The script had been written and the first act was done. If Jono was found alive, he would know she had grassed him up, opened up Pandora's box to reveal their terrible secret. Instinct told her he was dead, and she was left to take the blame for what they had both done.

Her solicitor was talking again. "It is a little more complex than that, but you are helping by cooperating fully, Mattie. I'll see you tomorrow."

And with that Mattie found herself back in the little room

again. This time the room had grey walls, but it was similar to the one in her nightmares. A prison. She sank down on the floor again, hunching over her knees, curling into a tight ball. What the hell was she going to do now, though? She had given up her freedom, when if she had been a little cleverer, she could have held onto her secret.

But that would have been wrong. "I'm sorry, Joy," she whispered, as the room spun out of control, the voices returned, and she screwed her eyes tight shut, like a child, blocking out the world. But for Mattie, the world inside her head was just as bad as the one outside. There was no escape. "I'm truly sorry, Joy, so sorry."

THIRTY-ONE

By morning, she found she must have slept a little, because she had torn at her wrist with her fingernails, and sharp scratches lined the soft skin of her inner arms. There were no mirrors in her cell, but when she was allowed to shower, she saw the scratches on her forehead were back too. Usually this only happened after the nightmares had visited, but she supposed as she was now living her own nightmare, it was her mind's way of letting her physical self know that things were not okay.

She had no idea of time in her cell, and she didn't really care. Her whole being was concentrated on staying huddled in her safe corner, letting her hair fall forward to hide her face, hugging her knees. A stray flash of conversation with Ned occupied her mind. His half-brother, Dami, had once said he was a regular churchgoer, and Ned had brushed this off as though it was something to be ashamed of.

Dami ran the legitimate side of the fish market business, and he took a lot of abuse from Ned. She recalled that one conversation was the only time she had seen Ned look uncomfortable, even though he had laughed at the reference to any former religious association, saying he preferred a life of sin.

Mattie wished she believed in something, anything that might help her right now. Because there was no getting away from it, she had helped commit murder. It didn't matter whether she had meant to or not, because nothing would bring Joy Maddison back from the dead. She hunched closer to her knees, buried her head under her folded arms and closed her eyes tightly.

A commotion outside made her jerk into alertness, but it was just another drunk being bodily pushed into the cell next door. He did some yelling and banging on the walls before he shut up. Soon after she heard snores from her new neighbour as he presumably slept off his intoxication.

DI Armstrong and another officer came to take her for her next interview. Her solicitor was present, and Mattie assumed they were now going to formally charge her or tell her which prison she was going to spend the rest of her life in. She was grateful the psych analysis had been postponed until this afternoon.

"Mattie, we need to discuss some new evidence with you." The DI looked rattled, she thought suddenly, focusing on his face properly for the first time since she had entered the room.

"Do I need to speak to my client in private before we hear this?" Mattie's solicitor asked sharply.

"I don't think that will be necessary," the DI said. "We have had forensic evidence back from the dig yesterday. Due to the high-profile case, we fast-tracked at the lab. Firstly, we have confirmed the body was not that of Joy Maddison, but of a woman named Stephanie Coultas."

Mattie blinked. "What do you mean? Of course it was Joy. I told you what happened, and you saw the video." She felt her heart pounding way too fast, mouth dry.

"DNA tests have confirmed the body was twenty-seven-year-old Stephanie Coultas, of no fixed address. She was a known drug user and has been charged with prostitution in the past. Did you know her, or have you heard the name mentioned?"

She shook her head. "No, no I don't know her... But the video?" Mattie blinked hard, rubbing her temples with her fingertips. Her head ached and her eyes were sore and gritty, swollen from crying.

"You can see for yourself it was poor quality, the light was bad, and although there is no question that a blonde woman was attacked, restrained and killed, then buried in the woods, at no point is there a clear identification shot. Forensics have identified the victim was dressed in the clothes Joy was wearing when she disappeared. Her physical characteristics match those of Joy Maddison, so I can see why you believed it was her."

He pushed a photograph towards her. "Stephanie Coultas could have been Joy Maddison's twin, unless you looked closely. She was only a year younger, and as I say, her physical characteristics, such as height and weight, matched Joy's almost exactly. Are you sure you never met her?"

"No."

"She was a dancer, and most recently worked at a lap-dancing club, the Pink Pussycat off Foundry Lane." He raised his eyebrows, as if hoping to jog her memory.

Mattie stretched her fingers out for the photograph again, pulling it towards her in trepidation. A pretty woman, laughing in a slightly blurred photograph. Long blonde hair, green eyes, a perfect pink pout. "I don't know her... but... are you saying we buried someone else in Joy's clothes? Jono switched the bodies?" She could feel her brow furrowing in confusion. "I don't get it." This was getting worse. They had stripped their idol of her clothes. Revolting. Strangely, she was more disgusted with herself for this act than she had been for anything else they had done. Was she finally losing her mind?

Mattie stared across the table. Both police officers looked edgy, shocked even, she would have said. Was there more?

Would they reveal a second body had been discovered and announce another murder victim? Perhaps before her, there had been Stephanie, or maybe Jono had been seeing them both.

Or, another thought popped up, like speech bubbles in her head, and this time her heart seemed to freeze inside her chest. Perhaps she and Jono had killed two women. Could she have been so stupid, so drugged up, she hadn't noticed she was living with a killer? Loveable, laddish Jono, who had an obsession with Joy Maddison, and any girl who looked like her, clearly had more secrets of his own than she could ever have imagined.

Mattie found her hands were making sweat marks on the table and withdrew them, wiping them shakily on her top. Her jaw was clenched so hard her facial muscles were hurting, and threads of a headache were spreading like electric shocks just above her eyes. The headaches always went after she started drinking, but there was no alcohol in sight at the police station. In prison she would have no alcohol either.

Just as the silence began to seem unbearable, and Mattie wondered if it would be okay to scream or burst into tears to relieve the pressure building in her brain, DI Armstrong cleared his throat, and looked her straight in the eye. "No, Jono didn't switch the bodies. Your DNA test came back, and it has confirmed you are in fact not Mattie Woods at all. You are Joy Maddison."

THIRTY-TWO

Lucy had not managed to sleep properly for forty-eight hours. To discover her CHIS had in fact been responsible for the murder of her sister had been almost too much to bear. Most of the time she had believed this, she had wanted to scream at someone, at anything, punch the wall or kick out a window in her lofty apartment.

To do them credit her colleagues had managed to keep the arrest from the press until Mattie took them to the burial site. As soon as the story broke it was a case of trying to keep Mattie's identity a secret.

But now everything had changed, and it wouldn't take long for the journalists to get their claws into the story of the year. Lucy dropped her head into her hands and tried to stay focused.

One tiny bit of sanity remained. She had been right. She wasn't going crazy, and her instincts had at long last proved to be correct. Mattie was her sister. Which opened a whole new can of worms. Now she would have to face her, ask her why she had done what she had done, why she had denied her true identity, and what had really happened on that night five years ago.

Her phone had been buzzing with messages and missed calls all morning, as specialist support officers broke the news to Emile and Frank. She couldn't, she just couldn't speak to anyone at all. The only person she needed to see right now was her sister, but she was afraid, so afraid of what she might say.

When her colleagues told her Mattie had been informed of the DNA results, Lucy managed to pull herself together enough to walk out of the office down the stairs and into the room where Mattie and her solicitor sat. It took a few deep breaths as she paused outside the door, before she found the strength to raise her hand and open it.

Mattie was clinging to the edges of her chair, apparently fighting for breath, head falling forward, limp, lank hair flopping across her face. Lucy heard a gasp that became a sob, and it took a moment before she realised it was her own. Tears were streaming down her face even as Mattie started to speak, and her whole body was shaking as conflicting emotions drowned her professional edge once again. Her sister was alive, sitting in front of her.

"Joy?" Her sister was still slumped forward, and Lucy's legs felt as though they might be about to give way. How many times had she dreamt of being reunited with Joy?

She didn't look up for a long moment, just kept her head down towards her knees, and Lucy could see her shoulders shaking. "*What is going on?* But I'm not Joy, I'm really not, I just look like her!" Mattie said. "This doesn't make any sense."

"Breathe, Mattie, breathe slowly and deeply," her solicitor said firmly but kindly, as Lucy knelt next to her sister.

"It's okay, it's okay," Lucy told her, as she watched Mattie struggling to control her panic attack, sipping at the paper cup of water, but spilling it all over her lap. She reached out and took one of Mattie's hands. She was touching her sister, their hands were clasped together, her own skin warm, Mattie's icy cold. Her sister was this scarred and haggard woman who had been living on the streets. She was a drug user, an addict. How had this happened? Lucy placed a tentative hand on Mattie's shoulder, horrified at how bony and thin she was, how her skin looked so unhealthy and pale in the harsh light of the room.

Gradually the tears stopped, and Lucy began to wonder who would speak first. She couldn't stop staring at Mattie, and Mattie refused to meet her eyes. Was she feeling guilty?

"Would the two of you prefer to be alone for a bit?" the solicitor asked kindly.

"No!" Mattie said sharply, just as Lucy started to say yes.

The woman smiled. "How about you chat, and I'll just grab a coffee. Then we can decide what we're going to do about the criminal charges. I know it's probably the very last thing on both your minds, but Mattie is still a suspect in a murder investigation, and she will need to be bailed."

Lucy waited until the woman had left the room, before she stood up and pulled a chair over until she sat opposite her sister. "It's okay, Joy, we can sort it out. Whatever you have done, we can start to make it right," Lucy said gently. She could see Mattie's... Joy's eyes shining with tears again. "We can sort out any charges, you can help with the investigation and explain it all from your perspective."

"I..." Mattie was rubbing her eyes with both fists, like a child waking from a nightmare. Her eyes, when she finally met Lucy's gaze, were bloodshot and red-rimmed. "Why would Jono and I have killed a random woman? This Stephanie... How did we know her? Jono told me we killed Joy Maddison. He told me the woman in the grave was... myself?"

It was heart-breaking, and desperate though Lucy was to get to the truth of Mattie's dual identity, she needed to help her sister deal with the immediate charges first. A soft knock at the door was the solicitor retuning.

"Shall we have a discussion about what happens next? I think we will be able to get them to agree to bail, especially with your sister being in the force. I'm sure she will take responsibility?" She looked questioningly at Lucy, who nodded.

"Of course."

"Mattie, you are safe now, and nobody is judging you. Can you tell us what really happened?" her solicitor asked. Her face was serene but her eyes just a little too bright and her voice a little too eager. Lucy supposed this was probably the most interesting case she'd had all year. It must make a change from giving legal aid to drunks and pub brawlers.

"I don't know... I really don't know, and I don't understand how I can be Joy. I am not that person!" Mattie dropped her head into her hands and ran all ten fingertips through her hair. "I don't get it... Is it possible the DNA test could be wrong?"

"No... I mean there is a tiny margin for error of course, but this shows 99.9 per cent who you really are." Lucy was watching her closely. "Do you really not remember, or are you afraid? Because either is fine. Just tell us what's going on in your head. Jono can't hurt you now, or Ned, if that's what you are thinking. Your evidence will get him banged up for a long time."

Mattie was still stumbling over her words. Her lips, her mouth, looked clumsy, as though she was struggling to spit out the sentences she needed. "But Jono *told* me we killed *Joy*. He's always reminded me on the anniversary. We had photos on our phones, videos... Living like we did, away from society. He said it was to keep us safe from anyone finding out we killed her..."

"It's probable he edited all the photos, created a stack of false evidence to keep you under control and away from anyone who might have recognised you," Lucy told her. "Stephanie was almost your double, so again, and I am just speculating, it's possible Jono was using her until he could get hold of you."

"But what happened to me? Are you still looking for Jono?"

She blinked hard and dug her nails into her palms. The pain steadied her, grounded her. "I mean are you looking for him more than you did when he was just another missing CHIS?"

"Jono? You bet we are." Lucy's mouth set into a hard line before she spoke again. "Not only is he caught on camera committing murder, and hiding the body, but he has now become the number one suspect in your disappearance. I am not personally involved in any of the searches, although the family liaison will keep us all updated."

"Hell's teeth..." Mattie put her hand to her forehead and massaged her temples, as though trying to push the headache away. "I mean... why? And why don't I remember anything? And Joy, she wasn't an addict, was she? And she didn't have scars and a lame leg!"

"Can you remember any of your childhood? How far back do you have actual memories. I mean personal ones, not with Jono?" Lucy's voice was gentle, calm and as she hoped, Mattie took a deep breath, and responded in kind. "It would help..." She glanced at the solicitor, who nodded. "It would help if you can tell us a bit more about Jono's treatment of you. It sounds like he was extremely manipulative. Were you afraid of him?"

Mattie twisted a frayed piece of hair in her fingers as she considered, before finally admitting the awful truth. "I don't have any memories from before I met Jono," she said softly, "but I was an addict for a long time, so I was used to blackouts, to gaps in my memory. Jono told me I was in foster care, but ran away, slipped through the cracks in the system, much as he did, and that I came to Brighton from Plymouth for a party, met him and never went home. He said I was an alcoholic then, but I can't have been, can I? Unless Joy was?"

"She wasn't," Lucy confirmed. "She liked to drink, and yes, she could be a party girl, but not to excess, and I don't believe she took any recreational drugs except that bit of puff as a juvenile. That's how we have her – your – DNA on file. It was a minor charge."

"So, everything has happened since... In five years, I've become... me? The drugs too?" Mattie sipped the water, staring at the wall opposite. "Jono said we followed Joy around if she did an event, hence all the photos, and that was our story. We were super fans and that's how we met and fell in love. I never questioned how or where, and if someone asked, Jono filled in the blanks. It became a habit, something he teased me for, even though secretly I was ashamed."

"But you have no actual memories of Plymouth? Of your supposed foster parents?" the solicitor probed.

"No," Mattie whispered, clearly more and more aware of the enormity of what they were contemplating. "He had filled in the blanks, and I just accepted it."

Lucy exchanged glances with the solicitor, who now spoke firmly and clearly. "I think the first thing to do is get you out on bail. Stephanie Coultas was murdered. The pathologist report shows her neck was broken, so it could have happened just as you described in your statement, and as we can partially see in the videos."

"So, I could still have killed someone?"

"It was Jono who killed her, and if you are correct it was him who then buried her. You assumed you held the camera and filmed the burial, but there may well have been someone else present. The fact you have severe memory loss means no kind of case can be brought against you without extensive medical reports and evaluations. I do have a little medical knowledge, my husband is a specialist, but have you ever heard of trauma-related disassociation amnesia?" The solicitor had pushed her shiny grey bob behind her ears and was tapping her pen on the table, observing Mattie thoughtfully.

Mattie shook her head, opened her mouth as though trying to force some coherent words to leave it, but the effort was too great, and she gave up. Lucy felt her own mouth dry, words jumbling in her mind. Did her sister really have no memory? Had she been a victim all along? She couldn't help but feel ashamed of the thought that Joy had run away from her family, left them all on purpose. But if she'd planned to disappear and then it went wrong...

She realised she had dreamt of this moment for so long, and yet now she hadn't even hugged her sister, was sitting opposite a person who was essentially a stranger. She could no more fling her arms around Mattie than she could pull a random person on the street into a hug. Mattie's confusion was tearing at her heart strings, but equally she was frustrated, cheated of her reunion moment, and for that she felt guilty. How would Emile, the kids and her dad cope when Mattie arrived at the door, not recognising any of them? It was a different kind of hell.

"Don't worry now, but we can get you medical help. As your solicitor says, we need to get you out, first."

It took a fast-tracked decision to grant bail, but with Lucy's assurance she would look after her sister and take full responsibility, it was done.

As Mattie faced Lucy outside the station, she was still fumbling for words, still struggling.

"Do you want to come back to my place? I can get someone to bring my car around. Emile, Dad, they can't believe it. You should hear the voicemails on my phone!" Lucy laughed, a little shaky, still awkward as Mattie stood with her thin shoulders drooping, eyeing her warily. The rear entrance to the police station was sandwiched between large buildings, with a high chain link fence and a few footpaths leading into town.

"I think... I need to collect my cats." Mattie's eyes were darting from Lucy to the fence and back again.

"What? You have cats?" Lucy asked.

"Yes. Nuala and her babies. Bobby has been looking after them."

"You had a cat called Nuala before," Lucy told her gently.

"I know. I know everything about Joy, about myself, but as an outsider looking in. It makes sense but it doesn't. How can this be happening? I thought I was a completely different person. How can I have zero memories?" The pleading, bewildered look was back.

"And so many injuries," Lucy said soberly.

Mattie touched the scar on her cheek. "Joy didn't have any scars, any tattoos, any limp, did she?"

"Nooo... Well, apart from the scar on her shoulder that I noticed. Mattie, I can go and get my car now. I don't think you should be alone, and apart from anything, you're out on bail, so you need to be extra careful."

"Extra careful not to get into trouble?"

"Not exactly, but if you were thinking of going back to Kingston Lane, I don't think that would be a good idea. You're known down there. Ned is currently going through the process of being charged, but his crew know you."

"You don't need to keep tabs on me, I'm not going to do anything stupid, I just need some time. Pick me up tomorrow morning and I'll be ready then, to do whatever I need to," Mattie said, desperately, stubbornly. "I need to... I need to touch base as well as get my cats. I need to try and work out what happened, and Kingston Lane is where I lived with Jono. Maybe, now I know who I am, if I go back there, I might remember."

"I'd still like to give you a lift down there. I feel like... Look, it's too far to walk. I'll get the car now." Lucy studied her, sensing she was torn between fleeing and facing up to the enormity of the situation. She couldn't imagine how it must feel. It didn't matter if Mattie did a runner, she had already admitted she was attached to her cats, and the only place she was likely to go was home. As soon as Mattie was out of sight, Lucy pulled out her phone. It was easy enough to keep her sister under surveillance. After losing her once, she wasn't going to lose her again. But instinct told her Joy needed to feel she was being allowed to make her own choices for once.

THIRTY-THREE

As soon as Mattie watched Lucy get around the corner of the building that was it. Her mind was totally blown, and she needed to touch base, to rearrange her thoughts. Too much had happened in such a short time for her to be able to process, and she just knew she needed to get away from her sister.

Moving as quickly as she could, she slipped out of the back area, between two emergency response vehicles and made her way home. Stumbling along the weed-encrusted footpaths, following the sweltering city's back roads and alleys, sweating, tears stinging her eyes. How could this be real? Was it real? Could a person split themselves into two lives and not even notice?

Finally, back at home, soaked in sweat and gasping for breath, she stripped off and had a cold shower, hauled on an old T-shirt Jono had left behind, the one with the holes under the arms.

Finally, still not allowing herself to think, she grabbed a mug of water from the tap, dropped onto the battered sofa, and texted Bobby:

> Need to see u asap. At home. Come by after
> shift?

He got back almost immediately:

> Finish at 1:30am will come to yours. R u ok?
> Been so worried doll. Cats fine. x

Taking her third cup of water, wiping drips from her chin, Mattie went to the next room to see her cats. Nuala welcomed her with a sweetly rusty purr, and her kittens chirruped next to her. Enchanted, she played with them for a while, trying to let her mind settle, wondering how long before their eyes were fully open. Would Bobby have them while she stayed in a hotel? Or would she go back to living in Joy's... *her* house up in Dyke Road?

She fed them, the routine soothing her, and then wandered around her home. It wasn't really her home. She wasn't Mattie Woods who worked in the fish market, had a side hustle as a police informant, and lived in a derelict house. So, who the fuck was she?

Certainly not perfect, beautiful Joy Maddison. Nuala watched, unblinking, as she pulled out the scrapbooks, the photos, everything she had on Joy.

Did she remember making these? She searched her brain and came up with a no. No, she didn't. Which meant Jono had made them, has gaslighted her into thinking she was someone she wasn't. Was that gaslighting? She wasn't quite sure, but she had heard Bobby use the term in connection with his former partner, when Col had liked to pretend Bobby was going mad and imagining things when he questioned whether abuse was part of a functional relationship.

How had she met Jono? Again, she found she didn't have an actual memory, only lots of photos of them at festivals and parties. She looked closely at the photos. Was it possible, as

Lucy had suggested, that they had all been edited? Which meant her whole life HAD been invented by a man she thought had loved her?

Mattie found a smiling picture of them both on her phone. He was a bit cheeky, a bit of a lad, even though he always said he was four years older than her. And the addiction? To what extent had it been Jono getting her hooked? Keeping her hooked, as Bobby had said. An enabler. Not just an enabler, it seemed, but a creator, of a whole new person, Mattie Woods. How had he replaced her memories as easily as slipping in a new phone card? None of it made any sense.

This man she had trusted, lived with, cared for... Was Jono the man in her nightmares?

She watched Joy's final video again, hoping to awaken some kind of memories, but no, she was still just Mattie watching Joy. She felt no closeness, no intimate bond with the beautiful, laughing woman on the screen. And yet she had *made* this video. She had run into the woods. Then what had happened?

There was no alcohol in the house, and she was too exhausted to contemplate even walking to the corner shop. Frustration and shock ensured she remained slumped, cuddling her cats, watching video after video, until her phone was low on battery. Lucy had texted her, anxious, and she had responded, reassuring her sister she was okay and did not need a visit. *Her sister!* She had a sister. She tried saying it out loud, but once again nothing chimed in her memory. Mattie did not have a sister.

She could see that Lucy struggled to understand why she needed to return to what was essentially a squatter's quarters, but she had nowhere else to go and she realised she was terrified to be anywhere else. Plus, the person she wanted to see more than anyone else was Bobby.

She fed the cats again, as they had finished the food, went back into the kitchen area, filled her mug once more, and drank it slowly as she sat on the mattress, not allowing any thoughts to wander through her mind. Mattie watched the vivid orange sunset glow through the cracks in her boarded-up window. Finally, as darkness crept across the sky, she lay down, telling herself she would just have a nap and wake up when Bobby arrived after his shift. He knew how to let himself in.

The smoke woke her, winding sour tendrils through her nostrils, alerting her primal senses. She moved, blinking in confusion. Fire was crackling through the house. Terror shot through her heart. Not for herself but for Nuala and her babies.

She fumbled her way towards the room where they had made their nest, shoving objects out the way. Why were there boxes and chairs in the hallways? Surely there hadn't been earlier? Dimly, through her terror, she could hear shouts, glass breaking, boarding crashing to the ground. A woosh as the flames leapt towards the stairs made her gasp for air, cough as soot and smoke filled her lungs. Shouts outside, she could hear people shouting.

Suddenly Bobby was there, grabbing her arm, shouting, a barely discernible figure in the depths of the swirling smoke. It took a moment for her to understand what he was yelling. "I've got Nuala and the kits. They're safe! Mattie, come on, we need to get out. *Move!*"

She forced herself out of her frozen terror and they began to fight their way out of the burning building, shoving falling walls and hot metal aside. Her hands hurt as she grasped something and pushed it away and twice Bobby shoved her roughly to one side as a larger piece of the ceiling came down.

"I called 999 as soon as I saw and got the cats out first, but there were police already here!" Bobby yelled in her ear. "Mattie, come on!"

She hesitated again, confused, disorientated, and convinced

he was leading her back into danger, to the heart of the fire. His hand was on her arm yanking her forward. They staggered towards the exit at the back door, but as they did so, a flaming rafter fell from the ceiling, blocking their escape route.

Panic was rising again. She couldn't breathe. The air was dense with soot and smoke, and the heat was so intense she was sure her face was burning up. But she knew where they could get out. The side window with the broken board. Now it was her turn to pull Bobby along with her, leading him, hand clasped in his, even as there was another crash, and he faltered, swore, clutching his leg.

"Come on!" She dragged him into the side room and shoved at the board. It gave after a couple of tries and she pushed her friend out first. She could see flashing blue lights, fire officers in breathing apparatus reaching in to help. Blinded by the lights, her voice just a croak, she fumbled her way out of the window.

Strong arms pulled her away from the flames, as with a crackle and flash the fire reached the room where, moments earlier, they had been standing. She twisted away from the fire-fighter who had taken her to a safe distance and looked for her friend.

"Bobby, are you okay? Where's Nuala?"

He nodded, bent double, panting and supported by a paramedic. "Fine, and she's under the hedge over there."

Mattie shook off the emergency services and headed straight for the hedgerow and scrub, right away from the boat, near the railway line. Bobby had been wise. In these conditions, one spark from the fire would have set the dry scrub alight, but Nuala was safe, crouched over her babies, still in the cat bed Mattie had bought her.

In the darkness interlaced with harsh lights, the deafening shouts and sirens and rush of hoses and water, the cat yowled in terror. Desperate for comfort, seeing Bobby safely sitting in the back of an ambulance on a stretcher, Mattie slipped into the hedge with Nuala, encompassing the little feline family in her arms, holding them tight, feeling their little hearts pattering alongside her own, rubbing her burning cheek against their soft fur.

It wasn't true, the nightmare wasn't real.

And as she watched the place she had called home burn to the ground she knew: there was no going back now.

PART TWO

JOY

THIRTY-FOUR

The events of the last few days have thrown us all into turmoil. Firstly, news leaked out that someone had been arrested for Joy's murder. I was ecstatic. The police would never chase after me if they locked someone else up.

My head spun a little as I processed the news. An odd mixture of relief, indignation and anger, all churned unpleasantly together and pulsing through my body like a virulent poison. The feeling has not abated.

Yesterday the papers, the forums, social media announced that Joy Maddison had been found safe and well after five years. Speculation was rife but most news channels were leading with the story that Joy had been abducted and kept prisoner all this time. She had somehow managed to escape her captor and take herself to the police station.

And this was the kicker: she had been in Brighton all along. Net curtains are fluttering in the suburbs, shutters are banging in Dyke Road, and the criminal underworld is pretty damn impressed. Who knows what goes on behind closed doors? And who would have guessed Darling Joy was being held in a basement near you?

I've joined in the general shock, the emotional outpouring. We are once again divided, with some of us already leaving gifts and welcome home bouquets at Joy's family home. Others are joining in with the conspiracy theory that Joy planned this all along. A bit harsh, I feel, given what she has been through. A few blurred photos have emerged, taken with lenses pushed up against tinted car windows.

A few drone shots showing the top of Joy's head, hidden by a hood. It could have been anyone. They are going to have to try harder than that to catch sight of her. And when they do, what will they say? No longer a beautiful princess, but the ugly sister.

I'm shocked, disappointed she is back, and also interested. How much will she remember? Has she learnt her lesson? Understood at last about the natural order of things? About the role she needs to play in society as a whole?

I do need to keep a watch on her, which will be hard, because she's bound to have a massive security presence, and that will be just to protect her from the press, not her fans.

Does she know what I did? Has she told the police? I'm guessing not, because nothing has happened in terms of announcing suspects. So many unanswered questions as I pace the room, continually scrolling through social media to find the answers. DI Merry is smart, and if anyone can restore Joy's memory she can. She obviously knows nothing of the natural order of men and women, but at least she doesn't flaunt herself to millions.

I pull up an older photo of Joy, posing in a bikini for a style shoot. There are other types of women more suited to this kind of job. But how far has this broken woman come from the old Joy Maddison, and can she ever fit the two halves of her soul back together? I realise I'm going to need to treat this as another experiment. How good a job did I really do? Part of me knows I should get further from the potential firing line, but I can't tear myself away. I want them all to see the new Joy, and I want them all to *have to make the decision whether to still love her, for who she is now.*

But most of all, she's been just mine for five whole years, and now she's moving further away again. But she can never truly escape.

We're all watching you, Darling Joy, we're all watching you.

THIRTY-FIVE

DI Lucy Merry watched her sister, so still and so fragile in the hospital bed. Her chest rose and fell reassuringly, but her eyes were still closed.

"What do you think?" she asked the doctor.

He smiled at her. "She's going to be fine. The burns are superficial, but..."

"Yes?"

"She shows signs of significant previous physical trauma. Did you say she has been sleeping rough for several years?"

"That's what we've been told. She was squatting in a derelict house near the port with her boyfriend."

"I see. She is also severely underweight and shows signs of drug abuse."

Lucy nodded, bit her lip in anxiety and waited to hear the worst.

"Her observations are normal and although we will have to wait for her bloods to come back from the lab, the tests we were able to do immediately show she was not under the influence when the fire started. Do you know how the fire started?" the doctor asked.

"It's too soon for the reports, but the fire crew said it was an accident waiting to happen in this dry weather. The electrics had been switched on, via a generator, but no precautions taken. The early theory is a spark from an overloaded socket caused the blaze," Lucy explained.

She was struggling with exhaustion and guilt. She had found her sister, and also nearly lost her again in the same twenty-four hours. Why hadn't she insisted Joy came home with her – kept her safe?

Because she had wanted to give her space, she told herself, but it was also true that just after Joy had left the police station, heading for Kingston Lane, Lucy's phone had rung.

It was a colleague at The Unit, reporting with an update. The best update. Joy's evidence against Ned had given various teams an excellent excuse to haul him in yesterday, just as he began a six-hour van journey to deliver a large portion of his drugs haul in person. Now he had officially been charged with a list of offences and the evidence against him was such that his solicitor had already been asking for leniency and protection if Ned grassed on various rival gang members.

But such a great result professionally now made her suspicious of the fire at Mattie's house. News travelled as fast in gangland as anywhere else in the city.

The police officer in Lucy couldn't yet discount the fact someone in Ned's close-knit crew had suspected it was Mattie Woods who grassed them up, and set the fire on purpose, but until she had the facts, she would run with the evidence as it was presented. She was also going to talk to Bobby Smith, who had arrived promptly just after the fire started. Very promptly. He had called 999, he said, as he was walking past the super-stores, which were located just after the speed camera. From this point he had a good view of the house where Mattie was sleeping.

Luckily, the two-person surveillance team outside Mattie's house had been able to alert fire services at the first sign of smoke, but with the heatwave leaving the bones of the building so dry, the house had gone up like a bonfire.

Other calls had come in from a variety of worried security guards at the port, motorists driving past, and other residences further up Kingston Lane. But Bobby had been the first to call, and he had known Joy had been home because she had texted him.

Lucy dragged her thoughts away from potential suspects, as the doctor was still talking. "...and as I say, physically she shows signs of abuse. There are numerous breaks consistent with a major trauma, and from the way they have healed it's likely she had no medical treatment for them."

"She mentioned a historic car accident, when she walked out in front of a vehicle. A hit and run. Her boyfriend looked after her when she was rehabilitating, but I initially presumed she meant when she came out of hospital." Lucy kept one eye on the steady rise and fall of Joy's chest, the other on the door. Was she still in danger?

"We checked and there are no records of Mattie Woods ever having been treated in hospital in this area," the doctor said. "The scar on her cheek, possibly a glass cut, or knife wound, may be so raised and unsightly because it wasn't sutured."

"What kind of timescale are we looking at?" Lucy asked, her gaze back on her sister, resting on the large unsightly scar, healed to a raised and rough-looking slash of skin, and running from her left ear lobe across to the bridge of her nose. Glass from a windscreen perhaps?

"Approximately four or five years ago. The X-rays and scans also show us injuries that are healed, and, to a degree, what stage the healing is at. If she didn't have any treatment, it would explain why there are no signs of medical intervention, and the breaks on her left femur and right tibia have healed slightly crookedly." He paused to consult his notes. "Under normal circumstances they would have been pinned. The scar on her cheek is probably from a wound that should have been stitched. The raised skin and uneven tone suggest perhaps it was also infected and reopened several times before the skin closed, and it healed."

Lucy leant back against the desk, arms folded, trying to think what this might mean, what story this might be telling them about Joy and what she had been through.

The doctor was watching her. "You said she's your sister?"

"Yes. She doesn't remember who she is though. I haven't seen her for five years. Is it possible she has had amnesia, maybe from the hit and run? Her solicitor suggested traumatic association amnesia. I mean... It sounds crazy, but is it really possible she could have forgotten who she is to the extent she accepted a new identity, and never questioned it?" Lucy was desperate to find Jono McQueen, who must hold the key to so many puzzles. Not to mention being wanted for the murder of Stephanie Coultas. But the man seemed to have truly vanished. Just like Joy all those years ago.

"Head injuries are complex, and the effects can be catastrophic, so I really can't give an informed opinion, but what I would say is your sister needs to be treated for her historic injuries, and then evaluated by the trauma team. That way she can get the help she needs and a proper diagnosis. If she went through a traumatic event, it's possible for her to be suffering from amnesia without evidence of a physical head injury, indeed, without her even suffering one in the first place..." His bleeper went off and there was a callout across the tannoy, alerting the crash team, calling them to Resuscitation Bay A. "Sorry, got to go. But you can reach out to me if you need to."

He smiled briefly before hurrying away in the direction of the Accident and Emergency department.

Lucy went quietly into her sister's room, and as she sat down in the chair beside her bed, the woman lying so still, her body shrouded like a ghost, opened her eyes.

THIRTY-SIX

Joy tried to focus on the room, but things were still blurred, spinning slightly out of focus, and she blinked hard. It felt like her eyes were still full of soot and smoke, and she had a weird burning sensation on her tongue. She turned her head a little, aware for the first time of the figure in the chair.

"Hello, Joy."

"What are you doing here?" But she knew, of course she knew. She just wanted to hear the woman say it. Her sister. Lucy Merry was her sister. She was Joy Maddison, she really was. Not Mattie who worked at the fish market, but a social media star. She couldn't get her head around it; it made no sense. Panic ballooned in her chest as the events of last night came sharply into focus. "Is Nuala okay? And Bobby?"

She nodded. "Obviously I came to see you as soon as I heard what had happened. I should have made you stay with me or got you a hotel or something. I'm so sorry."

"But I..." Joy pushed herself up on one elbow and winced. It must be one of her crazy dreams, she thought. God she was thirsty, but even as she stretched out a hand Lucy was quick to push a pillow under her back, passing her the cup of water.

"How did you know I wanted a drink?" Joy asked, when she sank back down. Her sister! She found herself staring at her, taking in the detail, desperate for some jolt of empathy, of memory, or something to bond them together. "Were we close? I mean, before I disappeared?"

Lucy's eyes filled with tears, and she brushed them away and apologised. "Sorry. Yes, we were. Mattie... Joy?"

"Yes?"

"What the hell happened to you?"

Joy shook her head with frustration. "I don't know. I can't remember anything except life with Jono. He was good to me, looked out for me, but before that, I don't know."

"Jono led you to believe you had killed yourself," Lucy pointed out. "Which is a total head fuck to begin with."

"He... I don't know why we thought—" she corrected herself "—I thought, that dead woman was Joy."

"Before you vanished, you spoke to me about how the pressure was getting to you, about the trolling, the perfect image you felt you needed to live up to." Lucy's eyes were fixed on hers and she blinked hard. "Joy, did you plan to run away? Maybe you met Jono and he helped you to escape? I'm not mad at you, I'm just too glad to have you back, alive, but I just want to know. Because if you felt so trapped that the only option was to run with this... this bloke, then we all failed you, let you down badly."

"No!" Joy felt the word crack in her throat, emotion pouring out, exhausting her. "No, I honestly can't remember, but if I think about it at all, I'm sure that wouldn't have happened." Lucy was looking sceptical. "But I know everything about Joy Maddison from a different perspective. I see from the outside looking in, and I don't know how I can weave myself back together, to get the memories back so I can be Joy again. Does that make sense?"

"Yes, of course it does. Your whole identity has changed

overnight, and not just to a stranger's, to someone you had up on a pedestal, from what you told us yesterday." Lucy smiled. "But Joy, the real you wasn't some perfect little doll. We still had arguments. Sometimes she liked a sneaky cigarette, or drank too much, or swore because the kids were driving her crazy. She was normal, but people see what they want to see, and for some reason she came across on camera like she was made of milk and honey and Brighton rock sticks!"

Joy laughed, then winced and clutched at her ribs. "Okay, that's good to hear. I guess it's just like you said, a head fuck. Mind-bending. I mean, I have a husband, and kids, and a dad, and you, my sister... and I don't know any of you. I... I'm terrified of seeing Emile, my poor kids, oh God my kids... It hurts so much I can't remember being a mother. How could I not remember something like that?"

"You might remember when you see them," Lucy suggested. "I need to ask something else. Did Jono ever hit you?" she asked, pain and concern showing in equal amounts in her face.

"No, I don't think so..." Her impression of Jono was reforming for her. How much did he know? Had he been involved in her initial disappearance? The obsession with Joy, that he had then projected onto her, suggested he had. It led quite clearly to the assumption he had somehow abducted her, and she had then lived with him quite happily as another woman. How would that have even worked? So many questions and theories buzzing in her exhausted brain. "Why would you think that he did?"

"Because your X-rays showed multiple broken bones from a possible trauma that happened around five years ago. You don't have to be afraid; you can tell me... Because we still have a body, and we need to find out what happened to Stephanie Coultas and where she comes into your story."

"I swear I don't... I mean there was the car accident, that

could be it, couldn't it?" Joy held her breath, seeing the shadows, the man in the mask again. Her drawings would be all gone now. All those months of waiting to see if she could unveil the man from her nightmares, wasted. She inched herself higher on her pillows, wincing at the pain in her lungs as she took a deep breath, the sting in her bandaged arms from the burns.

"What are you thinking?"

"I have these nightmares... Worse since I got sick after Jono left. That was when I started getting off the drugs and booze, just because I was so sick, I couldn't leave the house. Bobby brought me food and water and checked I wasn't dead." She smiled slightly, remembering the heavy sweats, the craving and the shaking so hard her body hurt.

"What kind of nightmares?"

"A man in a surgical mask. He yells at me, hits me, makes me pee on the floor..." Joy shivered, and stuffed her hands under the blanket.

"Is the man Jono?"

"I don't think so... No, I don't think he fits. I did wonder for ages if it was, but the nightmares are stronger now and I'm stuck in a room with the man. He won't let me out and he tells me how bad I am, how stupid and sick..." Joy whispered. "Every time he tells me I'm a murderer. And I need to be punished for what I did. I always thought he was referring to Joy, but maybe it was Stephanie."

"What is his voice like? Does he have an accent?" Lucy was leaning forward, her hand resting gently on her sister's, her eyes bright with interest.

"I don't know because I only hear it in kind of echoes, but I don't think it was Jono." She sighed. "Or maybe I just don't want it to be."

"I suppose the first thing to do when you are physically fit is to get you home. Emile, the kids and Dad are all desperate to see you, but the medical staff told them to wait until you got out of hospital."

"Why?"

"You know, the press are desperately trying to find out what's going on with Stephanie's murderer, that would be you at the moment, and the story already broke that you were abducted and have been kept a prisoner for five years. If our family come here, the whole hospital will be under siege."

Her family. "But I wasn't..." Joy started to say, before Lucy cut her off, speaking urgently.

"Joy, we need to protect everyone, and we need to protect your CHIS identity too. Don't you see this makes everything harder? We can't have it getting out you were working as a police informant. The story has been vetted by our media department and people will believe it. You were abducted and imprisoned. It works. It's plausible and it's easier for people to swallow than the fact you've been walking around Brighton all this time with memory loss."

Joy flashed her a look, slightly afraid of the intensity in her sister's voice, but she only said, "Did Bobby call?"

"He came in while you were sleeping. He's fine now and was about to be discharged. He's got the cats still and I told him you'd call him when you were ready to come home. He's a sweetheart, isn't he?" There was an edge to her voice though, Joy thought. "Bobby said you asked him to come by after his shift last night, and he could see the smoke as soon as he walked past Lidl. Do you remember that?"

"He called 999, and he rescued me." Joy clenched her fingers on the sheet. She could tell Lucy wanted to ask more about her relationship with Bobby. But the jump from murderer to victim was not complete. Even as Joy, she must have been involved in Stephanie's death, so the nightmares were not over. The fire was the least of her worries. An old house, a heatwave, it had gone up like a box of matches in a bonfire.

"What's the furthest back you can remember? Properly remember?"

Joy considered, delving inside her brain, pushing back against the mass of darkness. "Pain. I remember being hurt from the car accident; I think Jono was looking after me soon afterwards, and putting a dressing on my cheek." She touched her scar. "Before, I remember walking or running out in front of a car, the hot metal as it touched my thigh. It gave me a limp, and ever since I've had trouble with that knee."

"Maybe that's how it started. A car accident. Perhaps that's how your run ended the night you went missing, whether by accident or design," Lucy said thoughtfully.

"You mean it might not have been an accident? Jono might have hit me with a car on purpose... How could that be true!" Even as the words left her mouth, she found herself thinking what a stupid thing that was to say. If Jono had kept her almost as a prisoner for five years, albeit a willing one, anything was possible. Joy put a hand to her mouth, pressing warm flesh against her lips. She had a family she didn't know, children she didn't love and a sister she felt a tiny connection with. Was any of it enough for Mattie to find her way back to being Joy?

THIRTY-SEVEN

Joy stared at the gates. Huge, wrought iron gates set in front of wooden ones. Double protection from prying eyes. Her home. Her mansion on Dyke Road, flanked by other millionaires, and by dense woodland on the right-hand side. The woods she had run through that fateful day when life changed forever.

"Do you recognise anything?" Lucy asked.

Joy shook her head. "I know what it looks like because Jono and I watched all the videos a hundred times, and looked at so many pictures, but I don't feel anything inside... Does that make sense?"

"I guess."

Joy could tell her sister was desperate for her memory to return, but she felt she was floating along, observing. It was the only way she could cope with coming face to face with the family she had left behind.

"Look, I know we talked about this before, and I can't imagine how hard it's going to be, but you can't use the name Mattie, or Martha, ever again. If anyone from your past life connects you with Joy Maddison, other than the people like Jono, who we assume have known all along, it would be a disaster. Bobby knows, and of course me and the police officers on your case, but nobody else," Lucy reiterated. "Even Emile and Dad only know an abbreviated version."

She nodded slowly. This was getting harder by the second. But the thought of Ned finding her, Harley appearing at the gates of Joy's/her home, her CHIS identity being leaked, was impossible to comprehend. "But Ned is going to prison after what I told you, isn't he?"

"I can't say for definite, but the CPS are letting the case go forward and I can't see any loopholes from our end."

"Ned wouldn't believe I was Joy anyway," Joy said.

"Unless he knew already," Lucy cautioned. "But we certainly don't want the press to know."

"I get it." Joy was still thinking about Ned. Could he have known? Even as she considered the possibility, she discarded it. If Ned had known he would have found a way to use the information, to make money, cause a scandal – anything. He had never treated her with anything but contempt.

"They want to see if I'll do something crazy," Joy said thoughtfully.

"You don't seem bothered by them."

"Did I used to be?" It was weird, but after the initial shock of seeing the group with cameras and microphones at the ready, she felt numb, insulated in her powerful car with the blacked-out windows, with her police officer sister beside her. *Her sister.*

"Yes. I would say you felt hunted, and you were terrified of what they said and did."

"It feels like they want to see another person. But I can hide inside Mattie, and the person I am now, and she shields me," Joy explained. "I'm not saying it doesn't freak me out a little, all this interest, and I worry someone from my life as Mattie will recognise me in the press. I heard what you said about Ned but he's got loads of followers who might have noticed me, or would notice me now."

"I told you, it's almost definite Ned's going to get sent away for a long time," Lucy said. "With that evidence it's an open and shut case."

"Funny how it's Ned's fault you knew I was still alive," Joy told her, squinting against the sunlight, still watching the journalists, the photographers camped out at her gates. "He did me a favour really. If I hadn't got involved with him, I would never be sitting with you now. You might never have found me. What? Why are you looking at me like that?"

"Because you're so strong, now. You were never weak, but you were insecure, worrying about little things you couldn't control, getting upset over trolls. Now you're like, fuck it and make way for Mattie."

She laughed bitterly. "Not really so strong. I've still lost five years of my life and somehow acquired an addiction problem. I keep trying and trying to remember the car accident, anything else about Jono, but I can't."

"You gained six cats too," Lucy pointed out. "It will come back, your memory, I'm sure of it. Perhaps it will come back as you become strong enough to face up to what happened to you."

"Maybe." The dream-like numbness was persisting.

"I like Bobby."

"He's an angel. When I was sick, if he hadn't looked after me, I would probably have died."

Lucy spoke urgently to their driver and then shut the privacy window again. The woman drove carefully past the press, indicating right, using the electric gates, which led them straight to the garages.

A short, well-muscled man, sweating in a black shirt and trousers, with an earpiece and a grim expression, was waiting, and he looked up and waved.

"That's Tony, head of your security," Lucy explained. She opened the car door and stepped out. "Tony, is everything alright?"

The man's eyes darted from her face to Joy's and back again. "Yes and no. Louise Major has done a tell-all about Emile's supposed affair and how it triggered Joy's disappearance. The amount of press at the gates is now doubling by the second. Are you okay if I call in an extra team and station them outside the main and side gates?"

"Of course." Lucy nodded. "Joy, it's fine. Do you remember Tony at all?"

Joy slid across her seat and stood awkwardly, avoiding the question. Because the answer was no. "Hi, Tony."

Tony nodded at her, professional as ever, but his smile was wide and genuine. "Great to see you back. Your family have been through hell and now here you are, alive and well."

"Did I hear that there is a problem?" Joy asked quietly, and she could feel eyes on her, but could also see, unexpectedly, Lucy's expression, and with it came the realisation. *She's like me; she doesn't trust anyone.*

"Nothing that can't be solved, but you have generated some headlines and this Louise Major wants to leech some publicity for herself," Tony explained, as he rubbed sweat from his forehead. "I think there's a storm coming."

Joy said nothing, not asking who Louise was. She licked her dry lips, her gaze was now fixed on her house, her front door.

"Thanks, Tony. Joy, shall we get inside before the drones start taking pot shots."

As Joy walked slowly towards the front porch, she could feel Lucy's concern. She still couldn't believe it was real. She just hoped the rest of the family could be patient, could understand a little even if she couldn't fully comprehend the past five years herself. It also occurred to her that memories might well come back now she was home and safe.

Lucy took Joy's arm, her hand warm, comforting, on her skin, and lowered her voice as they walked along a gravel path lined with late-blooming purple lavender. "Just before we get to the house, in case anyone mentions it, you should know the fire at the house in Kingston Lane wasn't an accident. It was arson. The chief fire officer found traces of accelerant."

"I thought it was just the old generator, or the dry summer sparking old electrics or something. Who would burn the house down?" Joy frowned in confusion, stopping dead to stare at her sister.

"It's unlikely it was connected to you personally, since you were there illegally. Could even be the owner finding out squatters were in his property, burning it down to get insurance," Lucy said reassuringly.

"You don't believe that."

"At the moment the evidence only tells us it was started deliberately, so I'm keeping an open mind on the who and why. Come on, it will be okay."

Joy pushed her hair back, self-consciously dragging the straggly ends into an elastic band. "It won't, Lucy, and you know it. I don't remember my own children, and I'm about to be reunited with them. What sort of terrible mother doesn't remember her own babies? I hate myself for the fact they have been without a mother all this time."

"You can't force it. Think, this is a medical condition, and it isn't as though you asked for it to happen. You are the victim in all of this, Joy."

Lucy thought she understood, but she didn't. How could she possibly understand? Apart from Nuala and her kittens, Joy had nothing left. All the scrapbooks, the mementoes, the few bits Jono had left behind, were gone. All her drawings, her nightmares and her life would have melted in the heat.

Lucy had been very interested in the drawings and keen to see them. Perhaps, Joy thought, as she continued walking towards her front door, perhaps someone was disappointed Joy Maddison hadn't vanished in the flames and the ashes, just as she had vanished five years ago. Either that or Ned's influence was extending way beyond the cell he was currently sitting in, awaiting trial.

Joy shivered. She thought she had been so careful, but now she had been forced to trust the police, to trust that anyone who knew about her would keep their mouth shut. It wasn't enough; snitches often ended up dead.

THIRTY-EIGHT

Glancing at her sister, Joy felt a wave of reassurance, warm and comforting like a soft blanket in a storm. It wasn't recognition she felt with Lucy, but it was a spark of a connection, something her subconscious recognised as familiar, and it made her feel safe.

Even so, when the reporters had been banging on the windows, running alongside the car, Joy had felt herself shrinking down into her seat. The windows were tinted so nobody could see her, but she felt naked.

Not just naked, but terribly afraid of slipping up with the numerous identities in her head. She was two different people and now she was being asked to kill one of those people. All the time she had thought her idol lived like this, with the photographers banging on her car windows, the interest and the noise, and now she had stepped into Joy's life.

She was Joy Maddison, back from the grave, returning home to her family. She said now, as they walked up the lavender-lined path, "I keep wondering if Jono *is* still alive, and if he'll see all the press coverage."

"If it was him who took you five years ago, he'll be keeping a very low profile," Lucy said fiercely. "The bastard." She reached down and snapped a lavender stalk between her fingers, rolling it on her palm, releasing the heady summer scent. "Here, sniff this. You always used to say it was calming. This whole garden was your idea, and you worked for months with the designers. It was your project after you were made redundant from the radio show."

Joy leant down and inhaled the soporific, slightly soapy, sweetness. For what felt like the millionth time, she searched her memory, willing the fog to part, willing herself to remember what had happened. But there was nothing but the familiar gaping black holes and numbness.

The noise of a helicopter and drones flying overhead made them both wince. Once more shielded by the security team, they were hustled through the front door, into the house.

Joy almost turned and ran. The terror she felt at meeting her family, her children, was beyond everything. The numbness, the unreality had vanished, and she was struggling to come to terms with the family she was about to invade. Her daughters and son, their expectation that their mummy was home turning to ashes as they saw this ragged stranger who didn't even remember giving birth. More than anything, she didn't want to hurt them any further. She would lie if she had to.

She wished she had Nuala with her right now, but Lucy had persuaded her to leave her pets with Bobby, promising to pop down and collect all six cats once Joy was in the house. She had a vague sense of being bribed, like a child, in the nicest possible way. Did her sister think she might run away?

To distract from the meeting, Joy found herself noticing every detail of the beautiful stone floor, the oak doors and beams. She stared at her reflection in the huge gilt-edged mirror at the end of the hallway. Mattie looked back, not Joy. Not even Joy's ghost peeking over her shoulder to help guide her through this.

Emile – who she'd seen so many times onscreen and in photos, and still couldn't believe was her husband in real life – was waiting in the hallway with the kids, and she held her breath as she walked towards them, shyly, uncertainly. She saw that his eyes were full of tears, and the kids were pressed against him for comfort. He was taller than she had ever thought, but just as good-looking, and then she looked at her children...

"Hello, Emile, hi, kids." Her voice sounded rough, but the emotion was only from the situation, not from genuine feeling. She felt she was watching the action in the room from a long way in the distance, or maybe as the audience at a play, waiting for the actors to be more convincing in their roles. *Come on, Mattie, what would Joy say?* She must know. It must be buried deep inside somewhere, this other half of herself?

"I can't tell you how amazing it is to have you home. When I came to the hospital while you were sleeping... I didn't think you were real. It was a miracle."

She smiled awkwardly, embarrassed, unable to speak to him.

"What? I told you not to come to the hospital because the press would see you. When did you sneak in?" Lucy said, exasperation and affection for her brother-in-law clear in her voice.

Emile shrugged and smiled.

The children stood, staring, eyes wide, but made no move towards her, and said nothing at all.

"Go and say hello to Mummy," Emile said, pushing them gently forward. He added, "Frank got held up in traffic but he's on his way." He came closer, with the kids, and she sank down to their level, crouched on her haunches smiling.

She knew Poppy and Daisy were twins, and they were ten. Bertie, the youngest, was just eight. He had only been three years old when she vanished, and her heart hurt at the thought of the pain they must have experienced when they lost their mother. At her pain at being separated from her children. Whatever had happened to her after her abduction, she must have fought hard to get back to her family. Mustn't she?

"I expect Dad wanted you to have some time together first," Lucy suggested. "Shall I go and make coffee or something?"

"No." Joy surprised herself by the sharpness of her tone, and she saw the kids had instantly registered she was scared. Their little faces changed slightly. The girls standing protectively, one either side of their brother. After the silence, they all started to ask questions at once, so quickly, and so garbled, so emotionally fraught that she wasn't quite sure who was asking which question. The worst thing was, these were mostly questions she couldn't answer.

"Are you really Mummy? You don't look the same."

"What happened to you, and why have you got a scar on your face?"

"We wanted to come and see you, but Daddy said when he went to the hospital you were sleeping. Why did you go?"

"Where have you been?"

"Where did you go?"

Lucy, liaising with the family and Joy while she was in hospital, had already agreed a basic story for general release, as far as they all knew it. They had gone over it several times, checking for anything that might lead a listener back to Mattie, but at last the family and the police had been satisfied.

So now Joy knew exactly what she had to do, and the kids were a trial run. Emile, who had sat down on the stairs, gently taken her hand, put his hand to her cheek briefly, knew something more of the truth as they suspected it, but not much. He watched her now, dark eyes soft with emotion.

"When I went out running, five years ago, we think I was hit by a car." She paused to gather strength. Still crouched, she was getting cramp in her calf muscles, and feeling seriously unnerved by those frank, direct gazes. These were her own children! They clustered either side of Emile, filling the stair, and here she was practically sitting on the floor in front of them.

All three kids were staring at her, drinking her in. Only one child, Poppy, had dared to touch her so far. "The driver of the car took me away, and I had a head injury that made me lose my memory. I've been with him ever since, kept away from you." She touched the scar on her face.

"But Lucy found you again," Poppy said flatly, her little face screwed up, one finger to her lips as though she was trying to work it out.

"Yes, she did." Joy glanced up at her sister, who smiled encouragingly. "I didn't know who I was." Joy sighed sadly, heavily and inched closer. They didn't move back. "If I hadn't lost my memory I would have been home much sooner."

"Do you know who we are now?" Daisy asked.

"Will your brain get better?" Bertie added.

"The doctors think it might do, but it will take time. Perhaps you can help me?" If she stayed talking to the kids, *her* kids, she didn't have to start talking to her husband, Joy thought.

To her surprise, Daisy bravely stepped up and gave her a tentative hug. The feel of small arms around her, the soft cheek and smell of clean hair. Something hit her deep inside and she almost cried out. It was a real, deep connection. Not a memory exactly, but something primitive and strong. A little like the feelings she had for Lucy, but stronger and differently formed.

She looked up, tears streaming down her cheeks, both at the situation and her own genuine feeling. Relief, so much relief she had a bond with her babies. Only a tiny thread of something, but it was enough to build on. Perhaps the doctor was right, now she was home, she might remember more and more of the past, and her mind might finally be able to reveal what had really happened that night.

Bertie came forward and hugged her too, though he kept his eyes downcast and gave her just the briefest of squeezes. Her heart ached for them all, especially her youngest. He had been just a baby, and Jono had deprived these children of their mother for five years.

After a while, as speech became easier, more natural, Emile stood up and suggested they play with Ella in the family room, while he talked to Joy. She smiled awkwardly at him. He was so tall and so good-looking, and she was... well, she must look like a ghost of the woman he had known.

"We can keep the door open," Joy said to them, as they clearly all thought she was going to vanish again. The connection might be there, but she didn't feel like a mum at all. Her heart knew she was, and her body probably did too, after the primal, instinctive recognition of her babies, but taking on the everyday duties of a mum, that was going to be terrifying.

Lucy softly excused herself, muttered about collecting the cats from Bobby and headed out of the front door.

Obediently, with lots of sidelong glances and some whispering, the children agreed to play in the room next door. As Joy stood up, stretching gratefully, Emile surprised her by pulling her into his arms, very gently as though she was made of glass, and he was afraid she was going to shatter. Or run away. She froze at his touch, tense and uncomfortable.

"Joy. I can't believe you're back." His dark eyes searched hers, and she didn't need to ask what he was thinking. There was a lot of love in his expression, and so many questions. And something else, something edgy. Was he just horrified by her appearance or was there more behind his genuine pleasure at seeing her back? His hands on her bare skin made her feel like shrinking away, not hugging him back.

Of course, she told herself, he *must* be shocked that he had lost his beautiful wife, and she had returned as this battered wreck of a woman, scarred and lost, she thought, suddenly remembering she wasn't Joy, not really. She was still thinking like Mattie, still looked like Mattie. This man was so far out of her league it was ridiculous.

They talked for a little, him asking careful questions, her gradually gaining confidence and asking questions of her own.

"Why did I do this?"

"Did I like this?"

"What did I think of this?"

When Emile went to make coffee and began to put cake on plates, she realised one of the reasons she felt edgy. Jono had created Mattie. He had answered all her questions, filled in her history, and she had just been inviting Emile to do the same. It was dangerous, she realised, to let someone else fill in the blanks. She needed to rebuild herself. She needed to remember the truth.

Saving her from saying another word to her husband, the doorbell rang, and the security team answered. Lucy, balancing two bags on one arm, brought the box of cats into the hallway, and Nuala yowled in fear at the change in scenery.

Of course, the children came streaming out into the hallway, and in introducing them to her pets, in soothing Nuala until she purred happily in her arms, Joy found she was talking, doing things, naturally, without questioning, without her words coming out stilted and unsure.

The cats were soon settled in the utility room, Nuala cautiously exploring, sharp protective eyes on her babies, Daisy filling a water bowl and Poppy and Bertie each cuddling a kitten.

Lucy was smiling. "I can see why you ended up rescuing her. You always did love cats."

"I know. I hope she gets on with the resident feline though," Joy said, nodding towards the garden, where a magnificent Siamese queen lay stretched out in the shade of a magnolia tree.

There was another commotion and before Joy had time to brace herself another man appeared. She felt a flash of anxiety at yet another face, another person she was supposed to know. She looked at the man as he walked towards her. Did she feel a shiver of recognition? Not the spark of connection she had with her sister, but... something.

Frank, her dad, was also tall, but broad, silver-haired, and beaming. He folded first Joy, then Lucy into his arms. "My girls. I never thought I'd see you both together again. How are you feeling, Joy?"

Oh God, this was her dad. And she felt... nothing. An elderly stranger coming through the door, his delight tangible, and she felt not even a twinge of recognition. "I... I'm okay. It's all a bit weird." She caught Emile's look and tried to smile at her dad. "In a good way. It's just, re-adjusting to who I am, I suppose."

As they talked a little, she thought he seemed nice enough, but there was no connection. At the back of her mind, she couldn't help feeling still that it was all a mistake, and the police would arrive and tell her she was plain old Mattie Woods who had murdered Joy Maddison. Maybe this was a dream, and she would wake, still hunched on the floor in her prison cell.

Her dad patted her shoulder, bringing her back to reality. This was her *dad... Come on, Mattie!* Lucy had told her that their mum was dead, and all the grandparents were gone. This man needed her.

"Lucy and I will go and get ourselves some of that wonderful-looking cake while you talk to Emile," he said gently, smiling at the purring cats and the children playing with them.

This time she had a hold of herself, making sure she arranged her face and didn't look totally panicked at the idea of spending time alone with her own husband. What had he been doing for five long years? And once again, as she caught a glimpse of herself in yet another gilt-framed mirror, she wondered, what *must* he think of her? A poor, scarred copy of his radiant wife. She felt crippled by shyness, by the shame of what she had become.

They walked into the living room, "Come and sit down, Joy." He smiled at her, transforming his rather solemn dark looks into a more boyish, cheeky grin. He gave a short laugh, breaking some of the tension. "Well, this is weird. Like you said. Very weird."

They were less than a foot apart on the grey and white striped sofa, stacked high with grey and white velvet cushions. The wallpaper behind the sofa was charcoal grey with large white roses. A feature. Joy had done a whole video on decorating her living room when they moved to the new house. Her house. It was her who had chosen this. She had chosen the furniture, the wall colours, the fancy white shutters at the tall, elegant windows. Her house.

Sitting, staring tenderly at her was her handsome husband. She knew he was fluent in three languages, that his heritage was French, Spanish and Moroccan. He was a celebrity chef, with a huge following, and several restaurants. But she knew all of this as Mattie had known it, as a fan, not as his wife.

Yet they had met at a party, flirted, fallen in love, had sex, cooked together, worked out together, become parents, for God's sake. And she remembered none of it.

Tears started to fall, and he leant over and wiped them away. She jumped back, still thinking how disgusting he must find her, but also with the instinctive reaction of being touched by a stranger.

THIRTY-NINE

"What's the last thing you remember, Joy?" her husband asked gently, and she was instantly reminded of Lucy asking the same question as she sat at her hospital bedside, the morning after the fire.

Frustration ripped through her body. "Nothing! I don't remember being Joy at all. I don't remember my childhood, my sister, my parents..."

"Me?"

"You. I don't even know how we met properly. Or at least..." She was trying to explain. "I know all these things from looking at my life as someone else. I don't know how I felt, or what I was thinking on our wedding day, but I know what you said when you proposed, because Joy, I, had it documented on the vlog, and it was in lots of magazines." She clasped a hand to her heart. "But I don't have any memories. It's like a massive black blur of images I want so desperately to see, but I can't. Like..." She struggled for comparisons. "It's like an old-fashioned print photograph being developed in a dark room, but it never quite comes into focus."

"I get it." His expression changed, determination showing

through the sadness. "Well, I want to help you to remember. This man, this Jono, who took you, do you remember him?"

"Yes. But the more I think about it, everything I think I know, came from him, right down to the car accident, and details from my childhood. He fabricated everything. He used my amnesia to rewrite my life. I suppose by convincing me we had committed murder it was an effective way of scaring me to keep under the radar." She shivered at the thought of Jono killing Stephanie Coultas. He could so easily have killed her too. And she had thought it was sweet that Jono had gone everywhere with her, had kept her so close.

It was such a leap to think of him as her possible abductor, rather than her boyfriend, that she found herself scrabbling to push the possibility to the back of her mind, trying to make excuses for him. How could she have willingly lived with a man who abducted her? He had told her he loved her on numerous occasions, had laughed and cried with her, had looked after her, for God's sake. Yet he had taken her from her family, from her babies.

Her husband took her hand. "The police told us you could still be in danger from this man. He sounds like a crazy fan who just tipped over the edge. I saw how much people loved you, thought they knew you, and I was always worried it might happen. Not an abduction, but just somebody getting too close, perhaps... We had some intruders trying to get into the house several times, which was when we hired a security team."

"Lucy showed me the NatterJack forum," Joy told him, adding quickly as his face changed, "It's okay, she just wanted me to be prepared. The police said the same thing to me about Jono probably being like a stalker. He must have known exactly where I would be that night." She tried hard to make her voice sound firm, confident, but the idea that Jono might still be circling around somewhere, hiding in the shadows, was terrifying given the enormity of his crimes against her.

Emile nodded. "We will help you to take your life back again, Joy. I can't tell you how much it means to us all that you're home again. I know this is so bizarre, but you're alive. *Alors*, I was convinced, we all were except Frank, that you were dead. It is like a second chance."

"For me too... The second chance, I mean," Joy said quickly, picking up on his words, sensing the awkwardness that perhaps wasn't just alluding to the current situation.

The security team had whispered when she had emerged from the car, and Tony had mentioned Louise Majors. There had been gossip Emile had been having an affair before Joy vanished. Jono had talked about it constantly, saying it was good because it had thrown the police off, making them think Joy had run away to be with another man, because she found out about Emile's affair. This way, he had lectured her, there was less chance of anyone finding out they had committed murder.

Now she was in the same room as Joy's husband, her husband, how could she even begin to ask him such a thing? Especially as she had been sleeping with Jono for the last five years.

Okay, she had mostly been high on drugs or falling down drunk when they did have sex, and it had been... okay, from what she did remember. Possibly far better for him than it had been for her. Not memorable for any other reason than she needed the reassurance Jono had wanted her. Well, now she knew the real reason for that. Bastard. There were so many emotions buzzing around her head she felt like she was going to explode.

But what of her husband since she had been gone? Emile was bound to have had relationships. He should have done. Why not, when they all thought she was gone forever. Her world had moved on without her, while a few miles away, she had been living in an alternate reality with her captor.

Struggling with the silence, needing to say something,

anything, she was struck by another wave of shyness, feeling her cheeks reddening, her words coming out in a croak. "Lucy said the cats would be a good icebreaker with the kids."

Emile seized on the subject change, his words also coming out in a rush. He must be finding this as awkward as she was? "Yes, she thought it might give the kids something else to think about, and she knew you'd want Nuala with you." Emile grinned suddenly, all at once making him more approachable, less remote. "You always loved cats. Nuala number two?"

Joy felt a genuine smile stretching across her lips for the first time since she had walked back through the door. "Yes, and hopefully it works a bit like Mummy coming home with gifts?"

He was looking right into her eyes, and she felt a flash of attraction, and something approaching awe. She had slept with this man, had *married* him. But attraction wasn't love, and as with Frank there was no tiny spark of connection like she had felt with her children, no deep well of emotion she had accessed with the cats and the ease she felt with her sister.

"Shall we go and find them all again? I can tell Frank and Lucy are hiding in the kitchen to give us time to talk, but I'm sure Frank is desperate to talk to you as well. I... I don't know if Lucy mentioned it, but your dad has had a few health problems since you were... abducted. That's why he walks with a stick now. We offer to help, but he keeps everything very close to his chest." Emile laughed. "He's just like you, very stubborn."

She stood up, slightly easier, and he took her arms, very gently as though she was made of glass. It was non-threatening, but he was too close, and she instantly wanted to wrench her arm away.

He smiled down at her, understanding instantly. "Too much too soon?"

"No." She slipped her arm through his, ignoring the cringing she felt inside, and was rewarded by his pleasure lighting up his face. If she could hide how she was really feeling, just say what everyone wanted to hear, keep them all happy, surely in time the real feelings would come back?

It couldn't be hard. She was *happy*, and lucky. She had gone from living in a derelict house, struggling with addiction (okay, that was going to be something she had to face for the rest of her life, but at least she was getting help), riddled with guilt at a crime she had never committed, to living the dream. All she had to do was be grateful for her own second chance, be grateful to be given her Cinderella moment. *Mattie Woods, you are now Joy Maddison.* Magic.

But the dark and terrifying voice inside her head laughed now, and although the instructions were faint, she could still hear them, still feel echoes of terror. She needed beyond everything to know the truth.

'You are Mattie Woods, and you are a murderer. Say it!'

'You don't deserve to be happy. You don't deserve to be alive. You are evil.'

Alone in the hall with her, Emile paused, squeezed her hand gently, where it rested on his bare arm, making her shiver. He looked down at her, his dark brown eyes strangely remote, but still compassionate. "Don't you think you deserve to be happy, Joy?"

FORTY

She spent some time exploring the large, timber-frame house, moving slowly from room to room. Emile told her it was only twenty-five years old, but the structure, all English oak and glass, blended beautifully with the views of the city on one side, and the South Downs on the other.

At the very top, on the third floor, was a stunning triangular room, with a skylight and floor to ceiling glass windows on two sides. One of these opened out onto a balcony area with potted miniature orange and lemon trees. She wandered outside, taking it all in. But with every room, she found herself checking the security, admiring the views but also wondering if Jono was still watching her. Why had he left her so suddenly? Had he found another Joy look-a-like, or had he been spooked by the DNA findings and realised it was time to bail out? Or maybe her initial reaction, to assume he had got in trouble with Ned, had been recognised as a grass and disposed of, still rang true.

As Mattie she had been more and more convinced he was dead, but now she was back as Joy, with the knowledge she had acquired in the past forty-eight hours, she thought he was far cleverer than she had given him credit for. A super fan. A man so obsessed with her he had stolen her life away. She shivered, glancing out into the garden, looking west towards the woods. They were thick oak woods, with huge tree canopies despite the drought and the heat.

Now Jono's crimes had been revealed, she couldn't help thinking if he had been smart enough to abduct her and keep her hidden under the noses of the police and her family for five years, he could have been smart enough to get out when the DNA was found on Elena's body in Hove. And smart enough that if he wanted to carry on watching her now, he could. Again the tremor of fear writhing in her gut. Jono had reformed in her mind since she discovered what he had really been capable of.

The timing worked. He had missed the anniversary. Mattie's Jono would never have done that unless he was dead. Or something or someone had told him he was about to get busted. If it was the latter, it meant he was still out there, maybe watching her, just as he used to do. Except now it was different. For five years she had been his plaything. Sickening. Joy put a steadying hand to the balcony rail in front of her. The wood was warm from the evening sun, and rough to her touch. Now she was her own person again. Not Joy Maddison but not Mattie Woods either.

"This was your yoga room, and sometimes you liked to work up here too," Emile said as she went back inside. He pointed at the desk in the corner, a mood board still pinned up and a box of magazines. "It was hard, you know. Sometimes I would convince myself we needed to hang on, that you would come home, and other times I saw we needed to move on, for the kids' sake. I couldn't have them hanging on for every doorbell, every phone call. Bertie was too small to understand, but Poppy and Daisy have been having therapy every week."

She was only half listening to what he was saying,

entranced by the room, distracted by danger. It was similar, although upgraded times one million, to the upstairs room she had used in Kingston Lane. "Did I used to draw?" she interrupted her husband. "Did I like art?"

"I... I don't think so. You were good at making graphics on Canva, you know for social media. Why?"

"It's something I've been doing while I've been away," she told him. "Maybe I could bring some pencils and paper up here?"

"Yes," he said eagerly, "I've heard art therapy can help in cases of amnesia." Emile looked slightly sheepish. "Ever since it was first mentioned I've googled the hell out of it, trying to understand what might have happened to you, trying to see how I might help you find your way back to us. Your mum was an art teacher," he added.

She smiled at him, feeling his concern, feeling for the first time no barrier, no ulterior motive lurking behind his words. Trust. But she had trusted Jono, had leant on him, depended on him, and now it seemed like the whole structure of Mattie's life had been based on a lie, a deception so horrific she couldn't even begin to get her head around it.

"I'm sure the kids won't mind if I borrow a few bits until I can get my own," Joy said now, walking over to the windows again. The view was so peaceful, and it was so quiet. But there was a uniformed security guard at the gate and another in a car at the rear entrance near the garden cottage.

When she turned back into the room, Emile was leafing through the magazines.

He might be keen to help, but for some reason she didn't tell him about the nightmare drawings. Only Lucy and Bobby knew. Would they still fill her troubled mind now she was sleeping back in her own house or had the demons been laid to rest by the discovery of Stephanie's body, and her own true identity?

. . .

The sound of footsteps woke her from a half sleep. The room was dark, but the blinds allowed a few shadows from the moon to illuminate the path to the door.

She sat up, tense, blinking hard. Her door opened and without realising it, she was already halfway out of bed. Mattie's instincts were ingrained so strongly. If there had been an intruder in her house she would have needed to fight or run, because nobody entering her house at night would have meant her well. Street law.

Two small figures in pink pyjamas, with long dark hair in plaits, padded hesitantly towards her bed.

"Girls? Are you okay? Do you feel sick or have a nightmare?" Relief at the sight of the children. But there was also relief when unexpectedly, totally without thinking, the words came naturally. Words that she supposed any mum would ask if their kids made an unscheduled 1:00am visit.

"Mummy?" She thought it was Poppy who had spoken, but the kids were standing so close together it was hard to tell.

"What's wrong?"

"You're still here."

"Of course I am. Is that what you were worried about?" Again, she could feel their confusion, their sadness.

"I woke up and heard a car in the driveway and thought you had left again."

"You heard a car?" She felt her heart rate ramp up again. A changeover for their security team, maybe.

Both girls came forward and perched on the end of her bed. This time it was Daisy who spoke. "I told her it was just Daddy, but she wanted to come and check."

Joy sat next to them, tucking her feet underneath her body. "Where was Daddy going?"

"Oh, he goes out quite a lot at night. He always gets back

before we wake up. When we asked, he said he has something to do that he couldn't do in the daytime. We saw him going out after you went away last time. It was the same week you disappeared, and we thought he must be going to look for you, but he said we should leave it to the police."

Poppy flashed a sidelong glance at her sister. "He said it was a secret and we shouldn't tell anyone."

"He leaves you alone in the house?" Joy couldn't believe it. Emile had come across as so caring, the perfect dad... What the hell was he doing leaving his kids while he drove off in the middle of the night?

Poppy fiddled with the ribbon on her long dark plait. "No, Ella sleeps in the room between us and Bertie, and Rachel, who looks after the house, sleeps in the garden cottage."

Right. She had forgotten about the nanny. And the housekeeper. Even so, where was Emile going on his night wanderings?

"Do you want me to come and tuck you back into bed? If this is part of Daddy's routine, I'm sure he'll be back when he normally is, and you have school tomorrow, don't you?"

They consented to let her lead them back to their pink and white room, with unicorn wallpaper and big gilt mirrors. Clearly Joy had had a thing for gilt mirrors, she thought with a wry smile, remembering the decor downstairs.

"Does Ella come and check on you at night?"

Poppy paused before she answered. "Sometimes. But mostly she talks to her boyfriend on her phone. She does video calls, so she gets cross if we interrupt her and make noise."

Joy looked out of the bedroom, and saw the nanny's door was firmly closed. She padded back across the floorboards, feet sinking into the deep pile white rugs, as her daughters slid underneath the covers.

"Now go to sleep, and if you need me, just come down to find me, okay?"

"Night, Mummy... Mummy?"

"Yes?"

"We're happy you're home."

"Me too, baby girls, me too."

There was a muffled giggle, and she paused at the doorway. "What?"

"Nothing. Only you always used to call us that before."

She smiled into the shadows and made her way back to bed. But as soon as she lay down, all trace of amusement gone, her mind was working on her husband's night activities. That would be an interesting conversation. A thought occurred to her, and she picked up her phone. The family had insisted she have a new phone with a tracker app. Every family member except Frank, who was sticking rigidly to his ancient Nokia, had a tracker.

Joy opened the app and located the green dot that was her husband. Devonshire Gardens. What the hell was he doing over there? More to the point, who lived in Devonshire Gardens that he could possibly be seeing at this time of the morning...?

Surprising herself, Joy passed the rest of the night peacefully, in the cool, pristine grey and white room, waking in clean white pyjamas and immediately opening the slatted blinds to a glorious view of the main gardens. A gardener was already working on a flower border, another was netting leaves from the swimming pool and the hiss of sprinklers keeping the sweeping lawns a plush emerald green was both soothing and alien to her.

The sky was washed a clear blue, and the view from this side of the house was across the Downs. There was no reason she should feel agitated and for her heart to be beating so fast.

Downstairs, the children were ushered out by Ella after a brief goodbye, clutching book bags and PE kits, so smart in their navy and grey uniforms.

She bent to kiss them goodbye, more confident after their night-time interactions, but she was very conscious of Ella standing frozen and scornful by the stairs, her red-gold hair in a high ponytail, pink top hugging her slender figure. "We need to get going, or they'll be late." The tone of her voice was very nearly rude, but the smile she flashed Emile, who was in the kitchen, was pure innocence.

"Bye, girls!" Joy ignored the nanny. They waved, and the door slammed behind them. At least her daughters seemed fine this morning, and nobody had voiced any fears that she might vanish in a puff of smoke during school hours.

"I made you some juice," Emile said, handing her a glass of freshly squeezed orange. "I've got a meeting with my agent, but Lucy is coming over in half an hour, and your friend Bobby is coming with her." He pecked her on the cheek. "I'm so sorry, but I can't get out of it. I'll only be a couple of hours."

It was nice, non-threatening, almost dream-like. This was Joy's life. It was how she lived each day. The danger was inside her head. "Thanks. Emile, did you sleep alright last night?"

His eyes didn't flicker. "Yes, fine. Why?"

"Oh, the girls came into my room about midnight, said they had heard a car in the driveway." She was watching his face, but it remained a carefully arranged blank.

"How strange. Security didn't say anything. Perhaps they just had a nightmare. I'm glad they came to you. It shows they are accepting you back, doesn't it?" With a smile, he changed the subject. "Now, your PR team want a Zoom meeting to discuss the media statements, AJ is over the moon you're back, but most importantly, you have a meeting with Dr Alores at 2:00pm. There will be physio to arrange, and more medical appointments scheduled for later in the week." He picked up a satchel bag, grabbed his laptop and headed for the door. "Now you're home we can start to get you better and work on that memory!"

The door shut gently behind him, and Joy, standing in the hallway, bare feet cool on the slate tiles, waited until she heard the crunch of tyres on gravel before she turned back to the kitchen. She wasn't sure what to think, except that her apparently perfect husband had already lied to her, and she hadn't even been home for twenty-four hours.

She wasn't alone for long, as the housekeeper and cleaners turned up at 10:30am, hugging her, exclaiming over her. The nanny returned from the school run, and in response to Joy's slightly awkward questions, assured her coolly that everything was fine with the kids.

"Oh, and it's my half day so I'm going out to lunch. Out with my boyfriend," she added. Her gaze, silently disdainful, and her cool attitude made it clear she was not pleased Joy was home.

"Sounds nice," Joy said, "I think I'll go and get dressed."

Ella didn't exactly say 'whatever', but she did make a dismissive gesture with her hand that basically implied she couldn't care less what Joy did. After the warm welcome from everyone else it was a little disconcerting.

But Ella was a new hire since Joy had been gone. Lucy had told her the girl had been employed here for just over a year, after the old nanny left. Her sister had also implied Ella had a crush on Emile.

Joy swiftly left the downstairs and locked herself in her bedroom, which luckily had an ensuite bathroom. She showered slowly, revelling in the luxury, the expensive products, the soft towels, the clean shower cubicle. Perhaps she could start helping some of the drop-in centres, some of the homeless hostels and halfway houses she had seen when she was with Jono. The thought occurred to her for the first time that perhaps she could use Joy's platform to do some good. She might be able to become a philanthropist.

But first she needed to lay the past to rest, and the only way to do that was to uncover the truth. She stood in front of the mirror, which had misted up after her long hot shower. She couldn't see her reflection clearly, just bits of herself, and on impulse she extended a finger and sketched out a shape. The condensation droplets ran down the mirror streaking the quick sketch. A man's profile, with his face in shadow.

I'm going to hunt you down, she promised him silently. As the mirror revealed more of her face, her serious bluey-green eyes, her cheeks flushed from the shower and her chapped lips, she added to the imaginary conversation in her head. *Was it you, Jono? Was it all you? If it was, I hope you're alive and I hope we meet again. But this time it won't be you in charge, it will be me.*

Joy started to dry her hair. So many skincare products, so many haircare products. All new, unopened under the sink. But she found she knew exactly which ones to apply and how much. When she faced the mirror again, she was bare-faced but expensively moisturized, and her skin felt comfortable. Even her scarred cheek didn't feel the usual tightness. She touched the rope of skin, lightly tracing the injury with gentle fingers, before turning quickly away to her dressing room. Was she still Joy on the inside? Discarding appearances, perhaps she could will herself into her own head again, and remember what she had been thinking, feeling that night.

A noise at the window made her jump, and she felt a draught of cooler air on her back. Surely she had shut the window before her shower, and pulled the blinds right down. She was positive. Joy lifted the blind, cautiously, hand shaking a little. As with the beautiful room at the top of the house, this level also had a split balcony area. There was nobody standing outside, yet the breeze blew carelessly, innocently from a wide-open window.

She peered right out, smelling salt and the sea. Was it real or half imagined? The sea was a long way down from Dyke Road. Shivering again, she reached and yanked the window tightly shut, pulling the blinds down again, hiding from any watchers, any imagined prowlers on her balcony.

Lucy and Bobby turned up as she made her way back downstairs, and the security team let them in the door. *See, you have a whole security team*, she chided herself, as she walked downstairs, *there is nobody stalking you now, nobody watching from the shadows.*

FORTY-ONE

She's back; been back two months now and I still can't believe it. Has she learnt nothing at all from the last five years?

She might be a shadowy, gnarled-looking copy of her former self but she is properly back, and she knows who she is, what she wants. I honestly don't think I have many choices left now. Gossip says her memory is returning. She tells her friends things she shouldn't, and she walks with her head held high and her shoulders square.

I don't want to kill, but I feel I'm being backed into a corner. The police are getting close now. The media coverage has been excellent, and I begrudgingly give a nod to whichever man put the press release together. It stands up to scrutiny. I could blow that apart in an instant, but it isn't in my interests to lead more people to Mattie Woods.

The dead Joy lookalikes is another great story that hasn't yet surfaced. It's only a matter of time though. Naturally these girls are not news to me. They are copies, dolls, fake idols. There wasn't much fuss when they all vanished, so I guess they don't mean much to anyone. Nobody put their disappearance together with Joy's.

I need to keep close to her, and I've been trying to think of the best way to do this, without making her suspicious. There are her flashbacks, which concern me. They are getting more detailed, I hear, as her mind begins to heal and fill in the blanks. What if she remembers? Luckily her security team is flawed, but she mustn't discover this.

I don't like the idea of her drawings. It seems harmless enough, but in Kingston Lane, in the abandoned house, some of her artwork was close to replicating scenes from the abduction, scenes in the months that followed. She didn't realise I was watching all the time, couldn't possibly have known there were cameras in the house. These were easy to remove when she was at the police station. I looked carefully at the drawings, and I looked around the house and realised it was all evidence that needed to go. The fire was easy to set, and there she was, all alone in that shithole of a house. Stupid girl!

I must be very careful, in case the police try to trip me up with their many questions, all under the guise of concern for Joy's wellbeing, just like they did before. I don't like talking to the police. It makes me smile though, imagining the media furore if Joy dies again, and who knows, it might even be an option.

I get ready for the day, gel my hair, add a swipe of face powder, smile at my reflection, and I'm done. That's exactly how I want people to see me, and most idiots never look past the surface to find out what lies underneath. We all know what lies underneath is always darker, always a far truer representation of a person's character.

We loved Joy because she was so transparent, but now she's back she has just proven again and again she wears the same mask as everyone else. Her fan base is divided. Some still love and adore her, and some still hate and abhor her. But we all want to watch her, to follow her, and we're all waiting, like addicts desperate for a fix, to see what happens next.

My black mood continues to dominate my mind as I look for

a coat. The heat is finally over, and this year the burning summer has finally delivered Joy back to her fans. But it's raining today, and for so many reasons September truly is a fucking awful month to be alive.

FORTY-TWO

The staff were calling to each other, music was floating through from the dining room. It was all too invasive, and Joy said as much after she, Lucy and Bobby had shut themselves in the garden room. It was really more like a huge, oak-beamed conservatory, with a small jungle in the corner, as Joy had suggested to Emile last night when she was driven back from her therapy session.

"It is a bit strange, probably, until you get used to it again. I suggested to Emile he might like to keep the staff away for a while, but he insisted you would want to get back to a routine," Lucy said.

Bobby was taking in the room as he always did, running a hand over the silky blankets laid on the sofas, admiring the two glass chandeliers hanging from the ceiling, spinning a full circle on his heels. "Plush pad, I don't think I've seen this room before. Doll, how are you coping with it all?"

"I'm okay..."

He raised an eyebrow disbelievingly. Eight weeks after the fire, and he still had a bandage on his right bicep and a dressing on the back of his neck, little mementoes of the arson attack that had nearly killed them both. His wounds were taking longer to heal, as he had succumbed to an infection, which had resulted in a short stay in hospital.

"Okay, not great," she admitted. "On the face of it, I'm bloody lucky to be living in paradise, so don't think I'm not appreciating the solid roof over my head, the hot and cold running water and clean sheets." Joy took a breath. "But it's like everyone is expecting me to just drop back into Joy's life and pick up where I left off. It's as though they've forgotten I might be charged with being an accessory to murder, that I don't know what the hell happened five years ago, that I'm still, and always will be, fighting addiction, probably thanks to whatever did happen when I vanished..."

"Joy, it's fine if you need time out, if you need to just press pause on everything until you reconcile Mattie with Joy," Lucy said. She passed over a folder. "I did what you asked and put down a timeline of your life and some photos. Dr Alores said too many might be overwhelming, so I just chose one for each year... Holidays, places and me, Dad and you. Some of Mum too..."

"Thanks." Joy took the red folder, and placed it gently on the chair next to her. Stupidly, she was almost afraid to open it. Later, when she was alone, she would try for the hundredth time to force some memories to return.

Bobby, apparently clocking her anxious face, added, "Is Emile putting pressure on you? He told Lucy he had scheduled a meeting with your PR team today. Is that a good idea? Because you don't have to do anything, doll. You can stay here or with Lucy, or your dad or me, whatever you want."

Joy sighed. "Not really pressure, well maybe... I do get it must be really hard for everyone else as well. The PR needs to be handled or we'll never get rid of the reporters outside the gates, I get that, but suddenly I have a schedule, and a buzzer going off on my phone for meetings. It's crazy." She took a sip of her drink, avoiding his concerned gaze. What if they all thought she was going mad? There was still so much to fill in, so much she didn't know about herself. So much to come to terms with. "You know it would really help if I could lay some ghosts to rest. I need to know what happened to me, and I need to know what happened to Jono."

"Deal with what has to be done, and then just stop everything, concentrate on your kids, your cats, getting to know your home again, friends, whatever you need," Lucy suggested calmly.

"Hey, have you done any more drawings?" Bobby asked suddenly.

She could see from their faces they wanted to know if the face had become recognisable, but she shook her head. "I mean, I have been drawing, but I haven't drawn any more from the nightmares."

"Are you still having nightmares?" Lucy asked, concern in her eyes.

"Yes, and..." Joy paused. "They are getting worse, but Dr Alores says that might mean some kind of breakthrough is coming."

That was the hardest thing, she thought. She held the key to all the secrets, but the key was stuck in the lock, and at the moment, no amount of pushing and pulling was going to make it turn. Dr Alores had suggested this image and Joy liked it. It was exactly how she felt.

"It will come. As you get stronger, I'm sure it will come back." Bobby patted her hand.

At always it was so easy to talk to Bobby, and Lucy, who was just sitting, listening, with her chin in her hand. Off duty she wore white linen trousers and a loose navy shirt. She was pretty in a stern and professional type of way, Joy thought. Actually, she was pretty amazing. Had she always been so much in awe of her elder sister?

Lucy picked up a jug of water and poured glasses for all of them. She seemed very at ease in the house, and Joy felt a flash of envy at her confidence as she accepted her drink.

"Joy, there has been a development in the investigation into Jono McQueen."

She stared at her sister, heart instantly beating faster. "You found him?"

"No. Sorry." Lucy paused as though choosing her words carefully. "We, well the investigating team, have linked Jono to two other missing girls of a similar appearance to you."

"Shit." Joy and Bobby both spoke at the same time, and her best friend laid a hand over hers, squeezing her fingers gently.

Lucy pulled out her phone. "Strictly speaking your liaison officer should be telling you this, but they okayed me to go ahead. They will want to talk to you later though, just to see if any of the details jog some memories. Right, Maggie Parsons was, unfortunately, just another missing person on a very long list. She was a nineteen-year-old runaway from Plymouth, Devon. Last seen eight years ago at a friend's party in Saltash in Cornwall. Her history seems very similar to Mattie's history, so I think we can assume that potentially you took on a lot of her identity and history."

Joy opened her mouth, but could only think of more expletives, so she closed it again.

"Lucinda Bailey was a twenty-two-year-old student nurse who went missing from Haywards Heath, in West Sussex, a year after Maggie disappeared. She had a lot of personal issues leading to a severe mental health breakdown just before she vanished." Lucy turned her phone around so Joy and Bobby could see photos of both girls.

"Fuck me, they look just like Joy," Bobby said.

Lucy scrolled to another photo. "As does Stephanie Coultas."

Joy found she couldn't speak; her eyes were shining with

tears. All three girls had wavy brown and blonde hair, and bluey-green eyes. All three faces were smiling, pretty and happy in their photos.

"But what happened to these girls? Why wasn't the bloody connection made when Mattie... sorry, Joy disappeared!" Bobby's eyes were blazing protectively, and his voice rose in anger. "Three other girls practically identical to Joy go missing a few years apart, and the police don't bloody notice? Really?"

Lucy spread her hands in a pacifying motion and shook her head. "I agree with you, but what can I say? All the departments are short-staffed, dealing with funding cuts, and although in theory it is now easier than ever before to share details of current cases and check for similarities, sometimes it just gets missed. Different areas, different reasons. None of these other three girls were flagged as priority, because the files suggested all of them may have left of their own accord." She paused. "Lucinda Bailey's family admitted she had talked about quitting her course, about getting away from the pressure, and the other two girls, well, friends and family weren't sure they hadn't left on their own. It wouldn't have been totally out of character."

"Did you find these girls?" Joy found her voice. Her mouth was dry, and she had to pass her tongue over her lips before she spoke.

"No. Apart from Stephanie Coultas, we have no girls and no bodies."

"But including me, that makes four?"

"It may do," Lucy hedged cautiously.

Joy met her sister's eyes, heart beating fast, the sick feeling swirling in her stomach. "You know it does. What you're saying is that for five years I've been living with someone who might have murdered three other girls, just because they looked like me."

FORTY-THREE

"He was having an affair. Your marriage was in trouble, he was jealous you were getting more followers and fame than him. He even suggested you might want to dial down the channel, take a step back." Kate's eyes were limpid and sincere. Huge baby blues fringed by huge fake lashes. Her white-blonde hair extensions reached down to her waist, and her full pout was unnaturally puffy and pink. Her cheeks were sharply sculpted and her forehead so smooth it looked like plastic.

Joy was silent, staring at her supposed friend. Now she had moved back home, started to get to know her life and her family, and she had decided to find out who her friends were. It felt like a huge step, interacting with these people, who may or may not be sympathetic to her.

The police were still investigating Jono and the connection between her case and the other three women who went missing, but it was taking so much time, and she felt guilt for nagging Lucy to provide her with answers.

So, she had chosen to try and move on as Joy Maddison. These women had constantly emailed and texted Emile, wanting her new mobile number. She had told him she didn't feel ready. But flowers and gifts had arrived. The best gift was from someone called Georgia and had been a potted lavender and some cat treats, complete with a card and phone number:

When you feel you can, let's catch up XX

It was typical that Georgia couldn't make it tonight. Joy hadn't actually invited any comments on her husband, but these women had been so keen to draw the conversation to Emile. After just a few minutes of air kisses and exaggerated inquiries into her well-being, she had known this was a mistake.

What the hell was she trying to do? She didn't have to prove anything. Well, actually, she thought, she kind of did. And she was curious, so curious about what it was like to be part of Joy's life, see the world through Joy's eyes.

She had been home for long enough to feel stable now. Not safe, but in a routine, as her therapist had suggested. The best thing of all was that her relationship with her children was flourishing. The nanny, Ella, was still sulky and shot her evil looks, but Joy had insisted on being part of the routine.

So she sat with them at breakfast, helping the twins with their reading practice, and she played Lego with Bertie after school, while the girls were at gymnastics practice. It took a lot of effort, mainly because she was terrified of saying the wrong thing, of destroying the fragile little bonds that were reconnecting her with her kids.

Everyone thought they knew what had happened, everyone was eager to fill in the blanks, and although Dr Alores had warned her to take things slowly, she was thirsty for knowledge, intrigued by Joy's life and her friends. And now quite repelled by her choice of friends.

Certainly, Emile couldn't have been nicer to her since she got back, showering her with gifts, encouraging her to make use of all the facilities and treats she had once carelessly enjoyed on a weekly basis. They were still stepping awkwardly round each other on the subject of his affairs, or potentially ongoing affair though, and she just didn't feel she had the right to question him. Not yet.

"What do you mean, take a step back?" Joy asked.

"We could all see how stressed you were when you bagged the Summer Style contract, and with your husband being a little unsupportive, it's no wonder you might have felt you needed to get away from everything."

"But I didn't..." Joy remembered what Emile had said: *'You had a small group of friends who you trusted absolutely, and then you had others who said one thing, but would gossip to the press behind your back...'*

"It's okay, darling, Emile's a hot husband, and I know him well, but is he really long-term?"

"You sound like you're trying to get me to divorce my husband, Kate. I only moved back in a few months ago," Joy remarked, trying to disguise the way her heart was pounding, her mouth was dry. "What about you? Do you have a partner?"

She tossed her hair back. "A few but nothing serious. Sex is the main thing, isn't it? Relationships are boring."

Joy bit back her next question, which would have been about Emile again. Surely, he wouldn't have slept with this woman? But there were those times she had caught him looking at her with a strange expression. When she questioned this, he told her it was like seeing a ghost every time she walked into the room, that he couldn't quite believe she was really home.

That was sweet, but she couldn't shake the strangest feeling perhaps he didn't really want her home at all... Was it just imposter syndrome? Thrown by the revelations that Jono McQueen might well be a serial killer, she had finally told Lucy and Bobby about Devonshire Place. She now knew who lived there, but she still hadn't confronted her husband. It seemed almost trivial in comparison to the police investigation.

Kate's words confirmed her suspicions, but who would trust this woman? In her tight pink dress, showing off a frankly impossible cleavage that had to be held together with stitches, she looked like Barbie. But Barbie didn't have that kind of blood lust in her eyes.

The three women, sitting elegantly on her garden furniture, all glossy hair and long tanned legs which defied the cooler autumn weather, couldn't be further removed from her own physical self.

As the conversation moved on, Joy reached for her glass of iced water. Her own hair was now short and blonde again, and her personal beautician had been called in to pamper her with facials and massages. Her nails were pale pink, and she had new clothes, and a few old clothes (mainly from Frank, who had refused to allow Emile to give many of them away). She was thinner than she had been before she disappeared, and she tried to hide her scars, her ruined veins, under long sleeves and trousers or maxi dresses.

She didn't remember having a choice over her tattoos, but she liked them. The stars, the crescent moon, and the intricate floral decorations were a little piece of Mattie, right there on her skin. Lucy had been right, they had partially covered the scar on her shoulder, the one she had from childhood, and a birth mark on her lower back. Marks which would identify her as Joy Maddison. Jono, because she knew it must have been him, had chosen well.

Kate was tapping her nails on one of the many gift boxes lying around the place. Boxes of products gifted from companies she had once worked with, and boxes of products from businesses who saw she was about to become even more famous. She intended to donate them to charities, to people who needed them.

There was a physiotherapist who came to the house, and medical appointments with various doctors to discuss her previous injuries and ongoing amnesia. And then there were the journalists. The girl who came home made a great story and the magazines, the papers, all the TV channels, wanted exclusive rights to her life.

Joy found if she maintained a light touch on reality she could just about cope. She still felt like a puppet going through the motions, and the only time she could truly be herself, whoever that might be, was with Lucy, Bobby or her therapist, Dr Alores. But her family seemed to be happy. Her dad was adoring and although it was a bit annoying he spent so much time at their house, pottering around the garden, or making cakes in the kitchen, she could tell he was lonely. He talked to her about her mother, about her childhood.

Her personal assistant was back, as were her PR team (headed by dynamic and over-enthusiastic AJ), her marketing team and all her friends. Natasha and Kate had insisted they were all best friends, but Lucy told Joy in private that Kate was a 'shallow bitch' and she had never met Natasha.

But what had Joy thought of them all? Who had she really liked and trusted, and who had she barely tolerated? Mattie had no friends, apart from Bobby, and in her world, if you trusted someone, you went for a drink with them. If you hated them, you ignored them. Or killed them. Death and dirt had been part of her everyday life, and it had been all about the struggle to survive.

Here in princess land the official line was that Joy had numerous besties and a huge circle of celebrity acquaintances. She would judge who was a real friend and who was not. They had all been fed the same line, but she could tell most of them knew it was just a cover story:

Joy was abducted and kept prisoner in an unnamed location.

She also suffered an accident leading to amnesia. It's an ongoing investigation and we can't comment.'

Everyone asked her about the last five years, but the police had advised her to keep the address vague, to say she just didn't recall anything before the accident, and not much in those lost years until her abductor had left the door unlocked and she had escaped. Nothing about Jono and her abduction, or her recent battle with addiction. Nothing about Stephanie Coultas, Maggie Parsons or Lucinda Bailey, or even about Mattie and Ned and Number Forty-Two Kingston Lane. So much to hide.

The journalists were never going to swallow such a bland story, and they had been pushing for more ever since. But on the whole, Joy's PR team justified their pay, keeping everyone at a safe distance, never even close to the truth. The police were saying nothing at all about the body of Stephanie Coultas, and the ongoing investigation. Hence the only thing for the journalists to report was that uninteresting gem of a *'no comment'*.

So mostly they contented themselves with writing about her past. There had been stories about Emile's supposed affair, her own struggles with mental health as the trolls *'drove her to the brink'*, and still a lot of speculation she had indeed just run away. The question they couldn't answer was: why had she come home?

It was a miracle nobody had linked the woman who had been arrested for Joy's murder with Joy's re-emergence into society, but Lucy told her carefully leaked information said the woman arrested had been suffering with mental health issues and had been released for further care.

"Joy, are you even listening to the gossip?" Kate interrupted her thoughts, and Joy realised she had zoned out of the barbed conversation, letting it flow around her without listening.

"Yes, I am. Sorry, I guess I was just thinking..." Joy smiled an apology at her. "I was just thinking what I was going to do in the future, you know. I have a lot to catch up on, but I do know it feels so right being back with my family, and Emile and the kids couldn't have been more welcoming."

"That's nice to hear. Of course, we all adore Emile, but he's a bit of a dark horse, and he likes to play up the dark and dangerous type. And after you were gone... we did become closer." Natasha, a blue-eyed brunette with a honey-gold tan lowered her voice. "Well, we can tell you everything you need to know, darling, but some of us feel you need to recover a bit more first. You aren't yourself at all, are you?"

Natasha was a beauty, a plastic beauty with swishy silky hair, but still beautiful. Joy's heart sank a little, as the ghost of Mattie sat on her shoulder and observed. She could see her husband dating someone like Natasha. Yet surely, as these women seemed to be implying, he hadn't been sleeping with *all* of her friends? That would be ridiculous. Not to mention cruel.

Kate tapped her arm with her long red nails, and Joy winced, moving out of range under the pretext of picking up a piece of watermelon from the huge silver plate in front of them. She knew she had to say something else, something to shut them up for a bit, to make them see how confident and self-assured she was, coming back into someone else's life with no memory. She had faked it being a CHIS, she could fake it with this lot.

Natasha, too, was supposed to have been one of the few people in Joy's inner circle she told all her secrets to. But how close had these women really got to Emile before Joy vanished? "Sorry, I was thinking about what Kate said earlier. I can't see it. He just wouldn't have had an affair."

"How do you know?" Kate turned wide innocent eyes on her, before sliding on her designer sunglasses, shaking out her hair with a seductive little wriggle. "How do you *know*, darling? Because you can't remember anything at all, can you?"

FORTY-FOUR

Natasha, and the third member of the gang, a small slender girl called Courtney, nodded in agreement. Courtney had a squeaky, breathy voice like a broken bath toy, and standard waist-length platinum-blonde extensions. She looked sweet. A bit daft, but more genuine than the other two women. She smiled at Joy. "Shall we take a look at all your goodies? And have you got your diary sorted, because there is so much going on, and so much you'll want to catch up on. There's a party at Soho House on Thursday... It's okay, but the pool is *tiny*. I suppose location is everything." The smile was broad, showing very white teeth, and two cute dimples. "Georgia's sad she couldn't come today, but she'll be there!"

She has no idea. Joy wavered for a moment, not wanting to deliberately make enemies, but the instinct she had used, had nurtured to survive on the city streets, won out. She had survived Ned and his gang, had survived Jono, and it had all strengthened her, made her surer of her judgement.

She didn't like any of these women. Courtney certainly didn't seem to have the brains to be malicious, but the other two... They clearly thought they were physically perfect, but they were rotten inside. Bobby, who had been with her when she was crawling around puking on the filthy concrete floor of her living room, was still the only friend she could really trust.

For some reason she flashed back to Ned and his snake. It was like being surrounded by half a dozen snakes, their heads swaying as they sought the best place to sink their fangs. If this had been Joy's best friend group, things were about to change, she decided.

"I can't explain how I know about Emile, but I just do. I'm sure there is a logical explanation," Joy told them dismissively. She swung her legs off the sun-lounger, forcing the confidence she needed to end the conversation. "Sorry, girls, I forgot I'd double-booked this morning. I need to see my solicitor in twenty minutes, and I have medical appointments later. Great to see you. I'll call you sometime."

She was pleased to hear how cool and confident she really sounded, when inside she had been terrified at meeting this lot, cringing at how they would view her beaten and scarred body, the other changes that had taken place in the last five years. Meeting them had triggered no memories or flashbacks. Perhaps it was because they meant nothing to her in her previous life?

For a moment, they didn't move, as though they couldn't quite believe Joy was dismissing them. When Kate finally reached for her handbag, she did blast out a final warning. "You can try and pretend all you want, Joy, but the truth will come out. Running away from something that's so obvious to everyone else won't help you. You haven't changed at all. Lots of us can already see that and it won't help you at all to keep up the attitude. We want to help you get on with your life, but you won't tell us anything."

It was her phrasing and the nuances that made a guess almost a certainty. *'Lots of us can see that...'* Lucy had shown her the latest NatterJack posts, the previous anniversary emails, wanting her to be prepared, wanting her to be careful. Lucy had also told her she suspected at least one of Joy's friends of being part of the NatterJack forum, of leaking stories to the press. The piece in the paper this morning from a *'trusted source'* had similar phrasing, and Kate, Natasha and Courtney knew all about the beautician visits and the physio *'...trying to make tragic Joy beautiful again...'*

Joy smiled at the blandly pretty faces, and thought of other pretty faces, the ones on Lucy's phone, the ones who had more than likely vanished forever, thanks to someone who called himself her boyfriend. "Yes, yes I have changed. I know who I can trust, and I know I can't trust shallow bitches like you. Stay out of my face. Go and ring up the papers and sell another story or add another post to NatterJack."

The satisfaction she got from seeing the smug smiles drop, replaced by raw, naked shock, went a long way towards making her day. Bobby would have been proud. She would tell him later and he would laugh.

"Oh, and Natasha?" She gathered her strength for one last shot as the defeated army departed.

The other woman paused, eyes now hidden behind her own designer shades.

"Nice pad you've got in Devonshire Place, isn't it? I might visit sometime. Say, around midnight? Because you're still up then, aren't you?"

Natasha froze, before she put a finger to her glossy pout in a shushing motion. "Stay out of what doesn't concern you, Joy. Just keep your mouth shut like you did before, and everything will be fine. We'd hate it if you disappeared again." She turned and staggered away on her platform sandals, pulling her tight pink dress down over her skinny bum.

Courtney alone lingered, confusion and concern on her face. "I hope you're okay, Joy. I mean" – tears filled her eyes – "I was really worried about you."

It wasn't much, but Joy smiled at her and thanked her as Courtney scurried after the other women.

That dress was definitely made for someone with curves, not a stick-like doll, Joy thought, almost amused as she watched Natasha vanish along the path. She wondered if running after her and smacking Natasha in the face was a civilised option. Nuala emerged purring from the house, and Joy rubbed a gentle finger across her furry striped face. "Did that Barbie bitch just threaten me?" Had Joy *known* about the affair and just gone along with it? Surely, she wouldn't have done. And yet... The lifestyle, the money and the gloss. Joy's brand was built on her happy family unit. How far would she have gone to maintain it?

In her mind Mattie and Joy had just moved further apart than ever before. It wasn't just the clothes and make-up; it was the attitude and mindset. At this stage, she was getting to dislike Joy quite a lot. Had she really been this insipid, easily led creature, living in such a shallow world? Someone who dodged the school run on a regular basis, who spent more time on her appearance than with her children.

Had she been afraid to challenge her husband about an affair, or had she just ignored it, so as not to cause a scandal? Or maybe, just maybe, it hadn't been true at all. Even if he was sleeping with Natasha now, it didn't mean he had been before she disappeared, did it? Or the dancer from that other club mentioned in the tabloids: Platinum Lace.

There had always been rumours about them. According to Lucy's careful timeline, two months before Joy was abducted, the gossip columns suggested she herself might be having an affair too. With a fellow influencer and DJ Reggie Holliday. She had studied his Instagram account carefully, staring at his face, trying to spark a memory. They shared the same agent, went to a lot of the same parties... But the idea they could have been lovers was baffling, almost amusing. There was no tiny spark of attraction, and more importantly no fizz of memory waiting to be released.

As she walked back to the house, still fuming at Natasha, trying to calm her possibly irrational anger at Emile, her phone buzzed with a text. Expecting it to be another warning from one of the three bitches who had just been sitting in her garden, she glanced down, ready for war.

What the hell? Shaking, everything else forgotten, she stared at the message:

> Hi Mattie, how's it going? I see you're back in princess land. Don't worry, I'll be watching over you. JONO xox

FORTY-FIVE

"She isn't really Mummy, I think she's just another woman pretending." Bertie's little face was stubborn, confused and Lucy's heart ached for all of them. She hoped this was just a blip after the honeymoon period.

"She is. She's just been through a lot since she's been away."

"Why did she go away?" he persisted, kicking a football against the wall, in a way that was forbidden. Lucy didn't bother to tell him off. This was hard enough anyway. "And why didn't she come back? Daddy says you had to find her, and Grandad says she didn't want to come home."

"She did want to come home, but someone wouldn't let her. Someone stole Mummy," Daisy said soberly, and her brother's eyes widened as he stopped kicking the ball.

"They might come back and steal you if you kick the ball indoors," Poppy added unsympathetically.

Bertie burst into tears.

"Poppy! There was no need for that," Lucy said crossly. Cursing the kids listening at doors, but sympathetic to Bertie's confusion, and relieved at the girls' stalwart defence of their mother, she hugged them, and they pressed close, bewildered.

She tried to imagine how she and Joy would have felt if their mother had turned up alive, instead of being told she was dead right from the beginning. They had been roughly the same age as Joy's daughters were now.

"We don't know what happened to Mummy yet, okay? We know she didn't want to leave us all, but something happened." Lucy tried her best to reassure them, passing Bertie a tissue for his snotty nose and picking up the ball to prevent further arguments.

"Something bad happened to Mummy?" Bertie persisted, recovering slightly.

"Yes."

"Was she *kidnapped*?" Poppy asked.

"Yes. And she was in a car accident so that might be why she doesn't recognise us. You know, we said she had a brain injury."

"She likes Nuala, her cat, but not us. That's why she doesn't remember us," Bertie pointed out dolefully.

"She remembered me and Daisy," Poppy told him smugly, and Lucy resisted the urge to give her a sharp retort. Poppy could be a brat sometimes, but she could tell this was coming from the child's pain. She was just lashing out because she couldn't express herself any other way. Thank God the kids were still having therapy.

"She isn't like Mummy. I know she is really, but sometimes I don't think she really is Mummy." Poppy's little face was sharp and concentrated now, and she pulled her long ponytail around, fiddling with the ribbon on the end, as she always did when she was stressed. "She's different and when I went into her room in the morning, she was talking to someone."

"Well, that's okay, isn't it?" Lucy queried. "Maybe she was on the phone?"

"There was nobody there, and she was looking in the mirror. Her phone was on the bed, I saw it," Poppy replied, her eyes wide. "Mummy was talking to someone called Jono, but she was the *only* person in her bedroom."

"Unless Jono is a ghost?" Daisy suggested.

"Oooh." Poppy considered the possibility, as Bertie watched them, his gaze going back and forth between his sisters like a spectator at a tennis match.

Lucy bit her lip, weighing this up. She was concerned for Joy's mental health, and the constant pressure coming from all sides must be taking its toll. Not to mention she had to take on a whole new identity. It would be weirder if her sister wasn't showing signs of the strain, she told herself. "Right, well... It's hard for everyone, and for Mummy too. But she is trying as hard as she can to get better. She wouldn't have been talking to a ghost, because there is no such thing as ghosts. We just need to be patient, and understand Mummy needs time to get better. Okay?" Lucy said, trying to inject some confidence into her voice.

"Nuala's kittens are cute," Daisy said, changing the subject and smiling at Lucy. The kids' expressions brightened at the thought of the distractions in the utility room.

Lucy began to usher them through the door to the hallway. "Why don't you go and find the cats? You know, Poppy, if you lose your memory, you can't just make the bits come back that you want to come back. It just happens. I think now she is home, she will start to remember more and more."

They stared at her, and she was grateful when a distraction appeared in the form of their nanny. "Oh, hi, Ella! The kids were just going to find the cats."

The nanny, carrying swimsuits and towels, plus her phone, came down the stairs and called to the girls. "Do you want to swim now? The rain has stopped, and I've just put the roof over the pool. Bertie has a playdate until four, so you can have the pool toys to yourselves. Bertie, Tassie's mum is picking you up in ten minutes, so get some shoes on!"

Ella turned to Lucy with a shallow, pretty smile. "It's still so warm for this time of year but I think there might be thunderstorms again later, so we need to make the most of it." She adjusted the shoulder strap of her flowered crop top and picked up a dropped towel.

Bertie, one shoe on and one off, had stopped and picked up his tablet, checking a screen notification with such a squeak of glee that his sisters crowded around.

"October is a funny time for a heatwave to end," Lucy agreed. The girl was so superficial, so obviously looking for Emile. When he was within earshot, she came alive, flirty smiles and extra cuddles for the kids.

To be fair, she did seem to be good with them, but her crush on Emile was a bit embarrassing really. Although Lucy still didn't think he had ever done enough to put Ella firmly in her place. She supposed it must be flattering to have a pretty young girl trying to catch his eye, but she hoped he was a bit above that. It was hardly a new thing for Emile...

"Lucy, I was meaning to ask." Ella glanced down at her feet, lowered her voice. "How is Joy really? Because she's been a bit odd with me... You know, a bit rude, and I just wondered... is she going to get her memory back?"

"I don't know." Lucy kept her voice steady, her face blank. "Perhaps you could try and understand what she has been through, and make some allowances. I don't imagine my sister is trying to be rude, but she has been through a lot."

"Yeah, I guess." Ella was still doing the wide-eyed concern, standing with her hands full and the kids waiting.

"Go and have some fun, and of course you can come to me privately with any concerns, Ella," Lucy said pointedly, hearing a note of annoyance slip into her voice. The kids appeared to be busy with Bertie's tablet, but still, Ella shouldn't be talking like this in front of them. "But like I say, just a bit of understanding. This is hard for everyone."

When Ella had taken the girls away, Lucy had made herself an iced drink, sipping it thoughtfully. Her dad had suggested maybe Joy should switch to another therapist, as they didn't seem to be making much headway, but she knew her sister would never agree. She trusted Dr Alores and often said she was the only person who could really get inside her head.

Emile strolled in, chucking his bag onto a chair and heading straight for the cafetière. "I just saw Ella and the kids on the way out. Are they still giving you a hard time about Joy?"

"Yes. I don't blame them. It's such a bizarre situation, and I can't explain it because we still don't know what happened to her either." Lucy sighed, crunching ice cubes. "I know she is remembering more and more, which has to be a good sign, and she looks a lot healthier. It doesn't help that the press are going crazy over the possible identity of her abductor, or the ongoing investigation. I'm really worried about her." She looked up at him, brushing her hair wearily out of her eyes. "Anyway, did you have a good meeting?"

He ignored her last remark, busy making his coffee, clattering a mug down from the cupboard and measuring the coffee beans ready to grind. "You said there was no proof Joy was really filming Stephanie's death?"

"There is nothing concrete to tie her to the scene either, but the woman was wearing Joy's running clothes so her DNA would be all over the body. Joy described a fairly accurate scenario of the victim's neck being broken and the video was on her phone. But she could have watched the video over and over, so she knows what happened. Lots of circumstantial evidence." Lucy shrugged.

"What about the other women this man supposedly abducted or murdered? It is shocking. I can't seem to get my head around it at all," Emile said. "Do you want coffee too?"

"Please. Ongoing investigation," Lucy told him. "Sorry, I know that's crap. This story is dynamite and the more coverage it gets the harder it is to get to the truth. So many cranks out looking for fame, and so much speculation on Jono's identity. If he is still alive, he will have gone to ground for sure."

Emile nodded thoughtfully. "And you still think a car accident caused a loss of memory? A loss of memory so bad that she then built a new life away from us. I know we've all seen the doctor's reports, but I admit I'm still trying to get my head around that too. I'm confused about this dissociation amnesia, even though I've googled the hell out of it."

"It's possible. I think the very fact that it sounds so crazy makes it plausible. If she was going to run, had planned to disappear, and I don't believe she did, she wouldn't have stayed in Brighton, would she?" Lucy was finding it hard not to sound defensive. She could completely understand Emile's frustration, but she felt so protective of her sister, she wasn't going to have her brother-in-law directing the merest breath of criticism towards Joy, whatever her worries on the state of Joy's mind.

"And this man she was with, Jono? Could Joy still be in danger?"

Emile sounded concerned, but she noticed he didn't seem to have all his attention on the conversation, his eyes kept flicking towards his own phone. She sighed. "I doubt if he could get near her, but I agree it is a worry."

"Joy thought he was dead," Emile pondered. "But we need him, don't we? We need to find him so we can make him tell us what happened, what he did to her and why." As an afterthought, he added, "And he can tell us about these other women too. Do you think he set the whole accident up to abduct her? Maybe he hit her on purpose?" He pulled a packet of biscuits out of the cupboard and set them down on the countertop.

Lucy picked up the shortbread he offered and frowned. "I keep telling you, I'm not on the case, and I must be a total pain in the arse to the investigating team. It's lucky I've got a friend who keeps me in the loop."

"Sorry, but what do you think personally?" Emile persisted, passing a mug to Lucy before sipping his own coffee gratefully. He leant against the counter, his eyes fixed on her face.

"From the planning, the mind games, and the potential other victims, I'm leaning towards planned abduction." Lucy spoke slowly, carefully, building the pictures in her mind. She had been over and over this, but something still didn't quite fit. "You can't rely on hitting someone and them having amnesia, so perhaps she really did run out in front of the car, and his lucky break was when she came round and couldn't remember anything at all."

"It doesn't explain why he concocted this elaborate story of them killing Joy, to the extent that he really did kill Stephanie Coultas in front of her. He can't have done that on the same night. The place was crawling with police," Emile pointed out.

"No. Stephanie Coultas was still alive and working at the club at the end of August. That's the last definite sighting we have, and it comes nearly two months after Joy vanished. So, what happened in those two months? Joy doesn't remember when she was told they had committed a murder. Perhaps, if she was recovering physically from her injuries, he took the chance to stuff her full of heroin, get her addicted so she was never fully in control again?"

"I'm so torn. It feels like a crazy dream, and of course I am so thankful you found her, but now this readjustment... I don't know if it will work. I'm not her husband to her, I'm a total stranger, and the kids, well, the kids are struggling too."

"She can have all the medical help she needs now, and the therapy is going well, isn't it? Emile, I'm not going to lie, she's been through a lot, lived a whole different life that you can't even imagine. For five years she has had to survive, and we only have a theory as to why. Nothing is proven yet."

"I wonder if he did run after he saw the news that a body had been discovered? Even though it turned out not to be connected. Or was it connected, maybe that was connected too," Emile queried. "By the way, she's still drawing. I keep going up to the room to check and she's doing a lot but still shadow images of the man she says kept her in a room after the abduction. Who must have been Jono, so I don't know why she can't fit it all together."

"I haven't seen any evidence to connect the cases, other than Joy's DNA being present," Lucy told him, choosing to answer his first question and avoid Emile's mention of the drawings. It annoyed her Emile was checking up on her, but she supposed he was also desperate for some kind of resolution. But regarding the Hove body, it was true that Elise, the victim, bore no resemblance to Joy, so didn't follow the other potential pattern the police had uncovered with Stephanie.

"Maybe he thought he'd been busted. I'd love to meet him, oh I know it won't ever happen, but this man basically took five years of our life. And the drug addiction? He must have got her addicted, like you just said." Emile scowled and his expression was bleak.

"Someone got her addicted. Because the Joy we knew previously never took any drugs, did she? Apart from that one time when she and I were teens."

"No." He pushed his hair away from his forehead with an impatient flick of his hand, changing the subject abruptly. "I need to get to the barber. Yesterday, Poppy asked if she could brush my hair, make a ponytail and tie one of her ribbons around it." He rolled his eyes.

Lucy smiled but noted the quick subject change. Was he uneasy about her question, or just frustrated by the whole conversation and ready to move on? She was sure her sister hadn't taken drugs, since that festival when she acquired a juvenile record. And thank God she had, or her DNA would never have been matched on file.

On the whole, Joy had also been a good girl and it had been teenage Lucy who experimented and rowed with their dad about staying out late. "It might be a whole new look for you to promote," she said lightly to her brother-in-law. "By the way, did you decide on that reality show?"

He looked slightly uncomfortable, she thought, but answered readily enough. "Yes, I told them I would do it, because since Joy came back, they doubled the offer."

FORTY-SIX

Joy studied her husband, her kids sitting together at the long table on the terrace and willed herself to remember. Dr Alores had told her firmly but gently to stop beating herself up. What kind of mother didn't recognise her own children? Didn't remember giving birth? These kinds of questions were now banned from her head. What kind of mother had she been really? Not so perfect, she thought, according to the NatterJack forum.

Had she really been the sort of person to use her kids for photoshoots and then leave them with a nanny for the rest of time? Apparently, she had, because she had spent a lot of hours with the coven of witches she had just dismissed.

Jono's text had freaked her out, but she forced herself to try and behave normally while she sorted it out in her head. Emile and the kids didn't need to be worried when she was trying to reassure her family everything was okay, and she was settling back in quite happily. No mention of affairs or of her own abduction could be allowed to ruin the precarious peace.

Joy told herself this was why she had decided, after much thought, not to mention Jono's text. She had responded to the message, but it just came up with the 'undelivered' symbol. She tried calling but the number wasn't recognised. Her next action (or even her first), should have been to tell Lucy. Joy bit her lip, thoughts whirling through her brain. If she told Lucy, the police would get straight onto it and try to track Jono down. That would be the best course of action.

But... he knew what had happened, what had really happened from the time she vanished to the time he vanished. She was desperate to understand what she had been through, to fill the gaps in her memory. Jono was her last link to sanity, and she wanted to talk to him herself, to make him tell her what she needed to know. He would never talk to the police.

If she couldn't remember on her own, Jono was the only person who knew everything and that gave him power. She felt tears start, and blinked furiously. He still had power over her. Not just her. There were now other families, other loved ones desperate to know what had happened to their own daughters, sisters and girlfriends. How had he got this hold over her? She wished she knew what had been done to her, then she might be able to work out how to undo it. Was it just the drugs? The fog in her mind hung frustratingly heavy, making her want to scream out loud. It felt like the answers she needed were just out of reach, but tantalisingly close at the same time.

Poppy and Daisy hugged her one by one as she reached the table in the garden room, all laid with fluttering white linen, glass and fancy plates that looked as though they had been hand-crafted into garden leaves. Bertie still watched, his dark lashes flickering as he shot wary glances across the table.

She forced herself to respond in kind to Poppy and Daisy because it would have been too cruel not to, and it was easier with the kids. She felt very protective of them. When Bertie shrank from her, she smiled at him instead and asked him about his football, about his Lego.

With Jono's message dancing through her brain, even when,

after the meal, her handsome husband pulled her close and rested his lips against her forehead, she still felt nothing. Nothing but a terrible desire to run away somewhere and be quite alone, except for the scream of the seagulls. Joy even felt she wanted to be back in her derelict house, sitting in the upstairs room, staring up at the sky. Ungrateful, that's what she was.

Still keeping her close, her husband asked playfully, "How was your chat with the girls? I bet it was great to catch up, but they are the gossip queens of Brighton, so don't believe a word they might say, will you?"

A *meow* from under the table gave her the excuse she needed to pull away from Emile, her heart pounding, head throbbing with secrets. She knelt beside the magnificent Siamese cat, who leapt up onto the spare chair and studied her with huge blue eyes. Honey, Poppy's cat. Nuala had her heart, but even so she felt something inside her respond to the blue gaze, and when she put her hand out to stroke the cat's head, she suddenly knew she had done this, in this place, a million times before, in this place in the garden room.

Unexpectedly, muscle and memory clicked into place. She knew she had planted catmint in the borders, next to the lavender, that cat food was stored just *there*, next to the sofa in the blue bin in the utility room. She could find her way back to the hall, and she needed to mind the chest because everyone always stubbed their toes, but Emile would never move it...

"Oh!" Joy stood up abruptly and gripped the garden chair in shock as her mind flashed with images, see-sawing uneasily between past and present, unable to reconcile either. The flood of images stopped as sharply as it had begun.

"Joy? Are you okay?"

Emile was close, way too close, wrapping a gentle arm around her, setting her onto the chair as though she was made of china. The smell of his aftershave made her feel nauseous, and she forced herself to speak calmly. "Dr Alores said now I was home it might trigger my memory, and I guess she was right. It's just taken longer than I hoped."

"What did you remember?" Daisy asked, fork halfway to her mouth, food forgotten. Her eyes were wide with interest. She was the only one still slowly picking her way through her dessert.

Joy told them about the cat-food bin and for some reason the tension was released, everyone finding it hilarious of all the important events she could have recalled, she knew where the cat food was. She crossed glances with Emile and could have sworn a flash of relief added to his laughter.

After lunch, she went to lie down in the cool, shady living room, with its overstuffed plush sofas and Nuala reclining with her babies on the stone floor tiles.

What had happened for Jono to turn her into Mattie? And finally, she thought, as she smiled and lay gratefully against the sofa cushions, shutting her eyes, who the hell was she now?

Two hours later, she was finally alone, rested and still thinking about Jono's text. She should tell her sister, and the police would try to track Jono down. He was a wanted man and they would try hard.

Joy picked up her phone again, and called Bobby.

"Hi, doll. How's it going? Hey, guess what? Emile put me in touch with Charmaine Davies, the woman Emile said you used to know. She's a comedian and actor *and* she just happens to organise comedy nights at Burger & Bird in Peacehaven. I've got another gig, and Charmaine said she can get me talking to an actual *agency*."

"Did you get the bar job?" Joy was thrilled for him, but Jono's message seemed to be pulsing through her brain. She kept glancing at the windows, jumping at small sounds in the house, and every light draught of air was his breath on the back of her neck. She wriggled round, so her back was to the wall, and she had full view of the doors and windows.

"Yes, so Ned can fuck off forever, now. He must have been trying to cut himself a deal inside because, I wasn't there, but Al told me the police turned up with riot vans and hauled off Harley and load of the main crew, and they haven't come back. After Ned got arrested, this will really screw things up." His voice was still high and excited, and she let him continue, "Looks like Dami is running the show until they find out what's happening, but he's legit so that'll put a stop to any drug runs. Sorry, I'm *way* too excited about everything. What's going on with you?"

Unsure quite what she was going to say before the words came, she felt something inside her switch and she told him about Jono's message.

"*Shut up, doll!* Do you really think he's alive? Because you always said Ned was dropping major dead body hints."

"I don't know, but what if he *is* watching me? I mean, what's he going to do?" She could hear her voice a little too high and sharp. "Bobby, I was thinking maybe I could get him to talk to me, and tell me..." Joy stopped, aware she sounded hysterical now, her reasoning way off.

"No way, that's far too dangerous. Tell the police. Ring your sister right now. If you haven't already?"

"I called you first."

"Doll, I get it, you want to know, and you might think you can rely on the connection you may have had, but you have to get into the mindset that he stole five years of your life. He's an abductor and a murderer, probably, of three other women as well. You know what gets me? All the time, he kept you just a few miles from your real family, living a lie. You also have to think, before you go spilling secrets via text message if he does respond, maybe it isn't him contacting you?"

"But I need to know what happened, Bobby. If he's still alive he's the only person who can tell me!" She was crying again, the raw sadness in her chest bubbling up and over. She knew if Jono was arrested there would be no chance of him revealing exactly what he had done to her. He loved being the big man, the one with the power, and he would hug it all to his chest, and keep those secrets.

"I know, doll, but he's also the only person who is a serious danger to you. You aren't thinking rationally, and I don't blame you after the shit you're going through. But you're wrong anyway. Your memory will come back, so you don't need him for anything."

She was silent for a moment, thinking it through. The shouting in her head had started again, probably in response to Jono's text. "It's definitely him. We used to call Joy's house 'princess land' and that's what he said in the text. He wants me to know it's him. It's a new number, so he must have a burner phone." Joy knew about these because Mattie knew about these. How far would things go before she was able to merge the two women into one person? She did know she was correct in saying Jono was key to that happening.

"You know I'm right, though. It's a huge issue he has your new number. If you don't ring Lucy right away, I'll do it for you. Mattie... sorry, *Joy!* You could be in serious danger from this bastard."

FORTY-SEVEN

We're all waiting to see what she does next...

I type the words into a burner phone, and then change my mind and delete them. Part of me is loving the chance to be able to properly pull her strings again. My little puppet, my doll, my little poppet, has no idea at all what is really going on.

I'm still in two minds about what to do. The police have confirmed my opinion of them: useless, bumbling idiots stumbling along, making mistakes at every turn. Shocking, when you think that so many of our police force are men.

Lucy might begin to put the puzzle pieces together eventually. She's always been a problem. I've been watching her too. When she was younger she was so competitive – in sports, at school, forever pushing people aside to get to the next level. Now she's been promoted again, and I know the other officer in the running for the same job was a decent man, with an excellent record. He must be so disappointed. Angry. I'm sure he is angry at being passed over for a woman. His whole career might have been dependent on the promotion, his family waiting, watching to see the triumph in his face when he reads the email. Or not.

Joy was never clever in the same way as Lucy, but as we all

watch, and wait, she seems to be gaining momentum with her flashbacks, putting the same jigsaw together. Will she remember what really happened? It will be interesting to see, after what I put her through, if her mind is strong enough to break through.

The story, parts of the story, about Emile's affair, and about the police finally putting together the missing girls and Joy's abductor. A potential serial killer. So sexy that story, as I knew it would be.

The news broke today, and she was suddenly trending on Twitter again. We were so proud. It was like the old days. We had something to get our teeth into, something tangible to tear apart once again. I couldn't resist looking at the pictures I took five years ago. Reliving the blood, the darkness, and the shadows give me a thrill of power. I broke her, and then I reformed her into someone else.

It was a harsh treatment, prescribed just for our Darling Joy, although I was impressed that she lasted out, that she fought me for as long as she did. Three months it took, to transform Joy Maddison into Mattie Woods. Three months of alternating drugs and brainwashing. Three long months of breaking down her spirit. It doesn't take long before the body craves artificial stimulants once you have it hooked. Every time she fought me, was stubborn or screamed for her kids, I plunged a needle back into her arm.

Once she managed to regain consciousness enough to stagger off the bed. I found her collapsed by the door and I was furious. Stupid girl! How could we ever trust one another again, and how did she think I could let her live a normal life if she wouldn't listen, wouldn't do as she was told?

I did a lot of research into the best techniques, which were basically based on the pain/reward principle. If you deprive someone of everything, including their dignity, it won't be long before they say what you want them to, do what you want them to. They become dependent on you for their basic needs, but also emotional needs. They will want to please you.

The physical transformation came early on and helped to break her. I admit I was exhausted after the sessions, and it was lucky I had someone to help me. Joy's fans have always worked best together. It was exciting to be creating our very own doll, from the wreckage of another.

Did you know social media is associated with brainwashing? It seems appropriate.

A true lesson from all of us to Darling Joy. But sent with XOX.

FORTY-EIGHT

"Emile, I need some time to process this. I told you last night," Joy said.

Her husband scowled at her, and her dad, who had just arrived, was leaning heavily on his stick in the hallway and looking anxious. "What's going on? Why don't you stay with me if you want, love, just until you feel more like your old self again."

Emile was watching her, his face shuttered, brown eyes cool, but finally he shrugged. "Whatever you feel is best. You always did get whatever you wanted, Joy, which is why I found it so hard to understand why you ran away."

"*Emile!*" her dad put in. "That's enough. She just needs some more time to adjust, that's all. What's happened?"

She took a deep breath and forced herself to approach her husband. "I'm not going anywhere. Let's sort this out. Dad, do mind getting yourself tea or something, while we just talk?"

"Of course." He still looked worried, but he left them alone in the vast, elegant hallway, with its large and slightly incongruous neon sign spelling LOVE hanging above the stairwell.

How had her fairy tale gone so wrong, Joy wondered, as she

stared at her husband, torn between a desire to run, to give up, or to stay and fight for the truth.

It had started last night, with her long-postponed confrontation of Emile and his little visits to Devonshire Place. Confidence boosted after a session with Dr Alores, she had decided this had gone on long enough. If there was going to be a chance her marriage might work, there needed to be an end to the secrets.

"How long have you been sleeping with Natasha?" she had asked, before he even had time to greet her.

He had set his wine glass down on the countertop. Despite her explaining it was easier for her if there was no alcohol in the house, he clearly didn't see why he shouldn't still enjoy a glass. As always she had fought to ignore the craving that rose deep in her stomach every time she heard a bottle open, heard the rich liquid poured into a glass, or caught sight of the alcohol and mixers, which were always served when the PR team came around.

It was a constant struggle, but by repeating inside her head, *one minute at a time*, she found she could get through it, and was ridiculously proud of herself when she went to bed each night, for sticking to her sobriety.

"How did you find out?"

"Phone tracker the very first night I was here. Do you remember I told you the kids came into my room, and you brushed it off as a nightmare?" She sighed. "I just want to know. Were having an affair, sleeping with her before I left, or is it a recent thing?"

"It's complicated."

"I'm sure."

"Don't try to make me feel bad, Joy, because I won't." He scowled at her. "It started *after* you left. She said being around here helped her grieve for you. We became close, but I didn't want it going official because we were still married. I was sure you were dead, but Frank, the kids and your sister, they were convinced of the opposite."

Joy turned her back on the wine and looked out of the window, into the evening mist. The leaves were changing from green to gold in the woods, and the unusually late summer heat-wave had given way to rain and thunderstorms. To be fair, it had been a tough situation for everyone. Why should he not have been allowed to move on? Dr Alores had been careful to remind her it was just as tough for everyone. But another thought niggled. Why had he been so sure she was dead?

"Joy, I was never sleeping with anyone else before, you need to believe that. You need to trust me, like I trusted you when you said nothing was going on with Reggie. At first, I went to break it off with Natasha the night you came home. I told her I needed space to find out who you were, and what you wanted – what we wanted." He paused to take a gulp of wine. "She went mad. Turns out she thinks I've been stringing her along all these years, waiting to find out what really happened. She thought now you were home I would finally have the closure I needed, get a divorce and be with her."

Joy, watching his face closely, found suddenly that it was more important that she could believe they had been happy before that fateful night. It had been real, Joy's life and her marriage, and the gossip queens of Brighton, the forums, the social media and beyond had been wrong. What happened from now on depended on what they could build out of the ruins of their relationship. It gave less credence to her running away, less credence to those gossipy bitches. Did Kate and Courtney really know, or had Natasha been wetting herself laughing, keeping her secret lover close to her chest, sure she was going to get him to herself at last.

The previous night had marked the return of her night-mares, and of the drawings she felt compelled to do, to move the darkness from her head into the light, into something tangible.

Terrible, dark drawings and violent flashbacks had her wondering if she was going mad.

Was she Joy or Mattie, or even Martha? The name popped up in her dreams. Sometimes she wasn't sure if she really had been a CHIS, had lived that life, had been the one responsible for Ned's arrest and subsequent conviction.

This was why she had booked an emergency visit to Dr Alores, who had reassured her perhaps now she was safe and healing physically any traumatic memories might be ready to come out.

Joy wasn't sure if she *was* safe. She hadn't received any more messages from Jono, the police had been helpful but evasive when she asked if they knew where he was yet. But equally she couldn't shake the feeling she was being watched, which then led to other feelings of paranoia, confusion as to who she really was, deep inside as well as on the brittle shell she presented to the outside world. She had tried to explain this to her therapist, who listened patiently.

"What are you seeing that is different than before?"

"The car. I have a flashback to the car, and it isn't hitting me or anything. I feel the metal or plastic on my thigh, but that's because I'm leaning against it... maybe leaning against the door talking to the driver."

"And who is the driver? Male or female?"

Joy shook her head. "I can't see. The flashbacks come in fragments and they're in colour, but the nightmares are black and white."

"Do you recognise the voice?" The doctor was tall and thin, her long legs elegantly crossed as she considered her patient. Her red hair was pulled back into a long swinging ponytail and her green eyes were steady and interested.

"No, it's the same as when I try to home in on the voice in the nightmares. But this one, in the car, I don't know if it's male or female." Joy's voice rose in frustration, and she clenched her fists in her lap. She was getting closer, but not close enough. And how could the police not have found Jono yet? Nor any more bodies. Perhaps he hadn't killed Maggie and Lucinda at all. Maybe the whole thing was just a jump too far, instead of the pattern Lucy had suggested.

"So, this person in the car. Could it potentially be a woman?" her therapist asked, breaking through her thoughts.

"Yes. But if I stopped to talk to someone the night I was abducted, they would have come forward. I was thinking... Could it have been Stephanie Coultas? Maybe Jono had help. I... I can't be sure, but I think there are two people in the car, maybe a man and a woman, which is why I can't work out who speaks, who is driving..."

"I can't speculate, and I know your logical self will be trying to sort this out, but if you can, just allow the images to come, in whatever order. Think of it as collecting pieces of a jigsaw puzzle. Once you have them all on the table, we can assemble the full picture."

Joy nodded. "It makes sense." She pushed her hair back. "You know what I'm now terrified of?"

"Tell me."

"What if I did all this myself. What if I somehow arranged to vanish and it went a bit wrong? Okay, it went a lot wrong," she admitted. "I know that's what Emile is thinking, at the back of his mind."

"Is there a reason you are starting to question yourself now?"

"I found some stuff under Joy's desk in the yoga room. There's a panel in the wall for air conditioning, and there was some stuff in there. Details of a villa in Spain and one in Ibiza, and some printouts of visa requirements to live in Spain. Why would I have kept those hidden?" Joy felt tears start again, "So when I had the flashback about the car, I wondered if I planned the whole thing. Emile has been a bit funny about the texts from Reggie that I had before I left or was taken. I really don't know if Joy, if I, was having an affair."

"Have you tried asking Reggie?"

"Yes, I spoke to him on the phone, and he said we were just friends. He sounds like a genuine bloke. He did say Emile was always very jealous and liked to check out my male friends."

"Do you find that odd? Controlling?"

"Not really, I don't think. I have found out he lost a lot of deals, you know, endorsements and things, after the gossip about him having an affair. That was around the same time as Joy... as I signed the deal with Summer Style and later with Elite." She considered, relaxing. This was the only space in her life where she didn't have to pretend, didn't have to keep anyone happy, consider anyone else's feelings. The relief was so great she always left her sessions in a semi-catatonic state.

"What about your husband's affairs? Has he brought them up? Denied them maybe?"

"I suppose I've been funny about the fact Emile was sleeping with Natasha. She implied they had been having an affair before I was abducted," Joy added.

"That's a lot to process, but don't assume you were going to run away. It's perfectly normal to explore options. Perhaps you were feeling trapped and were thinking of the future. Maybe you wanted to keep it a secret until you had decided if you really wanted to go. Perhaps you had been thinking of taking your whole family abroad."

"Oh. I didn't think of that," Joy said. She immediately felt slightly better. Maybe she had been planning to present her ideas to Emile, take the kids and her husband to live in the sun somewhere. After all, Emile was a fluent Spanish speaker, and she knew they had holidayed in Ibiza several times.

Dr Alores glanced at her watch, and made some notes on her laptop, "Joy, I can understand you feel confused, frustrated, and that is perfectly natural. The trauma you have been through, not just physically, but also mentally, will take years to come to terms with. Dissociation amnesia is different for everyone, and personal to your own unique experience."

Joy was frowning again. Her thoughts always flooded out here, in this quiet room, high above the busy main road through Hove. All her worries, her bewilderment, could be left in this house. She was free to be her messy, sometimes tear-stained self, and to allow her mind to jump from one topic to another without fear of judgement. "Then there was the text from Jono! The police haven't found him yet."

"Yes, you mentioned that on Monday. It must be terrifying to think he is out there, but he can't get to you, Joy. Again, I understand how confusing this is, and I wonder if you need to lay down some ground rules with your family. It is very hard for them too, but you can help by explaining what makes you feel safe."

"Like what? Because if I mention anything out of the ordinary my family are starting to think I'm paranoid. Hell, I'm starting to think I'm going crazy at times." Her words seemed to hang in the air between them, branded with fire and crackling with truth.

FORTY-NINE

Her therapist frowned but said nothing.

"I know logically nobody could get in, and we're spending a fortune on security, but I don't feel *safe*." Joy thought of the bathroom window, the rearranged clothes on the back of her bedroom door and her missing shoe. Little things that she kept telling herself were nothing. But always, there was the sense of someone watching, waiting, the hairs on the back of her neck standing up, or a cool breath on her cheek. Was she going mad?

"Less speculation, and more routine, but not routine like the full work schedule you described. From what you have told me, everyone managed the honeymoon period after you first returned fairly well, but since then, there has been too much pushing, too much baggage for you all to carry. You need peace and quiet, and your family need to understand we may never know the full story."

"So, what should I do?"

"It's up to you. How are the kids doing now?"

"They seem okay. It's so much for them to take in, but Daisy especially seems to have accepted me back. Bertie is a bit anxious and distant."

"Do you think it would be harmful to them if you were to, say, stay with your sister for a weekend, try to break the cycle of negativity?"

"I... I don't know. Maybe. I don't want them all to think I've gone away again." She considered, coming to a swift conclusion. "No, I couldn't. I promised them I wouldn't go away, and I've only been back for a few months."

"As I said, these things can take months, years, to piece together. You and your family and friends have the added stress of not only being in the media spotlight, but also the police investigations, and all the unresolved family issues. Put together, Joy, none of this is good for you. Potentially, I'd even go as far as to say, it's a ticking time bomb." Her round face was very serious, wide green eyes candid and concerned. "I want to give you my mobile number and I want you to promise to call if you start to feel you can't cope for any reason, or if you have any more nightmares and flashbacks revealing further information that shocks you."

When Joy got home, as usual after a session, she felt calmer, more in control. She found Emile in the kitchen, making eggs and toast for the kids, who were watching TV in the living room, sprawled across the rugs with the cats, and two new additions: sausage dogs called Minnie and Roo.

Her husband had his back to her, and she could tell by the set of his shoulders he was tense. Marshalling her courage, her newfound strength, she walked up to him and laid a gentle hand on his arm, until he turned and faced her. "Emile, I'm sorry for what you have all been through, and I'm sorry you might have a sneaky suspicion it was all my fault, that I deliberately planned to run away. I don't know what happened yet, but I am trying my hardest to find out."

He said nothing, shrugged and washed up a couple of mugs, drying them with exaggerated care.

"Emile, don't blame me for this please. I *want* to remember."

He moved away, gently pushing the connecting door shut. "We can't be sure. You get all stirred up about me and Natasha, but for five years you've been sleeping with someone else. Maybe that's what you wanted?"

"It wasn't!" But she couldn't know that, and he obviously didn't believe her.

"Maybe, Joy, it's a case of you don't want to remember. You've had your adventure and it went badly wrong. By a series of coincidences, you are home, but now you don't seem to want to be here either. Make up your fucking mind!"

"You don't want me back." It was out before she could stop it.

"What do you mean?"

"I heard you talking to Lucy that second week I was home. You said I was rough, with my scars, tattoos and my limp."

For the first time in days, she saw tenderness in his eyes. "And if you had carried on eavesdropping, idiot, you would have heard me say none of those things matter because inside you are still the Joy I love."

"Am I?"

"Yes, but if you keep pushing me away, what am I supposed to think?"

"I just need time. I know the girls were trying to wind me up, and I believe you about Natasha, I really do. But all this extra drama, it's keeping me from focusing on finding out what really happened. And I am going to focus on the nightmares, because they seem to be triggering my flashbacks now. If I have a really bad night, the next day I get more memories back," she told him, a rush of fear and determination keeping her voice steady.

"That's great. I mean, look, I think we can only get past this if we find out what really happened when you went missing. I need to know, but you do too. Because otherwise, I'm not your husband, I'm just some random good-looking guy." He was watching her with concern. "Be careful though, won't you? I know you said you've been thinking someone is watching you again, but I, we, are concerned you might have a breakdown or something. Okay, I heard you talking to Bobby. Talk to me as well? Please!"

"Now who's been eavesdropping?" She smiled, relaxing, feeling what? Not a bond or a memory, but not fear and cold either. Perhaps it was a start. Although she was slightly annoyed with his remark about her sanity. Nobody knew more than she did about treading that delicate line.

From behind her Nuala started purring and she reached out a hand automatically, fingers caressing the soft fur, feeling a little damp nose nudging her wrist, turning to look at her cat. Nuala was in the basket by the radiator, but she looked up from washing her kittens to meet Joy's eyes. Yes, there was hope, but she would need to face whatever demons were haunting her and that would mean screwing up her courage and allowing her mind to take her back to those dark places, to the man in the mask.

The sun went in abruptly and as she looked out of the window; dark clouds were gathering over the woods, which were now turning gold and orange in their seasonal plumage. Autumn was here and she was still struggling, still trying so hard. *You can do this.* A tiny spatter of rain hit the windowpane, making her jump.

"Hello, Joy, I didn't realise you were back already." Frank pottered in the back door, a handful of plant clippings in his hands. "It's getting quite cold now. I think even with the roof pulled over it might be time for the kids to say goodbye to the swimming pool for this year."

She had forgotten he was here. Again. Her dad was often around the house and garden. He was a comforting, non-threatening presence and much in the same way she felt protective of her children, she hated the thought of anything upsetting Frank.

Now her dad was smiling at her. Emile was still close enough for her to feel the warmth of his body, but she remained by the window, frozen in time, suddenly engulfed by a sudden tidal wave of memories.

"Joy?"

Frank sat down on the window seat, next to her. "Did you remember something?" His voice was so hopeful, so concerned, and she wanted to scream because everyone kept asking the same question. "Emile?"

Emile was slipping an arm around her shoulders, saying her name, gently but urgently. She couldn't speak, couldn't breathe, as the waves crashed over her, drenching her in pictures, in memories.

And the memories were not of Jono, or Emile or her children. They went much further back:

Two little girls sitting at the kitchen table while their parents toasted some celebration with glasses of wine, and the rain battered the windows.

Shouting and arguments later on as Lucy slipped into her bed and told Joy to go to sleep. A scream and door slamming. Later, much later, her dad crying, saying it was all his fault. There was a car too, the sound of a car engine revving, driving away fast over gravel.

After that the bright sunlight that beat down on the funeral party in the churchyard as she and her sister gripped each other's hands tightly and stared at their shiny black shoes. Tears dropped on the shoes, sliding onto the wet grass.

"Joy?" Emile's voice was panicky, and Frank was asking about calling an ambulance. "Joy, come back, darling..."

Gradually, focusing on their voices, on the pressure of her

husband's arm on her back, she began to come back to reality, to swim to shore. She realised she was kneeling, palms pressed against the stone tiles, as if she was desperate to ground herself.

"Emile?" Her voice was a thread of a whisper, and she was so tired, so bone tired as though she had indeed been struggling to survive a stormy sea.

"Thank God. Joy? What happened?"

Instead of answering, she just sank back against the soft cushions of the window seat. What secrets was her memory going to bring to the surface? They brought her a mug of tea and she managed to tell them she had remembered some of her childhood. A big chunk, and yes it was good memories, happy ones. She was just shocked, and yes, she would ring Dr Alores and tell her, no she was fine now, just very tired...

FIFTY

Somehow she managed to get through dinner, brushing off their concern with a hopefully plausible explanation. "I remembered me and Lucy as kids, and then being here, right in this spot when the kids were little. Nothing bad, it's just the way the memories come, it's exhausting. Sorry, everyone."

"Did you remember us?" Poppy asked, eyes bright and hopeful.

Joy felt bad for lying but told herself it would only make her daughter happy, and in her heart that was what she wanted more than anything, for them all to be happy and safe. "Yes, I did, when you were little toddlers."

After dinner, in the special two hours she had carved out for her and her children, she played with them, read stories and drew cat pictures. She had come to treasure this golden time, when Ella wasn't hanging around, when she could concentrate on getting to know them again, on building their relationship.

Emile popped his head around the door, just as she was starting to think about bath times, saying he was off to meet a couple of friends for a quick drink. "Get to bed when the kids are asleep. The more rest you get I expect the more you will find your memory comes back." He smiled at her. "Night, kids, be good for Mummy."

The front door banged. She didn't question whether he was off to see Natasha, she was still struggling to bind her soul back together and understand what she had seen in her head. Mattie and Joy currently seemed to be at polar opposites again.

"Can you read my story in the bath?" Bertie asked. "And can we have *Stick Man* again?"

Joy forced herself to be normal, to smile, to read stories. Actually, reading the stories was also so precious. Little faces entranced by tales of dragons (Poppy) and Pokémon (Daisy and Bertie). Bertie also insisted on *Stick Man* in the bath, which caused mutiny from the girls, who said their brother had had *two* stories and they'd only had one each.

As soon as the lights were out, and she had said goodnight to Ella, who emerged briefly to ask if Joy needed anything, before retiring to her own suite of rooms, Joy called Dr Alores. The brief conversation reassured her. Her therapist seemed pleased to hear childhood memories were resurfacing, even if they were traumatic.

"It is part of the healing process. It is probable you have unresolved traumas relating to your mother's death and that would be perfectly natural."

"You mean every single traumatic thing might just come back to me in date order?" Joy asked, torn between relief and horror. What else might her mind be harbouring? So many secrets, so many memories.

"Not necessarily. It might just be the traumas where your mind feels there are things to resolve. Childhood trauma is quite often something we are unable to process at the time, and losing your mother at such a young age, so dramatically, must have made what I would call a psychological footprint on your mind." She paused. "That isn't a technical term, by the way, but I find it a useful visualisation tool for my clients."

Joy thanked her therapist, ended the call, and after a second's hesitation called her sister.

"What's up?" Lucy answered immediately, almost as though she had been expecting Joy.

"You said our mum died in a car accident?"

"Yes, when I was ten and you would have been seven. Why?"

"I remembered something," Joy said and told her sister what she had seen. "You said, on the timeline you made for me, that she had crashed the car going out that night."

"Yes." There was a pause like Lucy was trying to work something out. "They had a row, and she ran out, got in the car and had an accident, went off the road into the woods. I didn't put all that on the timeline, because it's bad enough I had to put she died."

"Was she drunk?" Joy thought of the full glasses, and the sound of a smashing bottle in her memory.

Another hesitation, as Lucy apparently probed her own memory, before she admitted reluctantly, "Yes. Dad said she used to drink a lot in secret and when she got her promotion, he asked her to stop because after everything she had worked for, she could sabotage it if anyone found out she was practically an alcoholic."

"She was? So, she ran out on him?" Joy felt the panic rising in her chest, hot and choking in her throat. What if her memories were showing history repeating itself? "Lucy, did I used to drink too much? Take drugs?"

"No! You asked me that before. Are you comparing Mum to yourself? You asked me before and I can honestly say I never saw you take any kind of drugs apart from the bit of puff at the festival that got you arrested. But not hard drugs, not even pills when we used to go to wild parties. I was thinking about this the other day. You might have got drunk occasionally, but you were nowhere near an alcoholic. You were normal, Joy. You weren't perfect, but you weren't bad either. Do you get that?"

"Okay." Joy looked around her peaceful bedroom, relaxing slightly until her gaze fell on a pair of fluffy slippers. On what should have been a pair of fluffy slippers. One was on the floor and the other was on her dressing table, loaded up with designer lipsticks, like a bizarre boat from one of the kids' books. What the hell? She whipped round as a faint chill of air slipped across her shoulders. The window to the balcony was open just a crack, allowing the draught and a tiny spray of rain to decorate the wooden sill. The darkness against the pale wooden mantel looked like a spray of blood. Joy wrapped her arms around her knees, huddled in bed, all her brave decisions made in the kitchen tonight just leaking away.

Lucy was talking again. "Maybe you're remembering this because it's linked to trauma. Perhaps your mind is starting to fill in the gaps, starting with an early traumatic event and working forward."

"That's kind of what Dr Alores said. Do you think the therapy might be working?" Joy couldn't work out why she felt so scared. There was nobody in the room, for God's sake. "I promised Emile I would try really hard to write everything down and to draw it when it comes into my head. Perhaps this is the beginning? Starting with Mum?"

Lucy was silent for a moment. "Before you disappeared, you were working on an ancestry project online. I think you got sponsored to do it, but I remember Dad giving you some old pictures of various grandparents."

"Did I say anything about Mum's death?" Joy was intrigued now, anticipating all her memories returning, banishing the shadows.

"Not that I recall, but you were asking where she might have been going, the night she ran away. You were very inter-ested, but said you were waiting on a few photos before you showed me the whole project. You said Mum's family had been really rich, and you were gutted we weren't related to any royalty."

A thought struck her, something chiming in her mind with Lucy's words. "Hang on, I'm going downstairs." She padded across the landing and down into the hallway.

Joy put the phone between ear and shoulder, sat down on the sofa and quickly opened her MacBook. It was her old one, returned by the police after the initial investigation, still containing all her files and search history.

"Sorry, I just had an idea. Listen..." She relayed the findings to her sister, before she stopped at one particular document. Joy, *she*, had made notes. It was a message from her old self to her new self and gave her the weirdest feeling. As she read it through twice, she found herself frozen amongst the comfy sofa cushions, listening to the rain drumming on the windows. Shock made her lips numb, but she managed to get the words out.

"Lucy, can you come over?"

FIFTY-ONE

"What do you think I was doing?"

Lucy had hardly had time to take off her coat when her sister dragged her into the living room and shoved the MacBook under her nose.

There was a document open onscreen, with just a few pages of notes, but the final line read:

WHAT IF MUM WAS DEAD?

Lucy wrinkled her nose, brushing stray raindrops from her cheeks. "I don't understand either. I mean, Mum *is* dead. The notes are just jottings of what happened the night Mum died. They aren't part of your ancestry project at all. Is there anything else?"

"I can't find anything," Joy said. "Sorry, do you want tea or anything? I've dragged you out in this shitty weather to show you something that doesn't even make sense. Emile is out with some mates, and I was just so confused."

"It's fine. It's not like I have a wild social life and I'm working tomorrow so I wasn't planning on hitting any bars."

Lucy smiled at her. Actually, she felt pleased Joy had called her first, before even telling Emile. It was tough getting to know the new Joy, and she had tried so hard not to crowd her. Trust was earned and she knew better than anyone else in the family what her sister had been through.

DC Alia Mattez, still working on The Unit, and shaping up to be one of the best handlers she had, often asked after Mattie/Joy in private, and expressed the confident view that Jono would be caught if he was still alive. *If*. The Unit had eyes and ears open, and the underground was where you got the real information.

"Tea would be great," she added, and watched as Joy went into the kitchen. Nuala leapt up onto the sofa, purring, and Lucy stroked her soft ears. "Where are your babies?"

Overhearing as she came back with tea and half a chocolate cake balanced on a tray, Joy laughed. "She leaves them to fight it out with the puppies sometimes now, so she can come and snuggle up."

After an hour poring over Joy's notes, and Lucy providing as much information as she could on their mum's death, they still hadn't got any further.

"I can't think why you would have written that, or even what you might have meant," Lucy said eventually, yawning.

"If only I could *remember*." Joy frowned in frustration.

She was looking more like the old Joy now, Lucy thought, studying her sister. She was putting on weight, her cheeks plumping out, and a better diet had given her skin some of the old glow. She wasn't wearing make-up though. The old version of her sister would wear make-up even if she was walking downstairs. "How's it going with Emile? Dad said you had a fight yesterday."

"We did. Sorry, I meant to text you, but I didn't want to bother you at work, and this is tough on you too," Joy said, now cross-legged on the sofa.

"Do you think you'll be able to work things out?"

"I think we might. It was almost as though we needed to stop tip-toeing around each other and clear the air."

"That's good then. And no more texts from Jono?"

Joy shook her head. Outside the rain intensified and a rumble of thunder brought both dogs into the living room. "It's okay. Poor babies. I don't know why but they hate thunder. Honey's probably still out hunting, and even the kittens don't mind at all."

Lucy sensed her sister didn't want to discuss Jono and changed the subject back to their mother. "I wonder if you just wrote it wrong. Maybe it's meant to say, 'What if Mum wasn't dead?'"

Joy frowned. "You think maybe doing the ancestry project just made me emotional, missing her or something?"

"Maybe. I'm not sure you need anything else to worry about just now." Her sister had told her about the misplaced slippers, arranged in a rather odd fashion, and all the other things going missing. Frank, who had found Joy's Jimmy Choos out in the garden a couple of days ago, ruined by the rain, had expressed the opinion her mind was under so much strain she was in danger of a breakdown. He suggested the paranoia might also be as a result of her drug use. And then he had bustled into the kitchen to bake another lemon sponge cake.

It was past midnight when Lucy finally left Joy's house, but she woke early the next morning for a 6:00am shift. The Informant Unit was running well, but her thoughts kept turning to what Joy had said last night. Her own memory of the night their mother died was hazy, but she thought she could vaguely remember telling her sister to go back to bed, when she woke to see Joy at the bedroom window.

There was an email update from DI Armstrong on Jono

McQueen. The last sighting appeared a week before Joy had said he disappeared. He was caught on a street cam crossing the road opposite the fish market. The image was blurry, but he was carrying a large rucksack, lending credence to Joy's theory he had run away in response to the DNA discovery in Hove.

Ned Carthy had been found guilty on all charges, but although he had been questioned extensively about his relationship with Jono, he had admitted nothing, and claimed he hadn't seen him since 'maybe June sometime'. There was no proof to tie him to any foul play, and no evidence anyway that Jono was dead. He was, however, now linked to the body of Elise Vorunchuk, who had entered the UK illegally via the port. The theory was that Joy had unknowingly transferred some DNA to the dead girl's clothing, when she had helped with the landing of Ned's illegal cargo. Which had raised further questions of criminal charges against Joy Maddison.

But we know she was under duress during this time, and that will be taken into account...

the DI added reassuringly at the bottom of his email.

Her phone rang and she answered quickly, eyes still on her computer screen. "DI Merry. Oh, hi, Jack, I just read your email."

"Hi, Lucy, just a quick one. We have found a witness who claims she saw Jono McQueen and Stephanie Coultas together the night Joy disappeared. She also claims Jono was a regular at the Pink Pussycat Club, and always asked for Stephanie to dance for him."

"Right." Lucy took a moment to process this. "But she didn't come forward when Stephanie also disappeared, a few weeks later?"

"No. She was scared. She works as bar staff at the club, and says she never linked the events before. Stephanie wasn't a particular friend of hers, and she only made a statement because we were back asking questions. So, who knows?"

"Thanks, Jack. Interesting. I suppose you'll want to talk to Joy?"

"Yes, I've got a couple going over to her place now."

Lucy hesitated, and finally just thanked him again and hung up. She pushed her chair back and went in search of coffee. Had Stephanie *and* Jono picked up Joy that night? Had she got into a car with strangers? She might have felt less threatened by a woman, and perhaps the pair had staged a breakdown. The tiny office kitchen produced a caffeine hit and she sipped gratefully, still thinking hard.

Did Joy know Jono and Stephanie before she vanished? She wouldn't have got into a car with strangers, unless... Unless there *had* been an accident. A minor one, say, planned to coincide with Joy running across the road. Maybe Jono said to Joy she could sit in the passenger seat while Stephanie called an ambulance.

It wouldn't be just chance he was driving past the woods where she ran. Everyone on YouTube knew her route. And Jono wasn't the person her sister had remembered and described, the cheeky lad who was the life and soul of every party. He wasn't even the same person who had worked as a CHIS, the power-hungry, small-time dealer arrogant little sod her handlers had described.

He was a man with a dangerous obsession, and he could easily have planned everything that night, kept a famous face hidden in the city where she was best known for five whole years. And he was still out there.

FIFTY-TWO

Emile poured Joy a glass of ginger beer and passed it across the kitchen table. The autumn wind howled outside, swirling leaves and debris against the glass doors, but she felt more settled than she had in ages.

"How did it go with the police?" he asked carefully.

She had not wanted him present when the two officers arrived at the house, and the revelation that Jono had known Stephanie didn't surprise her. She had already fixed in her mind the woman had somehow, maybe entirely unintentionally, played a part in her abduction.

"It was okay. I mean, they know I didn't do anything wrong, and they don't think I'll face any charges because there is no proof I videoed Stephanie's death and burial." She glanced at him, noting the relief in his expression, mirroring her own. Quickly, she summarised what they had told her about Jono and Stephanie. "Afterwards, I started thinking about... you know, the future."

His face was blank now, but his eyes were hopeful. The two sausage dog puppies were snuffling around the corner by the fridge. "Minnie! Roo! Stop it and go and lie down."

The pair gave him a baleful look and slunk off to their designer dog beds. From behind, in the cat basket, Nuala gave a faint hiss. She disproved of the puppies but they, in turn, seemed to acknowledge a superior species and kept a suitably low profile when she or her kittens stalked past. Honey, the Siamese, after initially trying to eat both dogs whole, had also now accepted them, but with clear disdain and frequent protests.

"Sorry, what were you saying?" Emile prompted.

Joy tried to focus. "It's been months now, and I need to work out what to do."

"Okay."

He wasn't going to make this easy for her, but she continued slowly, watching his frown, his eyes fixed on her hers. "I think, if it's okay with you, I'm ready to try to make sense of my new life."

"With me?"

A flash of emotion across his otherwise still face. Randomly she remembered he had also been good at card games, with his poker face. *She remembered!* The jolt of triumph this induced gave her the courage to carry on. It was up to her to make things right between them, to give him the choice. "Of course with you, idiot. As long as you meant it when you said you really didn't want to be with Natasha?"

"She can have as many tantrums as she likes, sell as many stories as she can, but I'm not leaving my family. Now that I have you home again, it feels so right. Don't you think?" He leant across the table and kissed her gently on the lips.

And it felt... It felt okay, but he immediately drew back as though he'd done the wrong thing. Joy put her fingers to his cheek. Still nothing like a tidal wave of love hearts and rainbows, but maybe the flicker of attraction that was there could be nurtured, as her therapist had suggested, into something real, something differently shaped but just as meaningful.

Her husband was also a great cook. After casserole and apple crumble, comfort food, as Emile put it, they sat curled on the sofa, him flicking through the channels, her curled against a cushion with her feet tucked underneath. "What would you like to see? A movie?"

"What was my favourite series? I must have some catching up to do." She smiled, feeling herself more relaxed with him than she had ever been.

"You were into *Silent Witness*, any police detective series, and anything like a crime thriller. But you loved an old school movie night with the kids. You know, popcorn and pick'n'mix with a dash of Disney thrown in."

"I might give the crime stuff a miss for a bit," Joy suggested. "Pick something easy to watch."

After the movie, they had coffee in the kitchen, just talking into the night, naturally and easily.

"What about a new career? You mentioned art?" he questioned. "Your drawings are amazing."

Joy considered, sipping her drink slowly. "I'm not sure. I don't think I could possibly go back to vlogging. What would I say? And Lucy said I was determined to go back to presenting, that I loved the local radio show, but I don't remember why I loved it..."

"Up to you. Everything is up to you, but I will support you one hundred per cent if you do decide to go back and work on your channel. The opportunities you were offered were amazing, and I'm not going to pretend the money didn't come in useful, but if you want to be an artist instead, or even just keep it as a hobby that's okay too." He smiled at her, put his mug down, reached for the stash of biscuits and added casually, "Have you done any more drawings from your nightmares?"

Joy wrinkled her nose, resenting the intrusion into a nice normal conversation, but she answered readily, "Some. I don't have any more to add, and I seem to keep drawing the same

scenes over and over. Dr Alores said I could be close to a breakthrough after I started remembering scenes from childhood."

"Like your memory has been kickstarted?" Emile froze, his
hands gripping the back of the chair. "Really?"

"Yes. Emile, about my channel... Kate said I was thinking
about giving it all up."

His shoulders relaxed a little, and his mouth twisted.
"Okay... Well, I wouldn't believe everything Kate says."

"You don't like her either? Lucy hates her," Joy told him.

Emile fiddled with the gold link bracelet on his wrist, not
meeting her eyes. "It's awkward, because she was your best
friend at one time. You met her at a blogger event in London for
a make-up brand, and after that you seemed to be suddenly
BFFs. But I always felt she was jealous because you hit the big
time and she didn't. She liked to lash out after you left, sell
stories. They all did. Georgia was the only one who seemed
genuinely upset, and she kept her distance. Have you spoken to
Georgia yet?"

"No, she sent a sweet gift and we texted, so she has my new
number, but she's been away in Dubai for work." Kate fragmented and reformed in front of her eyes. Joy didn't feel quite
so relaxed and sure of herself anymore, and the conversation
halted abruptly. She felt like she was hovering on the edge of a
panic attack. Had it been the mention of her channel, the
money or Kate? "Would *you* want me to start vlogging again?"

Emile turned away, looking out of the window, his tone
abruptly distant. "It would be up to you. You would have total
control, but the way I see it, you worked hard to get up there,
and someone took it all away from you. Now you're back you
have the opportunity to make some serious money, maybe. A
book deal, endorsements... We talked about getting the finances
sorted for the kids, paying off the mortgage and buying a little
place in Ibiza. Just a secluded bolthole on the north of the
island."

"We did? I like the idea of a hut on the beach," she told him, pleased to have this particular niggle settled in her mind. "It's whether I want to take back the kind of pressure that, according to Dad and Lucy, nearly finished me last time."

"You were stressed, yes, but you enjoyed a lot of it. You were, you are, a businesswoman, and I was proud of everything you achieved." He turned back to face her and shrugged. "Everyone has part of their work they like and parts they don't. You need to find a balance. And not all your influencer friends were bitches. You had... you have real friends in that community and outside it. I would guess they don't like to reach out right now, because it's clear you have had so much to deal with, but when you're ready, they're there."

That was nice, she thought. Maybe she hadn't been such a bad judge of character after all.

"The reality show I've been offered... Natasha has been offered it too."

Joy heard her own breath shorten, and she waited to process this bit of information before she answered, now was not the time to get mad. "Do we need money?" she asked him outright now. "I mean are we in trouble financially? That's the *only* reason why you would be considering doing a reality show with Natasha, isn't it?"

He glanced down at the table, finally met her eyes and nodded as though relieved. "I took my eye off the ball after you were gone, carried on spending, and the bills have been piling up. But I can sell one of the restaurants rather than cause you to make a bad decision. We have a bit of time to decide."

Joy nodded, put her hands tentatively on his arms, and snuggled against him, enjoying the feeling of peace that swept over her, and as usual, doubly appreciating her full belly, warm blanket and the huge house sheltering them from the autumn storms. He hugged her tightly, almost fiercely.

"As long as you push Natasha out the boat on the way to the

island and personally hold her under until she drowns, I don't care if you want to do it. If it's the money and you hate the thought of it, we'll work something out. I have a lot of offers just waiting for me to be ready to pick through." She smiled up at him. "And AJ is desperate for his cut."

He was laughing at her. "And she's back!"

"What do you mean?"

"Every day you get more and more like yourself. Joy, you seem to have this weird notion old Joy was some kind of meek, mild, sweet girl, who was basically taken in by everyone, used and abused until she couldn't take it anymore. She wasn't. *You* weren't. She, and *you*, were and *are* feisty, funny, sour, sweet, crazy, sane and everything in between."

Although they paused on the landing as they went to bed, and Emile pulled her in for a gentle kiss, by silent consent they both went their separate ways towards their bedrooms.

Joy, as usual, couldn't resist peeking in on her children, smiling, her heart hurting a little for what she had missed, as she watched them sleep for a few minutes. When she made her way to bed, she smiled to hear the comforting noises of the wind, the patter of rain, the house creaking slightly. The storm had rolled inland and outside the clouds were starting to clear. The chill of autumn was making itself felt at night now, but she was lucky. Warm and dry with her family.

Annoyingly, she couldn't find her bed socks. She was sure she had put them neatly on her duvet cover, ready for tonight. After a fruitless hunt she gave up and slipped between the crisp sheets.

She woke at 1:00am, finding herself sitting on the edge of her bed, with no idea how she got there. Convinced someone was in the room with her, she could hear her own gasps of fear, and became aware she was flailing around in the darkness, as though she could beat off the intruder.

As awareness crept slowly back, so did the memories. Unable to do anything but ride out the torrent of colourful images, she sat hunched, gripping her knees, shoulders tensed, watching herself.

She was running in the woods, and she stopped to cross the road onto the next footpath. Instead of passing, the car pulled up and the driver leant out the open window. She heard herself laugh, talk to him.

A woman laughed too. Pretty, with long blonde hair falling across her shoulders. . She heard herself ask a question, then she walked around to the passenger side and got in the car. It was hot and her bare legs stuck to the seat.

The memory changed to another car, another woman sitting where she was in the passenger seat, but this time she wasn't in the car, she was watching from her bedroom window. The weather was rainy, and it was night. A Halloween pumpkin sat next to the gate, and she watched as the car pulled away with the woman slumped in the passenger seat.

Joy felt like she was on a surfboard, riding one huge wave after another, finally missing her moment and being thrown, tumbling underwater, spinning and gasping for air.

She was back in the other car, in the blinding sunlight. It was evening but so hot still. Joy reached for her seat belt, and as she did so, she felt a sharp scratch on her upper arm. An insect bite? She turned in surprise, batting at her arm, expecting a wasp or horsefly, but the woman in the back seat seemed to be shocked, also staring at Joy's arm, asking a question of the man. Terror and disbelief flooding her body, her mind and she began to struggle, to call out. Finally, there was acceptance as her body, her mind, slid into unconsciousness, slumping against the hot metal of the car door, the sweaty seat. The smell of leather and strong aftershave lulled her away into dreamworld and she could hear the man laughing. He was laughing, excited, triumphant.

As soon as she could walk, Joy headed for the airy room at the top of the house, desperate to pick up her pencils. On her way upstairs, she found herself jumping at shadows, wincing from the contact of her bare feet on the wooden floorboards. The door to her room was shut. She froze. She always left the door open.

Joy put unsteady fingers to the handle, afraid for a moment it had been locked. She pushed it, and in a reckless rush of courage forced herself to step through. The room was empty, and, now the storm had passed, was flooded with the pale wash of moonlight. There was nobody there.

Quickly, she moved to her table, clicked on the little desktop light, and picked up her pad, drawing, sketching fast and furious.

After half an hour she had the woman from the car on that hot summer evening. Stephanie Coultas. She also had the woman from the other car. A car from a different time in her life. Her mother. But the driver of both cars remained as a half profile. Two cars. One shadowy entity.

FIFTY-THREE

When, eventually, she finished drawing, she sat down in the corner of the room, head on her knees, arms wrapped around her thighs. Invisible in the shadows.

Joy stayed hunched in the same position for a long time, almost afraid to move, even though her memories had slowed to a mere trickle and were just a confusing montage of playing with her kids, drinking shots with Emile and zipping up a pink dress.

When she finally uncurled herself, she snapped the lights fully on, half expecting the figures from her mind to be present in the room. As Dr Alores had instructed, she reached for the notepad on her desk to write down what she had remembered. But her fingers were stiff and slow from drawing and her whole body ached. In frustration she threw the pad across the room.

If the notepad didn't work, she was supposed to record on her mobile, but her phone would be in in her bedroom, where she had left it. Instead, her drawing would have to suffice: a message to herself from herself.

She rubbed her forehead, confused, and clambered to her

feet. Her drawings looked like a storyboard for a movie. Each one was intricate and detailed, and they followed in chronological order. The first strip was of her mother: in the kitchen drinking wine, in the car in the passenger seat, head lolling, then her gravestone.

The second strip was herself: running through the woods, in the car with Stephanie, and a man. Was she sure it was a man? Her drawing showed, for the first time, his hair was touching his shoulders. Jono had favoured the look, so it shouldn't come as a total surprise. In her next drawing she was in the room, lying on a bed. Again, this was the first time she had been able to draw what had happened from an outsider's point of view. Tears were trickling down her cheeks as she looked at the woman in the bed. The last picture was another shock. Two people, a back view so no faces, were bending over the bed, while the woman who lay helpless had her head turned to the side, lolling unconscious in the same way as her mum's had.

Two.

Was it because they had been talking about their mother that she had become confused, merging the alternate reality with what had happened to her? There was no question in her mind now that she had been abducted. She had been taken. Had she met Jono before then? Of course, she must have done. He had been a superfan, he told her so. If she had met him at events, perhaps she was familiar enough with him to have sat in his passenger seat. Had he been giving her a lift?

And Stephanie? She had been part of it. Perhaps that was why she had been killed, or perhaps it was just because he didn't need to pretend anymore, he had the real Joy Maddison now. Stephanie had been bait, and perhaps the others just practice.

But her mum? That didn't make sense at all. Her mum had driven off and crashed her car herself. There had been nobody else in the car with her. Had there? She looked at her drawings. The car was black in the summer scene, her abduction scene, a little like the black BMW Emile had been loaned to promote once.

In the other drawing, the one with her mum, the car was black too, but old and a little shabby. In the memory she had seemed to know the car, so assumed it must have been the family car her mum took.

As the clock on wall showed 4:36am she stood and stretched, exhausted. After carefully leaving the door ajar behind her, she began to walk back to her room, passing another spare bedroom as she did so. She stopped, looked back. This bedroom had the balcony too, and there was someone standing on it, in the moonlight, their back to the open glass door, cigarette smoke drifting across the night air.

Joy froze, her breath coming in jerky little gasps, fists clenched as if to defend herself from an attack. Surely it couldn't be Jono?

It was impossible to tell if the figure was male or female, but the figure looked small and slight and this gave her the confidence to tackle it. Silently, she crept across the room, adrenalin buzzing around her bloodstream, giving her a much-needed hit of energy.

Who the hell was it? Joy reached the doorway and breathed in the chilly night air, gasping as the figure cursed and spun around to face her. On some level she registered that at least she wasn't the only one getting shocks tonight. Her heart was still hammering and her limbs shaking, she leant briefly against the doorframe, trying to recover her composure.

"Hello, Ella," she said.

"Shit! Joy, you freaked me out. You look like a ghost." Ella had one hand pressed to her heart, the other gripping the balcony rail. At her feet a cigarette smouldered.

"Put that out," Joy said sharply, and the girl obediently ground out the cigarette with her foot. "Sorry I scared you, but it might be time for us to have a talk." The terror that had been flooding her body had turned to anger.

Ella was scowling at her, pretty features contorted, her red-gold hair scooped up in a pink clip, strands escaping to frame her face. "Fine."

As Joy leant on the balcony rail next to Ella, the night air was cool on her face, and she could hear the buzz of insects, the faint noise of traffic on the road in front of the house. A siren was blaring somewhere in the distance.

"So what's the problem?" Ella asked at last.

"I know you've been moving my stuff, I know you don't like me" – Joy was pleased to hear how calm and steady her voice was, as guesses became a certainty – "but I don't actually care. You might have a crush on my husband, but you are employed to look after my children." Ella said nothing, but Joy could see anger, hurt and resentment painted all over her face.

She continued, "So now you have a choice: you can grow up, suck it up and behave like an adult with a well-paid job, or you can leave next week."

Silence for a long beat, before Ella pulled a packet of ciga-rettes out of her pocket, extracted one with a shaking hand and snapped the lighter. After she had taken a long drag, she spoke. "You're right, I was screwing with you. I can't say I'm sorry because it feels so weird that you just walked out on Emile, your kids, this life. Then you got found out and came home, and you're expecting everything to be like it used to be!"

Joy considered this, pushing down her first instinct, which was to snap that Ella didn't know what the hell she was talking about. "I understand it's hard for everyone, and there are a lot of things we can't share with you... but Ella?"

The girl took another drag and blew smoke into the darkness, where it spun, danced and then vanished. "What... I mean, what were you going to say?" Her shoulders had dropped a little, the defiant stance and the aggressive tone gone.

Joy moved a little closer. "I would never willingly leave my family. Someone took me away and I can't even begin to tell you how painful, how raw that makes me feel. Someone took me away from my children, my husband and my home. But I don't need to explain myself to you."

Another silence before Ella nodded. "Okay, I'm sorry... I do love the kids and I love working here." The beginnings of a smile creased the corners of her mouth. "Plus, my mum would kill me if I ditched the job. She thinks Emile is like the best ever..." A sideways glance. "So do the other nannies."

Joy found it was easy to smile back at the girl, although she still had reservations. "If you're staying, sort out the attitude."

Ella nodded. "Got it. Sorry, I was being a bitch."

"Apology accepted." Joy shivered. "Now I'm going inside, but I have no problem with you coming out here to smoke, or whatever you were doing, so carry on."

"Goodnight, Joy."

When Joy turned to slide the door closed, she saw Ella's green eyes were still fixed on her, a thoughtful expression on her small face. She padded softly towards her bedroom.

Joy woke the next morning gritty-eyed and exhausted. There was so much going on in her head, so many unanswered questions, that as soon as she opened her eyes, she could feel her heart racing, nerves jangling. At least she felt she had gone halfway to resolving the situation with Ella, but really, a stroppy nanny was the least of her worries.

As she swung her bare feet out of bed, she smiled slightly to hear her children racing downstairs for breakfast, and for a moment the tension in her shoulders eased. She reminded herself how far she had come, brushed tentative fingers across the unopened pages of the gratitude journal she had been sent as part of a glossy PR haul. Not yet. Jono was at the forefront of her mind, creating little jitters of electricity around her body, making her heart thump too hard and her jaw clench.

She needed to end this part of her life before she could move on properly, and this morning she couldn't wait to unload last night's revelations onto Dr Alores. But when she called there was no reply, either to the main work number, or her own private mobile number.

Having dispatched the kids to school with Emile, Joy wondered whether to go up and see Ella, who had told her husband she was 'feeling a bit poorly and didn't want to give any germs to the children'. Joy wondered if she was mulling over the conversation last night, but decided she didn't really care enough to get into another heart-to-heart with the girl, so she discarded the idea, and picked up her phone instead. The itching feeling along her arms and chest, the dry mouth, told her where she was currently headed.

Worried about her ability to cope with the panic and cravings alone, to stay away from the bottles in the kitchen, she went to call Bobby, before she realised his gig was tonight. The last thing he needed was her dumping a whole load of complex shit on his lap. *You've got this, Joy*, she told herself firmly. This was why she needed to move on, to be free from Jono.

She quickly texted her best friend instead.

> All ready for tonight? Good luck & so proud of you! X

He got back almost immediately, and she could tell he was terrified.

> U r still coming???? X

Of course. See you at 9. Love you & you'll be
amazing.

She added several heart emojis and sat down on one of the
chairs in the kitchen. A big mug of coffee sat in front of her,
steaming gently. The morning was misty, with long swathes of
smoky fingers wrapped around the garden and house. Deep
breaths in, deep breaths out, box-breathing, Dr Alores called it,
and it helped a little. Every plant, every stone glistened with
moisture, and a weak ray of sunshine elevated her view to fairy-
land status. Princess land. She and Jono always said she lived in
princess land. *Jono.*

As the panic began to rise in her chest again, and she felt
the old cravings start, the desperation to blot out the memories
she had been so desperate to regain, she knew she needed to call
someone. Before she started opening a bottle of wine. But even
as she processed the thought she found herself in the kitchen,
taking a bottle of vodka from the cupboard, unscrewing the top,
inhaling, imagining. She tilted it to her lips, desperate to blot
out the craziness and confusion, but retched as the first
mouthful hit the back of her throat. No! She wouldn't do this.
Strength and sanity returned.

Flinging the open bottle down on the tiled floor, not caring
that glass splintered everywhere, that the alcohol swirled in
useless puddles across the kitchen unit and dripped down the
cooker. Joy grabbed her phone, breathing fast. *Lucy.*

Her sister arrived within an hour, breathless and concerned.
Joy was pacing the house, having cleaned up the vodka mess,
but dropped her coffee mug and spilt the contents all over the
beautiful floor tiles. In the confusion she'd cut her finger trying
to clear up, and now blood dripped from a makeshift bandage,
mingling with fragments of blue china.

"What's happened? Joy?" Lucy's voice was sharp with

worry, and as Joy felt tears slide down her cheeks, her sister moved in close, strong arms wrapped around her shaking body.

For a while they stayed, clinging together, but slowly, as her sobs began to subside, Joy told her.

"Wait, wait, start at the beginning," Lucy said, calmly and gently, disentangling herself and surveying the mess. "You sit over there and start talking, while I clear this up, and make some more coffee. Deal?"

Joy nodded, sank obediently onto the purple velvet armchair near the doorway and began to tell her. Gradually, as she spoke, her words seem to get into a rhythm, and her frenzied heartbeat slowed. She tried to explain about things being moved, her feelings of being overwhelmed by the questions left to answer. "I've been scared a lot since I came back. Things happen, like my shoes are mixed up in the hall, or my make-up or toiletries are moved around. Just random stuff. And I keep thinking someone is in my room." She knew now this had been Ella, but she wanted to explain just how stressed she was, and really didn't want to discuss the nanny just now. Not when Jono was smiling in her head, laughing at her, hurting her.

Lucy frowned, and Joy could instantly see she was concerned, but also sceptical. "Are you sure it isn't the kids or even the cleaners tidying up?"

"It sounds very simple now I've said it out loud," Joy sighed. "And with a simple explanation, but inside my head all this is building up into a massive crisis. Already built into a crisis really. It's like I can't calm down, can't stop all the chatter and the anxiety."

They sat at the kitchen table, surrounded by cats and dogs, listening as the bustle of cleaners and gardeners started.

"I'm not surprised you feel this way." Lucy laid a warm hand over hers. "Don't take this the wrong way, but what you have been through, what you are still dealing with, would be enough to send most people off the rails."

Joy shrank from her sister's worried look. She trusted her, but instantly felt she had shared too much. This was stuff for Dr Alores. And she hadn't told her about their mum yet, either. "I need to know who I really am and what really happened. Jono knows how I became... what I became. He knows what happened that day. Everything!"

"Oh, Joy." Lucy's eyes gleamed. "I want that too, and I want to find Jono and have him banged up for life for what he did to you and the others. Just... when we do catch up with him, we can only piece together so much, and I wonder if you might need to start thinking about the future, moving forward." She brushed her hair behind her ears, a decisive and brisk gesture. "We can't change the past."

Joy shook her head. "But... everyone, and I'm not saying this to nark, everyone seems to think I'm going crazy. You, Emile, Dad... I can see your little glances, your not-so-subtle ways of checking up on me." She raised her hand as her sister tried to speak. "No, it's okay, like I said, I get it, I sound crazy even to me."

"You don't. It's just how we process trauma. Everyone is different."

"It's fine. I just need time to sort things out in my head," Joy agreed. She finished her mug of tea, set it down on the table with a little thud, and stared away from her sister, out of the window, forcing herself to sound calm.

There was silence for a long moment before Lucy said, "By the way, I checked, and your therapist reported an intruder last night. She was burgled by all accounts. No wonder she isn't answering her phone, but I agree it's tough when you've had this breakthrough."

"Poor woman." Joy was instantly empathising with Dr Alores waking, possibly hearing someone creeping around her house in the darkness.

"Did she give you anyone else to call, if it was an emergency?"

"No. I guess I just need to deal with this and move on. I guess I'll ring the police liaison officer, Holly, just in case it helps the overall case."

"Oh, it will. Every detail you can bring to the table gets us closer to the truth, to Jono. Can I see the drawings you did last night?"

Joy led her upstairs, and they studied her sketchbook together.

"I don't think there is any doubt you are going to remember what happened, and hopefully your other memories will come back too. What about the stuff with Mum? You said on the phone there was something else?"

"There is," Joy told her, watching her face carefully. "Why doesn't Dad keep any pictures up of Mum's graduation, or have any of her certificates on the wall?"

"Maybe it's too painful. He said he thought they were happy before she started going for more qualifications and promotions," Lucy suggested. "Why do you ask?"

"There is something in the arguments, intertwined with everything else and for some reason I keep focusing on the wall at Dad's, the one above the table in the kitchen."

"What about your dream?" Lucy demanded.

"Don't you think you might be trying to make something more of it than it was? I was seven, I could easily have it out of sequence, or something." Joy was getting agitated. This was another problem. The more she remembered, the more she felt back in touch with reality. The worries of her other life as Mattie, like staying off drugs and booze, wondering where Jono had gone, and being able to pay for food, had been real, tangible things. Now, she could only wonder if her newly awakened memory was playing games with her.

"No. Go through it one more time," Lucy insisted.

"You're treating me like a suspect!"

"I'm not. Joy, trust me. There is something here and I want to know what it is."

"I woke up when they were rowing. I heard shouts, I crept down to the stairs. I saw the blood on Dad's head. Then, through the window a while later, I heard the car start. When I looked out, you know, from the little round window on the stairs, I could see them drive past."

"Them. Exactly. And Dad was in the driver's seat?"

FIFTY-FOUR

"Yes." Joy went over this in her head for the hundredth time. She could feel the dull thump of a headache brewing at the base of her skull. "He was driving, and Mum was in the passenger seat. They drove past slowly, heading for the gate to the road."

"What did you do then?" Lucy was scribbling notes now, in professional mode, Joy thought.

"I wanted to wake you, but I was still confused, scared. I peeked into your room, but you were still snoring, so I went downstairs."

"What did you see? On the way downstairs, and when you got to the ground floor?" Another note on her pad.

"The kitchen was a mess, like they'd had a meal and left all the dirty plates out. There was a bottle of wine tipped over, dripping onto the lino, and the broken glass in the sink. There was blood on the floor, and on the edge of the countertop." Suddenly her vision cleared, the pain briefly abated, she could see it as clear as she had all those years ago. "Lots of blood, like a pool."

"And when they drove past, was Mum sitting up in the

passenger seat? Slumped forward?" Lucy suggested, pausing to drink more tea.

"I... I think so... She was leaning back against the headrest."

"So, she might have been unconscious?"

"Shit... I suppose so." The pain was back, and Joy felt her breath shorten. She knew what she was saying, what she had seen, but hell, it was much worse saying it out loud to her own sister.

"We can ask Dad. I mean, I don't want to stress him, but if you feel like there is something unresolved in your own mind about that night..." Lucy said, reluctance in her voice. She put the pad back in her pocket and pushed her hair back with all ten fingertips, as though trying to cleanse her thoughts, her own memories.

"No! Well, I don't know... I'm saying there is something Dad isn't telling us." Joy rubbed her forehead with her fingers. "Mum keeps coming up in my nightmares. They're getting worse since I started therapy. She appears in almost all of them, even if my mind then switches to another topic, there's always a link back to her. Like the cars, or the bottle of wine or... I don't know, something."

Lucy was silent for a moment. "Perhaps your amnesia works like that. Old memories come back first, and they bring the newer ones with them?"

"I bloody hope not. It might be years before I remember what happened to me, and this is tough. You know how much it will mean to all of us if I can remember, but every time it happens, I feel like I've had some kind of attack or fit."

"On the night Mum died, I remember bottles of wine," Lucy said slowly. "I think they had been celebrating her promotion, hadn't they?"

Joy stared at her. "Nothing else? You honestly can't remember anything else?"

"They had a row and she stormed out, drove away and went

off the road. But I was asleep, I can't remember anything apart from early next morning and Dad sitting on my bed crying."

Joy frowned at her sister. "Let's go over to Dad's. He should be coming back from walking the dog by now. I need to know what's going on. I need to know if my memory is right."

"Okay, but just bring it up slowly. I honestly, hand-on-heart, can only think you are relating Mum's death with your own trauma, because she was driving the car. There was nobody else involved."

The drive to Frank's took ten minutes, and Joy spent the whole time sitting in the passenger seat trying to calm the coils of tension in her shoulders, in her stomach. Lucy said nothing at all, simply pulled in at the cottage when they arrived and marched up to knock on the door.

Frank opened his front door, accompanied by Bessie's yaps, and beamed when he saw who it was. As Joy had feared, given the circumstances of their visit, he was clearly delighted to see them.

"My special girls! Sorry, did I forget you were coming round?" He opened the door fully, fumbled in his pocket for a treat for the dog, who was still on the lead and jumped around in excitement. Still smiling, but his brow furrowed, puzzled, he moved aside and opened the door fully.

"No, we just wanted to see you," Lucy said. "To ask you something."

"Of course, come in." Frank unclipped Bessie's lead, ushered them into the hallway and kitchen area. The black and white dog yapped round the table, tail wagging furiously as she greeted first one, then the other. He smiled at the two women. "Would you like tea?"

"Yes please. I'll make it, Dad, you sit down," Lucy told him.

Joy sat on the wooden dining chair, propped her elbows on

the table, resting her chin in her fists. Exhaustion, disbelief, were making her doubt herself. The dog sat panting next to her, head cocked on one side. She focused on the dog as she spoke to her father. "Dad, I'm not sure how to say this but... I've been having nightmares about Mum," Joy told him.

A beat of silence while she turned away from the dog and watched his face. There was sadness in his eyes. "What kind of nightmares? Is your memory coming back properly?"

Lucy brought mugs of tea to the table and set them down. "We think perhaps Joy is focusing on Mum's death as a sort of focal point for her trauma, and if you can go through what happened it might help her to move on."

Joy opened her mouth to speak, but behind her dad's back Lucy put her finger to her lips.

"Well of course. I mean, I hate to talk about it, but if it will help with your memory, love." He smiled at Joy, but his big hands were clenched together on the table, and the smile looked to be merely a facial expression, without the customary warmth. "What are your nightmares about?"

"I don't know, and I don't want to upset you, but my therapist said it could be important to go through any issues. I was going to call her today, but she had a burglary last night," Joy said.

"Do you remember what happened five years ago yet?" he asked slowly. When she shook her head he added quickly, eagerly, "And have the police made any progress on tracking down Jono?"

"No. But Lucy suggested, and this kind of ties in with what the doctor said, that it might be the way I'm healing, to start at the beginning. So, no secrets, don't try and protect us, because I need to reshape who I am, and I can't do that without building from the truth upwards," Joy said firmly.

He smiled at her, properly now, the warmth back in his eyes, hands relaxing as he bent down to pet the dog. "I'm so proud of you, of both my girls. I can't tell you how it makes me feel to have both of you back together again, and safe. But okay, I can tell you if you think it will help. But just know I was trying to protect you. Anything I have ever done has been to protect you two."

"We know that, Dad, but we just need to understand what happened," Lucy added. She leant back in her chair and crossed her legs, with every appearance of being completely at ease. But Joy, who was next to her, could see the fingers on her lap gripping the fabric of her jumper so tightly her knuckles where white.

He took a slightly shaky breath and checked in his pocket for a silver blister of tablets, popping one with a swig of tea, before he began to speak. "Beatrice had started drinking heavily about a year before she died. The pressures of taking on a failing school, and it was tough, don't forget I taught there too, so I knew how bad it was, were getting to her. I was very proud of all that she accomplished, but I could see she was getting in way too deep."

"You didn't want her to be headteacher?" Lucy queried.

"I wanted her to go for it, for many reasons, but at the same time I could see what it was doing to her. She would come home later, work late in the evenings, trying to fill the jobs of two, three or even four people." He was speaking slowly now, and his gaze was distant, as though he was watching the events unfold in his head.

"Did she enjoy her work?" Joy asked.

He sighed heavily, and coughed a little before he continued. "She did. I think initially it was the challenge. But the drinking got worse. I begged her to get help, but she wouldn't. She kept saying she would cut down on work and stop drinking when she was finally made head, or when the school was finally out of special measures."

"I remember arguments," Lucy said suddenly. "A broken

glass. You. You with blood on your head." She touched her own head, just above the bridge of her nose.

Frank nodded, took a moment to take a great gulp of tea before he spoke again. "She threw the glass at me when I emptied a bottle of wine down the sink. When she ran out that night, she had drunk too much to drive, but not so much she should have crashed. I think she had had enough. She could see what I was saying made sense, but she couldn't stop what she had started. She couldn't see a way out..."

"Go on," Lucy said gently.

"Sorry, just got to me for a moment." He massaged his forehead with a finger and thumb. "We argued, she was drunk, and she pushed me. Oh, not hard, but I stumbled, fell over, possibly hit my head. I'd been drinking too don't forget. It had been a celebration. She was nominated for this national award." He paused, as though choosing his words. "When she drove away, I heard the car, but it didn't register. I was stunned, shocked, by what had happened."

"What did you do then?"

"I ran after her. The car was going far too fast, out of the driveway, and she came to the junction and turned left, down the hill, instead of right to continue on the road."

"Wait, you think she crashed on purpose? You think she died by suicide?" Lucy asked.

"I... I'm not sure. The police report showed there was nothing wrong with the car. She was over the legal amount of alcohol in her blood, but she could always take her alcohol, your mum. They thought... we all thought she might have just, for one crazy moment, had enough." He picked up a glasses case, opened it, fiddled with his reading glasses. "Sorry, I'm so sorry, girls, and I can't imagine how awful this is to hear."

Joy glanced at her sister and saw the same stunned expression mirrored on her face.

"That's why you might think I've been so overprotective,

fussy even," he said, acknowledging their exchanged glances, "but I was terrified of the same thing happening to you. Joy, when you started to get famous, I was terrified. I almost thought, when the police told me you were missing, when Lucy came in crying, that you had..."

"That I had followed in Mum's footsteps?" Joy whispered.

He nodded, eyes shining with tears. "And Lucy, you just keep rising up the ranks at work, so again I worry about the pressures of that, the dangers." He sighed. "But I'm not stupid, I do realise I'm a fussy old fusspot, as my charming grandchildren call me." He coughed, put a hand to his chest, and reached for the silver blister tablet sheet again.

"Are you alright, Dad?" Lucy got up and fetched a glass of water.

"Fine. Just got to keep on top of the medication." He brushed her concerns away. "I'm sorry I kept that from you, but I hope you can understand why."

Joy found she had to ask. It was eating her up, not knowing if she was remembering the truth, or if the meaning was being twisted by her own mind. "Dad, was there anyone else in the car when Mum drove away?"

He stared at her, lips still wet from the water he had just drunk, eyes shining with the remnants of tears. "What do you mean?"

"She didn't call anyone, and nobody came to meet her?" Lucy said softly.

"No. I didn't see her get in the car, because as I said, I was incapacitated, but no, of course not. The emergency services only found her, and by the time I had run to the gate..." He was frowning now, wrinkles creasing around his watery eyes, the deep trenches of grief dug across his forehead. "No, I couldn't see because it was dark, but why would there be another person in the car?"

Joy picked up her empty mug, wrapping her hands around

it for comfort. "Because I had a sort of nightmare last night. They aren't really nightmares and it's hard to explain, but in my memory, I see Mum in the passenger seat, sort of slumped, and someone else in the driver's seat as they pull away. And I see this from my bedroom window."

Her dad was pale with shock now, and Joy felt a surge of guilt. "I... I don't know what to say. Do you think? I mean, I don't see how there can have been anyone else... I don't..." His hand went to his chest again and Lucy stood up.

"It's okay, Dad, it's okay." Lucy hugged him as he sat, shoulders hunched. "Joy has been remembering a lot of things and we aren't sure all of them are true representations of what actually happened, or if the trauma of her own abduction is influencing what she sees."

Joy said nothing, although she tried to smile at her dad, tried to smile at her sister, who made another cup of tea, offered to make dinner and finally, firmly took herself and Joy out the door.

Joy waited until they were in the car before she spoke. "I wasn't muddled, it was true. I know it was true."

Lucy indicated left at the end of the single lane road leading to their dad's house but made no move to pull away. She turned to her sister. "You are saying what? That Mum was leaving with someone else? That *Dad* was driving her away?"

There was little traffic on this road at this time of the morning. Rush hour had ended, and the road only led to another housing estate further down the hill.

The tension in the car was making Joy feel claustrophobic. "You're the copper, you work it out. I'm not saying I am right, but what if Dad was more involved in the crash than he let on? They had a row, a fight even, she goes unconscious, not him, he puts her in the car, drives to the bend, gets out, and lets the car go down the hill into the woods."

"Fucking hell, Joy, you're basically accusing Dad of

manslaughter, based on a dream! Do you even realise what you're saying?"

"Yes! Yes, I do, and I think you're blinkered by your love for him, but I'm coming back in, not knowing him at all. I think he's a nice old man, devoted to his kids and grandchildren, but that doesn't mean he hasn't done something bad in the past, made a wrong choice in anger. It happens! You know it does!"

Lucy drove back towards Joy's house in silence. When they arrived, parked safely behind the automatic gates, away from the press, she turned to her. "I am on your side, okay? Always, and whatever you remember I want you to tell me, but I can't accept this. I'm sorry, unless there is any firm evidence, I can't see the point of wrecking our family on the strength of a dream. I lived through it too, remember, I lost Mum too."

Joy, hot and flushed with a strangely unpleasant mixture of embarrassment and rage, simply picked up her bag and got out of the car without a word. As she walked towards the front door, she heard wheels crunch on gravel as her sister drove away.

FIFTY-FIVE

When I said I had help with Joy, it was true. One of those chance meetings, a time when everyone is off their head and secrets come out. Silly secrets mostly, that nobody cares about, but sometimes, if one of you isn't quite as out of it as you thought, you might find yourself being blackmailed after you blabbed.

This is exactly what happened. My dad introduced me to those kind of clubs. He let me see a different kind of woman worked in places like that, totally different to Mum at home, but he said it wasn't a bad thing and everyone had to make a living. So, I knew all the places you might not have expected me to know and hung out with the kind of people you might look down on. And you know what? Because I was careful, I was invisible.

My mum was a good housewife, and my aunt too. If they did anything below standard, like there was a stain on the washing up, or a crease on my uncle's shirt, harsh words would be used, but next time, the washing up would be sparkling and the shirts would be steamed to perfection. I had other male family members who would visit from America. They would all have a big meeting, and the women were allowed to serve drinks and snacks, before being banished to the kitchen.

My dad let me see some notes from their meetings, explained to me that in the natural order of things we should venerate the housewife. Men should have lots of money, fast cars and the top positions at work. It was the natural order of things, he kept saying.

Stephanie was a sweet girl. Not too bright, but she liked to chat, and she was happy to stroke egos, and to stroke other things for extra money when a big group of men came in. I could tell straight away she didn't feel threatened by me, and I was careful to keep it that way. The way she dressed, the way she was, she was asking for it, but I almost admired that she seemed to know this.

After I got to know Stephanie, after I realised that she was just one in a line-up, and I had my plan right there. At that point I wasn't sure she would need to die, but it became evident later on. Loose ends must be tied up, and this pretty, bland girl, with the soft laugh, short skirts and the aquamarine eyes just like Joy's was just another loose end.

My dad would have said she was one of those women, and not the type anyone really cares about so it didn't matter but I didn't enjoy killing her.

FIFTY-SIX

After her row with Lucy, and the revelations of her drawings, Joy decided the best thing she could do was once again get on with her life, and try to keep everyone happy. She might have her strikes in a secret notebook rather than the wall, and she might live in a castle rather than a slum now, but the same reasoning applied. In a way her sister was right, she needed to move on, to make herself happy, to make everyone else happy too. Sooner or later, she would have to trust her memory would either return or not.

About her dad, she refused to think anything just yet. Lucy was correct; she, Joy, had no right to come back and tear the family apart with insinuations that might just be part of her damaged mind healing itself. It would be different if she could believe her dreams were all memories, and there was no doubt, but she was getting muddled, doubting her own integrity, her own sanity.

She had felt suddenly like it was important to challenge herself, to get out and show she could still do it. First, Bobby's gig at Burger & Bird in Peacehaven, and afterwards back into the centre of Brighton for the event. Her first proper event since she came home. It was the launch of a new lipstick brand, held in a bar in central Brighton. She had dressed with extra care, in a long white dress, with floaty lace sleeves, and Emile had been by her side the whole time.

Burger & Bird was a proper comedy night, not just the corner of a pub, and she could tell Bobby was nervous.

"You'll smash it. Honestly, you are really funny," she told him, before they went to take their seats.

Charmaine, who organised the nights and was also a professional comedian, kicked off the night. She was sharp and witty and her impressions of everyone from Amber Heard to Adele soon had the audience in stitches.

Bobby was in the middle and although he came out with his head down and a deer-in-headlights expression, he managed to get through his opener, looked incredulous when the audience laughed, and gradually warmed up. By the end of his slot, he was in full swing, and Joy could tell the audience was on his side. She was so proud, so emotional for him, she could feel herself tearing up. Again. She seemed to be crying most of the time now, whether she was happy or sad, she chided herself wryly.

Driving back into Brighton, Bobby told them Charmaine had booked him again and given details of an agent who might be interested. "Imagine doing this for a living!" he said, eyes sparkling. Then he gave a smile. "I do realise it'll probably take years to get established, and I might have to keep the bar job for a while, but it's such a buzz."

There were a few photographers outside the bar and a few more inside, calling out to the influencers to pose with the brand lipstick, but it was still okay. Her make-up had been professionally done, and her hair fell in waves over the scarred side of her face. She remembered how she had watched Joy walk on her channel at events, shoulders back, elegant and smiling.

Emile stuck close initially and Bobby made her laugh with his dry comments on the crowd inside the bar. But as soon as Emile was called away to talk to some of his friends, and Bobby went to get her a non-alcoholic cocktail, the witches landed beside her.

"Hi, Joy, how are you feeling?"

"Fine thanks. You lot getting ready for Halloween?" Joy supposed the irony was lost on them, because they just looked confused.

"We heard your memory is coming back."

"That piece in Just Now *magazine, where they did a psychological profile of you... Don't you want to know what happened?"*

"Maybe your brain is, like, protecting itself from what he did to you. That's what he said in the profile, that maybe you don't want to remember."

"Did you have sex with this man? No wonder Emile seems a bit off. Must be freaking him out."

"I expect you've already booked in for surgery. Must be hell finding out what you used to look like."

Joy zoned out as their voices, whiny, breathy and downright annoying, buzzed around her, but this last comment from Kate hit home. The woman was waiting expectantly for her to speak, her pursed shiny pink lips and blue eyes far too close as she inspected the scar on Joy's cheek. Her perfume was cloying and sickly.

"Why would I get surgery?" Joy moved back slightly. She knew why, and it was something she was considering, but from a health point of view rather than anything cosmetic, but this woman was pissing her off, and it felt good to be able to focus some of her emotions.

"You used to have such flawless skin and now, I'm not being mean, babes, but you need to get some work done, and a serious makeover. You've aged..." Kate put her hand over her mouth. "Sorry, I'm so unfiltered, aren't I? I didn't mean it to sound bitchy. We'd love to help you in any way we can. I mean, we know you haven't been yourself at all, so we didn't worry about what you said last month, about not wanting us around. Like, we knew it wasn't *you* talking."

There was a chorus of agreement from the other girls, and Joy found herself more amused than anything. It was truly amazing how they had managed to spin the truth to suit themselves. How had she spent time with such vapid, poisonous women? Only Georgia looked genuinely uncomfortable. The others were staring at her in barely disguised delight.

Natasha smiled and leant close – another one who had been heavy-handed with the perfume bottle, Joy thought.

"Come on, Joy, you can pretend all you like, but we knew how much was fake. You liked a drink and a line of Charlie as much as the rest of us."

Joy frowned at her, trying not to push away her anger, to shrug it off. Lucy had been adamant Joy had not been doing drugs when she disappeared. This woman was just trying to get at her. Hopefully.

What had Jono repeated so many times? '...*a poor man's copy of Joy Maddison.*' And so she was, a shadow of her former self, the ghost of a glitzy, glamorous influencer. She should have been more upset, and there was a little pain, but there was also that little nugget of sparkling strength that had carried her through the hard times.

Bobby wandered out onto the patio area, passed Joy a sparkling juice drink, and they shared a look.

"So, Bobby, you knew Joy from when she was basically kept prisoner. What was she like? How was it even possible you met her, if she was being kept in this house?" Kate was wide-eyed and poised for gossip.

Joy watched as Bobby sipped his drink slowly, considering, still glowing from the success of his gig. "It's an ongoing investigation so I can't answer that. Joy was amazing back then and she still is."

"Wouldn't you love to see her get a makeover though. If we all put some style together, I'm sure we could do it."

"No. She doesn't need a makeover. She looks gorgeous," Bobby told them seriously, his blonde hair gleaming as he brushed it out of his eyes. It was an elegant, natural gesture, and so far removed from the flutterings and dramatic hand sweeps of the women in front of him, Joy thought.

"Maybe I'm happy as I am," she suggested. "Maybe I'm just glad to be alive, to see my family again. And maybe, just maybe, it isn't all about appearances."

They stared at her, confused. Clearly it was indeed all about appearances. From the furthest seat, Georgia gave her a wink.

Kate was the first to start moving, making a big show of gathering up her bag. "Well, it's been *lovely* to catch up, but Alejandro is taking me to the do at The Ivy tonight, so I need to get properly party ready."

Bobby eyed her tight red dress and matching heels. "Oh yes, I'm sure you can do better than what you're wearing now."

Ignoring him, the others followed, blowing air kisses. "Call us when you're feeling better. Got to move on now, there's a club opening in North Street and then we've *got* to look in at a fashion launch."

Only Georgia and Bobby were left, and when they caught Joy's eye, they burst out laughing.

"What the actual fuck was that? A coven of witches?" Bobby asked, putting an arm around Joy.

Georgia sighed. "Unfair to witches. The trouble is, if you don't go along with them, they just cancel you. I mean, they have so many endorsements and followers, and I have to see them on press trips and everything. It's hard to keep out of their way."

"But are they so important? Because they have more followers than you?" Joy asked. "Stay for another drink, Georgia. They won't notice, because they've got *important* stuff to get to. Please don't tell me everyone is this world is like them."

The other woman grinned, pulling back her cloud of black hair and tying it with a silk patterned scarf. "Of course not. Lots of us are just normal and we have a right laugh. I'm out of favour with Kate and co because my boyfriend just ghosted me."

"Was he famous?"

"No... Well, sort of. He was a footballer. Albion."

"What do you do? Are you another influencer?" Bobby asked.

She laughed. "No, I'm an actor slash comedian. God, that slash sounds so pretentious, doesn't it? I haven't really got a good break yet, you know, hundreds of auditions and a bit part in that fabulous Roy Grace series. But I do get bookings for adverts and sometimes a slot on stage. I don't suppose Joy remembers but we met on the radio show, where I had a part-time gig. We used to giggle so much during ad breaks."

"Are you funny now?" Joy asked. She had been seriously questioning her own judgement when it came to friends but Georgia seemed sound so far. And a long-standing friend seemed better. Someone who had been part of her life before she attracted attention.

Georgia picked her phone out of her bag and began scrolling through links, pulling up her YouTube channel.

Bobby and Joy leant in to watch. She was funny. She presented a totally different character on stage. Soon Bobby was telling her about his recent gigs, and they were comparing notes on the trials and tribulations of a career on stage and in front of the camera.

Joy sat back, letting the conversation flow over her, relaxing for the first time since lunch, sipping her mocktail.

"You know what, Joy." Georgia turned back to her finally. "There is something I wanted to say, and the reason I kind of wanted to speak to you on my own." She held up a hand as Bobby started to move. "No, it's fine if you stay. I meant the girls... and Emile."

Joy felt ice start to drip on her hand from the tongs as she helped herself to another drink. The longing to grab a bottle and add some alcohol still ebbed and flowed, but despite everything that had been thrown at her in the last few weeks, she was still sober. It was a bloody miracle, she thought wryly. "Go on, Georgia."

"Natasha... Natasha had a really deep convo with Emile a few days after you went missing. They were in her apartment, and when I arrived, she tried to say Emile had just dropped in to help her with some contractual thing."

"Emile is a chef, not a lawyer," Bobby pointed out.

"Right, well anyway, she shoved me into the living room, but I heard them talking. They were talking about making sure the car was never traced." Her brown eyes were wide. "They were scared, and kept saying about how it would really screw things if the car was found."

"Fuck me." Bobby turned to Joy. "What car?"

She blinked and dragged a hand across her eyes. "How would they even know about that, though? They couldn't possibly. Nobody knew. I mean, Jono hit me by accident. Or maybe he didn't. It was *Jono*. Shit... How could you plan something like that?" Joy felt herself choke up, and clutched at her chest, breathing hard.

"Did you tell the police?" Bobby asked Georgia, slipping a hand into Joy's and squeezing it gently.

"No, because I didn't know there was a vehicle potentially involved in your disappearance until you just told me. I didn't connect the dots at all. They never mentioned you, Joy, so I thought... I don't know what I thought, but maybe they had been having an affair, or Natasha was having some drama with her boyfriend. You know, well, you don't, but he, Ricky, has two drink driving charges, and a load of other stuff like driving without insurance."

"I thought she was with someone called Alejandro?" Bobby questioned.

"Oh, that's Kate. I think Alejandro slept with Natasha first though... In fact, they only broke up recently."

"Did Natasha hook up with Alejandro before or after you all heard I was coming back? Because she was still sleeping with my husband until recently," Joy queried, recovering slightly. She was struggling to fit the puzzle pieces today, to sort out what was and was not true. In a way it was the same as her frustration with her memory, but in another way different. Here, she had the pieces needed to make the full picture, she just needed to put them in the right order, but with her memory, she had to just wait. And wait.

They talked for a while longer, before Georgia, after planting a soft kiss on Joy's cheek, departed for another event.

As Emile also had to go on to yet another party, Joy and Bobby got an Uber home, and went to sit in the garden room, side-by-side on the sofa, just as they had done at Forty-Two, Kingston Lane.

"Wow! Doll, this just gets more fucking twisted every day." Bobby lit a cigarette. "This bunch of toxic bitches, the way your husband might have been playing around with one or more of them, or the shit-hot nanny who keeps giving him slut eyes. I hate to say this, but Jono seems like a nice straightforward guy compared to this lot."

FIFTY-SEVEN

"It was clearly all going on before I was abducted. Something involving my supposed friend and my husband having an affair?" Joy felt like she'd been punched in the head. "It feels like everyone has so many secrets, and some of them are connected to me, but I don't know which ones are relevant."

"Well, you know what you need to do, don't you? Identify the man in the mask and the man in the car. You said your latest drawings show two different people."

"What?" Joy blinked, jolted from her thoughts.

"That might be why you can't get the face to fit in your drawings. You're trying to make Jono fit two different people. Whether it's Stephanie and Jono or Stephanie and someone else, maybe you need to allow your brain to consider that option."

She considered this. "Right. Simple. But there can't be two potential serial killers slash obsessive Joy fans living in Brighton, surely?"

"I was thinking about that, actually. Following on from what I just suggested, perhaps you are intentionally blocking it, just because it's too much to process that you lived with the man who took you and abused you. I don't think there can be any question, logically, it was Jono who abducted you, and the police say that too, don't they? But he involved Stephanie, why shouldn't he have involved someone else too?"

"Maybe. I mean, yes it makes sense, but I'm so scared a lot of the time and I know everyone thinks I'm going crazy. Now, just when I think I've got myself sorted out a bit, and my relationship with my family is moving in the right direction, Georgia suggests Emile might be someone I need to be wary of."

He watched her with his bright blue eyes fixed on her face, lips pursed. Bobby didn't contradict her, never said he thought she was mad, and listened as she talked him through her nightmares. Eventually, he yawned. "You aren't mad, doll, just trying to process everything. Keep doing what you are doing."

"Should I try and get Georgia to tell the police about the conversation between Emile and Natasha?"

"Yes. I think she would anyway. She seems like a breath of fresh air compared to Kate and Natasha. You won't get in shit with Emile, and you don't even have to tell him you spoke to Georgia, do you?"

"I guess." She lay back against his arm and they sat cosy and relaxed as, outside, the sky deepened to twilight.

Into the peace came the sound of gravel crunching under car tyres as her husband arrived home. A murmur of voices as the security team welcomed him back, the bang of the car door.

It was the sound of the car that opened another door, just briefly. Maybe it was because she was relaxed, distracted by the events of the day, but somewhere, somehow, her brain clicked into place, just as it had two nights earlier.

A car engine, herself getting in the passenger seat, leaning over to kiss the driver, laughing with him and with the woman she now recognised as Stephanie. The sun was low, just like now, and there was a chill in the air. Joy had bare arms, just like in her drawing. Then as she turned to pull her seat belt across, there was pain in her arm, sharp, like an insect bite or a sharp scratch. Again, she turned to bat away the wasp.

But this time her memory took her forward, away from the hazy car journey. She woke in a dark room. No windows and so much pain. So much shouting. The man in the mask was shouting and she was crying, shouting back. Another figure stood by the side of the bed, watching, just watching.

What did he want her to say?

"You killed her, you murdered Joy Maddison. Say it! Confess and you can have some water."

"You're crazy!"

"You are Mattie Woods and you killed Joy Maddison. Say it!"

"No!"

Every time she denied it, the sharp scratch in her arm was repeated, the man shouted. Even in her sleep he shouted. And the sharp scratch wasn't a bite, it was something she was familiar with, should have identified when she first dreamt about it. It was the sting of a needle entering her flesh.

And then she was alone, no shadowy figures, but the voice went on and on, so loud she tried to cover her ears, but she couldn't because her hands were tied.

"Joy?"

Bobby's voice, his arms around her, shaking her gently, his face white and scared. "Joy?"

"It was a recording," Joy said, suddenly returning to the room. "Sometimes he was there and sometimes it was just his recorded voice telling me over and over, I was Mattie Woods and I killed Joy Maddison."

"Fuck me, doll. Can you see his face? Joy, try really hard. It's okay, I'm here. Is it... Is it Jono?"

"Bobby! The car..." She was on her feet, breathing fast, clutching her chest in a frantic clawing motion, aware for the first time her face was wet with tears.

"Calm down, doll. It's okay. What did you see?" His voice reassured her, and she moved her hands, gripped the arms of the chair, desperate to make sense of it all.

The words were coming fast now. "I got in the car, and I was okay. There wasn't a car accident, not then. I was talking to him. It was the man in the mask again, I think, but I... I must have *known* him. To get in the car and kiss him on the cheek. The engine was going, but he was pulled in at the side of the road. Stephanie was laughing, talking to me."

"Could you have willingly gone with them? Was it planned after all?" Bobby looked sceptical.

"I don't know, I don't..." She knew the feeling in her arm now, had identified it, grappling through the fog, searching her memory banks. The sharp scratch. "I think whoever I got in the car with drugged me. It wasn't an insect bite I was feeling, it was a bloody needle. And the car, I know the car... And I know the man."

Bobby just stared at her, as footsteps came through the kitchen and Emile appeared at the door.

"You two look very serious. What's going on?" He was smiling, silhouetted against the sunset, very good-looking, very sure of himself, and just maybe, Joy thought, shocked to her core, just maybe guilty as hell.

FIFTY-EIGHT

"You think *Emile* was involved in your disappearance now?" Lucy was shocked, peering closely at her sister.

Joy seemed calm enough, but her mouth was tight and the lines around her eyes seemed more pronounced today. Lucy was getting seriously worried. First her dad and now her husband. Joy seemed to be spinning out of control with these dreams, allowing them to become more real than the world around her.

"I don't know." She met Lucy's gaze, and sighed heavily. "There are so many undercurrents going on, so many secrets and tensions, I can't tell who is taking advantage of me not being able to remember."

"But these women, your friends are suggesting he was somehow involved?" Lucy picked up her drink, sipped the hot chocolate slowly, letting the rich, dark liquid melt the cream on her tongue. She had told Joy it was her favourite drink, how they used to love autumn, even though October was a tough month: the anniversary of the death of their mother.

"Not really, well, I told you Georgia thinks he may have been having an affair with some other woman as well, so after I had that flashback, coupled with what she said, I began to wonder. He would have known exactly what I was doing that evening, he has money to pay someone like Jono to abduct me."

Lucy watched her sister, trying to logically consider it. But it felt wrong even as she put her suspicions into words. It felt treacherous to her brother-in-law, and almost as though she was trying to mould her thoughts into a shape that they couldn't be part of. The wrong piece in the jigsaw puzzle, but Joy was now so desperate she would file down the edges to get it to fit.

"What are you thinking?"

Lucy considered, but she dealt in facts, not rumours and gossip. "I wasn't part of the investigation into your disappearance, for obvious reasons, but I can tell you I know the DCI, a DI and a lot of the team who were working on it and they are up there with the best. Emile was interviewed, but there wasn't a shred of evidence to tie him to what we now know was an abduction."

Joy slumped in her chair, biting her nails. It was a fairly new habit, but compared to some of her old ones, it could be worse. "I don't want to suspect him of anything. He's been so nice to me, so kind when it must be weird to suddenly have your wife back, especially looking like I do."

"You're still beautiful, Joy," Lucy told her firmly and fiercely. "Scars and wrinkles, they just show how much you've been through. They are battle scars. Nobody can take away the essence of you, and it's still sparkling."

Joy blinked hard and Lucy could see a tear glassy on her cheek, running over the ridge where her skin had healed itself.

"I'll speak to a few people, and you can certainly sit down with your police liaison and tell him about your newest flashbacks. I assume Georgia is happy to give a statement?"

"But if it doesn't lead anywhere, what's the point?"

"You don't know that. Have a bit of faith, and it must be good you're getting these flashbacks."

"The doctors said it was. I had an appointment about my knee last week too. I'm booked for surgery at the end of November."

"Well, there you go."

They were silent for a moment before Joy said, "I'm sorry I upset you and Dad. I think that my past and present traumas are somehow colliding, and I can see how hard it is for you, for all my family. I don't want to go around accusing any of you, but I have to go on what I see."

"Even if what you see isn't the truth?" Lucy suggested gently.

"Maybe."

On her way home, Lucy called her dad. "I just wanted to let you know I saw Joy and she seems fine."

"Are you sure? I didn't... I didn't like to pop over in case she is still, well, you know..." His voice trailed away.

"You're right, she is struggling, but I think her therapist might be right, and all this sudden surge in nightmares and drawing might mean she's nearly there, she can nearly tell us what happened."

"What about Jono? Has she had any more texts?"

"No. She's still scared, but more in control."

"I'm so worried about her, Lucy, I really am."

"Me too, Dad, me too."

FIFTY-NINE

Joy got her driver to take her down to the coast road. She left him in the Lidl car park, walked away, head down, shoulders hunched, and stood by the port, opposite the remains of the house she had once lived in. There was scaffolding up around the buildings, and boarding stretching down to the road. Five years of her life, gone in a flash, stolen by someone, maybe even stolen by her own husband. Was she being crazy to rely on her memories, and her dreams?

She had seen in Lucy's eyes that she was starting to think she was crazy, losing it completely after everything that had happened. But if she couldn't rely on what she was remembering, how was she ever going to know what really happened, to come to terms with it?

And her mum? Thinking it through in the chilly, drizzly light of day she was still convinced of what she had seen. She fiddled with her phone, turning it over and over in her pocket. Lucy had tried to pressure her into seeing another therapist again, but Joy was adamant she wouldn't see anyone else. Dr Alores knew she was on the brink of a breakthrough, and Joy knew that when she could, she would respond to her panicked voicemails. It was a lifeline she was hanging onto.

She walked a bit further, hood pulled up, remembering what it was like to walk to work this way, remembering the cold, the heat, the dust and dirt, the gnawing hunger, and the sick cravings that ruled her life.

Joy leant against the wall, watched the fishing boats, the taller ships, the Border Force vessel. On the far side, on Brighton Wharf, the cement ship was loading up. Or maybe unloading. She never could be quite sure, but the mechanics, the huge cranes and equipment still fascinated her as they had during her years as Mattie.

Gigantic piles of sand, asphalt and pebbles were laid out in neat pyramids, and beyond, piled high like Lego bricks, were the stacked shipping containers. Blue, orange and brown for this particular company. Workers in fluorescent vests and hard hats walked swiftly between the machinery, and the chimneys of the vast power station belched smoke upwards into the silver grey and faded blue of the late autumn skies.

Joy shivered, pulling her soft, cashmere hooded cardigan around her, wriggling her toes appreciatively, feeling wool socks and snug boots. Normally when she watched the port she was freezing cold, her feet like blocks of ice encased in sodden, smelling trainers. She had been cold for five years. Cold and utterly lost.

If she kept having flashbacks, and the person responsible for her five-year purgatory thought she might remember the truth, there was a flicker of hope... The danger she felt at home, with her friends, even talking with Lucy, it prickled across her shoulder blades, and made her catch her breath when a sharp sound reached her ears.

It was almost like her body knew the truth and her mind was trying to catch up.

"Hello, Mattie. Didn't think I'd ever see you again."

She looked up and saw Dami, Ned's half-brother. Immediately she knew it had been a mistake coming back to her old haunts.

Harley, she heard from Lucy, had bartered his way down to more minor charges. Most of the others from Ned's crew had been sent down for a long time, but Dami had always been on the fringes, trying hard to find a way of making Ned go straight, fiercely defending the legal part of the business.

"I heard you were dead."

She turned around to face him, reassured by the constant buzz of traffic on the coast road, the bustle of the port, the daylight chasing away her fears. "What do you want, Dami?"

He raised both hands, palm upwards. "Nothing. I just saw you and thought I'd say hello. Heard you were badly injured in the fire."

The police had done well after all, and the seeds had been sown. And now she had almost wrecked it. Keep it vague, Lucy had said. "I nearly did. I was in hospital for ages, only just got out," she invented. "I'm actually moving away, right away. I've got a friend in... Cardiff."

"That's good then." He shifted from foot to foot. A hefty lump of a man, with a shock of sandy hair already receding from his forehead. "What about Jono?"

"What about him? I'll say goodbye then," she told him, picking up her bag and starting to walk away.

"Wait!"

She turned.

"I want to tell you something."

"Go on then." He hadn't given any hint he knew who she really was, and she supposed as it had never been made public, perhaps he hadn't made the connection between Mattie's death and Joy Maddison's sudden reappearance. Why would he?

"Jono wasn't good to you. When you first moved in, and when you first started working for Ned, he used to watch you the whole time, like a frigging prison guard. You were scared of him, I could tell. Do you know what I'm talking about?"

She searched through the haze and shadows and reluctantly shook her head. "We probably didn't have the best relationship. I don't think we were good for each other."

"Right. I want you to know it's okay, I wouldn't grass on you, because I know why you did it. You deserve to have a good life."

"I don't get it. What are you saying?" Joy's heart thudded faster, and her palms, clutching the bag, were sweaty.

Dami bent closer, but carefully, as though he was afraid of frightening her away. "I saw you."

"What do you mean?"

"I know you killed Jono. I saw you, but I won't say anything, don't worry."

She froze, and the port seemed to spin slowly, crazily, like a snow globe shaken and then replaced when all the snow had fallen in different places, on different ground. "What... what did you see?"

He pointed to the hatch over the drainage system, near the abandoned warehouse, flanked by some pyramids of sand that must be over thirty metres tall. "You were arguing, up on gantry. He pushed you, not hard but a little, and you staggered near to the edge. I was going to come over, but then you suddenly charged at Jono, and shoved him hard in the chest. He obviously wasn't expecting you to do that because he was caught off balance and he fell, straight into the pile of silicon sand stuff from the cement works, through it and fell sideways into the old drainage tract."

Joy stared at the doors next to the huge sand piles. It wasn't far from where they were standing. There was evidence of a little repair on the right-hand one. Subtle, but true. Piles of ancient rope, broken containers, even an upturned rowing boat merged with the weeds in this area. A mould-encrusted, battered TO LET board swung sadly from one rusty screw, and huge concrete bollards sat next to fallen chain-link fencing. It was a nobody's land, similar to various plots all along this coastal road, long fallen into disrepair.

Echoes of conversation flooded her brain, like vibrations bouncing back and forth from Jono's grave. That was his final resting place according to Dami, just metres from where she stood. Jono was dead. She had known all along.

"Look, Mattie, this wasn't how I imagined it, and I don't need the money anymore, so you can learn how to live on your own."

"What do you mean?"

"You really never guessed, did you?" Jono was laughing, "None of this is real. It's all make-believe and you swallowed it. But even fucking you, and let me tell you that isn't as great as I thought it would be, doesn't make up for having you trail around like a lapdog. I am sick of having to be on call to make sure you don't get into trouble, to top up your doses, keep you out of sight and under control. It's got boring. I want my own life back."

Mattie was staring at him, frozen, small and defenceless against the backdrop of the port.

Joy, looking down from her vantage point at the wall, watched the scene replaying as though she was an outsider, perhaps as if she was at an outdoor cinema screen, and the whole stretch of port was somewhere she had never been before. It was no longer about the images in her head, she was watching an action replay, watching herself kill Jono.

She could see Mattie, small and ragged, standing on the edge of the wharf, her mouth and eyes still wide with shock and confusion. Mattie took a step forward, and as Jono turned to walk away, she moved faster, grabbed his sleeve. With the movement, Joy felt herself merge back into the scene she was watching and the shock of it made her gasp. She was Mattie again, hurt, shocked and ashamed.

"I don't understand. What do you mean?"

"It was all just a chance to have you all to myself for a while and the cash offered was beyond everything I could ever have made with Ned. But the novelty's worn off, babe, and I don't see how this will end well for me. It made sense in the beginning, but now..." He smiled self-deprecatingly. "Maybe I've just grown up, but I'm not waiting for the end game, because I know who will be first in the firing line."

"You're leaving me?"

A slow hand clap. "You're so slow, Mattie. Or is it Joy?"

"What do you mean?"

He told her then. An abbreviated version she didn't fully comprehend, couldn't take in, but as she tried to ask more, approaching him with her hands outstretched, pleading for truth, for clarity, he pushed her away. The spark of anger and confusion turned to a full-blown forest fire. Her hands met his solid chest full on and he stumbled, too astonished to cry out.

There was a sharp crack as he fell backwards through the dry, rotted timber door. And then he was gone.

Mattie stood alone in the darkness, breathing heavily. She knew what was behind the door. She approached warily, but there was no sound. The sheer drop, the long disused concrete and metal mechanics of an overflow drainage system, must have killed him. Living in a world where life was cheap and death an easy way out, she felt nothing but pain at another death.

She refused to think about what Jono had just told her. It didn't make sense. He must have been lying. She never questioned how he could make up such a fantasy story, she simply put it out of her head. It was too difficult, too shocking to process, and if she thought about it at all, she found she could hardly breathe.

So, Mattie Woods turned and went home to Number Forty-Two, coughing a little. The sore throat she had been harbouring all week was a little worse and by morning, after she had drunk a litre of vodka, passed out, vomited and drunk some more, the hot flush of infection was creeping across her body. Mattie lay on the dirty, cold mattress, hardly able to focus, barely able to stagger to the tap for water.

When Bobby texted, twenty-four hours later, all she could think about was her fever, and for the next six weeks, she was aware only of his coming and going, looking after her as she suffered.

SIXTY

The drizzle and salty breeze brought her back, and Joy found she was gripping the top of the wall so hard the concrete had left imprints in her palms. Dami was still hovering, watching her anxiously.

"Sorry, Dami, what did you say?"

"I said, nobody deserves to be treated like he treated you, especially not a woman." He ducked his head shyly. "I figured it must have been you that got Ned put away too. The business is mine now. I've been running it for years since Dad passed, and all the while Ned played drugs king and criminal mastermind." Dami nodded, as though she had spoken. "He used to call me slow, just like Jono had a go at you, said I was a lapdog too. Now look who's laughing, ay?"

He raised a hand in farewell and walked slowly away, shrugging his black leather jacket closer to his huge muscular shoulders. His voice floated back on the autumn breeze, mixed with salt and something that could have been respect, a whisper of affection. "Good luck, Joy!"

Joy stared after him, unable to move, until he loped across the road and got into a white van with the familiar fish market logo emblazoned on the side. Really? He had launched the equivalent of an atom bomb on her life, and he was just going to walk away. Life was cheap down here, in Ned's world, she remembered, and Dami wouldn't want to get into trouble now he had the business.

She felt a wave of nausea rising up at the sight of the logo, but her mind was blown by the latest revelation. It wasn't like the other dreams, the other memories. She knew without questioning that Dami was right, remembered every detail, knew she had locked it away from herself.

If she was a killer herself and could manipulate her own memories, what else could she be doing? Panic made her whirl around, breathing fast, scanning the traffic on the road without seeing it. Perhaps Lucy was right, and the memories couldn't be trusted.

Right on cue her phone buzzed with a text:

> Just checking u r ok? Did you go to the gym?
> Can give u a lift home as passing that way in 10
> mins. Corner of Eastern Road. X

Emile, also checking up on her.

Perhaps she had gone completely mad, and all this was an illusion. Was she in some kind of institution or virtual reality, or was she having a really bad trip and still sleeping on the dirty mattress with Jono, dragging her aching body to the fish market after a night of poisoning it with drugs and alcohol?

Joy slipped a hand inside the arm of her cardigan, pinching herself, hard. It hurt and she swore. The sound of her own voice steadied her a little, but the aftermath of shock still floated across her brain. Who knew what was real and what wasn't anyway? She started purposefully towards her car and driver. The only person who could take back control of her life was Joy herself, and she would start right now.

As she paused at the pedestrian crossing, her phone buzzed

with another text. She looked at it impatiently, expecting Emile again.

Instead there was a message from a ghost:

> Hi babe, how's it going? Did you get your memory back yet? You and I know things aren't always what they seem so don't rely too much on those nightmares, will you? Watching you.
> Jono XOX

Joy found she was shaking. What if it wasn't true? What if he hadn't died in the fall, just taken the chance to get away? She tapped out a reply with unsteady fingers:

> WTF do u mean. Where are you? I thought u were dead.

This time, instead of undelivered, her phone buzzed with a reply, and she stood there in the sudden pouring rain, having a conversation with a ghost, while traffic splashed her jeans, soaked her shoes, and turned her hair to dripping rattails.

> Wtf me dead?

She paused now, unwilling to commit herself, remembering Bobby questioning whether this was Jono or someone else playing games, someone who didn't know Jono was dead. If he was dead. Jesus! *Be careful, Joy, be very careful...*

> After u left, I thought Ned had taken u out

> Still here, still watching. We're all still watching you, babe.

> We? Who is we?

> Everyone who loves ya Joy.

Tell me what happened?

Jono???? What happened to me????

But whether it was Jono playing games with her, or someone else, this round was clearly over, because her texts were met with the familiar undelivered message.

Either she was on one hell of a trip, Joy told herself, or she was getting close to the truth about her disappearance. But if Jono was still alive he would have been badly injured surely, and this wasn't just her memory, it was Dami's too. Dami had nothing to gain by inventing a story like that. He had been sure.

She quickly texted Emile she had the car and driver so not to bother picking her up and left a voicemail for Bobby saying she needed to see him urgently.

Bobby had been the only person she saw, spoke to, for the six weeks after she had killed Jono. She would find out what he knew. Funny, it was as though she had known all along. After the initial shock, the heart-stopping terror that Dami was going to try and blackmail her or tell the police what she had done, she felt numb. Or was that just because she was having text conversations with a ghost after seeing his grave? Mind games. It was all about mind games and someone out there was still playing with her sanity.

SIXTY-ONE

Bobby hadn't got back to her, but when she arrived home, Joy greeted her husband cordially, pretending nothing had happened. She would trust nobody, she had decided on the way home, and keep everything to herself. But even the decision made little stray wisps of panic start to form in her chest, as the paranoia made her check all the windows in the room when Emile wasn't looking.

'Come on, Joy, it isn't you going mad, it really isn't.'

But wasn't talking to yourself a sign of madness? And what was madness anyway? Who decided you were crazy? She dragged her thoughts away from this dangerous area and concentrated. Dr Alores would provide the safe space when she finally got back to her, but even then, she would tell nobody the truth about Jono's disappearance.

She was so close to the truth, she could feel herself reaching trembling hands through the foggy curtain in her mind. Every so often the cloudiness would lift, and she could see part of the jigsaw in crystal clarity.

Heading upstairs for a shower and to change her soaked clothes, she took her phone with her.

"You should have let me pick you up!" Emile called after her. "Then you wouldn't have got drenched..."

Alone in her bedroom, she rang her dad, apologised and suggested a visit. "I just want to talk, and it's all been such a bizarre journey, I guess I'm getting muddled. I'm so sorry to have upset you too."

"That's perfectly okay, love, and I'm just glad you're feeling better. Lucy did say you'd been so stressed and not yourself... But the dreams could be your brain's way of trying to cope with what happened to you?" He sounded hopeful, reassuring.

"I think you're right." She felt the need to say more, to clear the air, regain trust, so she explained she had been so shocked and traumatised by the sudden memories she probably *had* been confused, agreed with him that her mother had been alone in car, added she had muddled the scenario with that of her own abduction, and then waited.

"I'm so glad," he repeated softly. "So very glad, and you don't know how much I love both my girls. It kills me to see one of you hurt, or worse. It makes me feel I haven't looked out for you, protected you properly."

She felt her heart catch a little at his words, and grief and guilt churning in her chest, even though she couldn't quite understand why.

But his relief at her apparent return to sanity was tangible, and she proceeded to further lull him into a false sense of security with some gentle conversation about his grandchildren. He was, as she had said to Lucy, a nice old man, but that didn't mean he didn't have a few dark secrets. Whatever the truth about her mother's death, it seemed to be part of the greater puzzle and she *would* find out what had happened.

"You look better, love," he said when she was finally standing in his kitchen, her childhood kitchen, the kitchen from her memories. The countertop wasn't there, and the place had been updated at some point, but the space was fundamentally the same.

"Thanks, Dad, I feel better. I'm finally starting to figure things out."

He gave her a one-armed hug and carried on stirring his cake mixture. "And what things would those be?"

She told him about her truce with Emile and the possibility of starting her channel again. "The offers coming in are really amazing and Emile thinks we should consider some of them." Nothing about her visit to the port, nothing about her text conversation with a ghost.

He stopped stirring and was looking at her with worry and an odd look in his eyes. "Joy, love, I really wouldn't advise you going back to that kind of thing – putting yourself back out there."

"You make it sound like prostitution," she said, laughing.

But he turned to face her, and his expression was almost frightening in its intensity. A fierce protectiveness, coupled with what? Guilt at having not managed to protect her from Jono, she supposed.

"It's not funny. I was so worried about you, and Lucy was too. You were at the end of your rope with all the trolling and pressure. Emile can sell his restaurants. I don't want you having to worry about money or anything at all. You're still too fragile. You are having all this trouble with your memories and the doctors said the amnesia might take years to recede, and maybe even never. Don't take this the wrong way, love, but could you be so desperate to get your memories back, you're confusing memory with imagination and dreams?" His eyes were holding hers, soft and concerned again.

He had hit a nerve, and she winced. There were still the flickering sparks of feeling threatening to burst into flames. "Dad..." She noticed once again how he beamed at the word. "I love how protective you are over me and Lucy, but we need to work things out ourselves. I'm much stronger now, and well... thinking about my channel, we could do with the money."

"Emile needs to sort that out. He is not to go pressuring you into anything." Her dad's lips set into a hard line, his eyes bright with concern. "Love, I didn't tell you this before, and I'm pleased it's all going so well with him, but Emile was jealous you became more famous than him. He was really quite snippy with you during the last few months before you disappeared. And once you were gone, he started spending like crazy. New things for the house, new cars, a new motorbike... The money which should have been saved for your children was trickling away. And now you are back, he wants you to start earning again. I like Emile, and I always have done, but my priority is you and Lucy, plus my grandchildren."

Joy nodded seriously, storing it all away, but she was also glancing back at the photos on his wall. She had been right, there were only pictures of him and his achievements. Her mother, Beatrice, only appeared in photos with Frank, never alone. There were lots of her and Lucy as younger children, but none that were up to date. She wondered idly if Frank kept scrapbooks, like the ones Jono had made for her, cementing his deception, their fake life. Once again Emile's face seemed to hover over the kitchen, so many question marks surrounding his innocence or not.

"But don't let me be the one to tell you gossip, love. I always say with a lot of these things, especially marital quarrels and the like: *least said, soonest mended.*" His eyes were very bright, and his voice choked with emotion, but this time she chose to ignore the lead.

"I'm sure you're right, Dad, and it'll all sort itself out in time. And I promise I will put a lot of thought into changing jobs, too." Her own voice sounded over-bright and fake to her ears, but again he seemed relieved, and patted her shoulder.

They talked about general topics, and after half an hour, she judged that her work was done. He was happy, reassured and off guard. Just as she got to the door, she turned to him. "I was just wondering... Lucy made me a photo album of family and friends, you know to help jog my memory, give me something to focus on. Do you have a picture of Mum at her graduation? Or any others of her?"

"I gave Lucy some pictures for the album... Let me have a look and see. I know your mother's parents kept a lot of her photos." He gave a short laugh. "They didn't like me much and we weren't on the best of terms. But a lot of stuff was lost in the house fire, and then of course they both passed away a few years later. It was tragic and Beatrice and I were very sad you and your sister never met them, but these things happen. We have good memories," he added brightly.

"Thanks. If you could find any more photos?"

"I'll go and have a look now and ring you if I find anything," he promised.

"Oh, and Dad?"

"Yes, love?"

"It matters a lot to me about Mum, just so I can get the memories straight in my head." She smiled at him. "I need to know what's real and what isn't, and I'm relying on my family to help me out."

He nodded seriously. "Of course, love, I understand. You can talk to me any time, and I would never judge you."

Joy went to bed late. The weather was still thundery and close, and there was a tension, a sense of something about to happen. She felt like she herself was setting everything in motion, acting out what she knew needed to be done, pushing people to the edge, just to see what explosions she might initiate.

She sat with a mug of oat milk latte, snuggled into the clean sheets, the soft feathery duvet, with the weight of a blanket comforting across her legs. A passing thought that Mattie would have been in heaven at the simple luxuries of warmth and a full stomach. But she didn't intend to sleep, she was tapping away at her laptop.

Joy had been looking at the property her mother's family owned before she was married. Beatrice had been an only child, and when her parents died, she inherited everything... Joy scrolled down the saved documents. Several were missing from a folder she had obviously found and scanned in. The property portfolio was incomplete, but it was certainly a shock that her mother, her mother's family, had been rich. She had no memories of grandparents on her mother's side, and only vague ones of her dad's parents.

Perhaps her maternal grandparents hadn't liked Beatrice marrying a schoolteacher? Even though Beatrice herself had been a teacher? As her dad had said, views had changed since then, thankfully.

But there was nothing else in the ancestry files to suggest Joy had discovered any dark secrets relating to her project.

She went upstairs to the room at the top of the house, reaching out her fingers to the drawings, touching the outlines of the figures. She had been drawing the children too, taken some sketches downstairs to show them. They had been inspired, instantly rushing off to get their own colouring pens and pencils, copying her as she sketched the cats, the dogs.

But none of these charming pictures interested her now. She paused at one page of her sketchbook, the most recent, showing the storyboard timeline and the two cars. A jagged tear showed where the page had been ripped out. Surely she hadn't removed a drawing?

Joy glanced up sharply, again feeling that breath of cool air on the back of her neck. It was quite dark outside and raining again. She suddenly felt very alone. The children were in bed, but Emile was downstairs working in his office.

Her phone buzzed with a message, and she drew it carefully out of her pocket:

> Do u miss me? Jono XOX

She considered her answer, her body shaking with adrenalin. Was it time to play games herself?

> I know it wasn't just you & I know you must have killed all those girls. You're pathetic.

As she had hoped, the reply came back quickly, angrily.

> You've got no idea, have you? I'm smarter than you can ever imagine. Stay in your own lane, Mattie.

Mattie now, not Joy? She examined her sketchbook carefully. The pictures preceding the missing one were of the car, Stephanie and the driver. This one had been... She screwed up her brow, trying to remember. This one had been half finished. She had started to draw the car from the outside, as she had seen it approaching in the road. She had started to draw the *number plate.* Was that why someone had removed it? And if so, who? Emile knew, Bobby and Lucy, of course...

Emile?

Joy turned back to her phone, took a deep breath and texted back:

> I know who you are. I just drew you in my sketchbook. And I don't need you to tell me what happened because I know now. I'm going to tell the police.

But to her frustration, all she got back was the undelivered message. Once again, he was one step ahead, and the phone had been switched off. She slammed her hand against her desk in frustration.

The night passed slowly. Every time she dozed off, she hoped she might wake, drenched in sweat, with nightmares and memories filling her mind. The last piece of the puzzle was so close she felt physically sick.

SIXTY-TWO

After seeing the kids off on the school run the next day she waited until Emile had gone to the restaurant and the staff had finished their morning duties before she allowed herself to relax. It was Ella's day off. The girl had been much more courteous to Joy since the night on the balcony, and when questioned rather delicately, denied taking the missing pages from the sketchbook. Still the kids seemed to adore her, and she was managing to control her attitude, whatever she really felt about Joy.

Joy had made a point of taking on more of the childcare duties, in the past few weeks, insisting she felt stronger every day, pushing herself to achieve the things she used to do and more. The school run was an ordeal, but she managed it, facing a gauntlet of lenses and garbled comments. She found more contact with her kids grounded her, reminded her why she was doing things, why she was still fighting.

The police told her they were making progress on Jono's last known movements, but she no longer wanted to hear this. She told them she thought he might have said he was going back to

Ireland, had mentioned he spent his childhood in Dublin, but she couldn't be sure.

If Jono wasn't dead, and he was back to torment her, it was one thing, but if he was dead, who the hell was sending text messages? Once again, she thought of her husband. He wasn't the man in the mask. She was sure of that, and it wouldn't have made sense, anyway. Lucy had told her, the police had kept a close eye on his whereabouts for months, seized his phone, his computers.

But that didn't mean he hadn't paid someone else to remove her from society. For now, she forced her mind away from the guilt she was currently feeling at suspecting Emile and concentrated on nothing but Nuala and the kittens, now big, striped and fluffy, as they rolled and played on the kitchen floor. After a quick text from Bobby, she reluctantly left her sanctuary, and Missy and Roo followed her into Emile's study at the back of the house.

Bobby arrived ten minutes later. "Hi, doll, I'm all set for a bit of snooping. God, I love that word." He was wearing tight dark blue jeans and a silk shirt that matched his eyes.

"You look far too glamorous to be a detective. Bobby, I feel like you're the only person who really knows me at the moment."

"That's because I am." He tossed his blonde hair out of his eyes. "Don't go soft on me, Joy. Let's get going."

"I'll make some more coffee first. We've got a couple of hours until Emile gets back. Um... when I was sick that time after Jono left, did I say anything?"

"Plenty of things. Why?" His gaze met hers with perfect innocence.

"I'm not sure. Did I talk about Jono?"

"You called out for him, the useless piece of shit, but no, doll, you were having trouble breathing, let alone talking. I spent most of time thinking I was going to have to call an ambulance."

"Do you think he's dead?" she persisted.

Blue eyes met hers. "I did originally think Ned probably had him knocked off, yes. But now I think maybe Ned just threatened him and Jono ran. Because you've had those texts, who knows what to think now?"

"That's what I thought. That he ran. Jono, I mean. He mentioned Ireland."

"Yes, he did."

They stared at each other for a moment. Joy was convinced he knew the truth but was unwilling to say it aloud and potentially incriminate both of them. In that split second, she came to the same conclusion as her dad: *Least said, soonest mended.* She was already involved in a murder investigation.

Emile's password would have been easy to guess, being the kids' birthdays, but in complete defiance of all advice, he had scribbled it down on a bit of paper wedged under the keyboard, apparently trusting nobody else would come into this room and poke around his computer.

"It makes me feel really guilty," Joy said, eyes darting to the window and back again.

"Sure you want me to do this?" His fingers paused, hovered above the keyboard.

"Yes."

Bobby was able to get into Emile's files and web history. "Okay, you said your friends, the witches, said he was in debt? Online gambling. Look at all these sites. Have you seen all the bank statements?"

"No, only the ones that were solely in my name, because I had to unfreeze them and get new passwords and cards. I never even thought about joint accounts, and Emile never mentioned them."

Bobby accessed Emile's bank account with ease.

"I can't tell you how scary it is how easy you can do all this."

"Well, Col was a cybercrimes pro, and I learnt a lot, but I've always been a hacker. A proper little computer nerd when I was a kid." He turned round and grinned at her. "Just because I'm pretty *and* funny doesn't mean I'm not smart too."

"Or big-headed." Joy rolled her eyes, and then studied the bank accounts. "Shit."

"The joint accounts were both drained within weeks of your disappearance. Check the dates but I think I'm right. That's over two hundred thousand pounds going right out into Emile's accounts and paying for all this stuff. Hotels, a car, clothes... tickets to Dubai. Shit, doll, what was he thinking?"

"Maybe his way of coping? He did admit he sort of went crazy after I vanished and that's one of the reasons we are in trouble financially now."

SIXTY-THREE

They read in silence, Joy pushing away the niggling guilt. She had to do this, had to find out who was lying to her.

Roo and Minnie were under the table, chewing up a red rubber ball, and Joy suddenly became aware of the time, and the fact that they were still in Emile's study. "We need to get everything turned off. And don't you sneak on me," she told the dogs, as they watched, tails wagging.

Finally, they shut the computers down, left everything neatly stacked and exited the study.

"I don't think Emile is the one behind your abduction," Bobby said decisively, as she made him more coffee. "Look at it logically, even if he was jealous because your star was rising and his was a little burnt by bad publicity, financially he had nothing to gain by removing you from the equation. If anything, he was becoming more and more dependent on the money you were bringing in."

Joy wrapped her hands around the mug and looked out into the misty autumn garden. "Perhaps I threatened to divorce him, if he was having an affair with Natasha, and right after this other stuff with the girl in the club? Maybe he really was having affairs and I knew about it, and ignored what was going on. Until suddenly I didn't ignore it and became a thing?" Again, she thought of the folder carefully stashed away. Having questioned Emile, she knew they'd had no plans to uproot their family and live abroad, and yet he had agreed it would be nice to get away and live in a hut on the beach.

She wanted to talk to Bobby about her dad, about her mum's death but it felt too much, and too personal, almost disloyal to Lucy. It also felt like she had so much drama she was a little worried Bobby would get fed up with her and her problems in the gilded castle. This beautiful, luxurious life, where she had never felt safe, not since she came back to Dyke Road anyway. How had she felt before she left?

"You want to know what I think?" Bobby dipped his hand into the biscuit packet.

"Tell me."

"Keep going to your therapist, keep struggling through the nightmares, and shit, doll, I can't imagine what it's like, but maybe if you stop pushing so hard, you will remember more. You said you're nearly there!"

"You mean, stop chasing around after potential suspects?"

"Right, all of that is not your job, it's up to the police to sort everything out. I like your sister, and I reckon she will have been a flea up someone's arse on the investigation team. She's in a much better place to find out stuff and make sure the momentum keeps going, so you can concentrate on readjusting and your future." He grinned. "Unless Jono turns up, then you can kick him in the balls, lock him in a room and call the police."

She nodded, and as Bobby went to get his bag from the living room, she put their mugs in the dishwasher and talked to the cats and dogs, who as usual were settled wherever the activity was. The kittens were adorable cuddly bundles of mischief now, and although Emile had half-heatedly suggested selling a couple, that so many cats and two dogs was too much, the kids had shouted him down, and Joy herself was glad. She still thought of Nuala and her feline family as saving her life.

Right on cue her phone buzzed with a text:

> Hey. How's it going today? Bet you're loving being queen bee again really. Good luck with it lasting a bit longer than it did last time. Oh, and I bet you don't know shit about what happened. Don't try and mess with me. See you very soon.
> Jono XOX

Breathing fast, she called out to Bobby. "I got a text! Another text from Jono. Oh shit, Bobby."

He came quickly into the room and reached for her phone. "Tell the police and see if they can trace it!"

Joy was still shaken. "I keep doing that and they always say it's triangulated, but they can't pinpoint the exact location, or switched off, or he's using another phone. I keep trying to go over how he could have got this new number, but I can't figure it out."

"What if someone has given it to him, not knowing who he is?" Bobby suggested. "Or what if it isn't him but his mystery partner. This might be someone nobody has suspected. How do we know Jono didn't have another girlfriend? Or the snaky hot little nanny? Or this might be someone trying to wind you up, because dead men don't send texts. What about that Natasha bitch? She was selling stories to the press about you."

Joy shook her head. "Natasha... I honestly don't think she has the brains to sort out a phone that doesn't link to her. And how would they know how to sound like Jono? And how would they have connected Mattie? Right down to the XOX. If this isn't from Jono, it's from someone who knew him, really well, was in contact with him, and might even have seen his texts to me."

Bobby considered, blue eyes blazing. "Text him back again."

"*What?*"

"You know, like you did before. Keep the conversation going. Ask him what the fuck he's playing at, just like you would if you were still just a pissed off girlfriend with a man who had disappeared. See what happens. You said you had a text conversation last time."

"I thought you said we should be leaving all this to the police?" But she started pressing the buttons on her phone:

> WTF are u and what do you want from me?

"Good. Now send it and wait and see what happens."

She did and they waited, peering at the screen. Two blue ticks told them the message had been read.

"Now follow it up with something like, 'the games are over'," Bobby suggested dramatically.

She did so and again the message was read. Joy rubbed her forehead. "My brain is fried."

Her phone buzzed with a reply and they both jumped.

> Playing games might be dangerous. You still don't know the truth, do you? Do you want to know the truth? Jono XOX

Bobby reread the conversations, as they both sat in silence. "Does it still sound like him? I mean did he always sign off with XOX? Does it still read like the kind of text he used to send you or are there any changes you can find?"

She tried to study the messages objectively. "The police asked me that, and yes, it does still sound like him. He used XOX a lot even though I told him he was an idiot for doing it. He knew it pissed me off. All the texts read like him."

"Is there any way you can think of that Jono could have got hold of your new number then?"

The police officers had taken her old phone, and she walked

into the living room, sinking down on the sofa, stroking the cats. "I can't think how he could possibly. The only people who have it are family, and a few friends, doctor, therapist, the nanny. But out of those contacts I'm sure it's only family who know I was Mattie."

"But if it is Jono then he can't be dead." Again the unspoken conversation they weren't going to have. "Because as I said before, dead men don't send texts."

Was it possible he *had* survived the fall? She went cold at the thought of blackmail, but no, if Jono had survived and was playing with her now, he had a plan, and it wouldn't be getting within spitting distance of the police. Her whole life as Mattie, and another murder. Jono knew about all of it. But it wasn't a murder if the victim wasn't dead, was it?

"Maybe he wants you back? Or maybe he just can't leave you alone and he wants to destroy your life?" Bobby suggested sombrely.

"Well, he doesn't want me back," Joy said. Which left the latter suggestion. He was trying to destroy her, to succeed where before he had failed.

SIXTY-FOUR

"We've found the body."

The police liaison officer, Holly, and her colleague, a tiny slender woman, with a high ginger ponytail, were sitting opposite Joy and Emile in the living room.

On the iPad in front of them was a smiling picture of a blonde girl with Joy's eyes.

Joy could barely look at the photo of the nineteen-year-old runaway, and Jono's first victim. *Maggie.*

"Looks like she was hit on the back of the head. There is evidence of blunt force trauma. She was discovered by a dogwalker in the woodland behind Princetown on Dartmoor. The remains were partially concealed in a plastic bag and must have been buried fairly deep. But the heatwave this summer caused the ground to crack, and wild animal disturbance has now brought the body back to the surface." Holly's voice was even and her eyes compassionate.

Hell, she was practically a family friend by this time. Joy thought, as she closed her eyes briefly, the room spinning, nausea rising. She almost shrank away as Emile put his arm around her. "You think she was Jono's first victim."

"Possibly. He was seen with her in a bar a few weeks before she ran away."

"Why didn't you investigate it then?" Joy said roughly, wiping tears away with her sleeve.

Lucy, who was also sitting on the sofa, passed her a box of tissues.

"It wouldn't be this force, it would be the local team, and unfortunately, she was nineteen, and said she was leaving. She had been bouncing around in foster care and had a history of running away. She later sent texts saying she was okay, a photo of herself at a festival in Gloucestershire to a friend a month later."

"We're not saying it's right, because it isn't, but the investigation would have been limited, as there were no red flags. She was a legal adult and free to make her own choices. So many people go missing every year. The ones you read about in the news are just the tip of the iceberg," Holly added.

"You know, you said I would be okay now, that there wasn't any danger now I was living back as Joy, instead of on the streets. But you were wrong, weren't you? Something is still going on, and I don't feel safe." Joy felt she needed to be careful what she said, and the extra knowledge weighed her down.

On the one hand, she was withholding information, railing at the police for not moving the investigation forward, but not telling them everything; on the other hand, she had already survived confessing one murder, and she wasn't about to needlessly incriminate herself again. You only got so many chances in life, and she considered most of her nine lives had pretty much been used up already. And she was scared, guilty, grieving for three women she hadn't known, who had died because they looked a bit like her.

Joy closed her eyes briefly. "What about Ned? Could he have had anything to do with my abduction?" Ned would have done anything for money, but was he clever enough to have been working with Jono all along? And that still left the question Jono had raised. Who had paid these men to keep her out the way, more who had paid them to destroy her?

Lucy leant forward to take her hand. "Joy, Ned is in prison, and we're keeping a close eye on all his known associates. It isn't unreasonable to think maybe Jono has been dead for longer, or that Ned or someone connected with Ned killed him. Nobody knows you provided that information, but it's very possible someone might think Jono did."

Joy frowned. "Ned was really smug about Jono disappearing. I swear he knew something he wasn't letting on. That was why I thought he must have killed him, but then of course Jono talked about going home to Ireland as well."

Emile looked uneasy at the talk of Joy's time away from him, and she smiled to reassure him. *Keep everyone happy.*

Later they sat in the kitchen, perched on the bar stools, drinking coffee and trying to make sense of everything.

"Are you sure Natasha didn't know about any of this?" Joy asked.

"No way. She wouldn't have a clue about Ned, Harley and the rest. It's not her world. I would never have told her." Her husband reassured her, his eyes shadowed with concern.

"Unless you talked in your sleep?" Joy suggested dryly.

"It isn't your world either," Emile pointed out, ignoring her comment.

"No, but it was for five years," Joy told him fiercely. "I had to survive with all of them for five years, and I can't tell you how much it eats away at me that we still don't know the whole story. Why did Jono take me really? Did he plan it? Did he go because the police found my DNA and he thought it was getting too dangerous? He could have taken me away from Brighton at any time, yet there we were, living in the same city I was abducted from."

"And now he's dead, and you can't get the answers," Lucy said sympathetically. "I get it, we all do."

"What about Ned?" Joy persisted, even though she felt she was going round in circles.

"What about him?" Lucy asked.

"He's in prison so you can ask him what he knows about Jono, if he knows anything about me and Jono."

"Joy, give the police some credit; the investigating team have already done that. Yes, the police make mistakes, and we are only human, but we do things right sometimes," Lucy said, with a defensive edge to her voice.

"You aren't the one who lost five years of their life, nearly died in a car accident, was deliberately fed drugs and alcohol until I was an addict. All just so I would stay with some fucking loser who called himself a fan and told me constantly how in love with Joy Maddison he had been." She burst into tears now, and the cats and dogs instantly migrated to her side.

Lucy had tears in her own eyes. "I can't imagine how awful this must be, and we want to know what happened too."

"I can't move on until I know everything," Joy said, talking to Lucy, but really targeting Emile. Out the corner of her eye, his face showed nothing but concern and mirrored her own frustration.

"Tough as it is, you might have to face we will never know exactly what happened that night, or in the past five years. But you will have to come to terms with it and move on." Emile looked at her, concern in his eyes. "If you keep bringing up the past it will never let you go. The nightmares and your memory might never fully return, but you need to balance out the good things. You are home and you are safe, with us."

"Am I safe though? Am I really?" She whipped round. "Because I don't feel safe at the moment."

She ran from the room, hearing the murmur of concerned voices, hoping nobody would come after her. She needed to think, to figure things out for herself. A thought occurred to her, and she found herself heading up the stairs to her little safe place. The Velux skylight showed her the stars, just as the broken ceiling had when she lived down by the port.

Calm flooded her, just like it always had when she drew. She sketched slowly, filling in what she knew, trying different eyes, nose. He had been the same height and weight as Jono but as always for some reason she couldn't make his features fit. Glancing quickly over her shoulder, she turned back and sketched her husband.

But this time, without the precursor of nightmares, she found herself adding details. After fifteen minutes, Joy laid down her pencil and stared at her drawing.

SIXTY-FIVE

The sadness overwhelms me at times, and I wonder what kind of person I would have been if I had chosen a different path, met different people. If I had chances instead of knockbacks.

They say you make your own luck, but I don't believe that for a second. I can hear children's voices in the other room, arguing, rising to a screech. Does it begin in childhood, or earlier, when we are still in the womb? Did I learn from my mother that women should be protected and subservient, or was it the nurture, was it watching the way my dad, my uncles, my male cousins treated the women in our family?

A child absorbs experiences like a sponge. And either accepts or questions. There was never a place for questions in my family and so my own ideas grew from their ideas. They were right, and I took those ideas forward into my adult life, soon discovering many people disagreed. But I knew I was right. It made sense on every level. But you can nurture a child in every way, instil correct values, love them beyond all love, and it can still go wrong.

I loved and idolised Joy, and look what happened? She told us all so many times on her channel that she never set out to be an influencer, that she was just like us – a busy mum, wife, trying to run a business. The business of sharing her life with millions of total strangers. But she wasn't like us. She was favoured with a sprinkling of fairy dust, collecting a hug from the gods as she came into this world, whatever you like to call it.

It wasn't just down to hard work, because if it was, I would have been a star and she might have had a life like mine. I think it might have started when the female students were given better marks than me at university, when I was passed over for jobs, and they were given to women far inferior to me. That simmering, bubbling resentment was creating a sour undertone to my personality for years until it boiled over into one violent act, one very final decision. But I got away with it, so one decision led to others, and now here we are.

Decision time again.

SIXTY-SIX

After Lucy had gone, and Emile had bid her goodnight, Joy went back to her desk, staring again at her drawing. There it was, but she couldn't quite believe it.

In total shock, unable to discuss it with anyone, she tore the page from her book and took it to her bedroom, dozing fitfully, waking in a panic.

Somehow Joy managed to get through the morning routine, numb and terrified. Could she be wrong? Could she trust what she had drawn?

Dr Alores was back at work, but Joy discovered to her horror she couldn't physically find the strength to go to her office. The effort of the leaving the house was too great. Shock, it must be the shock, she told herself. She picked up her phone.

"Joy, if this is what you have drawn, you need to consider firstly if it might feel plausible, and secondly, if it does, you need to tell the police," Dr Alores said, after they had greeted one another.

"I can't... I don't think I can. I don't understand why."

"You wanted to understand what happened, to remember what happened, now you say that you do, and not only that, but you can also now identify your abductor, and the other two people involved." Dr Alores' voice was calm and measured as ever.

"It was Jono who killed the other three girls." Joy's tongue felt loose and clumsy in her mouth, her thoughts skittering around like a kid on a frozen pond.

"Other people were involved, according to you," her therapist reminded her.

"Yes." Joy considered, trying to control her thoughts. "Last night when I drew their faces, I just knew it was right, the pieces were falling into place. In my mind, I could remember almost exactly how it happened, but it wasn't some kind of floodgate that opened all my memory."

"Maybe, now you have released this trauma, your other, happier memories, will follow," Dr Alores suggested. "Joy, I think you know what you have to do, and if you trust me, you need to take into account I am agreeing with you."

Much later, Joy sat alone in her room, cross-legged on her bed, waiting. The kids had gymnastics tonight, so wouldn't be back until six. As the winter months inched closer the darkness was already, at 4:00pm, spreading across her garden in long smoky shadows. The gardeners had been burning rubbish, and the acrid tang floated on the chilly air. A few gold and orange leaves had fluttered in and lay crisp and colourful on her sheepskin rug. But she didn't want to close the window. Not yet.

Her phone buzzed and she checked her messages:

> I'll tell you what really happened, but are you ready to face up to your lies? Meet me at Heaven's Gate, round the back of the café at 10:00pm. If you tell anyone I'll just disappear, and you'll never know the truth. Jono XOX

Joy found herself sitting frozen, unable to process. She already knew the truth, didn't she? Or did she? Dropping her head into her hands she felt tears on her cheeks, and a desolation that ached in her chest grow stronger.

Should she call Lucy? Tell Emile or the police? But deep inside she still felt it was her battle to fight. It was easy to get out undetected. Emile was in a meeting with his production team until late, the kids would be in bed, and Ella would be watching TV.

After picking at her dinner, dumping most of it in the bin, she came to a decision and called Frank. "Hi, Dad."

"Hi, love. Are you okay?"

"Yes, fine. I just... I wondered if I could come round later, when the kids are in bed?"

"Of course. You haven't had another argument with Emile, have you? I told him not to pressure you..."

"No, Dad, I'm fine, honestly."

"If you're sure, love. Lucy's here too. What?" He spoke to her sister and Joy could hear muffled conversation. "Lucy says she was heading home in about half an hour because she's got an early shift, but do you want her to wait?"

"No, it's fine. I'll come over later, when I've got things sorted. Does it matter what time?"

His voice was puzzled. "No, love, I said it didn't. I stay up late anyway now I'm old. I need less sleep and the meds aren't conducive to dropping off on the sofa." He laughed. "Just turn up, Joy, whenever you want."

"Okay, say in an hour?"

Later, Joy put her head around the nanny's bedroom door. "Ella?"

The girl looked up from watching a YouTube gamer, her pretty freckled face intense. "Yeah?"

"I'm just popping out for an hour. If I'm not back by 11:00pm, can you call me?"

"Call *you*? Yeah." She went back to her TV screen, apparently uninterested, but Joy caught a flicker of something in her face. Suspicion?

Back in her own room, Joy changed into jeans, trainers and a thick jacket and after a moment's thought, she slid open a drawer at the back of the dressing table. The knife slipped cool and deadly into her hand. Mattie's knife, Joy's knife. Jono himself had given it to her, taught her how to use it. She had taken it to work, deep at the bottom of her bag.

Now, she picked up her small gym rucksack for her purse, but slid the knife into the pocket of her coat. Easy access.

At least she had her driving licence back now, and, after a few tries, was happy pottering around the top roads of Brighton. She hadn't managed the city centre or the A27 yet, but Heaven's Gate, a local beauty spot, was only a ten-minute drive.

She parked round the back and walked past the café. The area was deserted at this late hour, and the café shut early in the low seasons, anyway. It was boarded up and shuttered with padlocks.

Joy paused beside a stunted hawthorn, her back to the café, dead leaves swirling around her feet. The pine woods loomed ahead of her, massed ranks of rough trunks, and strong-smelling needles dropping steeply into the fold of the Downs. "Jono?" Either she was making the second-biggest mistake of her life (the biggest being going out on that ill-fated run) or she was about to learn the truth about what had happened. Not just the truth as she now saw it, but the reason it had happened in the first place. Funny, it had been the memory she had been craving all along, but now she had to know why. The betrayal was intense, a punch in the guts that blindsided her, shocked her.

She texted Bobby quickly, frowning as her signal dropped, but waiting expectantly as the two blue ticks indicated the text had been read.

She walked carefully into the trees, breathing fast and shallow, eyes darting everywhere. The land shelved so steeply here, falling in terraces to the smooth valleys of the South Downs. Joy could no longer see the café when she turned her head.

SIXTY-SEVEN

Lucy spent the evening with her dad, holed up in his cosy kitchen, giving in to his *'just one last cup of tea before you go'* routine because she felt guilty leaving him. He was lonely, she knew he was, but she was exhausted after a tough day at work.

"What do you think is the matter with Joy now?" he asked, concern in his voice.

"Dad, I don't know." Exasperation, then guilt made her sharper than she should have been. "She's been through so much and we just have to accept she isn't the person we remember. She is trying though." She propped her elbows on his scrubbed wooden table, breathing in the smell of the wood fire, the stew he had made earlier, and the faint tang of disinfectant. Her dad was amusingly obsessive about tidying, about cleaning.

"I know, I know." Sadness touched his face. "Sorry, it's just, I worry she's heading for a breakdown, even though this therapist keeps saying her memory will come back. It's too much pressure for anyone to bear." Frank began to stack plates in the sink, squirting washing up liquid.

Lucy yawned and looked at her watch. Half ten. "Let me do that!"

"Don't be silly, it's my house and I'll do the cleaning. I'm still very concerned, Lucy."

"I know, and I'm really worried about her too, but just now I've got work in the morning, so I need to go. Thanks for dinner, and for goodness' sake let me give you a lift to the hospital next week for your consultant appointment." She yawned again and went to get up. God, she was so tired. All this worry about Joy, and a huge workload getting The Unit straight.

"I'll tell her to ring you tomorrow afternoon, shall I?" Frank's grey hair was spiked out around his face, as his shoulders hunched over as he reached for his stick. "And thank you, love, that would be kind if you could give me a lift to my appointment."

He finished the small amount of washing up, popped the rest in the dishwasher and started the appliance, pottering around the kitchen, talking about Joy, about Christmas, and she knew she really, really needed to get going. But she was so very tired. Her legs felt boneless, weak, like she had the flu. Maybe she was sick.

Or maybe she was just so very exhausted... She felt her head drooping, her fingers missing the almost empty mug as she reached for it. The wood fire burnt merrily, flames dancing and crackling at the edge of her vision. She blinked hard, reached for the mug again and dashed it to the floor in her effort to pick it up.

"Lucy? Are you alright, love?" Her dad's worried voice. *"Lucy!"*

She could hear a rush of footsteps. Heavy footsteps moving far more swiftly than her dad with his stick. Was someone else in the house?

Her dad was shaking her arm now, and then he moved, and the frantic footsteps continued. Furniture was being moved, the sound of cups in the sink. But her head was spinning so much she had to lay it on the table. Her limbs were heavy, and although she was aware of hands on her body, of voices, she couldn't see, couldn't respond. There was no fear after the initial flash of panic, and she thought she could hear herself laughing.

Lucy thought she turned her head at the sound of a loud crash from the hallway, and the last thing she remembered was thinking the intruder had tackled her dad.

Some time later she surfaced again, still dazed, the light above her head too bright and the shadows at her feet too dark.

Lucy opened her eyes fully, her brain foggy and her head rolling agony. As she struggled to place herself, she saw Joy, unconscious beside her, blonde hair hanging limply over the edge and at the same moment became aware of danger. Danger close to home.

"My darlings, it's such a shame you had to keep pushing, not to be content with the lives I gave you. Just like your mother. Too much ambition."

The words drifted across Lucy's brain even as she fought sleep. Again, she tried to speak, but her lips felt clumsy and numb, her throat closing. A bolt of terror shot through her body, momentarily driving away the sleepiness.

But the drug was too powerful, and the last thing she remembered was her dad tucking her coat around her. His hands were gentle as he tucked the edge under her head, making a soft pillow. How many times before had he kissed them goodnight, made sure they were safe and warm, before the lights went out and the shadows spilled in?

Beside her, Joy flung out a hand and muttered. At her movement, the man at the window looked up, as if startled. His face was wet, and a spatter of rain was pulling her back into alertness, but it wasn't enough.

"Dad?" She felt her mouth framing the word, but no sound came out. She could smell petrol, could feel the leather of a car seat under her palm, under her cheek as she sank back into the shadows, and the car began to move.

SIXTY-EIGHT

And now I need to finish this, before anyone notices they are missing. It's harder this time, because I haven't had time to plan, and my sadness at their ungrateful natures is making me angry.

Joy was punished, but she still came back and began to think she could do what she wanted. Poor Emile, having a wife who wanted to be better than him. I know how he feels and it's shaming.

I run a hand over Lucy's soft hair again. Their childhood comes flooding back, and again grief and anger collide. My girls, my babies, but they don't know what's best for them. Joy has taught me she learnt nothing from her lesson, and Lucy doesn't listen to me when I tell her she needs to stop climbing up the ranks and settle down.

My efforts to bring Lucy's drinking to the notice of her superiors has failed. She was confused, annoyed when she told me about the complaint, but I can't do more without drawing attention to myself. She would have figured it out, that I was responsible, sooner rather than later.

Just as they have both drawn their own conclusions tonight. But despite the experience, the lessons learnt, they both fell down because they still love me. They don't obey me, but they still love me. Blinded by the blood ties we share.

I thought they were coming close when they questioned me about their mother. But I was able to instil enough doubt that even Joy backed off. She still suspected something though, I saw it in that guarded expression in her eyes. They underestimated me, as their mother did. It was after that, as Joy started to remember more and more, I knew I was being forced to make another decision. History was repeating itself.

In my haste, maybe I didn't have enough to give a full dosage, and they are young and strong. They are waking up, laid on the back seat. Panic hits me. This can't be happening. Or maybe that bastard Luca sold me a bad batch. This is more likely than a dosage error on my part. He took advantage because he could see what state I was in. I'm disappointed in him, and furious at myself. I'm a chemist, and I should not be making a rookie error, after everything I've been through.

But my brain tinkers with this new plan, finds it good and eventually, as I work, I settle down. But when I turn around, I fancy they are both awake and Beatrice's green eyes watch me. The shape of their chins, the curve of their mouths, are all hers.

Female dominance. Nothing about those girls is me, nothing at all. I'm working myself into a rage, because subconsciously I know I need to be in the same state I was when I beat Joy, to be able to kill them. When I'm angry I have power, but when I'm not it's all just thoughts and talk.

I can feel my body shaking, the rage building like fire inside my heart. They have done this to themselves. None of this is my fault. When I look back their eyes are closed. It's much easier that way.

I start to drive along the road. I need to be quick, and careful, but I can do this. I have to do this.

A hastily arranged plan, but what else can I do? There is no choice as I regretfully, swiftly, prepare to kill my darlings.

SIXTY-NINE

The car was still rolling as Joy regained consciousness. She was propped in the driver's seat. She tried to raise her hands, to look around. What the hell was going on? Her brain was still fuzzy, her movements awkward.

There was a man jogging beside the car, his gloved hand on the steering wheel, controlling the car. They were going slowly, approaching the bend in the road.

She knew the man and she knew what he was going to do. It had all been real, her nightmares, her memories. They had all been true. Beside her, she became vaguely aware of another shape, another soft body flopping from side to side, head lolling in the shadows thrown by the headlights.

Joy would never have survived or been about to do what she was going to do, but she was Mattie too now. The knife was still in her pocket.

As the man reached to spin the wheel sharp left, Joy hauled at the handbrake, then launched herself at him, throwing him off balance. He swore, tried to twist free, but she held on.

"You can't do this!" Joy screamed at her dad. "Stop the car

now." The vehicle slowed slightly, but they were close, so very close to the deadly corner and that steep drop.

But he was wild with fury, and, yanking open the door, shoved her roughly to one side, turning the wheel sharply as they reached the corner. She reached for the handbrake, again, tried to stamp on the clutch, fighting him with all her strength. Joy felt her knife hit home.

A sudden spurt of blood and Lucy's yell as she too regained consciousness, but it was too late, and the car was already beginning its descent off the road, down the hillside, into the bushes.

Joy was dimly aware of holding tightly to the steering wheel and two bodies were hurled across her own. The airbags blew, and the rush and spin of the crash suddenly stopped. The grinding of metal and the hissing of steam sounded loud in the darkness.

"*Lucy?*" She was struggling for breath, desperate for light, but some freak chance had knocked the electrics out.

"Joy, I'm here... Are you alright?"

"Yes... What about... what about Frank? I can't see him at all."

"I saw... I saw him running alongside the car, and he... he was carrying me, I think, to the car, but I can't remember."

It seemed like hours, but could only have been seconds, before Joy was able to adjust to the shadows, to regain control of her movements. She wriggled around, helping her sister to emerge from the wreckage. The car was wedged between two trees, and although she couldn't see, she could sense a long drop below.

"It was him all along, Lucy. He killed Mum and he was going to kill us. I finished my drawing yesterday, but..." She took a ragged breath, and felt a sharp pain across her ribcage. "But I couldn't believe it. Then, today, tonight, I knew it had to be him, because it all fitted."

"But... But why?" Lucy's voiced was clogged with confusion, with horror.

"I don't know."

Finally free from the vehicle, Joy stepped over the broken bumper, which had become detached from the car, and onto something warm and soft. "Jesus!"

He was gasping, glaring, and she could smell the sweet metallic scent of fresh blood. A wounded animal. A father who had tried to destroy his daughters.

"Why did you do it, Dad? Why?" Lucy was leaning heavily on Joy's shoulder, her face bloody and one hand supporting her arm. The tears were running down her face and she was wincing in pain at every step.

Joy registered with some part of her brain that Lucy had been as shocked as she herself had been, but once she knew, she didn't need to question. She asked why, but not where he was guilty. The suddenness of Lucy's acceptance filled her with relief, but also guilt. She had caused this, forced the situation, taken away her sister's father as well as her own.

He said nothing at all, but a small trickle of blood slipped from his lips, and his hands hooked like claws.

Lucy made a move towards him, but Joy blocked her. "No. Look at all the blood. He's going."

Joy leant down. "Why did you do it, Dad?"

His voice was faint, so full of hatred and despair she instinctively moved back a step, "Because you were asking for it. We knew... we all knew..." He closed his eyes.

"Fuck!" Lucy said viciously. "Knew what? What do you mean?" She bent down and shook his shoulder, but his eyes remained shut. "Wake up!" In her horror and disbelief, Lucy stumbled and almost fell.

Joy moved from her position next to the dying man and, reaching over, took her sister's hand, helping her awkwardly back to her feet, pulling her away.

Slowly, carefully, they began to walk up towards the road, climbing steadily through wet brambles and gorse, tangled shrubs that pulled at their torn clothes. Every now and then they paused, to rest their injuries, to exchange glances, but Joy knew, because she felt the same, that Lucy couldn't speak as they left their father behind.

"We're still here," Joy whispered finally, fiercely under her breath, and Lucy looked at her and smiled through her tears.

"We're still here," she repeated, devastation making her voice faint. But she clung to her sister.

When they reached the road, emergency vehicles were already arriving, Lucy was puzzled. But Joy looked at the massed ranks of emergency services and picked out a figure slipping away from one of the cars, coming to meet them. "There's Bobby!" And tears clogged her throat again as she sat heavily in the wet grass.

Lucy sat awkwardly, painfully next to Joy, as Bobby hampered the efforts of medics and flung himself at both of them. "Well, you two look like shit, but, dolls, I deserve a medal for bringing in the coppers, don't I? Don't you want to know how I knew where you were?"

"Later, mate." A police officer pushed him gently but firmly to one side, as Joy hugged her sister close, her cheek crusted with blood, hair mingling with Lucy's, she gripped her sister's hand tightly, glanced down at their entwined fingers. There was blood under Lucy's fingernails.

SEVENTY

I am dying.

I can feel blood soaking my clothing, can smell the stench of fuel and I know one little spark from a lighter will send this whole mess, me, the car, up in flames. I don't have a lighter.

There are shouts, blue flashing lights, and car engines, but I close my eyes, blocking it out.

I met him on one of my visits to Suzy's Attic. I liked the name and I liked to delve into the underworld, just getting my feet wet, before I returned to my respectable life.

For six months, I'd occasionally see him in passing and as we sat in the waiting room, watching the girls, enjoying the drinks, I saw him on his phone, looking at Joy. Jono loved Joy, was truly obsessed by her.

Our conversations got longer, and I found out just how much he idolised Joy Maddison. As soon as I found this out, it was easy. I caught him out, got the evidence and the next time our conversation was private. He was receptive to my point of view, agreeing women should be wives or whores, but explaining, in his mind, there was another type of woman. Women like Joy, who transcended both categories. He was wrong, but I let him think he had made an impression on me.

I had the money and the means, and he got the girl of his dreams. It was a good bargain, and although he was initially confused, he went for it. Of course he would. He was an obsessed killer, a loser with grandiose dreams of entitlement. I was presenting him with a deal that would see him right for a good few years.

I never was sure how long it would last. I wanted her here, in Brighton, so I could watch her, and him. He knew I was watching, and he knew what I had on him. He had nothing concrete on me. I was careful with what I said, what I did. The money was cash and passed from hand to hand. We exchanged texts on burner phones, which I was careful to chuck in the landfill when I passed.

Maybe I was waiting for it all to unravel, because I don't think, in my heart of hearts, I thought it was forever. It was a punishment, an experiment, a show of power. All of those things made me more confident I was doing the right thing.

But when Jono disappeared, I was busy, distracted, maybe I had become a little complacent. And in that time, that window of opportunity, Joy began to find her way back. If I'm completely honest I was impressed with her tenacity, but also at the same time annoyed. She didn't seem to have learnt her lesson well enough.

The hours, weeks, we spent in the house on Kingston Lane, before I handed her over officially to Jono, were enough to change her for a few years, but clearly would have needed repeating for a long-term success. She could have died numerous times, mixing with the people she worked with. The addictions could have killed her, and the fire could have killed her, but she's still here.

Again, I'm torn between admiration and anger. Do some people just have a stronger will to live, an instinct to survive, than others?

She will see that all the way through I have only had her best interests at heart, but she consistently broke the mould. Not in an obstinate steadfast way like her sister, who should never have risen in the ranks in what can only be described as a profession for men. Women are never taken seriously in positions of power, and for their own protection they should keep in their own lanes. It's a scientific fact that women are weaker than men, both mentally and physically. I am a scientist.

Earlier today, I leaked a few stories, and laid a few trails alluding to the two sisters' desperate state, and how their mental health has deteriorated. I may have told a few lies, but some of the papers will be happy to go with it, simply adding the information is from 'a source' and 'it is alleged'.

The drugs were easy enough to get hold of, with my contacts and my knowledge. I'm amazed the police never looked harder at me when it came to Joy's abduction, but my alibi was unshakable, and they were diverted by bigger leads. I'm not saying they're clueless, because they aren't, it's just that I have an inside source, and I have always been the smartest person in the room. I have no heart condition, no medical issues, but all people saw was a pottering old man, and that was exactly what I needed them to see.

My wife knew that I was stronger and cleverer than her. Beatrice should have remembered that. Lucy seemed to understand once, but not now, not for many years.

When I sent the car off the end of the road, tumbling downwards just as their mother had, drugs in their systems, Joy's suicide notes already scheduled to be posted on social media, I thought I had it nailed. The ketamine worked like a dream, for a while...

We would all know why Joy had done it, and that she was really responsible, and we would show the world we were right about her all along.

The internet is a wonderful thing; once you know who to talk to, you order your drugs as easily as your Deliveroo pizza. On a different phone, of course. Did you think I was stupid? I'm sure you didn't, because you're one of us, aren't you? A fan, a lover and a hater.

The day has been full of weak sunlight and strong emotion, all washed down with a touch of bitterness that it has finally come to this, my last feeble struggles as my body prepares itself for death.

My chest is tight, and already it becomes harder to breathe. I am lying on a ledge, where they left me. I am safe enough I suppose, but I can already see uniforms scaling the side of the hill, bright searchlights seeking me out.

With my last bit of strength, I roll stiffly to one side, away from the light, and feel myself falling, as light as a feather. I think I can hear the sea, hear my father calling me home. It is the natural order of things.

EPILOGUE

"Hello, my darlings! It's been a long time since I made a vlog and things have changed so much in six years." Joy paused, and then smiled. "I wanted to tell you some stuff and also to let you know I am going to pick up vlogging again. This time it will be with a different perspective though."

Joy stopped again, deliberately allowing the sunlight to play across her blonde hair, to light up her scarred face, before she continued, "I went through a lot, and I saw a lot, and I'm still trying to rediscover who I am. My family and friends have suffered deeply through the selfishness of one man. But I have found out how strong we really all are, and I am hopeful for the future. So, I want to thank you for having faith in me, for caring and for never giving up on me."

She smiled again, beautiful blue-green eyes looking straight at the camera, straight into the hearts of her followers, the lovers and the haters. Resting her hands on the garden gate, just as she had done exactly six years ago, she signed off. "I'll see you soon, my darlings, and from the bottom of my heart, thank you."

Joy turned, and walked away from the woods, and as the

camera panned out, she could be seen heading for her house, where her family were waiting by the door. Before she reached them a large silver tabby cat leapt out of the flower bed and escorted her carefully, proudly on her way. The rustling and vigorous waving of the purple lupins indicated perhaps the flower bed was hiding a few more animals...

Her sister, DI Lucy Merry, who would have never appeared in one of her vlogs before, stepped forward to kiss her on her cheek, and her husband and children wrapped the pair of them in laughter and more hugs.

The video was posted at 6:00pm and by 9:00pm it had over five million likes. When Joy looked at it later, she felt a quiet sense of peace, fulfilment, pride even. She didn't look at the comments at all.

Full circle.

July 26th: Error message: The NatterJack Forum is now offline until further notice due to an administration error.

Six months later, Joy read the news as she sat on the beach, Bertie curled into the crook of her arm, lips moving silently, small fingers slowly turning the pages of his book.

The body of forty-one-year-old Jono McQueen, who had been missing for nine months, had been discovered washed up on the beach at Camber Sands, East Sussex. McQueen, Joy read, had been wanted for questioning over numerous serious offences, but although foul play was suspected, it was thought the body was too decomposed for any definitive tests to be carried out as to cause of death.

Joy scrunched her toes into the sand and pebbles of the beach while she digested the news. She adjusted her denim shorts, pushed her sunglasses back onto her head, and she glanced over at her two daughters, playing in the surf with her husband. Finally, she turned back to her phone, and read the short paragraphs again. There was no raw emotion, no sadness or anger, just a slight quickening of her heart and she registered it was finally over.

The part Jono had played in her abduction and her reincarnation as Mattie, the girls he had killed, almost paled in comparison to the evil her own father had perpetuated. That still hurt, in a dull ache that went all the way around her chest. She and Lucy had talked and talked, to each other, to therapists, trying to make sense of the loving dad, the twisted narcissist, the doting grandparent. The murderer.

Her phone rang and she smiled. "Hello, I was just thinking about you. How's it going?"

"Okay. I just finished a twelve-hour shift, but it's going well. Let me guess, you're lying on a beach chilling with the family?" There was amusement and affection in Lucy's voice, and the sound warmed Joy's heart. For a while, she had been terribly afraid their fragile relationship wouldn't survive Frank's death.

"Guilty. How was therapy?"

"Better..." Her sister paused. "I'm sleeping again now, properly sleeping without the nightmares."

"That's good. Are you still coming over at the end of the month?"

"I've booked my flights."

"Wait until you see the house..." And Joy found herself chatting easily about her home plans, the olive grove, the kids and Emile. Normal things. They talked for an hour before she rang off. Bertie was fast asleep on her arm, which was getting pins and needles. She made a pillow from a towel, slipped it under his head, heart catching as she looked at his freckled, tanned little cheeks, mop of sea-tousled hair and bare feet covered in sand.

A lot of decisions had been made, and a lot of changes to their family dynamic in the past few months. Yet each change had been made after consideration, and Joy felt she was back in control, in a place she loved, both personally and professionally.

One of the biggest changes had been selling the Brighton house and moving abroad. There had been enough money to buy a penthouse apartment on Chichester Terrace, a part of the city she had always loved. It was an investment, and currently rented out. She was discovering she was actually pretty good at managing money and had taken over the family's finances.

Emile had been highly amused that one of her biggest worries was taking her growing brood of animals with them. Nuala, the undisputed queen, had instantly settled in, to Joy's relief, and the others followed suit.

Without having to look, she could almost sense, a few miles behind her, the half-renovated farmhouse, a traditional stone building, which stood amidst tangled, long-neglected olive and lemon groves. They were renovating the property a few rooms at a time, often finding the foundations composed of the ugly concrete patching and the beautiful ancient stonework, so tightly interwoven they would be impossible to separate without bringing the whole building down but forming an integral part of its history.

Joy loved the sense that they were building on the solid foundations. She was relaxed, at peace here, she thought happily, tasting salt on her lips, feeling the sea breeze in her long hair, hearing the laughter of her family and the peace of the Mediterranean Sea so close to their new home.

Her sister and Bobby were frequent visitors. She had new friendships and she had Georgia, who visited from Brighton, talking excitedly about her career breakthrough, a presenting gig on a TV show.

She scrolled back over the news story for the last time, before deleting the page, and turning back to her language app, tapping to activate the next exercise.

"*Quién eres tú?*"

"Who are you?"
"Soy Joy Maddison."
"I am Joy Maddison."
And finally, she was.

A LETTER FROM THE AUTHOR

Dear Reader,

Huge thanks for reading *You Know Her*! I hope you were hooked on Mattie/Joy's journey. If you want to join other readers in hearing all about my new releases please sign up here:

www.stormpublishing.co/de-white

If you enjoyed this book and could spare a few moments to leave a review that would be hugely appreciated. Even a short review or star rating can make all the difference in encouraging a reader to discover my books for the first time. Thank you so much in advance!

The setting is always important to me, and after writing twenty books, I still get inspired by the 'feel' of places. *You know Her* initially unfolds during a July heatwave, and summer along the south coast and especially in Brighton is the absolute best time: the heat and dirt, the coffees at Carats Café, the comedy nights at Burger & Bird, and the cocktails at Rockwater. I was born in Brighton, and also lived there as a child, before I returned in recent years to the south coast with my own children. I love driving along the coast road, with the port holding a particular fascination, watching gradual development, the pockets of dereliction interspersed with industry, and new housing.

This was Mattie's place, and I knew it quite early on. Just as I knew Joy would live in Dyke Road, behind high security gates.

The influencer world can seem extremely fickle from the outside, and indeed from the inside, but in the course of my research I also found strong friendships, and a genuinely supportive and collaborative community, especially amongst the 'mumpreneurs' (a term which many of them hate!).

I am extremely lucky to have such amazing friends, who know this world intimately and who were happy to share their experiences, from being pursued by press photographers, to online trolling, and how they deal with it all. What you see on the socials, in the glossy magazines, and at events is very much not what happens behind the scenes. But it didn't want *You Know Her* to be just about influencers, so my starting point, after establishing the setting, was what if (always the author's best friend!) you took the glossy, the perfect, and you stripped it bare. What would you find? In Joy's case it was a strong and brave woman who survived in the most horrific circumstances.

I did a lot of research into coercive persuasion, and Stockholm syndrome in relation to Joy's story. During the course of this research, I also read many articles on social brainwashing. This particular quote from *Psyche* magazine (Joel E. Dimsdale) stuck with me:

'If we ignore the potential developments of brainwashing in the twenty-first century, we will be defenceless against it.'

Thanks again for being part of this amazing journey with me and I hope you'll stay in touch – I have so many more stories and ideas to entertain you with! I also spend far too much time hanging out with the book community on TikTok and Instagram, so do feel free to connect using the links below for a chat!

D. E. White x

KEEP IN TOUCH WITH THE AUTHOR

www.dewhiteauthor.com

facebook.com/DaisyWhiteAuthor
x.com/DEWhiteAuthor
instagram.com/d.e._white_author
tiktok.com/@d.e.whiteauthor

ACKNOWLEDGEMENTS

I do hope you have enjoyed reading *You Know Her*! Book number twenty – can you believe it?

I had the idea for this book back in 2021 and spent the winter juggling deadlines, trying to find the time to write it. The port is central to my starting point and like my protagonist, I am fascinated by the ever-changing scenes from the road.

The setting for *You Know Her* is my hometown, Brighton. I was born and bred, as they say, in this UK coastal city and it remains, in all its crazy, wonderful, filthy messed up imperfection, one of my favourite inspirations. I love the people and I love the vibe.

There was a lot of research and as usual I am so grateful to Eric and Dee Storey for their input into the police procedure. Thank you also to Graham Barlett (policeadvisor.co.uk) for his valuable input regarding Sussex policing, and Brighton in particular.

Thank you to my ambulance colleagues, and other medical professionals for their input on Joy's injuries. Any inaccuracies are purely down to my fictional plot twists, not the wonderful advice from these above people.

Hugs also to my influencer and celeb friends who shared the highs and lows of the crazy world they have found themselves in. To Emma Nicolet (a Joyinfluencer!) for patiently explain how it all works, to Cat Sims, Emma Norton Comedy, Michelle, Lucinda, Tashy, Josie and many, many more for all providing inspo for the character of Joy.

It's so important when threading the story together that I don't stray too far from the facts and my wonderful professional friends are so generous with their time and are excellent at helping me problem solve my way around this.

This is my first standalone for a couple of years, and it was a story that appeared in my head, almost ready written.

I have taken some geographical liberties with my locations. Ramon and Sons fish market does not exist, but it would be placed on the road somewhere between Shoreham and Portslade. A few pubs, roads and clubs are fictional, but the house on Kingston Lane is somewhere I have driven past for years. I knew that was where Mattie was going to start her journey, long before I knew exactly what her journey would entail. There is a new housing development next to the house now, and the whole area has been transformed.

Thank you to everyone who has bought the Detective Dove Milson series. Writing that series, and the readers' positive response to it, gave me the confidence to write another standalone thriller. It also gave me more of an idea of the kind of books I wanted to be writing.

Thank you to all my wonderful readers, to the bloggers, the vloggers, the bookshops, the libraries, without whom our books would never travel so widely, or be read by so many people. In this age of technology, one of the best ways to get book recommendations is still word of mouth and I am so grateful to all the people who facilitate this. Just a few who have been with me from the start, and who deserve special thanks are Jill, Bev, Alyson, Carol, Lesley, Abi, Danielle, Alan, Richard and Tracey.

The book community truly is a wonderful tribe, and I love how fellow authors, readers and anyone connected with books are always ready to support one another. Books create a special bond.

Huge thanks to my amazing agent, Kate, at the Kate Nash

Literary Agency, for always being there, and working so hard for us all. We appreciate everything you do!

For wise words of advice, honest critique, and huge support thank you to Lisa B, Laura B, Matt, Hayley, Steve, Debbie, Keri, Val, Amanda, and the Savvies (Tracy Buchanan, thank you for creating such a wonderful group). And to my wonderful new writing family at Sussex Writing Retreats, who include Vic, Ali, Julie, Sue, Catriona, Lesley, Jonathan, Caro and many more. You inspire me to work harder.

Huge thanks to Storm, for welcoming me into their book family (especially my amazing editor, Vicky Blunden), who took a chance on this book, and who are just the most incredible entrepreneurial bunch of people.

Two very important pieces of advice I try to abide by:

From Emma Grundy Haigh, "It's not the getting up there, it's the stickability that counts." I'm still working on that one, and publishing is a very rocky road!

From Amanda Brittany, a bestselling author and lovely friend, who reminded me to celebrate each small win along the way, "Eat cake and drink wine every time you have a book published!"

Finally, thank you to my long-suffering family, for propping me up when it all goes wrong, and celebrating those small triumphs when it does go right. Love you!

If you are interested in hearing more about my books, and in particular new releases, please do sign up to my newsletter, which you can find on www.dewhiteauthor.co.uk or follow me on Instagram at d.e._white_author where I spend far too much time chatting, filling my tbr list and procrastinating.

Best wishes,

D. E. White

Printed in Great Britain
by Amazon